Praise for
DEVIL'S CLAW
and other JOANNA BRADY novels by
J.A. JANCE

Books by J.A. Jance

Joanna Brady Mysteries
DESERT HEAT • TOMBSTONE
COURAGE • SHOOT/DON'T SHOOT • DEAD TO
RIGHTS • SKELETON CANYON • RATTLESNAKE
CROSSING • OUTLAW MOUNTAIN •
DEVIL'S CLAW

J.P. Beaumont Mysteries
UNTIL PROVEN GUILTY • INJUSTICE FOR
ALL • TRIAL BY FURY • TAKING THE
FIFTH • IMPROBABLE CAUSE • A MORE
PERFECT UNION • DISMISSED WITH PREJUDICE •
MINOR IN POSSESSION • PAYMENT IN
KIND • WITHOUT DUE PROCESS •
FAILURE TO APPEAR • LYING IN WAIT • NAME
WITHHELD • BREACH OF DUTY • BIRDS OF PREY

and

HOUR OF THE HUNTER
KISS OF THE BEES

J. A. JANCE

DEVIL'S CLAW

AVON BOOKS
An Imprint of HarperCollinsPublishers

AVON BOOKS
An Imprint of HarperCollins*Publishers*
10 East 53rd Street
New York, New York 10022-5299

Copyright © 2000 by J.A. Jance
Excerpt from *Paradise Lost* copyright © 2001 by J.A. Jance
ISBN: 0-380-79249-4
www.avonbooks.com

First Avon Books paperback printing: August 2001
First William Morrow hardcover printing: July 2000

Avon Trademark Reg. U.S. Pat. Off. and in Other Countries, Marca Registrada, Hecho en U.S.A.
HarperCollins ® is a trademark of HarperCollins Publishers Inc.

Printed in the U.S.A.

10 9 8 7 6 5 4 3 2 1

For Judi and Jack McCann

PROLOGUE

The yellow school bus rumbled down the long dirt trail known as Middlemarch Road, throwing up a thick cloud of red dust that swirled high into the air behind it. Approaching a shotgun-pellet-pocked CURVES sign, the bus slowed and then stopped beside a peeling blue mailbox sitting atop a crooked wooden post. Switching on the blinking red lights, the driver, Agnes Hooper, waited until the trailing dust blew past before she opened the door to discharge her only remaining passenger.

Moving slowly, Lucinda Ridder dragged her heavy back-pack down the center aisle. Even though she had been alone on the bus for several miles, Lucy Ridder never left her designated spot in the very back row. That was the place where some of the older kids had decreed she sit two years earlier, when she had first enrolled in Elfrida High School, and that was where she remained to this day—in the back of the bus. To Agnes Hooper's personal knowledge, none of the other kids ever spoke to the scrawny, homely girl with her bone-thin arms and her thick, eye-shrinking glasses. Lucy had come to Elfrida's high school after attending grade school in Pearce, a tiny community just up the road, but she had evidently been just as friendless there. None of the other girls ever offered to share that lonely backseat spot with her or whispered silly secrets in her ear. No one ever offered her a bite of the afternoon snacks that sometimes found their for-

1

bidden way onto Agnes Hooper's supposedly food-free bus. It seemed to Agnes that the girl's stubborn silence had rendered her so invisible that the other kids no longer even noticed her. In a way, that was a blessing, since it meant they no longer bothered to tease her, either.

The bus driver's kind heart went out to this strange and fiercely silent girl. After all, it wasn't Lucinda Ridder's fault that her father was dead, that her mother was in prison, and that she herself had been forced to come live with her widowed grandmother, Catherine Yates, whose own great-grandfather had been a noted Apache chief. Lucy's Indian blood had been diluted enough by both her grandfather and her father, so she didn't *look* particularly Indian. Still, in that part of rural southeastern Arizona where what went on during the Apache Wars still mattered, people knew who she was and where she came from. And, as far as Apaches were concerned, what could you expect?

Peering into the hazy reflection of her dusty rearview mirror, Agnes tried to catch Lucy's sad, downcast eyes as she trudged disconsolately down the narrow aisle of the bus. Agnes was struck by the girl's obvious reluctance to exit the bus. Everything about going to school and riding the bus had to be pure torture for her. Still, on this blustery spring afternoon, it seemed to Agnes that whatever fate awaited her at home must be far worse.

As Lucy finally stepped off the bus onto the weed-clogged shoulder, Agnes called after her. "You-all have a good weekend, now," the driver said as cheerily as she could manage. "See you on Monday."

Lucinda Ridder nodded, but she didn't answer. Once clear of the bus, she stood watching while Mrs. Hooper switched off the flashing lights and ground the bus into gear. It took several moves to maneuver the ungainly bus in the narrow turnaround space that had been bulldozed into the shoulders of the road. All the while, Lucinda Ridder gazed in that direction. Caught by the stiff spring breeze, her hair fanned out around her face in lank brown strands. She squinted her eyes to keep out the dust, but she didn't raise a hand to ward off the flying gravel and grit. Her fingers remained frozen stiffly at her side until the turn was complete and the bus had rumbled back past her, down the road, and out of sight. Only then did she raise her hand in a half-hearted wave. Of all the people at Pearce Elementary and Elfrida High schools, Mrs. Hooper—the bus driver—was the only person who had ever shown Lucinda Ridder the slightest kindness.

Once the bus was gone, Lucy opened the mailbox. She pulled out several pieces of mail and stowed them in her frayed backpack. But while the backpack was open, she removed another envelope. This one, previously opened, was addressed to her in pencil. Sinking to the ground along the rock-strewn shoulder, she raised the flap and fumbled out a scrap of cheap lined notebook paper. Standing there with the paper flapping in the breeze, she read her mother's note through once again, shaking her head as she did so.

Dear Baby,

Guess what? They're letting me out. Friday of this week. Don't tell Grandma. I have some things I need to do before I come home, and I want to surprise her. I probably won't be there until Sunday afternoon or so. See you then.

Love,
Mom

The last words swam on the paper, blurred by the tears that filled Lucy's eyes. For years—ever since the morning eight years earlier when she had awakened to find her father dead and her mother being loaded into a police car, Lucy Ridder had been afraid this would happen. She had prayed that somehow her mother would never return, that she would die in prison, but clearly those prayers had not been answered. Or, if God had answered them, his reply was no. Her mother was coming home, and that would ruin everything. The kids at school had almost forgotten who she was or why Lucy had come to live there all those years earlier. Once her mother showed up, though, once people caught sight of Sandra Ridder in the post office or the grocery store, everyone would remember, and the ugly torment and teasing would begin anew.

Unconsciously, Lucy reached up and touched the solitary charm she wore on a fine silver chain around her thin neck. It was a tiny silver-and-turquoise replica of the two-pronged gourd called devil's claw. Her great-grandmother, Christina Bagwell, had had it made for Lucy by a friend, a silversmith who lived in Gallup, New Mexico. Even though Christina had been dead for nearly five years now, just touching the charm which had been her great-grandmother's last gift to Lucinda still comforted her, putting her in touch with her great-grandmother's spirit as well as her wisdom.

Lucy had received her mother's disturbing note three days earlier, and she hadn't mentioned a word about it to her grandmother—not so much because Sandra Ridder had wanted her daughter to keep her impending arrival secret, but because Lucy herself had not yet decided what to do. Now, on the day of her mother's scheduled release, Lucy made up her mind.

Sighing, she refolded the single piece of paper several

times—first in half and then into quarters. Finally, when she had folded it as small as she could, she tore it up. Once the letter had been shredded into a fistful of tiny, confetti-sized pieces, Lucy tossed them up into the air and watched as the wind blew them away, scattering them far and wide. When the last traces of the letter had disappeared into the newly plowed field across Middlemarch Road, Lucy did the same thing to the envelope itself. Then she rummaged in her pack once more and retrieved a worn square of deer hide, which she placed over one narrow shoulder.

Rising to her feet, Lucy hiked the backpack onto her other arm. With her feet spread wide, she threw back her head and let out a wild, piercing scream. The high-pitched screech was loud enough to travel great distances over the seemingly empty and parched terrain at the foot of the Dragoon Mountains. Moments later, the eerie sound was greeted by an answering, keening cry.

Far away, across a tangle of blackened, winter-dead mesquite, a big bird took wing. Majestically, the red-tailed hawk rose high into the air and then circled lazily overhead, his wings spread wide and dark beneath an azure sky. For the better part of a minute he stayed there, floating gracefully on the updrafts, before putting himself into a steep dive. He plummeted straight toward the girl who stood, head unbent, waiting. Mere feet away, the falling bird banked sharply. Striking his great wings, he settled softly onto her shoulder with a gentle flap and clamped his golden talons harmlessly on the scrap of protective leather that covered Lucy's long-sleeved shirt.

"How's it going, Big Red?" Lucy whispered. Turning her head, she nuzzled the bare skin of her cheek against the down-soft feathers of his breast. "Hope you've had a better day than I did," she added.

With that, she turned and started up the desolate dirt track that led home. As Lucy walked, the bird was forced to sway from side to side with each stride in order to maintain his perch. Anyone watching the two of them from a distance might have thought this apparition to be a monster of some kind—a poor deformed creature cursed to live its life with the burden of two heads.

As far as some of Lucy Ridder's nastier classmates at Elfrida High School were concerned, that unkind assessment wouldn't have been far from wrong.

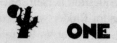

ONE

Lucy waited until she knew her grandmother was asleep before she left the house and quietly wheeled her bike out of the shed. The afternoon's bitter quarrel had continued to torment her the whole time she had sorted through the few possessions she would need to take with her—a bedroll, a few clothes, a heavy, sheepskin-lined jacket, a canteen of water, some food pilfered from the kitchen, her grandmother's .22 pistol, and, of course, the diskette. Her mother's precious diskette. The diskette that had meant more to Sandra Ridder than anything else. That diskette, Lucy Ridder knew, was the whole reason her father had died.

It was cold enough outside that she could see her breath. Across the Sulphur Springs Valley the full moon had risen high over the horizon, casting enough of an eerie yellow glow across the landscape that Lucy could see to ride. After pushing the bike for the better part of half a mile, Lucy stopped and once again sent that same wild and keening cry off across the night-still desert. She called and waited. Moments later, she was rewarded by the flap of Big Red's wings overhead. Once he settled gently onto her leather-thong-wrapped handlebar, Lucy no longer felt nearly as alone or as frightened.

"Will she come, do you think?" Lucy asked the bird.

Big Red didn't answer, but then he didn't need to. After

all, Lucy knew the answer to that question herself. She had known it all along. Of course Sandra Ridder would come, just as she had eight years earlier—in secret, in the middle of the night, and without Grandma Yates' knowledge.

Big Red had learned to ride on the handlebars of Lucy's bike long before he could fly. From the time he was little more than a ball of fluff, he had loved riding perched on the leather-wrapped handlebar with his wings half-spread and his hooked beak pointing into the wind. As he had grown, it seemed to Lucy that Big Red's partially unfurled wings always served to make them more aerodynamic.

They often took long weekend jaunts to the upper end of Cochise Stronghold. In the wild and protected reaches of the cliff-bound canyon where the noted Apache chieftain, Cochise, had often secluded his band, Lucy and her unlikely companion would while away the long weekend hours. This, however, was the first time that the two of them had made this pilgrimage together in the dark of night.

Three different times Lucy heard vehicles approaching from behind, and twice she met vehicles driving toward her. On each occasion, Lucy wheeled the sturdy mountain bike off the road. While Big Red hustled onto low-lying branches, Lucy disappeared into underbrush to wait until the danger of discovery was past.

Pumping along, Lucy felt physical warmth seeping back into her body right along with the anger she harbored toward her mother. And as she rode, the memory of that other night-time trip to Cochise Stronghold—one made from Tucson and in her mother's old Nissan—was still vivid in Lucy's mind.

Sandra Ridder had come to the Lohse YMCA to collect her daughter. Even though the ballet class had barely started, she had ordered Lucy to get dressed and come along. Her face had been bruised and bleeding and she seemed so agitated that at first Lucy had thought Sandra was drunk. That did happen at times, although it happened far less frequently now that Lucy's father had gone to treatment and quit drinking.

Once in the car, Lucy learned that her mother wasn't drunk. She was angry. Furious! As soon as the car doors closed, she had wrestled Lucy's backpack away from her daughter and dug through it, pawing all the way to the bottom.

"That son of a bitch!" she had exclaimed at last, pulling out the diskette Lucy's father had given her at lunchtime.

"I knew it had to be here!" Sandra continued. "They looked everywhere else, so I knew he must have given it to you."

Lucy didn't know who "they" were. But she did know that her father had placed the diskette in her backpack. She also knew that real physical danger lurked in her mother's anger, and right then fear overpowered everything else. She had shrunk into the far corner of the car seat and had tried not to listen as her mother ranted and raved about her father and about the terrible things he had done.

After they left the lights of Tucson behind them and all the time they were driving the familiar roads to Cochise County's Dragoon Mountains, Lucy had assumed they were going to see her two grandmothers. Grandma Yates, her mother's mother, and her great-grandmother, Christina Bagwell, lived just off Middlemarch Road in the foothills of the Dragoon Mountains. Instead, Sandra had driven her Nissan someplace else—to a place that was nearby and almost as familiar as Grandma Yates' ranch—Cochise Stronghold.

The Ridders and Lucy's two grandmothers had often had family picnics in the campground there. This time, though, Sandra had pulled over and stopped right beside the entrance. As she put the car in park, Sandra had told Lucy to get in the backseat. "Go to sleep," she said. "And don't you make a sound."

Lucy hadn't made a sound, but she hadn't gone to sleep, either. Instead, peering out through the back window, Lucy had watched as her mother carefully removed a stack of fist-sized rocks from beneath the rough-hewn FOREST SERVICE sign at the entrance to the park. Then, once the rocks had been moved aside, Sandra had hidden something deep in the earthen cavity created by the missing rocks. In the dark, Lucy had been unable to see the object her mother was so carefully and secretly burying, covering it over once again with the stack of rocks. Lucy assumed it had to be the diskette Sandra had retrieved from Lucy's backpack, but in the dark there was no way to tell for sure.

Sometime later, breathless with exertion, Sandra Ridder had returned to the car. By then Lucy was lying flat in the backseat, breathing deeply and pretending to be asleep. She had expected that once her mother finished whatever she was doing they would go to Grandma Yates' to visit and maybe have something to eat before heading back to Tucson. They had not. Instead, Lucy had ridden all the way back to Tucson listening to her stomach growl.

Somewhere along the way, she had fallen asleep for real. She did not remember arriving back at the little brick house on Seventeenth Street, nor did she remember her mother carrying her inside from the car. What she did remember, all too vividly, was awaking the next morning to find the house full of policemen. Her father, his body covered by a sheet, lay dead in a chair in the living room and her mother was being hustled into a police car.

At the time of Sandra Ridder's arrest, no one had been particularly interested in what her daughter had to say. Within days the child had been shunted out of town and sent off to live with her grandmother and great-grandmother. Instinctively, Lucy had known that the diskette and whatever else her mother had hidden that night had to have something to do with her father's death, but she didn't know what. And she didn't know what to do about it. Her father had come to school earlier that day, at lunch. He had taken her across the street for a doughnut and had warned her that Sandra might be in some kind of trouble at work. He had said something about Sandra being a spy, but that had seemed too silly, too far-fetched to be real. That was something that only happened in the movies or on TV.

Grieving for her father, lost, angry, and isolated, Lucy had kept quiet. She had told no one about that nighttime trek to the entrance of Cochise Stronghold, not even her Grandma Bagwell. Instead, Lucy had waited. It was almost two years later when, leaving the house without permission, she had taken a solitary hike back to Cochise Stronghold.

Working quickly, she had wrestled the heavy rocks out of the way. Underneath, she had discovered one of the plastic containers her father had used to pack canned peaches or pears into their sack lunches. Inside the container, Lucy had found two things—the blue computer disk and a tiny gun. Touching the metal handle, Lucy recognized that this wasn't a toy. It was a real gun, and Lucy knew at once that this was most likely the weapon—the long-missing weapon—that had killed her father. Her fingers shrank away from the cold steel, but she grabbed the diskette. This was something her father had given her, something Tom Ridder had obviously meant for Lucy to have. Her mother had taken it from her, and now Lucy was taking it back.

Now, once again within yards and spying distance of the entrance to Cochise Stronghold, Lucy walked her bike off the roadway and hid it in the brush. She walked up to the sign. She was relieved to see that none of the rocks seemed to have been disturbed. That meant that if her mother was coming here, she had not yet arrived.

Returning to her hiding place just beyond the crest of the creek bank, Lucy snuggled herself deep into the protective warmth of her bedroll. With Big Red keeping watch from the branches of a nearby oak, girl and hawk settled in to wait. Despite her intention of staying wide awake, physical exertion worked its magic, and Lucy fell sound asleep. She might have missed the whole thing if a warning squawk from Big Red hadn't brought her wide awake.

The last time Lucy had looked at the entrance sign it had been bathed in the faded glow of moonlight. Now it was fully illuminated in the glow of headlights from a nearby parked car. And on the ground, under the sign, was a woman on her hands and knees, struggling to shift the rocks from place to place.

With a catch in her throat, Lucy watched as her mother—a woman she hadn't seen in almost eight years, a woman she had hoped never to see again—carefully moved the rocks to one side. Lucy found herself paralyzed by a storm of emotion. She wanted to speak to Sandra, and yet, at the same time, she didn't want to. In the end, not knowing what to say, Lucy stayed where she was. She was still sitting there as unmoving as a carved wooden statue when a car pulled up and stopped beside the sign.

"Do you need help?" a man asked from inside the idling vehicle.

Quickly, Sandra Ridder stood up and walked over to the car. Lucy couldn't hear all that was being said, but evidently it was enough to satisfy the guy's curiosity. "Okay, then," he concluded at last. "Since you're all right, I'll just go on and go."

Sandra and Lucy both watched as the vehicle's taillights disappeared behind a tangle of underbrush and scrub oak. Momentarily distracted, neither of them saw the figure of another man suddenly emerge from the gloom into the bright glow of headlights.

"Well, well, well," he said with an audible sneer. "Imagine meeting you here!"

Lucy heard Sandra's sharp intake of breath. She stepped back one full step. "What are you doing here?" she gasped.

"What do you think?" he growled, closing the gap between them with one long stride. "I came to collect what's mine." He paused then and looked around. "What a clever girl," he added. "To think you'd hide it out in the open like this, hidden and yet almost in plain sight."

"Hide what?" Sandra asked.

He lunged at her then and grabbed her by one arm. "Don't go all coy and innocent on me, Sandy, honey. I know the score here. I know all about it."

"Stop," she said, squirming and trying to free her captured arm. "You're hurting me."

"And I'm going to hurt you a whole hell of a lot more if you don't give it to me right now! Now, for the last time, where is it?"

Sandra seemed to go limp in his grasp. "There," she said, pointing.

"Where?"

"Under the sign. I buried it."

"Well, suppose you unbury it?" With that, he flung her

away from him and sent her stumbling forward. Only by catching and steadying herself against the body of the sign did she keep from falling.

Barely daring to breathe, Lucy watched the ugly drama unfold. For the next several moments the man loomed over a kneeling Sandra Ridder while she removed several more rocks. And the whole time it was happening, Lucy was all too aware of what her mother had yet to discover. If what the man wanted was the diskette, it was no longer where Sandra Ridder had left it all those years earlier.

"You little bitch," he said as she worked. "Whatever made you think you could hold out on me? Whatever made you think you could get away with it?"

"I didn't. I just wanted—"

"Shut up and get it. Now!"

Part of Lucy wanted to call out to her mother and warn her. "Look over here," she wanted to say. "The diskette is right here in my pack." But another part of her—that primitive but still powerful instinct for self-preservation—kept her as still and silent as a frightened fawn.

At last Sandra wrested one final rock out of the way and plunged, elbow-deep, into the hole. She seemed to struggle for a moment, searching with her fingers. Then a look of utter disbelief crossed her face, but she said nothing.

"All right," the man said impatiently, holding out his hand. "Don't be so slow about it. Hand it over."

Obligingly Sandra Ridder removed her hand from the hole. When she did so, Lucy caught the smallest glint of metal and knew that Sandra was holding the one thing that remained in the container—the tiny gun that had been entombed right along with the diskette.

"Stop right there," Sandra ordered, aiming the weapon at the man who, even then, was bearing down on her.

But he didn't stop, and, unfortunately for Sandra Ridder, she didn't pull the trigger. From Lucy's hidden vantage point, what happened next seemed to do so in slow motion. The two separate figures of man and woman merged into one writhing mass of flesh. The two-headed creature fell to the ground, rolling this way and that. When the gunshot came, it was so muffled between the two clenched and struggling bodies that, bare yards away, Lucy hardly heard it. There was a single high-pitched shriek of pain, then slowly the two co-joined figures drew apart. When they had separated completely, the man was standing upright with the gun in his hand while an injured Sandra writhed and sobbed on the ground.

For several long seconds, nothing happened. Then there was an ominous click as the man tried to fire the gun while holding it at point-blank range inches from Sandra's head. "Shit!" he muttered after attempting to fire the weapon one more time. "The damn thing must be empty."

Leaning down, he grabbed Sandra Ridder under both arms and dragged her toward the waiting vehicle. "Open the door, for God's sake," he ordered. "Can't you see I need some help here?"

Behind the blinding curtain of headlights, there had been no way for Lucy to tell who was in the waiting vehicle. Now, though, the rider's door swung open, pushed by an invisible hand. In the dim glow of the dome light Lucy could see the figure of a woman seated behind the wheel of the vehicle, but lighting and distance both made it impossible to sort out any distinguishing features.

Muscling the door the rest of the way open, the man shoved Sandra Ridder's suddenly limp body into the backseat, then he went back to the hole. For several minutes he searched fruitlessly, cursing all the while. Finally he returned to the car and clambered into the front seat. "Now you've done it, you stupid bastard!" the woman muttered.

"Just shut up and drive," he told her. "Get us the hell out of here! Step on it."

He slammed the door shut, and the white car's engine roared to life. Too stunned to move, Lucy watched while the once again invisible driver made a tight turn. Sending a spray of dirt and rocks into the air, the car sped back down the road. It all happened so quickly that there was no chance of seeing the license plate, and once the car was gone, Lucy made no effort to follow. Instead, sobbing and shivering, Lucy ducked deeper into the folds of the bedroll that had burrowed deeply into the sandy floor of the dry creek bed.

Lucy had earnestly prayed for her mother's death, and now that prayer had been answered. Sandra Ridder was dead, and it was all Lucy's fault.

Several long minutes passed before Lucy finally calmed herself enough to creep from her hiding place. By then her eyes had once again adjusted to the moonlit darkness. She barely paused at the blood-spattered spot of sand where her mother had been shot. Instead she raced down the roadway to retrieve her bike. Once on it, she went pumping after the long-disappeared vehicle as if by overtaking it she might somehow be able to help.

Within a hundred yards or so, she knew it was hopeless. She stopped and stood still. As soon as she did, Big Red came gliding down out of the darkened sky and landed once again on her handlebar.

Walking the bike now because she was crying too much to see to ride, Lucy continued down the roadway. "It's got something to do with this stupid blank disk," she told Big Red. "It's why my father died and it's why my mother is dead now, too. And if that guy ever figures out I have it, he'll kill me as well. And maybe even Grandma Yates. What are we going to do, Red? Where can we go?"

Big Red gave no answer, but he made no effort to leave either. And for right then, that was answer enough. At last, squaring her shoulders, Lucinda Ridder climbed on her bike and rode back the way she had come to retrieve her bedroll.

 **TWO**

"Mom," Jennifer Ann Brady called from the bathtub. "Tigger's drinking out of the toilet again. It's gross. Come make him stop."

Sighing, Joanna Brady opened her eyes and forced herself up from the couch where she had inadvertently dozed off while waiting for Jenny to finish her bath so they could both go to bed. "Tigger," she called. "You come here."

But even as she said the words, she knew it was hopeless. Tigger, Jenny's half golden retriever/half pit bull, was one of the most stubborn dogs Joanna had ever met. Simply calling to him wouldn't do the job. Walking into the steamy bathroom, she grabbed Tigger's collar and bodily hauled the dripping dog out of the toilet bowl. Then, closing the door to keep him out of the bathroom, she led him through the kitchen and into the laundry room.

"There," she said, pointing at the water dish. "That's where you're supposed to drink."

Except, even as Joanna said the words, she realized the water dish was empty. And not just empty, either—it was bone-dry. Reaching down, Joanna picked up the dish and filled it at the laundry-room sink. As soon as she put the dish down, Sadie, Jenny's other dog appeared in the kitchen doorway as well. The long-legged bluetick hound and the shorter, stockier mutt stood side by side lapping eagerly from the same dish.

That's odd, Joanna thought. *That's usually the first thing Clayton does when he comes over to do the chores. He lets himself into the house to feed and water the dogs.*

Clayton Rhodes was Joanna's nearest neighbor. A bow-legged, spindly octogenarian, Clayton was a hardworking widower whose 320 acres were situated just north of Joanna's High Lonesome Ranch. For years now, ever since Joanna's husband's death, Clayton had come to the High Lonesome mornings and evenings six days a week to feed and water the ranch's growing collection of animals. The man was nothing if not dependable, but now, watching the thirsty dogs, Joanna recalled the unusual attention Sadie and Tigger had focused on the dinner table that evening while she and Jenny ate.

"Did he forget to feed you guys, too?" Joanna asked. "Do you want to eat?"

At the mere mention of the magic word "eat," Tigger left the water dish and began his frantic "feed me" dance. Shaking her head and half convinced the dogs were lying to her, Joanna collected the two individual food dishes and filled them as well. While the dogs wagged their tails and enthusiastically crunched dry dog food, Joanna went out onto the back porch to check the outside water dish. That one, too, was empty.

"Poor babies," Joanna murmured as she filled that dish as well. "He must have forgotten about you completely."

For Clayton Rhodes, forgetting to feed or water animals was totally out of character. Joanna wondered if something had happened that afternoon to distract him. Briefly she considered calling and checking, but a glance at her watch convinced her otherwise. It was almost nine o'clock. She knew that as soon as Clayton finished his hired-hand duties on High Lonesome Ranch, he returned home, ate his solitary dinner, and went to bed almost as soon as the sun went down.

"Early to bed, early to rise," he had told Joanna once. "That's the secret to living a long healthy life." And it must have worked. Only three months earlier, at age eighty-five, Clayton Rhodes had finally sold off his last horse and given up horseback riding for good.

A few minutes later Joanna was back in the living room with the sated dogs lying contentedly at her feet when Jenny emerged from the bathroom wearing a robe and toweling dry her mop of platinum-blond hair. "Can I stay up and watch TV?" she asked. "It's Friday. I don't have school tomorrow."

"You may not have school," Joanna conceded, "but tomorrow's going to be a busy day. We'd both better get some rest."

Jenny made a face. "More stupid wedding stuff, I suppose," she huffed.

Joanna's scheduled wedding to Frederick "Butch" Dixon was a week and a day away. It wasn't that Jenny was opposed to the match. As far as Joanna could tell, her daughter exhibited every sign of adoring Butch Dixon and of looking forward to having a stepfather. Nonetheless, within days of dealing with pre-wedding logistics—something Joanna's mother, Eleanor Lathrop Winfield, seemed to adore—Jenny had been bored to tears with the whole tedious process. In fact, as wedding plans continued to expand exponentially, Joanna was beginning to feel the same way herself. Even now, at this late date, she was tempted to back out and settle for a nice, uncomplicated elopement, just as she had years earlier when she married Jenny's father, Andrew Roy Brady.

Her penalty for running off to marry Andy in a hastily arranged, shotgun-style wedding had been years of unremitting recrimination from her mother. Right now, though, with Eleanor Lathrop Winfield functioning in fearsome, full-scale mother-of-the-bride mode, the idea of eloping a second time was becoming more and more appealing.

"Let your mother have her fun," Butch had said early on. "What can it hurt?"

Famous last words. Little had Butch known that once Eleanor Lathrop Winfield took the bit in her teeth, nothing would stop her or even slow her down. Since she had missed her daughter's first wedding, Eleanor was determined to make this second one a resounding social success. Butch had said those fateful words *before* the guest list had burgeoned to over a hundred and fifty—a crowd that would fill the sanctuary of Canyon United Methodist Church to overflowing. It would also test the considerable patience and capabilities of Myron Thomas, the man who ran the catering concession at the Rob Roy Links in Palominas, the county's newest and most prestigious golf course and the only place in Cochise County where what Eleanor termed a "four-star reception" could be held.

By now even Butch's easygoing good nature had been stretched to the limit. He was the one who had pointed out that Jenny's twelfth birthday on the fifth of April would fall right in the middle of their upcoming honeymoon. He had suggested that the three of them—bride, groom, and Jenny—abandon the wedding roller coaster for a day or two in order to spend that weekend focused on Jenny and her birthday.

"Not wedding," Joanna said in answer to her daughter's question. "Birthday. How would you like to go up to Tucson tomorrow and do some shopping?"

Jenny brightened immediately. "Really?" she said. "Can Butch go too?"

"Since it was his idea in the first place," Joanna replied, "I don't think wild horses would keep him away."

"Where are we going, Tucson Mall?"

"Maybe," Joanna said evasively. "But maybe not."

"Where?" Jenny asked. "Tell me."

Joanna shook her head. "It's a secret," she said.

Actually, she and Butch and Jenny's two sets of existing grandparents had already agreed on a joint gift. For some time, Jenny had made do with secondhand tack for her horse, a sorrel gelding named Kiddo. Now that she was getting ready to go barrel racing on the junior rodeo circuit, her ragtag collection of used equipment no longer quite fit the bill. As a result, the adults in Jenny's life had agreed on a birthday purchase of a new saddle in addition to all the accompanying bells and whistles.

"Well, then," Jenny said, "I guess I'd better go to bed." She turned and started from the room.

"Wait a minute," Joanna said. "Didn't you forget something? What about my good-night kiss?"

Jenny rolled her eyes. "Mom," she said. "I'm almost twelve. That's too old for good-night kisses."

"I'll decide what's too old for good-night kisses. Now come here!" Joanna commanded.

Shaking her head, Jenny came across the room, planted a glancing kiss on the top of Joanna's head, and then darted away before her mother could capture her in a hug.

"You're a brat," Joanna told her.

"A nearly twelve-year-old brat," Jenny agreed with a grin, then she disappeared into her bedroom and closed the door.

For some time, Joanna remained where she was, sitting on the couch and wondering how it was all going to work. In the time since Andy's death, she had grown accustomed to having the house to herself in the evenings, to doing things her own way, without having to consult any other adult about how the place was run. She and Jenny had hit on a reasonable way for the two of them to share the house's single bathroom. And all the while Butch had lived the same way—on his own. How would all the logistics work out when they tried to combine two separate households and lifestyles together?

Financially, they would be fine. With Butch's income from selling his Roundhouse Bar and Grill and Joanna's salary as sheriff, the two of them would be rich by Cochise County standards. They had talked about the possibility of selling High Lonesome Ranch and moving into a place that was neutral territory—a house where neither of them had lived before. But Joanna didn't want to live in town, and neither did Butch.

High Lonesome Ranch was only a few miles east of the Cochise County Justice Complex where Joanna worked, but it was far enough away to offer a retreat from some of the stresses of her job. It was a place where Jenny could have a horse—more than one, if she wanted—and multiple dogs as well. As for Butch, the ranch offered a perfect hideaway for someone dealing with the tortuous process of writing his first novel. In the end, Butch and Joanna had decided that the High Lonesome was where they would stay.

The upshot of that decision had Butch moving into Joanna's house with an eye toward doing some serious re-modeling—adding another bedroom, an office, and an additional bathroom, as well as totally redoing the kitchen. He was enthusiastic about the prospect of tackling this ambitious project and confident in his ability to get the job done. Joanna had her doubts. Her misgivings stemmed from having lived seven years of her childhood in an ongoing construction project while her father had spent all his off-work hours trying to remodel the family home on Campbell Street to Eleanor Lathrop's demanding and ever-changing specifications.

Shaking herself out of her reverie, Joanna got up and headed out to the kitchen to finish loading the dishwasher and cleaning off the counters. As she put in the soap and turned on the dishwasher, Sadie strolled over to the back door and whined to be let out.

"Time to go for a walk, girl?" Joanna asked as she went to open the door. "Come on, Tigger, you, too. Out you go so we can all come back inside and go to sleep."

While the dogs went wandering off to relieve themselves, Joanna stood on the back porch. The blustery wind that had blown all day long had died down, but even without the wind, the thirty-degree drop between daytime and nighttime temperatures left Joanna feeling chilled. She shivered while looking off across the sparsely settled Sulphur Springs Valley to where a golden sliver of full moon was beginning to rise up over the Chiricahua Mountains.

Sadie was already back in the house and Tigger was nosing his way up the walkway when Joanna heard Kiddo neighing from his stall in the barn. Kiddo's whinny was soon joined by a chorus of unsettled mooing from Joanna's several head of cattle out in the corral. That struck her as odd. Usually, once the sun went down, the livestock didn't make much noise. They lived on a schedule similar to Clayton Rhodes' early-to-bed-and-early-to-rise credo.

Standing listening, Joanna found herself wondering if maybe the dogs weren't the only ones who had missed out on food and water. Returning to the laundry room, she grabbed her lined denim jacket off the peg and stuffed a flashlight into her pocket. Then she hurried out through the yard and across the clearing between the fenced yard and the barn. As she passed the garage with its motion-activated light, the bare dirt clearing was brightly illuminated. She glanced down, looking for tire tracks in the fine dust. There was no sign that Clayton Rhodes' truck had been there at all that day. *Maybe the wind blew them away,* she thought.

But once in the barn with the lights switched on, Joanna knew that wasn't true. Kiddo was locked in a stall that clearly hadn't been cleaned that day, and the door to his paddock, which should have been open, was closed. His water barrel was dry, his feeding trough empty. Fuming to herself, Joanna used a hose to fill the water barrel. Then she poured out a measure of oats and wrestled some hay out of a new bale.

Out in the corral, her ten head of cattle were in much the same shape, although at least the float in the stock tank allowed their water to fill automatically. She fed the cattle along with her collection of chickens and rabbits. At first she was more angry than anything. If something had happened to Clayton—if he was sick or something—the least he could have done was to call her at work or at home and leave a message saying he wouldn't be in to work that day. But by the time Joanna finished the chores, her anger had changed to concern. Clayton Rhodes had always been totally reliable. Something serious must have happened to him. And for an elderly person living alone in the boonies, Joanna worried that whatever it was might be even more alarming.

With the animals fed and bedded down, she hurried back into the house and headed straight for the phone in the living room. She had taken messages as soon as she came home. None of those had been from Clayton. Now she scrolled through the screen on her Caller ID module. No calls from him showed there, either.

By then it was well past ten o'clock and that much later than Clayton's usual bedtime. Nonetheless, Joanna picked up the phone and dialed his number. She listened impatiently while the phone rang seven times without any answer. Ending the call, Joanna dialed Dispatch at the Cochise County Sheriff's Department. Tica Romero answered.

"What's up, Sheriff Brady?" the night-shift dispatcher asked.

"Have you logged any nine-one-one calls today from my neighbor, Clayton Rhodes?" Joanna asked.

"No. How come?"

"He didn't show up for work today," Joanna replied. "Evidently not this morning and not this afternoon, either. Who's patrolling this sector?"

"Nobody at the moment," Tica replied. "Deputy Pakin is assigned there, but he just responded to a serious-injury accident on Highway eighty out east of Douglas. Deputy Howell is finishing up with a domestic over in Saint David. I could check and see how long it would take her to get here."

"Never mind," Joanna said. "I'll go check on him myself."

"Keep me posted," Tica advised. "If you need backup, just call."

Putting down the phone, Joanna considered what to do next. She didn't like the idea of leaving Jenny alone in the house while she went to investigate. Still, worried about what she might find at Clayton Rhodes' place, Joanna didn't want to take her daughter along, either. And, as late as it was, it would take too much time to call someone to come stay with her.

Walking over to Jenny's bedroom door, Joanna noticed a tiny slash of light showing along the floorboard. As soon as she turned the doorknob, the light disappeared. "Jenny," Joanna called across the room. "Are you still awake?"

Doing an excellent job of feigning being awakened out of

a deep sleep, Jenny turned over and switched on her bedside lamp. "What's wrong?" she mumbled.

"I need to go check on Mr. Rhodes," Joanna said. "Will you be all right if I leave you here by yourself for a while?"

Making no further pretense of having been asleep, Jenny sat up in bed. "Really?" she asked excitedly. "You'd do that? Leave me here alone?"

"If it bothers you, I can maybe call someone to come—"

"No, Mom. Don't. I can stay by myself."

"You're sure. I'll lock the doors when I leave. I probably won't be gone very long, and you'll have the dogs—"

"It's okay, Mom," Jenny interrupted with a smile. "I'll be fine." With that, she settled back down on the pillow. "And thanks," she added.

"Thanks?" Joanna asked.

"For the early birthday present."

Joanna was mystified. "What early birthday present?"

"For treating me like a grown-up even if I'm not."

"You're welcome," Joanna said. "I'd better go."

"Well, go then," Jenny urged. "What are you waiting for?"

"I'm going," Joanna replied. "Don't rush me."

"Be careful," Jenny said.

Feeling her throat tighten, Joanna took Jenny's hand and squeezed it. "I will," she said. "Sleep tight," she whispered, reaching up to switch off the lamp. "Don't let the bedbugs bite."

Leaving the room, Joanna found herself fighting back tears. *Be careful.* That's what Jenny had said. Those words were never far beneath the surface in law-enforcement households. They were especially hard-hitting in a family like Jenny's. Her father, Andy, had died at the hands of a drug smuggler's hit man, and her maternal grandfather, Sheriff D. H. "Big Hank" Lathrop, had perished after being hit by a drunk driver. The last part of that sentence was never spoken, but it was always understood. *Be careful so you don't go away and never come back.*

In her own bedroom, Joanna unlocked the rolltop desk where she kept her weapons. Her Colt 2000 had proved undependable and had been relegated to the status of collector's item. As an engagement present, Butch had prevailed on her to replace that and her backup Glock 17 with a new pair of Glocks, a 19 and a 26 with interchangeable magazines.

Joanna's trip to Clayton Rhodes' place wasn't really an official police matter. It was more a case of a concerned neighbor looking in on someone else. There was no reason to show up armed to the teeth like some latter-day gunslinger. Still, if something was amiss up the road, it was best to be prepared. In the last few months, Cochise County had been overrun with hundreds of undocumented aliens making their illegal and dangerous journey from Mexico into the States. It wasn't at all out of line to worry that maybe Clayton had run afoul of a gang of UDAs more interested in the easy pickings of banditry than they were in harvesting strawberries or melons.

Leaving her shoulder holster with its heavy-duty 19 where it was, Joanna strapped on the compact 26 in its inconspicuous small-of-back holster. Then, putting the denim jacket back on and adding both her cell phone and flashlight, she hurried out the back door, carefully locking it behind her.

After clambering into her county-owned Blazer, Joanna headed for the Rhodes place. As the crow flies, Joanna's house and Clayton Rhodes' were little more than a mile apart. To get there, however, Joanna had to drive almost five miles of rough dirt road—first from her house out to High

Lonesome Road, north on that for the better part of two miles, and then back up another winding road into the hills.

By now the nearly full moon, high in the sky, cast a silvery glow over the nighttime landscape. That was something Joanna appreciated, and something that caught most city dwellers unawares. People who live in the artificial glow of streetlights have no idea that away from the pollution of manmade light, a full moon can make the nighttime desert bright enough to render headlights unnecessary.

Clayton Rhodes' house dated from pre-air-conditioning times and had been built into the cleft of Mexican Canyon where it was naturally sheltered during the worst of the Sonora Desert's afternoon heat. Carefully nurtured cottonwoods had grown up around the house, adding a much-needed layer of summertime shade. As Joanna drove into the silent yard, those cottonwoods, still bare-branched, stood like ghostly sentinels with their arms stretched skyward. The windows of the house were totally black. The only light was the eerie reflection of moon glow off the house's old-fashioned tin roof. There was no sign of life. Joanna remembered that, months earlier, Clayton had sold off the last of his livestock and taken his arthritic old dog, Biddy, to the vet to be put down.

"Won't be gettin' me another dog, neither," he had told Joanna then. "I'm too dang old. Wouldn't be fair."

And so, in Clayton Rhodes' yard, there was no welcoming chorus of barking dogs to announce Joanna's arrival. Nor was there any sign of a parked vehicle to indicate someone was at home.

Here, as on High Lonesome Ranch, the yard had been fenced to keep out marauding livestock. Joanna parked the Blazer in the gravel outside the closed gate. Before getting out of her vehicle, she pulled the radio's microphone out of its holder. "Tica," Joanna told the dispatcher. "I'm here now—at Clayton Rhodes' place. It looks pretty much deserted. I'm about to go inside."

"As in breaking and entering?" Tica asked.

"The man's in his eighties," Joanna returned. "He may be inside, sick or hurt. I know for a fact that Clayton isn't much of a believer in locking doors. But if it comes down to breaking in, I'm not above doing it."

"I've contacted Deputy Howell," Tica responded. "She's on her way, but she's coming from Saint David, so it's going to take some time for her to get to you."

Leaving the Blazer idling where it was, Joanna let herself in the gate, walked up onto the creaking porch, and knocked hard on the wood-framed screen door. "Clayton," she shouted. "Are you in there? Are you all right?"

She reached down and took hold of the knob. It turned easily in her hand and the door swung open, squawking noisily on elderly hinges. The house smelled musty and unkempt. Clayton had been a widower for years. Clearly he wasn't very interested in doing much of what he always considered "women's work."

"Clayton," Joanna called again. "Are you in here? Are you all right?"

No answer. Using her flashlight, Joanna located an antique push-button light switch. She pressed the upper button and an equally antique hanging light fixture with a single bulb cast a wan glow around the dingy room.

Making her way across a threadbare rag rug, Joanna walked through the dining room and into the kitchen, where she found Clayton's antique wood-burning stove cold to the touch.

"Clayton?" she repeated. Still nothing. He wasn't in the kitchen or on the screened back porch, either. Leaving the kitchen behind, Joanna hurried back through the sparsely furnished living room to check the two tiny bedrooms and the spacious bathroom that had been carved out of what had once been a third minuscule bedroom. Nowhere did Joanna see anything out of order. There was no sign of a struggle— nothing that indicated Clayton Rhodes had left his home under any kind of duress.

Shaking her head, Joanna went back outside. She had been listening so intently for a reply to her continuing calls that her hearing seemed to have been tuned to a higher level than when she had first exited the Blazer. Now, in addition to the steady rumble of the Blazer's engine, she could hear something else as well—the sound of another vehicle. It was muffled and faint and stationary— with none of the rises and falls in engine noise that would have occurred in a vehicle making its way on the rough road that wound up Mexican Canyon from High Lonesome Road.

Bounding back to the Blazer, Joanna quickly switched off the engine and then stepped back outside to listen once again. Without interference from the Blazer's idling engine, the muffled sound Joanna had heard was much clearer now. Following it, she walked toward a collection of outbuildings, including the sagging clapboard barn with a lean-to shed that Clayton used as a makeshift garage to shelter his beloved vintage Ford pickup truck that dated from the early fifties. As she neared the shed, Joanna smelled the heavy scent of exhaust and the distinctive odor of an overheated engine.

Sprinting now, she raced up to the windowless shed and tried the door. Nothing happened when she yanked on the outside handle. Too heavy to be raised by hand, the door refused to respond to her pulling. Pounding on the garage door, she shouted again. "Clayton! Are you in there? Answer me!"

This time Joanna heard no answer other than the continuing low growl of an idling engine. She turned and raced back to her Blazer. First she grabbed up the ax and crowbar she kept in the back cargo area. Then she paused long enough to use the radio.

"Tica," she said urgently. "Send an ambulance. I'm pretty sure Clayton Rhodes is locked in his garage—with a car engine running."

Back at the garage, Joanna made short work of beating a hole in the door. As soon as she did so, a thick cloud of acrid exhaust boiled out around her. Holding her breath, she crawled in through the jagged hole and felt her way through the oily exhaust up to the front of Clayton's old pickup. Through the murk she could just make out the shape of a human body slouched over the steering wheel. Blindly she reached in, felt along the dashboard for the ignition key, and switched it off.

Only then did she reach for Clayton. As soon as she touched his cold, lifeless hand, she knew it was far too late. By then she had run out of breath. As soon as she breathed, her lungs filled with smoke. Coughing and choking, she stumbled back outside, pulling out her cell phone and dialing as she went.

"Nine-one-one," Tica Romero responded. "What are you reporting?"

"Cancel that ambulance," Joanna told the dispatcher. "It's too late. Clayton Rhodes is dead."

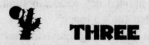 **THREE**

Agnes Hooper looked back longingly at the good old days—before CNN. Once her husband had watched the news only twice a day—after work in the evenings and again at ten o'clock. That was back before Wayne's heart went bad and before Dr. Loomis put him on total disability. The next thing Agnes knew, he had installed one of those little satellite dishes up on the roof. Now the news went on and on, hour after hour, all day long, with the same smiling faces endlessly repeating the same stories over and over.

Tonight the big story was from Tennessee, where some kid had gone berserk and had shot up a school bus, killing the driver as well as two children and injuring three others before some of the other kids on the bus tackled the shooter and wrestled the gun out of his hands.

"He was just a regular kid," a tearful principal was saying into the microphone someone had shoved in his face. "Something of a loner, but he never gave his teachers any trouble. This just came at us out of the blue, with no warning."

"See there," Wayne said. "Now they're turning school buses into war zones. You should stop driving that thing, Aggie. The way kids are today, it's too dangerous."

The stricken principal's words had already chilled Agnes Hooper's heart. *Loner,* she thought. *Never gave teachers any trouble.*

"That's what people say about Lucy Ridder behind her back," Agnes said softly. "That she's a loner."

Wayne turned away from the blaring television set and studied his wife's face. "Lucy Ridder," he said thoughtfully. "Isn't she that Indian kid who lives with her grandmother out on Middlemarch Road?"

Agnes nodded. "Lucy's the last one off my bus in the afternoon and the first one on in the morning."

Wayne covered his face with both hands. "Dammit, Aggie!" he exclaimed. "I wish you could quit that damned job. Just haul off and quit. Walk away from the whole stupid mess."

But they both knew quitting wasn't an option. Driving a school bus didn't pay beans, but the benefits were good. And it was Agnes Hooper's medical benefits with the Elfrida Unified School District that were keeping her husband alive.

"You know I can't do that, hon," she said calmly. "It's just not in the cards."

Wayne shook his head. "It's not right," he said. "I'm the one who should be out working and taking care of you. That's how life's supposed to be, not the other way around. The last thing you should have to do is be out dealing with a bunch of crazy kids day in and day out!"

"They're good kids," Agnes said soothingly, wanting to calm him down. Dr. Loomis said it was bad for Wayne to be stressed. "They're not crazy. As for Lucy Ridder, she's never given me a moment's trouble."

"Right," Wayne Hooper said with a despairing shake of his head. "As I recall, that's the exact same thing that principal just said about the kid who shot up the school bus back there in Tennessee—he never gave anybody a lick of trouble."

After finding Clayton Rhodes' body, Joanna shifted into automatic and made all the necessary calls. Once George

Winfield, Cochise County's medical examiner, had been summoned to the scene, there was nothing for her to do but wait. She did go inside the unlocked house as far as the little telephone table. There she came face-to-face with a much younger image of Clayton Rhodes in a framed, formally posed wedding picture taken of him and his late wife, Molly. Bony and bow-legged even then, Clayton looked grimly uncomfortable and out of character in a dark, double-breasted suit. The youthful, sweet-faced Molly, slender in her bridal finery, bore little resemblance to the broad-hipped, heavyset woman Joanna remembered meeting years earlier, when she had first come to High Lonesome Ranch.

Turning from the picture, Joanna donned a pair of latex gloves and rummaged through the drawer in the table until she located a small, leather-bound address book. She remembered Clayton's daughter's first name—Reba—but she had no idea what her married name might be. Consequently, Joanna had to page through almost the whole notebook until she finally located the name under the letter *S* for Singleton—Reba Singleton. The address listed was in Los Gatos, California. Jotting the address and 415 phone number down on a scrap of paper, Joanna returned the address book to the table drawer and punched up her cell phone.

"I'd like the number for the Los Gatos, California, Police Department," she told the operator.

"The emergency number?" the operator asked.

With Clayton dead, the emergency was long over. "No," Joanna said. "The non-emergency number will be fine."

She spent what seemed like several long minutes waiting on hold before a desk sergeant finally took her call. "My name is Joanna Brady," she told him. "Sheriff Joanna Brady of Cochise County in southeastern Arizona. We've had a death here—a man named Clayton Rhodes. I understand his daughter lives there where you are—in Los Gatos. I need someone to do a next-of-kin notification."

The desk sergeant sounded terminally bored. "Name?" he said.

"Clayton Rhodes."

"No. The daughter's name."

"Reba Singleton."

"Address."

"943 Valencia," Joanna returned, followed by the 415 area code telephone number.

"You say this Singleton woman is the stiff's daughter?"

"The deceased's name is Clayton Rhodes," Joanna returned sharply. "The man happened to be a friend of mine— a good friend."

"And this is the most recent address information you have for his daughter?"

Joanna was losing patience. "It's the one that was in Mr. Rhodes' address book," she answered somewhat testily.

"That may be true, but it could be out of date. The phone number is."

"What do you mean?"

"Our area code's been 650 for years now. If the dead guy didn't bother to fix that in his book, the address listed may be out of date as well. What did he die of, by the way—murder, natural causes, old age?"

The word "suicide" stuck in Joanna's throat. She wanted to find a way to cushion the blow for Reba Singleton. Learning a loved one has died is hard enough. Being told that person has taken his or her own life is infinitely harder on the people left behind. Joanna had never met Reba Singleton, but already her heart ached for her. By not saying too much right now, perhaps Joanna could give Clayton's daughter a chance to prepare herself.

"Tell Ms. Singleton that the cause of her father's death has yet to be determined," Joanna said. "I'll give you several numbers where I can be reached. Or else, if she'd rather, Ms. Singleton can speak directly to George Winfield, our medical examiner. I'll give you his office and home numbers as well. That way, once your officers have notified her, she can call one of us for more details."

"I'm sure that'll suit our officers just fine."

"Will you notify me once they've talked to her?" Joanna asked.

"That's not how we usually do it," he said.

"I'd appreciate it if you'd do it that way this time," Joanna said firmly. "Let me know one way or the other, whether your people locate her or not. I need to know either way."

"We're not equipped—" he began.

Joanna cut him off in mid-excuse. "And what did you say your name was?" she asked.

"Carlin," he replied after a short pause. "Sergeant Richard Carlin."

"Thanks so much, Sergeant Carlin. You've been most helpful. It's always a pleasure to work with someone who really cares about inter-departmental relations."

She hung up before he had a chance to reply. Then, shivering against the cold, she turned on the porch light and waited on the front steps of Clayton Rhodes' house to see who would be the first to arrive. The winner was Deputy Debbie Howell, followed closely by George Winfield. Somehow Joanna didn't have the heart to go back to the shed and work the crime scene. She stayed where she was and sent Deputy Howell along to assist the medical examiner and catalog evidence. Not wanting to pay any more

overtime than absolutely necessary, Joanna had put off sum-
moning one of her two homicide detectives until after hearing what the medical examiner had to say.

Sitting alone on the top step, Joanna lost track of time.
She was surprised by the amount of anger she felt toward
Clayton Rhodes—toward a dead man. *What was happening
that he would have committed suicide over it?* she wondered. *Was his health going bad? Did he have money worries that he never mentioned? And why the hell didn't he tell
me about it? Maybe I could have helped. Or at least been
there to say good-bye.*

Clayton Rhodes hadn't given Joanna that opportunity,
and right then that omission on his part seemed utterly un-
forgivable.

She was still lost in thought some time later when Deputy
Lance Pakin showed up fresh from his traffic investigation.
She directed him to assist Debbie in bagging and loading
Clayton's body into the medical examiner's van. While the
two deputies went about doing that, George Winfield came
up the gravel walkway and sat down beside her. "How's
tricks?" he asked.

Dr. George Winfield was a permanent snowbird who had
come to Arizona from Minnesota. Hired by the Board of Supervisors, his initial position had been that of county coro-
ner. Now, though, he held the recently created title of
Cochise County Medical Examiner. Due to his equally recent marriage to Joanna's mother, Eleanor, he was also
Joanna Brady's stepfather.

She looked up at him and gave him a wan smile. "Not so
hot," she answered. "Why'd Clayton go and do that,
George? Why did he have to commit suicide?"

"Who said anything about suicide?"

"Well, I thought . . ."

"You thought he locked himself in that garage with the engine running on purpose?"

"Didn't he?"

"Deputy Howell," George called out. "Mind bringing that bag of evidence over here?"

Debbie Howell came toward them carrying a clear plastic bag. Inside it were several glassine envelopes. George held it up to the light and pointed to a rectangular black-and-white object inside. "What does that look like?" he asked.

"A garage-door opener?"

"Right you are. And guess where I found it?"

"I don't know."

"In Clayton Rhodes' shirt pocket—pressed tight up against the steering wheel. My guess is the garage door was open when he turned on the engine. But then something happened—a heart attack maybe, or possibly even a stroke. We won't know exactly what until the autopsy. Whatever it was, he slumped forward onto the steering wheel. When that happened, the weight of his body pressed against the button, shutting the door."

"You're saying he didn't commit suicide after all?" Joanna asked wonderingly.

"Are you kidding?" George Winfield returned. "To do that, the place would have had to be airtight. And it's not. Definitely not. If there wasn't plenty of air, the engine wouldn't have been running when you got here. In an airtight garage the engine would have quit long ago due to lack of oxygen."

"So you're saying he most likely died of natural causes?" Joanna asked.

"Or smoke inhalation. That could be the culprit as well. In any event, for right now I don't believe Clayton Rhodes took his own life. You didn't find a note or anything to indicate otherwise, did you?"

"No."

"Well, he wasn't bright red, either, which pretty well rules out carbon monoxide, but as soon as I have autopsy results, I'll let you know. Meanwhile, what about notifying next of kin?"

Joanna glanced at her watch. To her surprise she realized two hours had passed since her call to the Los Gatos Police Department. What wasn't the least bit surprising was that Sergeant Carlin hadn't bothered to call her back.

"I found Clayton's daughter's address and telephone number. Reba Singleton lives in Los Gatos, California," Joanna replied. "Someone from the local police department there is supposed to notify her and report back to me once the notification has been made."

"Good. Glad that's being handled."

"What next, Sheriff Brady?" Debbie Howell asked. "You calling in the homicide guys?"

Joanna considered for a moment. From what George Winfield was saying, a full-scale homicide investigation might not be necessary, which meant that neither would an overtime visit from one or both of her two homicide detectives.

"If we need detectives, they can look things over in the morning. Meanwhile, you and Deputy Pakin do what you can to secure the scene," she answered. "You've got the house keys?"

Debbie Howell nodded. "Right here in the bag."

"Let's close up for tonight," Joanna directed. "Take the tarp from your vehicle and cover the hole I made in the door. Then put up crime-scene tape around both the barn and garage. I'll take care of locking up the house."

"Will do," Debbie said.

As Deputy Howell walked away, George Winfield peered questioningly at Joanna through the top of his bifocals. "How are you doing personally, Joanna?" he asked solicitously. "I know the man was a good friend of yours."

The likelihood that Clayton Rhodes hadn't committed suicide should have made Joanna feel better, but it didn't.

She shook her head. "I've been sitting here all torn up that Clayton had the unmitigated nerve to go and die without giving me any advance notice. Like he should have been thoughtful enough to pick up the phone and say, 'By the way, Joanna, I think I'm going to cork off now, so maybe you'd better make other arrangements to feed your own goddamned animals for a change.'"

"Sounds to me like you're blaming yourself," George observed.

"Maybe I am," Joanna replied. "And why shouldn't I? If I'd been smart enough or observant enough to notice that the dogs' water dishes were empty this morning when Jenny and I left the house, maybe I would have realized something was wrong and come over to check on Clayton early enough to make a difference. If I had done that, maybe he'd still be alive."

George shook his head. "I doubt it," he replied. "I don't think your getting here sooner would have made any difference at all. The way it looks to me, once he slumped over onto the steering wheel, I doubt he even twitched. We're dealing with something catastrophic here, Joanna. It's the kind of thing from which there would have been no recovery, other than life in some kind of vegetative state. And from the stories I've heard about Clayton Rhodes—about the kind of man he was and the active life he led—that would have been a nightmare. He wouldn't have wanted to end up that way, not at all."

"I suppose you're right," Joanna agreed with a sigh. "He would have hated being helpless. That would have been hell for him."

George reached over and gave her shoulder a gentle pat. "So, there you are then, Joanna. Let it go."

"I'll try."

George stood up and rubbed his hands together. "Back home in Minneapolis, this would have been considered balmy weather for late March. People would have been ready to haul out their shorts. But I have to admit, it feels chilly tonight, even to me."

Joanna stood up. Despite the sheepskin lining in her denim jacket, she, too, felt chilled.

"I'd best be getting back home to your mother," George added. "She doesn't like it when I have to be out late at night—even when I'm off on official business and in the company of her very own daughter."

"Truth be known, Eleanor doesn't like her daughter being out late, either," Joanna said with a laugh.

"You want me to stick around while you finish up?"

"No need. I'll wait until my deputies leave, then I'll go, too."

George started down the walkway, then turned back. "How's Butch holding up?" he asked. "With all the wedding preparations, I mean."

"Fine," Joanna answered. "Better than I am."

"I know things are turning out to be somewhat more complicated than either one of you originally envisioned," George added, "but I appreciate it. Ellie's having the time of her life making all the arrangements. She's in her element and loving every minute of it. By the way, she wanted me to ask when do your new in-laws arrive?"

"On Monday. They're driving into town in their RV. They

wanted to come a few days early so they'll have a chance to visit with Butch before the wedding. He tried to talk them into coming a little closer to time, but he doesn't seem to have any better luck with his mother than I do with mine. In other words, his folks will be here for the better part of the week. Since they'll be staying at that new RV park down by the Elk's Club, it shouldn't be too bad."

"I'll try to see to it that Ellie and I do our fair share of entertaining," George said. "Your mother will be in tall cotton and cooking up a storm. I'll probably gain ten pounds."

With that, George Winfield waved and continued down the gravel walkway. Joanna watched him go out and shut the gate, then she let herself back into the house. Talking with George had helped. She had worked with the man long enough to have real confidence that his initial assessment of the situation would most likely be on the money. There was little doubt in her mind that the official finding would be that Clayton Rhodes had died of a sudden massive stroke or heart attack or hemorrhage rather than by committing suicide or falling victim to foul play. Now, as Joanna went back through the house to make sure all the doors and windows were locked, she did so with a sense of loss that was no longer contaminated by guilt. It was all right to feel sad that Clayton was gone, but here on Rhodes Ranch where he had lived and worked most of his eighty-five years—here in the modest home he and his wife had loved so much—it was okay to feel thankfulness as well.

Clayton had lived a good life—a long and useful one. He had worked for Joanna not so much because he needed the money, but because he needed to be needed—because he knew that taking care of Joanna's livestock made her life easier. He had been in full possession of his faculties right up until the moment he died. Instead of lingering helplessly as an empty shell of his former self in some sterile hospital-bed prison, he had been up and about and on his way to work when death overtook him—when it caught him on the fly. Clayton may have had to give up on horseback riding, but as far as Joanna was concerned, he had died with his boots on in the best sense of the phrase.

Before turning off the living room light fixture, Joanna made one last survey of her surroundings. Once again she examined the stiffly posed wedding picture of Molly and Clayton, but this time, as she did so, she realized it was the only picture in the room. There were places on the wall where other pictures had once hung, but all of them had been removed, leaving behind a ghostly testimony of their existence in the form of clear rectangular-shaped pieces of wallpaper pattern in an otherwise sun-faded room. Joanna found herself wishing that the pictures had been left behind long enough for her to see them. Old photos might have told her a little more about the long, productive life of her dead friend, Clayton Rhodes. They might have given her something to remember him by.

As Joanna pulled the front door shut and stuffed the graceful old skeleton key into her pocket, she felt as though she were closing the door not only on a chapter in her life, but on a whole era as well. Once in the Blazer, Joanna followed her deputies back out to High Lonesome Road and as far as the turnoff to her own place. When she drove into the yard, she was startled to find Butch Dixon's Subaru parked next to the gate. By the time she had parked and locked the Blazer, he was coming out through the back door to meet her.

"What are you doing here?" Joanna asked after kissing him hello.

"I called to tell you good night," Butch replied. "When

Jenny answered and told me what was going on, I decided to come over and wait up for you. How's Clayton?"

"He's dead," Joanna said hollowly. "George thinks he suffered some kind of catastrophic physical incident—a heart attack or a stroke maybe. It looks as though Clayton was on his way here this morning when it happened."

Butch reached out and put a comforting arm around Joanna's shoulder. "I'm so sorry," he said.

Joanna leaned against him. "Me, too," she returned.

"Does he have any family?"

"A daughter, Reba Singleton. She lives in California."

"Have you been in touch with her?"

"We tried. I left word for her to call here if she wants additional information. There haven't been any calls, have there?"

"Only from your mother," Butch said. "I checked caller ID to screen the call. When I saw it was Eleanor, I decided not answering was my best bet. After all, what Eleanor doesn't know won't hurt her."

Joanna grinned up at him. "You're learning," she said.

They went into the house. "I may be learning with your mother," Butch replied, leaning against the dryer while Joanna removed her jacket and hung it on the peg. "But I almost blew it with Jenny," he added.

"You did?" Joanna asked. "How so?"

"By coming over to wait up for you. She was so bent out of shape when I showed up that for a while I didn't think she was going to unlock the door and let me in. She thought you had sicced me on her—sent me out as an emergency baby-sitter. I finally managed to convince her otherwise."

"How?"

"By telling her that baby-sitting was the last thing on my mind. That I had come out here primarily because I had designs on her mother's body."

Joanna was shocked. "You didn't tell her that!"

Now it was Butch's turn to grin. "I did," he said. "Scout's honor. Got me right out of the dog house. Turned us into co-conspirators."

"Butch," Joanna objected. "Jenny's only eleven!"

"Almost twelve and going on thirty," he replied. "Believe me, that kid knows all about the birds and bees."

"She shouldn't," Joanna huffed.

"Maybe not, but she does. Now come on. You wouldn't want to make a liar out of me, would you? Besides, you feel like a chunk of ice. I know just the thing to warm you up."

Joanna started to argue, but then she didn't. She *was* cold. And, as far as Jenny's knowing or not knowing what was going on between Butch and Joanna, the damage was done.

"Come on, then," she said. "Will you still be this horny after we're married?"

"Absolutely," Butch Dixon said, once again assuming his now lecherous grin. "I promise."

 **FOUR**

A tiny sound right next to Joanna's ear brought her fully awake. She opened her eyes. The sun was up. Jennifer Ann Brady, completely dressed and with her blond hair already neatly combed, stood beside the bed, grinning from ear to ear and bearing a cookie sheet laden with two steaming cups of coffee. Seeing her fully clothed daughter, Joanna was instantly aware that, except for a concealing mound of covers, she herself was stark-naked.

"It's about time you guys woke up," Jenny declared airily as she set the tray on the bedside table nearest her mother. "We're supposed to be going to Tucson this morning, remember? And don't worry. I won't tell Grandma."

With that, Jenny turned and flounced from the room. Behind Joanna, on the other side of the bed, Butch Dixon groaned and rolled over. He was no more dressed than Joanna was.

"Oops," he said. "Bad move. I meant to be up and out by now. We must have overslept."

"Overslept doesn't quite cover it," Joanna told him crossly. "I believe the correct term is caught with our pants down."

"Not just down," he said. "Mine aren't even within grabbing distance. Sorry about that." He swung his legs over the side of the bed and sat up. "I'll get dressed right away."

"Forget it," Joanna said. "You already spilled the beans last night, and since Jenny brought us coffee, we could just as well drink it before we crawl out of bed."

She pulled a pillow up behind him. Once Butch leaned back against the headboard and drew the sheet back across his bare chest, she handed him his cup of coffee.

"Somehow it seemed like a better idea last night than it does now that the sun's up," he told her ruefully. "What do you suggest we do now?"

Joanna was glad to hear that Butch sounded almost as embarrassed as she was. "Brazen it out, I guess," she answered. "We sure as hell can't put the toothpaste back in the tube."

At that, Butch leaned over and planted a kiss on her bare shoulder. "By the way," he said. "Did anyone ever tell you that you keep pretty ungodly hours—for a girl?"

The use of the word "girl" was standard fare in Butch's unending lexicon of teasing. Most of the time Joanna ignored it, but for some reason on this occasion it hit her wrong and put her on the defensive.

"Wait a minute, pal. We're not even married yet and already you're complaining about my job?"

"Don't get your nose out of joint," Butch assured her. "All I'm saying is don't expect me to wait up for you every night. Obviously I need more beauty sleep than you do."

"Oh," Joanna said, but she was still a little grumpy about it.

There was a knock on the bedroom door. "More coffee?" Jenny asked, pushing it open a crack.

"Hadn't we better get up and take care of the animals?" Butch asked.

That's when Joanna remembered that Jenny didn't yet know about Clayton Rhodes. No one had told her.

"No, thanks," Joanna told Jenny. "We'll be out in a minute. We'll have more in a little while."

When Jenny retreated from the door, Butch pulled on his shirt and pants and then hotfooted it into the bathroom. Joanna retrieved both her nightgown and bathrobe from the closet and then went in search of Jenny. She found her daughter curled up on the couch in the living room reading a book. Tigger, snoring like a locomotive, lay with his head in Jenny's lap, while Sadie sprawled on the floor at Jenny's feet.

Joanna could tell from the faded blue cover that the book was one of her old Nancy Drew mysteries. "What are you reading?" she asked, easing herself down on the couch in a way that didn't disturb either one of the sleeping dogs.

"The Secret of the Old Clock," Jenny said. "When I get my driver's license, can I have a roadster? Nancy's sounds neat."

Joanna shook her head. "You were born sixty or seventy years too late for a roadster," she said. "You'll probably have to make do with my old Eagle—if it's still running."

"But that's a station wagon," Jenny protested. "I want a convertible—a red convertible."

Joanna sighed. "Don't we all. Seriously, though, Jenny, there's something I need to tell you."

"Mr. Rhodes is dead, isn't he?" Jenny said at once.

Joanna simply nodded. "How did you know?" she asked.

Jenny shrugged. "I sort of figured it out. I mean, I followed the clues, just like Nancy Drew."

"What clues are those?"

"Well, you went over to see him and didn't come back for a long time. And then this morning. When I get up to watch Saturday-morning cartoons, Mr. Rhodes is usually already here, but today he wasn't. I went outside and looked for his tire tracks, but there weren't any. So I went ahead and fed the animals myself."

"All of them?" Joanna asked.

"You didn't think I'd let them go hungry, do you?" Jenny asked indignantly.

Joanna laughed. "No," she agreed. "Of course not."

"And after I fed them I made coffee for you."

Joanna was stunned. It wasn't that Jenny didn't know how to feed the animals or how much to give them. On Clayton Rhodes' days off, Joanna and Jenny usually did the chores together. Still, she was struck by the fact that Jenny had done the chores all by herself and also on her own initiative. Butch was right, Joanna realized then. Jenny was growing up—in more ways than one.

"So what happened to him?" Jenny asked. "To Mr. Rhodes."

"He probably had a heart attack or else maybe a stroke," Joanna replied. "At least that's what Grandpa George thinks."

"Grandpa George will have to do an autopsy, won't he—to find out for sure?"

Jenny had lived all her life in a law enforcement household where the pieces of homicide investigations were regular components in ordinary, everyday conversations. "Yes, he will," Joanna replied.

Jenny rolled her enormous blue eyes. "Well," she observed, "Mr. Rhodes wouldn't like that."

"What do you mean?" Joanna asked.

"Grandpa George is nice and all that, but he's still a doctor," Jenny said. "Mr. Rhodes told me once, after he hurt his leg last year, that he never wanted to go see a doctor again. But I guess if he's already dead, it won't matter."

Joanna was a little taken aback by Jenny's unemotional,

almost clinical response to news of Clayton Rhodes' death. After all, the man had been an important part of their daily lives. As Jenny's mother, Joanna would have preferred some show of sadness and even a few tears.

"Clayton Rhodes was a nice man," Joanna said. "I'm sorry he's dead. Aren't you?"

Jenny shook her head. "I'm not," she declared. "Mr. Rhodes told me once that he was old and ready to go anytime the good Lord was ready to take him. He said he missed his wife and could hardly wait to see her again."

Joanna felt as if she had been left standing in the dust. "Just when did you and he have this long conversation?" she asked.

Jenny shrugged. "I don't know," she said. "It was one time when we were out in the barn and he was cleaning Kiddo's stall. He told me he wished he had a granddaughter just like me. He said he had grandsons, but that he didn't like them much. He said they were spoiled rotten. I told him I liked him, too. And I did. But now he's in heaven with Molly and his little boy—"

"Molly and Clayton had a son?" Joanna asked. "I didn't know that. When?"

"Oh, a long time ago," Jenny answered. "During the war. At least I think that's what he said. That the little boy was born and died while he was away at war and he never even got to see him."

Joanna was nothing short of amazed to discover that Jenny had known so much about Clayton Rhodes' life. Somehow Jenny had managed to glean details that Joanna herself had never suspected while the old man was still alive.

"When is the funeral?" Jenny asked. "Will we have to go?" The child's blue eyes darkened as she asked the second question.

"I don't know when it'll be," Joanna answered. "As of right now, I don't even know for sure if his daughter has been notified. But whenever it is, we should probably go, don't you think?"

Jenny nodded. "I guess," she said after a moment's hesitation. "I don't like funerals, but that's what friends are for, isn't it?"

Joanna reached over and gave her daughter a hug. "That's right," she said. "That is what friends are for."

Just then Butch emerged from the bathroom. "It's all yours," he said to Joanna. Then he paused, glancing first in Jenny's direction and then in Joanna's. "This looks like a pretty serious discussion. Should I make myself scarce?"

"No, it's fine. Jenny and I were just talking about Clayton Rhodes' funeral," Joanna told him. "Jenny thinks we should go, and I agree."

Butch nodded. Then he added, "Speaking of Clayton, I'll head outside and get started feeding the animals."

"Don't bother," Joanna said. "Jenny's already done it."

Butch looked at Jenny. "You did?" Jenny nodded, beaming with pride. "Good for you," Butch added.

Joanna hurried to the bathroom to take her turn. She was just finishing applying makeup when Jenny knocked on the door. "Phone, Mom."

"Who is it?" Joanna asked as Jenny handed her the cordless phone.

Jenny shrugged. "Somebody from work," she said.

"Hello," Joanna said. "Sheriff Brady here."

"Hi, Sheriff. It's Lisa."

Lisa Howard was the weekend desk clerk at the Cochise County Sheriff's Department. Joanna's heart sank. If there was some new emergency at the department, Joanna's planned day-trip outing with Jenny and Butch might have to be canceled or postponed.

"What's the matter?" Joanna asked.

"Nothing. We've got a reported runaway out in the valley, but that's about it. There was a message that came in for you overnight. Since it didn't seem especially urgent, the night shift decided to let me pass it along to you when I came on duty this morning."

"What is it?" Joanna asked. "And who's it from?"

"Sergeant Carlin."

"In Los Gatos," Joanna supplied.

"Right. He wanted you to know that Mrs. Singleton has been notified."

"Good," Joanna said. "Anything else?"

"He did say one other thing."

"What's that?"

"He said, 'Good luck.' "

"What's that supposed to mean?" Joanna asked.

"I don't know," Lisa returned. "I thought maybe you'd understand what he meant."

"Well, I don't. But that's all right. The point is, Clayton Rhodes' family members have now been officially notified; you can release the news of his death to the press. And you should probably pass that word along to the medical examiner's office as well in case anyone comes asking Doc Winfield for information."

"Will do," Lisa said. "Anything else?"

"Not right now. Jenny and I are on our way to Tucson to do some shopping, so if anything comes up, you may need to contact Chief Deputy Montoya. I told him about it yesterday, so he knows he's on call."

Hanging up the phone, Joanna headed for the kitchen. "What's for breakfast?" she asked.

"French toast," Jenny replied. "At Daisy's."

"Whose idea was that?" Joanna asked.

"Mine," Jenny said. "Butch said that since I took care of feeding the animals, I could have whatever I wanted, and going to Daisy's is what I chose."

"So that's how it's going to be?" Joanna asked. "Whatever you want you get?" She turned to Butch. "You're going to spoil her."

"I know," he said. "But it's her birthday celebration, too. And I figure this way will be faster—if we leave right now, that is."

They took Butch's Outback—the newest vehicle in their stable of rolling stock—and headed for town. Daisy's Café was already crowded with the Saturday-morning breakfast crowd. Standing just inside the door, they waited for a clean table.

"Hey, Junior," Jenny called across the room. "How's it going?"

Junior Dowdle was a fifty-six-year-old developmentally disabled man who had been abandoned by his court-appointed guardians and left on his own at a local arts-and-crafts fair the previous fall. The priest who had found him had turned Junior over to the care and keeping of the Cochise County Sheriff's Department. Through Joanna's own efforts and those of her people, not only had Junior's mother been found, so had a new set of local, Bisbee-area guardians. Moe and Daisy Maxwell, the owners of Daisy's Café, had taken on that demanding role.

With infinite patience, Daisy and Moe had taught Junior how to bus tables. Now he spent several hours each day helping out at the restaurant. And, for the first time in his life, Junior Dowdle was earning his own spending money. One look at Junior's beaming countenance offered mute testimony as to how well that arrangement was working.

Grinning from ear to ear and carrying a plastic pan loaded with dirty dishes, he came hurrying toward Jenny. On the pocket of his shirt he still wore the sheriff's badge Joanna had given him the day she had brought him home from the monastery in Saint David.

"You come," he said, motioning for them to follow him toward a booth he had just finished clearing. "You come and eat."

From behind the counter, Daisy Maxwell watched, nodded, and smiled her approval. She waited until the party was seated before she followed with coffee and menus. "Most of the time Junior remembers menus," she said. "But not when he sees someone he knows. Then he gets too excited. Come to think of it, though, you guys probably don't need menus. What'll you have?"

Removing the stub of a pencil from her beehive hairdo, Daisy took two orders for choriso and eggs and one for French toast along with two coffees, one milk, and orange juice all around.

"I just heard about poor Mr. Rhodes," Daisy said, once she returned her order pad to its customary place in her apron pocket. "It's too bad. He was the one who usually did your chores for you, wasn't he?"

Joanna nodded.

"What are you going to do now? Who are you going to get to help out?"

Joanna glanced slyly at Butch. "I don't know," she said with a laugh. "I guess I'll just have to get married."

Daisy looked at Butch and grinned. "Sounds like a good idea to me. We women have to stick together and make sure you men pull your weight." With that, Daisy Maxwell marched off to the kitchen.

That leisurely breakfast at Daisy's was the beginning

of something Sheriff Joanna Brady didn't have too many of—a wonderfully carefree day. Together she and Butch and Jenny drove to Tucson and spent several hours in Guzman's Horse Hotel, Saddlery, and Tack Shop on the far east end of Fort Lowell Road. Once Jenny's all-new matching saddle, bridle, halter, and saddle blanket had been loaded into the back of the Subaru, they drove to Tucson Mall and spent some time mall-crawling. Then, after a late lunch at La Fuente, they headed back home.

Jenny, in the backseat next to her saddle, was once again lost in her book. "A penny for your thoughts," Butch said softly to Joanna, somewhere beyond Saint David.

"What?" Joanna asked.

"Where are you?" Butch asked. "We've driven sixty miles and you haven't said a single word."

"I was thinking," Joanna said.

"About what?"

"Cleaning house."

"Are you kidding?"

"No. Your mother's coming to town day after tomorrow and my cabinets haven't been properly cleaned and neither have my closets."

"Don't worry about it," Butch offered consolingly. "My mother's a terrible housekeeper."

"No, she's not. You're lying."

"If my mother didn't have a cleaning lady—her name's Irma, by the way, and she's cleaned Mom and Dad's house for years. If not for Irma, my folks would have been buried under clutter years ago. Believe me, you don't have to clean house on account of my mother."

"Yes, I do," Joanna insisted. "And tomorrow's the only day I have to do it."

"So you're saying tomorrow's out as far as fun is concerned?"

"Cleaning can be fun," Joanna told him. "Bring rubber gloves. You can do the oven."

Butch shook his head. "I'm serious, Joanna. My mother isn't going to look in your oven, and she isn't going to white-glove your cabinets or closets, either. Now, as far as my cabinets and my closets are concerned, that's another story entirely. But don't worry, please. Your house is fine."

Sighing, Joanna returned to staring out the window and saying nothing. Right around Tucson, the paloverde and mesquite had begun leafing out. As they climbed up out of the valley, though, the blackened mesquite trees looked as though they were dead for all time.

"In other words, you don't believe me," Butch said at last, reaching out and taking Joanna's hand.

"You're right," Joanna said. "I don't. You're just saying that because you want to make me feel better."

"No," Butch returned with a wry grin. "It's because I don't like cleaning ovens."

It was almost four in the afternoon as they turned off High Lonesome Road onto the rutted track that led to Joanna's house. Two hundred yards up the dirt road, they rounded a bend and found their way blocked by a white stretch limo, a Lincoln, that was high-centered on rocks in the middle of the steep wash. A man in a dark blue suit knelt on his hands and knees beside the vehicle and peered underneath it while behind him a woman in a pair of dangerously-high high heels tottered back and forth, pacing and gesticulating wildly.

"What the hell!" Butch muttered, stopping just short of the wash.

Joanna leaped out of the Subaru before it came to a full

stop. "Who are you?" she asked. "What seems to be the problem?"

The woman stopped pacing long enough to reply. "We're stuck, that's what the problem is. Seems to me that even an idiot could see that much. Who the hell are you?"

The woman's slender figure was clad in a black wool two-piece suit that screamed of haute couture. The thin-skinned, carefully made-up face looked as though it had been artificially augmented more than once, and her mane of hair had been highlighted within an inch of its life. She might have been quite attractive had it not been for the aura of prickly hostility that surrounded her like a dark thundercloud.

"My name's Joanna Brady. It so happens that this road leads to my house. What are you doing here?"

The woman's face hardened into a demeaning sneer. "So this is the incomparable Joanna Brady! Sad to say, you're the very reason I'm here. I had to come get a look at you for myself. I wanted to see the woman who killed my father."

"Killed your father?" Joanna echoed. "What are you talking about?"

"Oh, yes, by all means. Let's play innocent, why don't we. Clayton Rhodes was my father, and you had no business working him into his grave."

Behind Joanna one of the doors on the Subaru quietly opened and closed. Butch got out. With a curt nod in the direction of the two women, he walked past them and then dropped down to his knees, where he joined the limo driver in studying the situation under the Lincoln.

"Mom," Jenny called from the car. "What is it?"

"It's all right, Jenny," Joanna called back. "Just wait in the car." She turned back to the angry woman standing in front of her.

Joanna Brady had been connected to law enforcement

most of her life, first as the daughter of a sheriff and then as wife of a deputy long before she herself had been elected sheriff. She had been around grieving survivors often enough to know that they might well turn their anger on whoever was handy, including any unfortunate police officers who might be close at hand.

Joanna took a calming, steadying breath. "You must be Reba Singleton," she said soothingly. "I'm so sorry about your loss. If there's anything my department or I can do—"

"You can tell me the status of the investigation."

"Ms. Singleton, please understand, your father's body was found late last night. I've been unavailable since early this morning, when the medical examiner was scheduled to do the autopsy—"

"I've already checked with Dr. Winfield," Reba Singleton interrupted. "He seems to be of the convenient opinion that my father died of natural causes."

"If that's the case," Joanna said, "I would assume no further investigation is necessary. I have the key to your father's house. Once we get your car freed from here, you're welcome to drive on up to your father's house and check things out for yourself. Although maybe that's not such a good idea. His road's quite a bit worse than mine. You might get stuck again."

"Let me get this straight," Reba said. "On the say-so of Dr. Winfield who, I'm told, also happens to be your stepfather, you're declaring that there will be no further investigation into the circumstances surrounding my father's death?"

Joanna contained an impulse to lash back. "Dr. Winfield may be my stepfather, but he is also a perfectly competent medical examiner. If he says your father died of natural causes, you can rely on that being the case."

Reba Singleton raised one pencil-thin eyebrow. "Really,"

she said. "And you can rely on my smelling a conflict of interest when somebody sticks one under my nose." With that, she swung away from Joanna. "Washburn?"

Slowly the limo driver got to his feet and dusted the sand from his pants and sleeves. "Yes, ma'am," he said.

"You do have a cell phone, don't you?"

"Yes, ma'am."

"And do you have a signal?"

"I don't know," he said, reaching for his pocket. "I can check."

"Why don't you do that," Reba told him. "And then, call Triple A and have someone come pull us out of this godforsaken place."

Joanna made one more effort to soothe the roiling waters. "Look," she said, "I have a four-wheel-drive Blazer as well as a winch and come-along up at the house. I'm sure we could pull you out."

Reba swung back around. "Like hell!" she spat. "I'd rot in hell before I'd have you pull me out."

That was enough for Joanna. "Suit yourself," she said. "Come on, Butch. Let's go on around them and leave them be."

Butch came back, dusting off his pant legs as well. "Are you sure that's a good idea?" he asked.

By then Joanna was already back at the Subaru and opening the door. "I don't see that we have any choice," she told him. "From the sound of things, they're not much interested in our help."

"Who's that woman?" Jenny asked when Joanna was back in her seat. "She looks mad."

"She's Clayton Rhodes' daughter," Joanna said. "And she is mad."

"How come she's mad?" Jenny asked. "Because her father's dead? I wasn't mad when Daddy died. I was sad."

"Most people are," Joanna said.

Butch climbed in behind the wheel. Without a word, he started the engine. He maintained his tight-lipped silence until he had used the agile Subaru's all-wheel drive to detour around the stricken limo. Only when he was back on the road to Joanna's house did he finally speak. "That woman's something else," he declared.

Joanna nodded. She was remembering the message Lisa Howard had passed along to her from the sergeant in Los Gatos. Now, having met Reba Joy Singleton, Joanna had a far better idea of what Sergeant Carlin had meant when he said, "Good luck." He had meant that Reba Singleton was going to be a problem. Just how bad that problem would turn out to be was anybody's guess.

 **FIVE**

As usual, Sadie and Tigger came racing down the road to greet the car and follow it into the yard. While Jenny took the two gamboling dogs and darted inside to change into jeans and riding boots, Joanna and Butch busied themselves with unloading the car. "What's her name again?" Butch said, nodding in the direction of the stalled Lincoln.

"Reba Singleton," Joanna replied.

"And she really is Clayton Rhodes' only daughter?"

"That's my understanding."

Butch shook his head. "It's hard to accept someone like her being related to him. Clayton always struck me as being the salt of the earth. Reba, on the other hand, acts like a first-class bitch. What do you suppose she meant with that comment about you and George Winfield having a conflict of interest?"

Away from Reba's bristling anger, Joanna was attempting to practice letting go. She shrugged in response to Butch's question. "Who cares what Reba Singleton says?" she returned. "After a sudden and unexpected death, survivors sometimes go nuts for a while and make all kinds of crazy accusations. They try to blame anybody and everybody for whatever it is that's happened in order to keep from having to blame themselves.

"I don't think Reba and her father were especially close.

62

In fact, I seem to remember some big family hassle about the time Molly Rhodes died. Molly was Reba's mother. I don't recall any of the quarrel's gory details right offhand, but whatever it was was serious enough that I don't think she and Clayton ever patched things up. Which means that right this minute Reba Singleton is walking around in a world of hurt. She's packing a full load of guilt and regret, and she's looking for someplace to dump it."

"Preferably on you."

Joanna smiled. "That's all right," she said. "I'm tough enough to take it."

Jenny came out of the house wearing her jeans, boots, and hat, and carrying the cordless phone. "It's for you," she said, handing the receiver to her mother.

"Who is it?" Joanna asked.

"Who else?" Jenny returned sourly. "Work."

While Jenny collected her new bridle and then went into the barn to retrieve Kiddo, Joanna turned her full attention to the phone. "Sheriff Brady here," she said.

"Hi, Joanna," Chief Deputy Frank Montoya said. "Sorry to bother you on your day off, but it's a probable homicide. And we have a standing order that you're to be contacted—"

"Did you say 'probable'?" Joanna said, interrupting him.

"Yes. The victim was shot and is currently being airlifted to Tucson. According to Lance Pakin, the first officer on the scene, she's in real bad shape and isn't likely to make it."

"Who is it?"

"We have no idea at the moment. The man who found her was walking by and happened to see her lying in a ditch. He doesn't look or sound like a suspect. In fact, if it wasn't for him, she probably would be dead by now."

Jenny emerged from the barn leading her sorrel gelding.

She led Kiddo over to where Butch stood holding the new saddle blanket at the ready. Joanna turned away from them and walked several steps toward the house as she spoke into the phone.

"Where and when did this happen?"

"Near the entrance to Cochise Stronghold," Frank Montoya replied. "Not inside the monument itself, but between there and Pearce."

Cochise Stronghold, in the Dragoon Mountains, was an easily defended cliff-bound hideaway where the Apache chieftain Cochise had often retreated with his wandering band of followers. It was now a national monument. In the winter these days Cochise Stronghold was stocked with a new population of wanderers—an ever-changing assortment of RV-driving retirees. In the summer the demographics changed as retirees were replaced by campers with school-aged children who pulled into the camping area and stayed as long as the law allowed.

"Since I was already in the neighborhood assisting a deputy on a runaway call," Frank continued, "it only took a matter of minutes for Lance Pakin and me to get here as well. In fact, we got to the scene before the EMTs did. Lance and I applied as much first aid as we could, but I'm afraid the EMTs are right in saying that the victim isn't going to make it."

"What happened to her?"

"It looks as though she was shot in the lower back. She was hit once at least and maybe more. She appears to have lost a good deal of blood and was hanging by a thread as they loaded her into the Med-evac helicopter."

Joanna sighed as she lost all hope of being able to stay home and spend a quiet evening with Butch and Jenny. "You mentioned something about a runaway? What's that all about?" Joanna asked.

"A fifteen-year-old Elfrida high school girl named Lucinda Ridder disappeared from her grandmother's house sometime overnight last night, along with her pet hawk. When the grandmother got up this morning, both the girl and the bird were gone. The grandmother, Catherine Yates, made such a fuss with the emergency operators that I finally went over to her place on Middlemarch Road myself. According to Grandma, Lucy's mother is due home today or tomorrow. Mrs. Yates is frantic that we find Lucy and have her back home by the time her mother arrives. I was at the Yates' place—the grandmother's place—trying to explain why we have a twenty-four-hour waiting period on missing-persons reports when the second call came in. I decided to come straight here and check just in case the gunshot victim and Lucy turned out to be one and the same."

"And was she?"

"No. As I said Lucy Ridder is fifteen years old. I'd guess the shooting victim is somewhere in her mid-to-late thirties."

"Wait just a minute, Joanna," Frank said. "There's a call coming in on the radio."

While her chief deputy was off the line, Joanna turned back to Butch, Jenny, and the horse. By then Butch had heaved the new saddle onto Kiddo's back, and Jenny was busy cinching it up. Watching the two of them talking and laughing together, Joanna felt a pang of jealousy. They were having fun while she could feel herself being sucked back into the world of work. It wasn't fair.

"Joanna?" Frank's voice came back on the line.

"I'm here. What's happening?"

"That was the pilot of the Med-evac helicopter. He says the EMTs lost her. She flat-lined on them and they couldn't bring her back. The pilot wants to know what he should do, continue on into Tucson or head back to Bisbee."

"Bisbee, I guess," Joanna said. "That way we only have to pay for one transport instead of two. Have Dispatch let Dr. Winfield know so he can meet the helicopter and pick up the body."

"You don't think you should call him yourself?" Montoya asked.

"Are you kidding?" Joanna returned. "If I do that, my mother will hold me personally responsible for wrecking whatever plans she had for this afternoon or evening. Better you should do it, Frank. What have you done about calling detectives?"

Ernie Carpenter and Jaime Carbajal were her department's two homicide detectives. Ernie was an old hand—a burly veteran with more than twenty years under his belt. Jaime, in his early thirties, had been promoted from deputy to detective early on during Joanna's administration.

"Ernie's out of town this weekend, so Jaime's up. He was in the middle of coaching his son's T-ball game when I paged him, but he's on his way."

"If Jaime's on his way," Joanna said, "I'd better be, too."

"You don't have to do that, Joanna," Frank said. "After all, this is your day off. I think we have things pretty well under control."

At the time of her election to the office of sheriff, Joanna Brady had lacked any kind of previous law-enforcement experience. After the election there had been some scuttlebutt that she had won solely on the basis of a sympathy vote, that her elective office had been a kind of county-wide consolation prize for having lost her husband in a line-of-duty shooting.

In order to quiet the talk and counter those assumptions—in order to put to rest all speculation that in her tenure as sheriff Joanna Brady would be little more than an administrative figurehead—she had been determined to turn herself into a hands-on police officer. Although not required to do so, she had taken and passed the same police-academy training that was required of her deputies. She had also made it a point to be involved as an active participant in every homicide investigation that occurred on her watch.

Joanna turned back to the corral just as Jenny finished cinching up the saddle. Then, with the help of Butch's cupped hands, she vaulted onto Kiddo's back and settled her feet into the stirrups. Nudging the horse's ribs with the heel of her boot, she wheeled him away from the corral and took off down the road at a swift canter. There was nothing Joanna liked better than sitting on the porch swing and watching her blond-haired daughter and the equally blond-maned horse tear off across the desert. This evening, though, there would be none of that. Just like Jaime Carbajal and his son's T-ball game, Joanna was about to lose her evening at home with her family.

"I'll leave here as soon as I go inside and put on my vest," Joanna told Frank. "It won't take much longer than half an hour for me to get there."

Butch walked up just as Joanna clicked off the phone. "That sounds bad," he said.

Joanna nodded. "I'm going to have to go. We've had a homicide out by Cochise Stronghold. No telling how long it's going to take. I'll call Jim Bob and Eva Lou and see if Jenny can spend the night there."

Jim Bob and Eva Lou Brady, Jenny's paternal grandparents, maintained a bedroom in their cozy duplex that was always at Jenny's disposal. On nights when it looked as though Joanna would be out beyond Jenny's bedtime, she often left her daughter with them.

"Don't bother," Butch said. "I can stay here until you get back. That way so can she."

"You don't mind? You took care of her last night, too."

Butch nodded. "And there'll probably be a whole lot more nights just like that in our future. But no, I don't mind. The only thing I have waiting for me at home is to clean my own house, and I didn't much want to tackle that anyway. Besides, this way Jenny can ride Kiddo as long as she likes. When she finishes up, I'll have her help me feed the animals."

"Well, then," Joanna said. "If you're sure."

"I'm sure." He leaned over and kissed her. "Now get going," he added, giving her an encouraging pat on the butt. "The sooner you leave, the sooner you'll be able to finish up and come back home."

Feeling guilty and relieved both, Joanna hurried into the house. In the bedroom she whipped off her shirt and donned her Kevlar vest. After retrieving her two Glocks from the locked rolltop desk, she put on both her holsters as well as her shirt and then headed for the door. On her way past the phone table, she paused long enough to check her caller ID. The blinking red light announced there were calls, but when she checked the LCD readout and saw there were ten new calls in all, she didn't even bother to scroll through them. Whatever messages there were would have to wait until Joanna was back home and could deal with them in an orderly, systematic fashion.

Grabbing her purse, the keys to the Blazer, and her recharged cell phone, Joanna hurried outside. Jenny was back. Just beyond the gate to the yard, she sat astride a winded and snorting Kiddo while Butch stood close to the horse's head, rubbing the long, arched neck.

"I have to go," Joanna said to her daughter.

Jenny nodded. "I know," she said dolefully "Butch told me. He says he's going to stay here to watch me."

"I didn't say watch," Butch corrected. "I said keep you company."

"It means the same thing."

Joanna shook her head. The last thing she needed right then was to become entangled in yet another debate about whether or not Jenny was being baby-sat. "You be good," she said. "And help Butch with the animals."

"All right," Jenny grumped. "I will."

And don't be such a sourpuss about it, Joanna wanted to add, but she didn't. There wasn't much point.

In the Blazer, she started the engine. Before she could back out of her parking space, Butch came over and knocked on the driver's window. Joanna rolled it down.

"Just because the women in my life are feuding doesn't mean I don't deserve a good-bye kiss, does it?"

"No," she returned, smiling and giving him a peck on the cheek.

"Drive carefully," he added.

"I will," she said.

Fifty yards from the wash and out of sight of the limo, Joanna spotted the driver, squatting on his haunches and dejectedly smoking a cigarette. When Joanna drove up behind him and rolled down her window, he stood up.

"Still no tow truck?" she asked.

The driver shook his head. "No such luck. According to the dispatcher, it could be more than an hour before they send somebody out."

"As I said before, I have a winch on this thing," Joanna said. "I'm sure I could raise you up enough to get your vehicle out."

"Thanks, but no, thanks," he returned. "Madame made it quite clear that she didn't want any help from you. She's using my cell phone right now to tell the American Automobile Association exactly what she thinks of their service, and that's all to the good. If she's yelling at somebody else, at least I'm not the target."

"Ms. Singleton did strike me as a little prickly," Joanna said.

"That's an understatement if I ever heard one. Just because she flew into Tucson International on somebody's private jet, she seems to think the whole world is supposed to bow and scrape before her. I'm hoping that Triple-A tow truck takes a long damned time to show up. As long as the battery in that cell phone doesn't run out of juice, it's no skin off my nose. After all, I'm being paid by the hour."

Joanna put the Blazer back in gear. "I'll be going then," she said. Suddenly remembering that she was still in possession of Clayton Rhodes' skeleton key, she stopped long enough to dig it out of her purse.

"By the way," she added, handing it over to the driver. "This is the key to Ms. Singleton's father's house. Under the circumstances it's probably better if someone besides me gives it to her."

The driver nodded. "I'm sure you're right about that," he said. "See you," he added with an offhand wave.

Down by the wash, Joanna followed the trail Butch's Outback had blazed through the sand in order to detour around the stalled Lincoln. Reba Singleton looked up as the Blazer went past, but she made no acknowledgment, and neither did Joanna.

Out on High Lonesome Road, Joanna settled back to drive. The crime scene was a good half hour away, well beyond the little farming community of Elfrida and outside an even smaller hamlet called Pearce. She was about to call into the department for directions, when Larry Kendrick, her lead dispatcher, beat her to the punch.

"Sheriff Brady?"

"Here, Larry. What's up?"

"I just had a stolen-vehicle alert come in from the Pima County Sheriff's Department, and I thought I should let you know about it right away."

"What is it?"

"A woman named Melanie Goodson called in early this morning and reported her Lexus stolen. She thinks the person who took it was a guest in her home last night. The name of this alleged car thief is Sandra Ridder."

"Ridder?" Joanna said. "Wait a minute; isn't Ridder the same name as that of the fifteen-year-old runaway Frank Montoya was just telling me about?"

"It is," Larry replied. "Sandra Ridder is Lucinda Ridder's mother. She went to prison for manslaughter and has spent the better part of the last eight years as a guest of the state of Arizona in the women's unit up at Perryville. She got out yesterday. Melanie Goodson was Sandra's defense attorney on the manslaughter charge, and the two women were on good-enough terms that Melanie drove up to the prison and picked Sandra Ridder up yesterday when they let her out.

"The Goodson woman was going to bring Sandra on down to her mother's place—to Catherine Yates' place— today. Instead, when Melanie Goodson woke up this morning, Sandra Ridder and Melanie Goodson's Lexus were both among the missing. Goodson called in and reported the theft right away. She told the Pima County officer that Sandra was probably headed this way. Unfortunately, vehicle theft is such a low priority up in the Tucson area that no one got around to shipping the report down to us until just now."

"From what you said, it sounds as though the two women are friends," Joanna suggested. "In fact, you'd have to be damned good friends for someone to make a two-hundred-mile round trip to pick up someone who's just been let out of prison. Isn't it possible Melanie lent her car to Sandra Ridder and doesn't want to admit it?"

"According to the report in hand, Ms. Goodson was very firm on that," Larry Kendrick responded. "She says that Sandra Ridder has been out of circulation for nearly eight years. That means she has no insurance and no valid driver's license."

"See there?" Joanna asked. "And if anything happens to the car while Sandra Ridder is driving it—if it ends up in some kind of wreck—Melanie Goodson's insurance will still be valid as long as she claims the car was being driven without her permission at the time of the accident. This also gives us a pretty good idea of how and why Lucinda Ridder disappeared. As soon as Grandma Yates goes to sleep, Sandra Ridder pulls up in the Lexus—stolen or not—and then she and her daughter drive off into the sunset."

"Do you want me to call this over to Chief Deputy Montoya?"

"No," Joanna said. "Don't bother. I'm almost there now. I'll tell him myself. In the meantime, give me all the pertinent information on that missing Lexus."

Driving with one hand, Joanna used her other hand to make a series of quick notes on the notepad that was mounted to the Blazer's dash. By the time she had jotted down the make, model, and license number of Melanie Goodson's missing Lexus, Joanna was driving through Elfrida.

Ending the radio transmission, Joanna watched as the little farming community sailed past her windows. Elfrida was a one-horse town, even more so than Bisbee. If gossipmongers in Elfrida were anything like the ones in Bisbee, having the mother of a local student get out of prison and come to town to retrieve her daughter would be big news. This was the kind of juicy tidbit that could keep jaws flapping for weeks. Maybe Sandra Ridder and Lucinda wanted a little privacy—a little family time to get reacquainted before facing the rest of the community. A desire for privacy was something Joanna Brady could understand, although stealing a car didn't seem like the right way to go about conducting a mother-daughter reunion.

At Pearce, Joanna turned left and started up toward Cochise Stronghold and the Dragoon Mountains. For a short while the road was paved. Just when the road surface changed to washboarded gravel, Joanna met a group of people—twenty or so—walking in groups of two or three along the sandy shoulder of the road.

Joanna's initial thought was that this was some kind of protest march. Then she remembered, a group of Volksmarchers had been scheduled to have an event that weekend—a ten-kilometer walk from Pearce to Cochise Stronghold and back. The very thought made Joanna groan. That's what every homicide investigation needs—several hundred sets of unidentified footprints walking through and over the crime scene.

She picked up her radio and had Larry Kendrick patch her through to Frank Montoya. "Did you know there's a Volksmarch scheduled for Cochise Stronghold today?" she asked her chief deputy.

"Sure I knew that," Frank responded. "The guy who's in charge of the march is named Hal Witter. I thought I told you about him. He's the one who found the injured woman lying in a ditch."

"You said someone found her, but you didn't happen to

mention that the guy had a hundred or so people with him when he did it."

"One hundred three, to be exact," Frank Montoya replied. "That's how many people are participating in today's march, but it turns out Mr. Witter was all by himself when he found the victim."

"Well, then," Joanna returned. "I guess we should be thankful for small favors."

 **SIX**

When Joanna arrived at the crime scene, her Blazer was third in line, behind both Frank Montoya's Crown Victoria and Detective Carbajal's Ford Econoline van. Frank Montoya, Jaime Carbajal, and another man Joanna didn't recognize stood pointing off the road into a brush-clogged drainage ditch.

"I know it would have been better if we hadn't had to disturb the crime scene," the unidentified man was explaining to Detective Carbajal. "But as long as there was a chance of saving her, I figured that took higher priority than preserving evidence."

"This is the spot then?" Joanna asked, walking up behind them.

The three men turned to face her. "Sheriff Brady," Frank said. "Yes, this is it. Down in the culvert. And this is Hal Witter, the man who found the victim."

Joanna held out her hand. From her height of five feet four, Hal Witter seemed tall. He was silver-haired and in his mid-to-late sixties. Distinguished-looking, he carried himself with the straight-backed bearing of a military officer.

"Glad to meet you, Sheriff Brady," he said. "I've had some dealings with your office over traffic concerns for our various Volksmarches, but I don't believe I've ever had the pleasure of meeting you in person."

"You say the victim was hidden in the culvert?" Joanna asked.

Hal Witter nodded. "Completely out of sight. I'm guessing she was there but unconscious this morning when we all walked past. It's a miracle we didn't miss her this afternoon as well. I was bringing up the rear. That's my self-imposed task assignment. I keep an eye out for stragglers. In Volksmarching, everybody walks at their own pace. I don't want to rush anybody, so I give everyone else plenty of space and let them go on ahead.

"I was walking by myself when I heard a moan. At first I was afraid one of my marchers was sick or hurt—that maybe someone had fallen and twisted an ankle. Sprains are pretty common at these kinds of events. As soon as I saw all the blood, though, I knew getting help ASAP was a matter of life and death. I used my cell phone. The cops and medics who showed up did what they could for the poor woman and then called in a helicopter. But I guess she was too far gone. Mr. Montoya here tells me she didn't make it."

Joanna nodded. "That's right."

Witter shook his head. "It's too bad, but I was afraid that's what would happen. I've seen gunshot wounds before. This one didn't look survivable."

"Where's that?" Joanna asked. "Where have you seen gunshot wounds?"

"In the service," he said. "I was in Korea and Vietnam both. Something like this brings that other stuff back—stuff I wish I'd forgotten."

As he turned away from her, Joanna noticed him brushing away a tear. Wanting to give the man some privacy, she focused her attention on Jaime Carbajal. Armed with a camera, the young detective had clambered down into the ditch and was snapping pictures around the entrance to the culvert.

"It's real sandy down here, Sheriff Brady," he reported. "And it looks like the EMTs pretty well tore things up getting her out of here. I doubt we're going to get any useful pictures out of this, and we sure as hell aren't going to get any usable footprints."

"Do the best you can, Jaime," Joanna told him.

By then it seemed Hal Witter had regained his composure, so Joanna redirected her attention to him. "Since you were first on the scene, Mr. Witter, is there anything you saw to begin with that may have been disturbed by all the coming and going?"

Witter frowned. "You might want to check the weeds here. See where they're mashed down? I suspect she was pushed or thrown out of a vehicle, rolled down into the ditch, and then dragged into the culvert. That's just my initial impression."

Joanna looked up and down the road. If a vehicle had been there once, now there was no sign of it. Other than the three parked official sheriff's department vehicles, the road was totally deserted in both directions as far as the eye could see.

For the next several minutes, Joanna and Frank Montoya scrutinized the winter-brittle grass along the roadside. As Hal Witter had suggested, broken stalks testified to the fact that something sizable had rolled from the roadway down into the ditch. Careful not to step inside the area, Frank and Joanna marked it off with a boundary of yellow crime-scene tape so it could be searched later for any kind of trace evidence.

Finished with that, Joanna turned back to Hal Witter. "You found no identification?" she asked.

He shook his head. "None, and I checked, too. There was no purse, but people sometimes wear medical identification tags. There wasn't one of those, either, but I did find a neck-lace—a little silver necklace with a strange turquoise-and-silver pendant on it."

"What kind of pendant?"

"It looked like a devil's claw," Hal answered. "You know, those funny two-pronged gourds? It resembled a tiny one of those, with a pearl-sized seed of turquoise showing through from inside the gourd and with the two prongs made of sil-ver. Why someone would walk around wearing a silver devil's claw around her neck is more than I can figure."

Joanna glanced in Frank Montoya's direction and was re-lieved to see that he was busily taking notes. For the time being, that meant she didn't have to. She was also relieved to know that the victim was wearing a piece of what sounded like very distinctive jewelry. Something that un-usual might possibly make the prompt identification of an unknown victim far more likely than it would be otherwise.

"What did the woman look like?" Joanna asked. "How old was she? Anything you can tell us about her would be a big help."

"Native American or Hispanic," Hal Witter said at once. "I'd guess she's somewhere in her mid-thirties. Dark hair—not really black—and going a little gray around the tem-ples."

"Wearing?"

"A sweatshirt—a red sweatshirt with nothing on it—no logo, no Walt Disney characters, or anything else. Jeans. Tennis shoes—Keds, I think. No socks. Nothing really memorable or remarkable about any of her clothing."

"Other than the necklace you already mentioned, was she wearing any other jewelry?"

Hal shook his head. "No watch. No rings, and no sign that she had worn either one recently."

"Why do you say that?"

"Because when you wear a ring long-term, it usually leaves an indentation around the base of the finger. And in this climate, watches and rings both leave pale spots wherever the sun doesn't reach. There wasn't one of those either."

Joanna shot Hal Witter a quizzical look. "That's pretty observant for a civilian," she said.

He grinned back at her. "Thanks," he said. "I trained as a cop once, years ago. After Korea and before I re-upped in the army, I was a trooper in upstate New York."

"Why'd you quit?" Joanna asked.

"Couldn't afford it," he said. "The hours were too long and the pay too low. I figured I was better off back in the army. The pay wasn't that different, but it came with a place to live and a chow line."

"Career army then?" she asked.

He nodded. "Retired Special Forces. Colonel."

Just then Jaime Carbajal's voice came from behind them, from the far side of the road opposite where he had disappeared into the culvert. "I may have found something after all. Look at this."

As the three people on the road turned to look, Jaime materialized at the far end of the culvert holding three plastic milk cartons aloft. Two were empty. One still contained a quart or so of water.

"UDAs?" Joanna asked.

"I think so," Jaime replied.

"But they could have been through here anytime. There's no way of saying they were here last night, is there?"

"Don't be so sure about that," the detective answered. "One of the handles is stained with something that looks a whole lot like blood. I wouldn't be surprised if it matches up with our victim's."

Joanna found the very suggestion chilling. In recent years the steady stream of undocumented aliens coming north from Mexico had turned into a vast flood, one that threatened to overwhelm the resources of local law-enforcement jurisdictions and of the Immigration and Naturalization Service as well. Increased enforcement in one place only caused the flow to move to some other likely crossing point. It seemed to Joanna that as soon as INS officers plugged one hole in the border fence, another opened up a mile or two away.

In the past few months, the UDA crisis had gone from bad to worse. Recently the number of illegals apprehended in rural Cochise County rivaled those captured in San Diego, with far fewer officers and far less money available to deal with the problem. As the number of illegals increased, a vocal group of ranchers whose properties lay on the most traveled routes had been raising a call to arms.

Several isolated ranch owners had been victims of unsophisticated burglaries. They complained that cattle had died after ingesting abandoned plastic bottles that the illegals used to carry life-sustaining water as they walked across long stretches of unforgiving desert. Ranchers reported that faucets on stock tanks had been left open, allowing precious water to drain out, that fences had been cut down, allowing livestock to stray onto roads and highways, and that their properties were littered with human waste. Several of the most vociferous of the frustrated cattlemen had threatened to take the law into their own hands. Their position was that if the government couldn't be counted on to protect them from foreign invaders, the ranchers would do so themselves and round up any illegal found trespassing on their land.

Joanna knew that she was dealing with an extremely volatile situation, one already rife with threats of vigilante justice. She dreaded what might happen once news of this incident was made public. The specter of armed illegals preying on lone women motorists along deserted stretches of highway might well ignite a whole new style of range war. It wasn't difficult to see how this added element of fear might provoke a few rabid individuals into shooting first and asking questions later.

Joanna stared at the bloodstained milk cartons as though they were leaking powder kegs.

"We'd better bag them up and get them to the lab," Joanna said. Her comment proved to be unnecessary, since Detective Carbajal was already doing that very thing.

"Not only that," Jaime continued as he entered the bagged cartons into the evidence logs. "It looks to me as though this end of the culvert wasn't disturbed by the EMTs. There are a few tracks just inside here that are probably worth casting. I'll go get my equipment."

With Frank Montoya's help, Detective Carbajal mixed up a batch of plaster of paris and set about making the casts. Meanwhile, Joanna took down the remainder of Hal Witter's information——his phone number and address in Mesa, along with the names and phone numbers of friends in Bisbee with whom he was planning to stay for the next several days. When she was finished and because it was nearing sundown, Joanna offered the man a ride back into Pearce.

"Oh, no," he said. "I'll walk. I want to finish the event. Accepting a ride would mean it doesn't count." He started away.

"One other thing," Joanna called after him.

"What's that?"

"I'd appreciate it if you wouldn't mention any of what you heard or saw here this afternoon. Of course, you're welcome to let people know that you found the victim. Good

Samaritans are always appreciated, but when it comes to disclosing pieces of our investigation that you may have overheard, I'd rather you kept those quiet."

"Certainly," he said. "I understand. Holdbacks and all that. No problem, Sheriff Brady. I'll be more than happy to keep what I've heard to myself. I just hope you catch whoever did it. Shooting some poor woman and then leaving her to die in a ditch like a run-over dog isn't what I call civilized. The sooner those people are off the streets, the better."

Once Hal Witter walked away, Joanna went over to where her two deputies were working. "I'm assuming the campground up at the Stronghold is full of RVers. Has anyone thought to check with those folks to find out if any of them saw or heard anything unusual last night?"

"We're on it," Frank Montoya returned. "Deputy Pakin went up there as soon as the helicopter took off. As far as I know, he's still up there. I wanted him to get cracking on interviewing possible witnesses in case some of the campers pull up stakes overnight. I don't want any of them leaving without letting us know what they may have seen."

"Good work," Joanna said.

By then the afternoon sun had long since slipped behind the Dragoons. The cliff-lined canyon that had once sheltered Cochise and his warrior band of Apaches was fast fading into deepening shadows. Even though she realized they were losing daylight, Joanna knew better than to try to hurry the painstaking plaster-casting process. Experience had taught her that with proper analysis, footprints can be almost as foolproof as fingerprints in testifying to a suspect's physical presence at a crime scene.

She spent the next several minutes pacing back and forth. She was considering the possibility of heading back home and leaving Frank in charge when Deputy Lance Pakin came wheeling up in his Blazer.

"Find anything?" she asked.

"Mostly no one remembered seeing anything unusual," Deputy Pakin answered. "I was about to give up when I ran into a guy named Naujokas—Mr. Pete Naujokas of Estes Park, Colorado."

"What about him?" Joanna asked.

"He and his wife have a winter home in Oro Valley, but they've been out here in the park for several days, camping with some friends who are visiting from Colorado. Yesterday afternoon Pete had to go into Tucson on business. He planned on being back here at the RV in time for dinner last night. Things didn't work out, though. First he was delayed leaving town, then he had car trouble that kept him in Benson for several hours. By the time he finally made it here, it was almost midnight.

"As he was coming up the road, he came across a vehicle parked up the road with its flashers flashing. He saw a woman down on her hands and knees by the Cochise Stronghold sign, and he stopped to see if she needed any help. She said everything was fine. She had lost a ring and was using the headlights to look for it. Since she didn't seem to be in any trouble and since there wasn't that much he could do to help, he went on his way."

"What kind of car?" Joanna asked.

"He wasn't sure. Late model. White. He thought it might have been a Lexus."

Joanna felt a sudden clutch in her gut. At mention of the word, she realized she had failed to pass along Larry Kendrick's message about Melanie Goodson's supposedly stolen Lexus. Now it seemed that a Lexus might play a pivotal part in this case as well.

Finished with their casting job, Frank Montoya and

Jaime Carbajal came walking toward Joanna. Between them they carried a collection of several plaster casts.

"What's this about a Lexus?" Frank Montoya asked as he loaded the casts into boxes in Jaime's van.

"One was seen near here late last night. Up by the Cochise Stronghold sign. And I believe we now may have a line on our victim," Joanna answered. "My guess is her name is Sandra Ridder."

Montoya frowned. "Ridder," he repeated. "Any relation to Lucinda Ridder, the runaway?"

Joanna nodded. "Sandra is Lucinda's mother. She was released from prison up in Perryville sometime yesterday afternoon. And it turns out she's so well-rehabilitated after spending almost eight years in the slammer that she took the first opportunity that presented itself to steal her attorney's Lexus overnight."

"When did this all come up and why didn't I know about it before now?" Frank Montoya demanded.

"Larry Kendrick told me about the bulletin on the stolen Lexus as I was on my way here. I meant to mention it to you as soon as I arrived, but with everything else that was going on, it slipped my mind. It wasn't until Lance here mentioned a Lexus that I remembered. Exactly how far is it from here to Lucinda's grandmother's house?"

"It's off on Middlemarch Road. Two miles, give or take."

"Maybe we'd better drop by and see her," Joanna said.

"Catherine Yates told me her daughter was due home either today or tomorrow," Frank replied irritably. "But she didn't say from where—certainly not from prison. All Catherine said was that she wanted Lucy home when her mother got there. Any idea what the mother was in for?"

"Manslaughter. I don't know any of the details. Just that she got sent up for ten years and served eight."

"All of which puts Lucy's disappearance in a whole new light."

Joanna nodded grimly. "Doesn't it just," she said. She turned back to Deputy Pakin. "Lance," she said, "I'm going to go with Chief Deputy Montoya in his car. You stay here and assist Detective Carbajal. When it's too dark to see, I'd like you to stay here and keep the crime scene secure until we can get a crew of techs back out here in the morning."

"Will do," Deputy Pakin agreed. "What about emergency calls?"

"Call into Dispatch and let them know you're on assignment. If the need arises, they'll have to bring in officers from other sectors to cover problems in yours. And when you go off shift, have the Night Watch Commander send someone else out here to take your place."

"Sure thing."

Leaving her Blazer parked on the shoulder of the roadway, Joanna followed Frank to his waiting Crown Victoria. Without a word, Frank got in, slammed the car door shut, started the engine, and then rammed the gearshift into drive for a tire-spinning, gravel-spattering U-turn. From the set of Frank's jaw, Joanna knew her chief deputy was ripped. For the next several minutes they maintained a strained silence, punctuated here and there by radio chatter.

"What's wrong, Frank?" Joanna asked at last.

He turned and glowered at her. "I'll tell you what's wrong. I feel like you left me out of the loop back there. Like there were things going on that I should have known about and nobody told me."

"Come on," she pleaded. "Don't make a big deal out of this. It was nothing but an oversight on my part. It certainly wasn't deliberate. We were all busy, Frank, and it slipped my mind. Besides, until Lance brought up the subject of the Lexus, there was no possible way for anyone to see a connection between the two cases."

"I suppose not," Frank grumbled, but Joanna could tell he was still provoked, and that made her uneasy. Not only was Frank Montoya her chief deputy, he had long been Joanna's greatest ally in the department. She could ill afford to offend him.

"Tell me about Catherine Yates," she said, trying to change the subject. "If she didn't bother to mention that her daughter was being released from prison, she wasn't exactly being forthright with you. What's her story?"

"I don't know. She's an Indian—part, anyway. Apache, I believe. She told me that her granddaughter has lived with her for several years. She implied there was some kind of family problem—a sticky divorce or something. But when I asked if Lucy might have gone off to live with her father, she said that wasn't possible. That he wasn't in the picture."

"Here's the turnoff to her place," Frank added, switching on the turn signal.

"Wait," Joanna said. "Stop here a minute and let me check something."

Obligingly, Frank pulled over next to a mailbox on top of a leaning wooden post and put the Ford in neutral. Meanwhile, Joanna plucked Frank's radio microphone out of its clip and thumbed the "talk" button.

"Larry," she said when the dispatcher's voice came through. "When Pima County sent down the information on that stolen Lexus, did they include a rap sheet on Sandra Ridder?"

"Sure did."

"Does it say what she went to prison for?"

"Man-one. Sentenced to ten years and served almost eight."

"Does it say who she killed?"

"Yup, her husband, one Thomas Dawson Ridder."

"Thanks, Larry," Joanna told him. "That's a big help. What about a mug shot?"

"We've got one of those, too."

She glanced at Frank. "Is your wireless fax working?"

Frank Montoya had spent months and several thousand drug-enforcement dollars turning his Crown Victoria into a fully equipped mobile office.

He nodded.

"Fax everything you have to Frank's computer."

"Will do, Sheriff Brady," Larry Kendrick replied. "But it's going to take a couple of minutes. I'm here by myself and another call is just coming in."

"Take your time, Larry," she told him. "No rush."

Putting the microphone down, Joanna turned back to Frank. "Being dead is a damned good reason for the father not being in the picture," she said. "So what do you think is going on?"

"This is how it looks to me." Frank held up one hand and began ticking off his fingers. "On the surface of it, it's easy to say that a marauding band of UDAs is responsible for whatever went on back there and let it go at that. But I've got a different idea. How does this sound? First Mommy whacks Daddy, and somebody sees to it that Mommy goes to prison. Later Mommy gets out of prison. As soon as she does, somebody whacks her. Immediately prior to that or else immediately thereafter, Baby Daughter disappears. Sounds to me like one way or the other, we've got a whole new set of reasons to go looking for Lucinda Ridder. Either she's a victim, too, or else she's something a whole lot worse."

Sighing, Joanna leaned back against the headrest and closed her eyes. "Let's go. By the time we finish talking to

Catherine Yates, we'll have what we need from Dispatch. In the meantime, I have to say, I hope to God you're wrong. I don't want to be stuck tracking down some nice, gun-wielding fifteen-year-old."

"That's funny," Frank said.

"What's funny?"

"That's exactly what Catherine Yates told me earlier this afternoon about Lucinda. She said Lucy's a nice girl."

"Right," Joanna returned sarcastically. "I'll just bet she did. That's what grandmothers always say—that their particular little darlings are nothing but sweetness and light. I'll bet if someone had asked Lizzie Borden's grandmother, she probably would have given the exact same answer: She would have said, 'Little Elizabeth's an adorable child. She's just as nice as you please and wouldn't hurt a fly if her life depended on it.' "

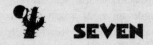 **SEVEN**

As soon as Frank's Crown Victoria pulled into Catherine Yates' yard, the porch light snapped on and the front door slammed open. A stocky woman in blue jeans and a flapping denim shirt came hurrying off the front porch of a tiny square house.

"Did you find her?" she demanded of Frank Montoya as he rolled down the driver's window.

"No, ma'am," he said. "I'm sorry to report that we still haven't found your granddaughter. I've brought Sheriff Joanna Brady along with me, Ms. Yates. She and I need to talk to you for a few minutes. We'd like to ask you a few questions."

Joanna stepped out of the car and went around to the other side, offering her hand. "How do you do, Ms. Yates."

Catherine Yates' work-hardened fingers closed around Joanna's with a surprisingly gentle touch. "Nice to meet you," she said grudgingly. "I guess I didn't really expect that the sheriff herself would show up."

"I came because we need to speak to you about your daughter," Joanna said.

"About Sandra?" Catherine asked. "How come? My granddaughter's the one who's missing."

"You told Frank that you were expecting Sandra home soon. Is it possible that she and Lucinda took off together?"

Asking the question, Joanna knew she was stalling for time, postponing the inevitable moment when she would most likely have to deliver the painful news. Joanna fully expected Larry Kendrick's mug shot would confirm that Catherine's daughter was dead. In the meantime, asking questions was an acceptable delaying tactic. Even so, if Sandra was the victim, the awful task of telling Catherine Yates that her daughter was dead couldn't be put off indefinitely. Notifying bereaved next of kin was Sheriff Joanna Brady's job—part of it, anyway.

Behind her, Frank switched off his Crown Victoria—his Civvie, as he preferred to call it—and emerged into the chill early evening air.

"No," Catherine Yates was saying. "That wouldn't have happened. Lucy wouldn't have gone anywhere with her mother."

"How can you be sure of that?" Joanna asked. "Her mother's been away for some time. Doesn't it stand to reason that she'd be glad to see her?"

Catherine Yates simply shook her head and said nothing.

"All right, then," Joanna said with a sigh. "Why don't you tell us what you know about your daughter's recent whereabouts."

Catherine glanced warily at Frank Montoya before she answered. "I heard from Sandra just yesterday afternoon," she said. "Sandy called from Tucson and told me she had been released. She said she was spending last night in Tucson with a friend. I told your deputies that earlier. I expect her home sometime today or tomorrow."

"What friend?" Joanna asked.

"A friend, that's all."

"Look, Ms. Yates, I'm sure this is all terribly painful for you to discuss. Otherwise you would have told Chief Deputy Montoya the whole story earlier. We already know that your daughter was released from prison yesterday afternoon, so it's no secret. Just tell us. Have you heard from her since then?"

Catherine Yates bowed her head. For a moment her face was obscured by a curtain of shoulder-length gray hair. Seeing her face in the dim glow of a yard light, it was easy to understand why Frank might have been in doubt about the woman's ethnic heritage. She could easily have passed for either Hispanic or Indian, although there was clearly some Anglo blood mixed in as well.

"No," Catherine said finally. "Sandra hasn't called me, and I haven't tried reaching her, either. In fact, I've been dreading talking to her all day long—ever since I realized Lucy was gone. I didn't want to be the one to have to tell Sandy that Lucy had run away."

"Who's the friend?" Frank interjected. "The one Sandra's supposed to be staying with?"

Catherine bit her lip. "Her name's Melanie Goodson, and she's not much of a friend, if you ask me. She lives somewhere out on Old Spanish Trail. She was Sandy's attorney years ago. She's also the one who let that stupid plea bargain go through. I don't know if she was lazy or what. I don't think she even tried to take Sandy's case to court. If she had, I'm sure my daughter would have gotten off. What happened between Sandy and her husband should have been ruled self-defense. He was abusive, and my daughter never should have gone to prison for manslaughter. After all, Tom Ridder beat her up. If I'd'a been her, I would have shot the son of a bitch, too."

Listening, Joanna remembered what Catherine had said earlier—about Lucinda Ridder not being willing to go anywhere with her mother. "How did your granddaughter feel about her father's death?" Joanna asked.

Catherine Yates was a stout woman. When asked that question, her broad shoulders seemed to shrink inside her shirt. She shook her head sadly. "Lucy loved her father," Catherine said. "All she remembers is this tall handsome devil in his smart army uniform. I've tried talking to her about it, tried explaining that as far as Tom Ridder is concerned, looks weren't everything. Tom looked a whole lot better than he really was.

"But it's like talking to a wall, Sheriff Brady, and it hasn't done a bit of good. No matter what I say, Lucy still blames Sandy for her father's death. You know how kids are. Once they get some wild idea in their heads, nothing short of an act of God is going to shake it loose."

"I take it Lucy wasn't necessarily happy that her mother was getting out of prison?" Joanna asked.

Catherine sighed and nodded. "Happy? I'll say she wasn't happy, not at all. Furious is more like it. In fact, we had a big fight about it just yesterday afternoon when Lucy came home from school. She told me that she had prayed every day that her mother would die in prison so she'd never have to see her again. I tried to explain how wrong and unforgiving that was. I told her there are two sides to every story, and that she needed to give her mother a chance to tell her side of it. Instead, Lucy blew up at me. She told me that she would never live in the same house with her mother, no matter what. She said that I'd have to choose between them—between Lucy or Sandy—because I couldn't have both."

"What did you tell her?"

In the glow of the porch light, Joanna saw Catherine's eyes fill with glistening tears. "I told Lucy that mothers don't work that way. That just because your child does something wrong, that doesn't mean you wipe them off the face of the earth. It's like Big Red and the kitten."

"Who's Big Red?"

"A hawk," Frank Montoya supplied. "Remember? I told you about him. Big Red is Lucy's pet hawk."

"A red-tailed hawk," Catherine added. "Lucy found him when he was nothing but a half-dead hatchling—a tiny little thing who had fallen out of his nest. Lucy climbed up and put him back. She waited and watched, but the parents never returned. Finally, rather than leave him there to starve to death, she brought him home and took care of him.

"For months we'd get up early several mornings a week and go find what we used to call fresh road-kill pizza. We'd drive along the highway between here and Elfrida or between here and the freeway and pick up whatever had been run over on the road overnight—rabbits, kangaroo rats, coyotes—and we'd give Big Red that for breakfast. Finally, though, he got big and strong enough to hunt for himself. And wouldn't you know, the first thing he nailed was a newborn kitten—a kitten Lucy had her heart set on keeping. She was mad about it for days, but I told her that wasn't fair. I told her that hunting is what hawks do to survive and that she was wrong to hold a grudge when Big Red was just doing what comes naturally.

"Yesterday I tried to explain that what happened between her mother and father was the same thing that had happened between Big Red and the kitten. I told Lucy that Sandy did what she did to protect herself—to save her own life and Lucy's."

"What did Lucy say to that?"

"She said it was all a lie, that her father never hit anybody. After that, Lucy stormed off to her room and didn't come out for dinner. This morning, when I got up, she was gone, along with her backpack, a bedroll, and some of her clothes."

"Was anything else missing?"

"Some food from the kitchen, her bike . . ."

"And?"

Catherine bit her lip and didn't answer.

"What else?"

"A gun," Catherine answered reluctantly. "A twenty-two. It belonged to my husband. I keep it for protection—for snakes, that kind of thing."

"Does Lucy know how to use it?"

"Yes. I taught her myself."

"Did you tell Frank earlier this afternoon that the gun was missing?"

"No. I was afraid if I told him she was armed that it would keep people from looking for her."

It wouldn't keep them from looking, Joanna thought. *But they'd be a hell of a lot more careful while they were doing it.*

"What about Big Red?" Joanna continued. "Have you seen any sign of him today?"

"No."

"So it's possible he's with her?"

"Probable more than possible, I'd say," Catherine answered. "The two of them spend most weekends together. They ride over to the Stronghold."

"Ride?" Joanna asked.

"Oh, yes. Big Red rides on her shoulder or her handlebars. He's done that since he was just a baby. When they get to the park, Lucy climbs up and down the cliffs and Big Red usually sticks around somewhere nearby. Out of sight, maybe, but not far away.

"I tried to warn Lucy about that, by the way. There are so many other people hiking and camping up there that I told her it could be dangerous for him. I tried to explain that turning wild animals into pets is a bad idea because once they grow accustomed to humans, they may not be afraid when they ought to be. But of course, by the time I told Lucy that, it was already too late. And maybe it's not as bad as all that. As far as I can tell, she's the only person Big Red'll have anything to do with. I can tell you, as soon as that bird catches sight of me, he flies off in a hurry."

"Does Lucy drive?"

"No. She's still too young to get a learner's permit."

"So you don't think Big Red would get into a vehicle with her?"

"In a car? No. But on the bike, no problem."

"Which means, if the bird is with Lucy, then wherever they are, they most likely traveled there on foot or by bicycle."

Catherine Yates nodded, and Joanna turned to Frank. "What about Search and Rescue?" she asked.

"They're aware of the situation," Frank replied. "By morning the twenty-four-hour waiting period will be up. I've made arrangements with Mike Wilson to have a Search and Rescue crew here by first light in the morning if Lucy hasn't been found by then."

Joanna nodded. Departmental policy called for the passage of twenty-four hours before taking a missing-persons report or calling in Search and Rescue. There were exceptions to that rule, especially in the case of lost small children or wandering elderly Alzheimer patients. Lucy Ridder's case fell in a gray area, unless she turned out to be a homicide suspect. In that case, all bets were off.

"Do you happen to have recent photos of your daughter and granddaughter?" Joanna asked.

"The one I have of Sandy is several years old, but I have last-year's school picture of Lucy. Would that help?"

"Very much," Joanna said.

"Well then," Catherine Yates told her, "come on in. You might as well wait inside. It's cold out here."

Joanna and Frank trailed after Catherine as she led the way onto the porch.

"When are you going to get around to telling her?" Frank asked, under his breath.

"After we have the fax with the mug shot in hand," Joanna whispered back. "I'd like to have a little more confirmation on that stolen Lexus before I blow this poor woman out of the water."

Frank nodded. "Want me to go back to the car and wait for it? That way I can bring it inside as soon as it comes through."

"Right," Joanna said, then she followed Catherine Yates into the living room of her tiny square-shaped house.

Joanna recognized the design. Larry Yarnell Homes, an early edition of modular housing, had been marketed in the late sixties and early seventies as a relatively inexpensive form of pre-fab housing—one step up from mobile homes and one step down from permanent frame construction. Because they were less costly to build, Larry Yarnell Homes had sprouted like weeds in rural southern Arizona. Now, almost forty years later, most of those houses had outlived their useful lives. Made of generally shoddy materials, some were little more than moldering, burned-out hulks. This one, however, had clearly been well cared for and kept in good repair.

While Catherine Yates disappeared into the back of the house, Joanna stood in the middle of the living room and looked around. The carpeting on the floor was threadbare but clean. The same could be said for the collection of old-fashioned but still serviceable leather furniture. On the wall, over a long sofa, two gold-framed pictures broke the monotony of cheap oak paneling. One was the photo of a smiling Korean War–era GI standing with one foot resting on the bumper of a 1952 Mercury convertible.

The other photo—in faded sepia tones—depicted a man who appeared to be a full-blooded Indian standing proudly at attention and staring, solemn-eyed, into the lens of the camera. He wore some kind of uniform—one that was unfamiliar to Joanna.

"The one on the right is Carter, my husband. The one on the left is my great-grandfather," Catherine Yates said, returning silently to the living room. "His name is Eskiminzin. Ever heard of him?"

Joanna shook her head.

"You should have. He was an Arivaipa Apache. He was also a chief, just like Cochise or Geronimo. Except he wasn't a warrior. He was a man who wanted to get along with the whites. Even after most of his first family was murdered in the Camp Grant Massacre, he still tried to make peace. My great-grandmother, my mother's grandmother, was his second wife."

Joanna knew enough about Arizona history to have a nodding acquaintance with the Camp Grant Massacre. What history books called the "Apache Wars" would, in the modern vernacular, have been termed "ethnic cleansing." Operating under the philosophy of "Manifest Destiny," the United States Government had engaged the Apaches in a war of eradication designed to remove them from their ancient lands and make way for Anglo settlers.

Worn down by years of fighting, in 1871 several separate

Apache bands had surrendered to the commanding officer at Old Camp Grant and sued for peace. Having been told that they could camp outside the fort under the protection of the United States Cavalry, the Apaches stayed there for the next two months while peace negotiations took place. Meanwhile, several Tucson-area merchants—Anglos every one—rounded up an expeditionary force made up of Mexicans and Tohono O'othham who had their own long-held grudges against marauding Apaches.

This band of mercenaries attacked the sleeping Apaches under the dark of night. Many of the younger men managed to escape into the hills, but women and children, along with the old and sick and helpless, were slaughtered where they slept.

"It was about this time of year," Catherine said softly. "April thirtieth."

Obviously, for Catherine Yates and her family, the Camp Grant Massacre wasn't some distant, dusty footnote to history. It was still a hauntingly vivid and painful part of her family's past.

"But the uniform . . ." Joanna began.

"After his family was killed, Eskiminzin still wanted peace. He became one of the first members of the tribal police on San Carlos. That's him in his policeman's uniform. Later on, he took his second family, left the reservation, and started his own ranch. Then there was another Apache uprising. Since he was a chief, he was suspected of being involved. His ranch was taken from him, and he was shipped off to Oklahoma."

"How do you know all this?" Joanna asked.

"A friend of his wrote it down," Catherine Yates explained. "John Clum was an Anglo who was superintendent of the San Carlos early on. Eskiminzin worked for him. Clum wrote a paper for the *Arizona Historical Review*. My mother, Christina Bagwell, was ten years old when he sent her mother, Eskiminzin's daughter, a copy of what he'd written, along with that picture—the one you see there on the wall. Otherwise it all would have been forgotten long ago."

Joanna had become so caught up in the story that she had almost forgotten her own purpose for being inside Catherine Yates' house until Catherine handed her two photos—two eight-by-ten school pictures in matching gold frames. Joanna took them and spent several long seconds examining them. From the hairstyles, it was easy to recognize that the two photographs came from different eras. Nonetheless, even the most casual observer would have noticed the striking family resemblance between Sandra Ridder and her daughter, Lucy.

Just as Joanna handed the two pictures back and was about to speak, Frank Montoya tapped lightly on the front door and let himself into the room. "Sorry to interrupt, Sheriff Brady," he said. "This just came in."

Frank made his way across the room without meeting Catherine Yates' anxiously inquiring gaze. As he handed Joanna the piece of paper he carried, he gave the slightest shake of his head. "It looks like she's the one," he said softly.

"Who?" Catherine asked.

Joanna looked down at the picture in her hand. In the mug shot, the woman in one picture appeared to have aged ten or fifteen years. "You're sure?" Joanna asked.

Frank nodded. "I'm sure," he said. "It's Sandra, all right."

Joanna turned to Catherine. "It's about your daughter, Mrs. Yates," she said. "I'm afraid we have some bad news. We're fairly sure that your daughter stole a vehicle last night, and now there's a good chance that she may be a homicide victim as well."

Nodding and moving in slow motion, Catherine sank down on the couch and wrapped her arms around her body. "I knew it," she said. "I knew when you kept asking me about Sandy instead of Lucy that it had to be something to do with her. What is it? What's happened?"

"This afternoon a woman was found in a culvert along the road between Cochise Stronghold and Pearce. She'd been shot. Unfortunately, she died while being airlifted to a hospital in Tucson. I didn't want to say anything to you about it until after we had more information."

"No," Catherine whispered. "I can't believe it! I just can't."

"I'm so sorry—" Joanna began, but Catherine cut her off.

"How could she?"

"As I said, the victim, she was shot. We didn't find a weapon, so we're currently treating this as a homicide. The vehicle she was thought to be driving is missing, and it's possible one or more UDAs—illegal immigrants—were involved in what happened."

"You're just saying that," Catherine said. "You're telling me that because you don't want to tell me the truth."

"What truth is that?"

"If Sandy is dead, I know who killed her, and so do you—Lucy! It has to be her. She's missing, isn't she, and so is my gun. I should have known. She as good as told me, but I never thought . . . Couldn't even imagine that she'd do such a thing!" Moaning softly, Catherine doubled over on the couch, rocking back and forth.

"You mustn't jump to conclusions," Joanna said carefully, even though she herself had made much the same kind of leap. "As I said, we did find some evidence that suggests UDAs may have been involved, and there may be some other explanation entirely. At this point, other than the fact that your granddaughter is missing, we have nothing to indicate that she's involved in what happened to her mother."

"You'll find it," Catherine said sadly. With that she leaned back against the couch and covered her eyes with one hand. After a full minute of silence she added in a hoarse whisper, "I can't do this again. I just can't."

"Do what?" Joanna asked.

"Go through all this." Catherine took her hand away from her face. The sorrowful eyes she focused on Joanna were smoldering coals. "This has probably never happened to you, has it," she added accusingly. "I'll bet no one you love has ever been arrested and sent to prison for killing someone else."

"No," Joanna admitted. "You're right."

"I thought so," Catherine Yates said. "Go away. Leave me alone."

"But we'll need to make arrangements to have you come to Bisbee and do an official identification. My detectives will need to talk to you . . ."

"Tomorrow will be time enough for that," Catherine Yates replied. "Right now, all I want is to be left alone!"

"You're sure you'll be all right?" Joanna asked.

"I won't be all right," Catherine said. "I've lost my daughter, and my granddaughter, too. I'm sure I'll never be all right again. But I'm a tough old bird, and I'll live. So go now, please."

Joanna started to say something, to warn Catherine about not going into Lucy's room or disturbing anything, but in the end she said nothing. The all-pervasive grief that distorted Catherine Yates' previously placid face, screwed up her mouth, and wrung a steady stream of tears from her eyes made any such cautions seem rude and unnecessary.

"I'm so sorry, Mrs. Yates. Really I am."

Catherine nodded. "I know," she croaked brokenly. "So am I."

 **EIGHT**

"It's interesting that Catherine Yates immediately came to almost the same conclusion we did," Frank said, as they started back toward Joanna's Blazer.

"It's not interesting," she countered. "It's sad. With all the UDA debris there in the culvert, we could be totally off-base even suggesting it. Still, Catherine knows Lucy Ridder better than anyone else in the world—including Lucy's own mother. If Catherine thinks her granddaughter is capable of murder, then the rest of us had better pay attention. Call Mike Wilson and cancel that Search and Rescue call for tomorrow morning. We're not going to send an unarmed S and R team out looking for someone whose own grandmother thinks she could be armed and dangerous."

"You're just going to wait for her to turn up then?" Frank asked.

"No," Joanna replied. "We'll send Terry Gregovich and Spike out to find her. That's why we have a canine team, but when you dispatch them, let Terry know that I expect both of them—man and dog—to be wearing their Kevlar vests at all times. I don't want to lose either one of them."

Terry Gregovich and his eighty-five-pound German shepherd Spike constituted the Cochise County Sheriff Department's first-ever K-9 team. Both man and dog were relative new-hires. Terry, a Gulf War veteran, had come over from

Search and Rescue. With the help of drug-enforcement
monies, Spike had been purchased directly from a breeder
who specialized in police dogs. After months of training and
working together, Spike and Terry had evolved into an in-
separable and valuable team. Six weeks earlier, a Phoenix-
area K-9 dog had been shot to death by a pair of fleeing bank
robbers. In the aftermath of that incident, Joanna had managed to find room in her budget to purchase a canine-fitted
Kevlar vest for Spike's protection.

"Do you want them to start looking tonight?" Frank
asked.

Joanna thought about that. "Tomorrow will be soon
enough. Catherine Yates asked to be left alone tonight. We
can give her that much of a break."

"Are you going to go for a search warrant?"

"With what?"

"Good question," Frank said.

Just then a call came in over the radio. "What's up,
Larry?" Joanna asked.

"Detective Carbajal called in a few minutes ago. He wants
you back up at the entrance to Cochise Stronghold pronto.
He says he's found something but he isn't sure what."

Frank flipped on both lights and siren. As he floor-
boarded the gas pedal, the rough surface of the road seemed
to smooth out. Joanna knew, however, that that was a dangerous illusion. The ride was smooth only because the tires
were spending so little time in contact with the roadway.
After several nerve-racking minutes, Joanna was more than
slightly relieved when they stopped on the outskirts of a
group of emergency vehicles parked around the carved red-
wood FOREST SERVICE sign that marked the entrance to
Cochise Stronghold. The sign was illuminated by Jaime
Carbajal's trouble light. The detective himself, on hands and

knees, appeared to be crawling through a scattered field of rocks.

"What's up, Detective Carbajal?" Joanna asked.

Jaime rose to meet her. "After what Deputy Pakin told us, I decided to come up here and take a look around. Over there are signs of what appears to be a serious struggle, including what looks to me like blood spatter." He pointed to a spot just to the right of the sign where a ten-foot-square area had been marked off with a border of yellow tape. "We'll be able to tell more tomorrow in the daylight. In the meantime, take a look at this."

He held up a bag that contained what looked like a small plastic soup bowl. Even through the glassine bag, Joanna could see that the outside of the once white bowl was yellowed with age and covered with a coating of grime.

"What's this?" Joanna asked. "The leavings from somebody's long-ago picnic?"

"I don't think so," Jaime replied. "Remember, Deputy Pakin's witness said the woman he saw was messing around with the rocks at the base of the sign, so I decided to come check. The cover was loose inside the hole, but the bowl itself was embedded in the dirt at the bottom of the hole."

Joanna took the bag and examined the bowl more closely. On the bottom, accentuated by clinging dirt, was a still recognizable Tupperware trademark.

"I tried selling Tupperware years ago, when Andy and I were first married," she told her astonished deputies. "The stuff's supposed to be airtight, waterproof, and capable of lasting forever. This looks as though it's been here for a long time. What's in it?"

"Nothing now," Jaime replied. "It was empty when I found it, but I'll bet it wasn't empty when the woman in the white car came looking for it."

Joanna walked over to the sign and the pile of disturbed rocks beneath it. With the help of a flashlight, she peered down in among them to where the outline of the bowl was still clearly visible in the soft, fine, insect-sifted dirt under the rocks.

"Assuming Sandra Ridder is the one who hid it, that would mean the bowl has been here for eight years at least," Joanna stated. "That's how long she's been in prison. What could be so valuable that, after all this time, she would risk stealing a vehicle her first night out of the slammer in order to come get it?"

"Whatever it was, it wasn't very big," Frank offered.

Joanna studied the container. "And it wasn't something Sandra wanted her attorney to know about, since she evidently stole Melanie Goodson's car to come get it. But shouldn't we ascertain once and for all that the person Lance Pakin's witness saw here really was Sandra Ridder? What's his name again, and is he still camped out up there?"

Jaime consulted his notes. "Mr. Pete Naujokas of Estes Park, Colorado," he said. "And yes, as far as I know, he's still up there. Third RV spot on the right inside the campground. But how can he possibly identify her?"

Frank held up a piece of paper. "The night clerk faxed me a copy of Sandra Ridder's mug shot."

Jaime laughed. "Frank Montoya's trusty mobile office strikes again."

Frank's technological additions to his Crown Victoria had been the topic of much good-natured ribbing both inside and outside the department. But at times like these, it was easy for Frank to rib back.

"It's only a little after nine," Joanna told her officers. "Even the most dedicated RVer won't have hit the sack this early. Frank and I will go show Pete Naujokas the picture and see what he says. That way we'll know for sure whether or not Sandra Ridder is the woman who was digging in the rocks."

Leaving Jaime Carbajal to continue his investigation of this new part of the crime scene, Joanna and Frank headed for the campground. The gravel road, little more than a trail in spots, was rough and winding enough to prove something of a challenge to Frank's Civvie. Once they arrived at the campground and saw some of the big RV rigs parked there, Joanna wondered aloud how they had made it up the road.

Frank looked at her and grinned. "Most of the guys who drive these are retired," he told her. "They don't care how long it takes to get from one camping spot to another. They're not on a set schedule."

Outside the Naujokases' RV, four people in folding camp chairs were seated around a blazing fire. "Mr. Naujokas?" Joanna asked, exhibiting her ID.

"That's me." A smiling, slightly built man stepped out of the firelight. "Most people call me Pete," he said.

"I'm Sheriff Joanna Brady, and this is Frank Montoya, my chief deputy. I was wondering if you'd mind taking a look at a picture we have here and telling us whether or not it's the woman you saw down by the park entrance last night."

Frank passed him the faxed mug shot, and Pete Naujokas walked it over to the fire in order to take a closer look. "That's her," he said, coming back to return the paper to Frank. "Who is she—or rather, who was she? Some kind of criminal?"

"Her name is Sandra Ridder. She went to prison for manslaughter eight years ago, after the shooting death of her husband. Her mother lives a few miles away from here off Middlemarch Road."

"But what was she doing here?" Pete asked. "At the campground?"

"We think she came looking for something, maybe something that had been hidden for years."

"Since before she went to prison?"

"That's right," Joanna told him. "We found an empty container, but there was no sign of what had been in it."

Pete shook his head. "Most likely not a missing ring," he said. "The whole thing gives me the willies." He shivered. "I guess I'm lucky she didn't accept my offer of help. No telling what might have happened then. When you hang around campgrounds like this, you meet up with a lot of really nice people. It lulls you into believing that everyone's pretty much the same. Know what I mean?"

Joanna nodded.

"I guess I'll be more careful after this," he added with a rueful grin. "Being a good Samaritan is supposed to be a good thing. On the other hand, being a dead good Samaritan is downright stupid."

"After you left the woman by the sign and came on up to the campground, did you hear anything?"

"You mean like a gunshot?" Pete Naujokas asked. "No, I didn't. I've asked around. As far as I can tell, nobody else did, either."

Frank and Joanna left a few minutes later. After a brief stop to check in with Jaime Carbajal, they continued back to Joanna's Blazer.

"That is weird," Frank mused along the way.

"What is?"

"If Sandra's mother lived just a few miles away, why not hide whatever it was on her mother's property instead of someplace as public as the entrance to a national monument?"

"Because she didn't want whatever it was she was hiding

to be connected to her mother or to her," Joanna said. "A weapon, maybe. What about the gun that was used to kill Tom Ridder? Was that ever recovered?"

"I don't know," Frank replied. "I can probably find out tomorrow. It would have to be damned small to fit inside that bowl."

"So we're looking for something that's small and valuable," Joanna added. "What about you, Frank? Supposing your house was on fire or about to be washed away in a flood, and all you could rescue was whatever would fit in a bowl that size. Given that set of circumstances, what would you have put in there?"

"My grandfather's Purple Heart," Frank replied with hardly a moment's hesitation. "My birth certificate, a couple of photos, and my wallet. That way I'd have some ID and my credit cards when it came time to start over. What about you?"

Joanna nodded. "I'd probably do pretty much the same thing, only instead of a Purple Heart, I'd save my father's sheriff's badge." As a teenager, Joanna had been given D. H. Lathrop's sheriff's badge after her father's funeral. It had been one of her most treasured mementos before she was elected sheriff. Now it was even more so.

By then Frank had stopped the Crown Victoria next to Joanna's Blazer. "See you Monday," he said as Joanna climbed out of the Civvie. "If not sooner."

"Let's hope not sooner," she returned. "I'd like to have one whole day to myself this weekend."

Driving back across the Sulphur Springs Valley toward home, Joanna kept mulling the same question. What would have been in a bowl that small? And why Tupperware? The one thing Joanna remembered from her abortive and relatively unhappy career as a Tupperware representative was that those sturdy plastic containers—especially the round ones—were supposed to be both air- and watertight. Driving through the night, Joanna smiled at a recollection of Andy teasing her back then, telling her that if nuclear warfare ever broke out, that, after hundreds of years, the only artifacts left to testify to human existence in the late twentieth century would be warehouses chock-full of still usable Tupperware and still edible Twinkies.

Part of what had made selling Tupperware difficult for Joanna had to do with the fact that many people in town were broke. Once the mines closed, most of Bisbee's economic base disappeared. For a long time the expected boom in out-of-state visitors had simply bypassed the little town. In those cash-strapped days, Tupperware had been hard to come by. You had to be invited to a party, go and play dumb games, and then fork over hard-earned cash in order to cart home a set of four of those stupid bowls. And, for Joanna, that had been the real difficulty in selling the stuff—she didn't actually believe in it. Her mother did. Eleanor claimed to adore the stuff. Joanna remained firmly in the camp of margarine containers.

Joanna couldn't remember her mother ever storing a dishful of leftovers without first using the distinctive little tab to raise the lid and let out excess air. And in Eleanor's fastidiously run household, no Tupperware-stored leftovers were ever allowed to spoil or go to waste.

The same thing couldn't be said of Joanna Brady's more casually managed existence. Containers of food were sometimes inadvertently shoved to the back of a lower shelf in her refrigerator where the contents might well mutate into a new life form before finally being rediscovered. With margarine tubs or cottage-cheese or sour-cream containers, there was never any question of what to do then—throw them out, leftovers and all. But Tupperware was different and came with an entirely different set of rules. No matter how disgusting what had been left to molder inside, those had to be cleaned out and rehabilitated with bleach, detergent, and elbow grease. To do anything less seemed un-American somehow.

Taking Joanna's own deep-seated prejudices and experience into account, that meant Sandra Ridder hadn't intended to lose her Tupperware bowl—ever. Not the first time when she hid it, and not the second time when she had gone back to retrieve it. And whatever she had stowed in the bowl all those years earlier, she had meant it to be protected from the elements.

By the time Joanna neared High Lonesome Ranch, she had left off worrying about Sandra Ridder's Tupperware and was dealing with concerns much closer to home. She wondered what had happened that evening in her absence. It was one thing to be a hands-on sheriff, but how about being a hands-on mother? What had her presence contributed to the investigation into Sandra Ridder's death, and how much had she missed by being away from the High Lonesome and Jenny and Butch? The fact that she wasn't alone—the fact that Joanna Brady was dealing with the daily ball-juggling contest of every other working mother in America—didn't make her feel any better about it.

Halfway up the winding road that led to the house, Joanna had to slow to negotiate the wash. A tow truck had removed Reba Singleton's stranded limo, but in the process the well-worn track across the dry creek bed had been obliterated. Boulders that hadn't been there before had been churned to the surface, while wheel-swallowing pits had been left behind in the sand. Using the Blazer's four-wheel drive to negotiate this new obstacle path was the only thing that kept Joanna herself from becoming stuck in her own driveway. As a result, Joanna wasn't thinking fond thoughts about tow-truck drivers, limo drivers, or Reba Rhodes Singleton by the time she finally pulled into her own yard.

She was relieved to see Butch's Subaru was still parked near the gate. Knowing Jenny had been looked after in the meantime was the only thing that made being gone so long possible or bearable.

The lights were on in the living room as she parked the Blazer, but as soon as she opened the car door, the back porch light came on and Sadie and Tigger came tumbling out of the house. Behind the two dogs walked Butch, in stocking feet, gingerly picking his way across the yard.

"You shouldn't be out here without shoes," she scolded. "Don't you know there are sandburs in the yard?"

"I do now," he said, hopping gingerly on one foot. "How are things?"

"It's late, and I'm tired," she told him. "How are things with you?"

Butch wrapped one arm around her shoulders and gently pulled her against his chest. "We had some company," he said, leading her toward the house.

"Not your parents!" Joanna exclaimed. "Don't tell me they turned up early."

"Not my parents."

"Who then?"

Butch waited until they were all the way inside the house before he answered. "Dick Voland," he said.

Joanna blinked. Dick Voland had been a long-term deputy with the Cochise County Sheriff's Department. He had served as chief deputy in the administration of Joanna's predecessor, Walter V. McFadden, and had continued in that capacity, sharing responsibility with Frank Montoya, once Joanna was elected. She had been able to deal with the man in the beginning, when he was simply gruff and overbearing. The situation had become much more complicated when Joanna discovered that he had developed a serious middle-aged crush on her. Voland had mostly pined in silence, but Joanna's betrothal to Butch had pushed him over the edge. The morning after her engagement was made public, Voland had turned up on High Lonesome Ranch, drunk and belligerent. He had handed in his resignation on the spot. Under the circumstances, Joanna had been only too happy to accept it.

Since then, Joanna had seen little of the man. She had heard that he was in the process of hanging out his shingle as a private investigator. She had also heard that he and Marliss Shackleford were now an item. Marliss, a columnist for a local rag called *The Bisbee Bee,* wasn't one of Joanna's favorite people either. When she heard Marliss and Dick were dating, Joanna figured that the two of them deserved each other.

"Dick wasn't drunk, was he?" Joanna asked carefully.

At six-four, Voland was a massive bear of a man who outweighed Butch by a good fifty pounds. "Not that I could tell."

"What did he want?"

"He didn't say. I offered to take a message, but he said he needed to talk to you. He wanted you to call as soon as you got home tonight. I left the number there on the table."

Joanna felt a sudden fury wash through her. "I know his number," she stormed. "And if it was that damned important, he could have called me on my cell phone. He knows *my* numbers, too. I sure as hell haven't changed them! He just wanted to come by, hassle me, and nose around in my business."

"Come on, Joey," Butch said, using the private nickname he had bestowed on her. "Don't be upset. He didn't cause any trouble, and he didn't say anything out of line."

"He should have told you what he wanted," Joanna insisted. "That was rude, treating you as if you're incapable of passing along a simple message."

Butch laughed aloud at that. "You don't understand very much about men, do you?"

Joanna frowned. "What's so funny? And what do you mean by that?"

"I mean Dick Voland and I were in a contest, and I won. Dick's the big loser here. I've got you, and he doesn't. Believe me, Dick Voland isn't ever going to sit down and have a long, heart-to-heart discussion with me. He hates my guts, and he's going to do his best to pretend I don't exist."

"What about you?" Joanna asked.

"I feel sorry for him, but not that sorry."

"Regardless," Joanna said. "It's late, and I'm not calling him back tonight. Whatever the big secret is, it's going to have to wait until morning."

"Good enough," Butch said. "Now, did you have any dinner?"

"No," Joanna answered, noticing for the first time that she was hungry.

"After that big, late lunch, all Jenny and I had were a couple of scrambled eggs and toast. Would you like me to make you some?"

"Please."

While Butch scrambled eggs, Joanna undressed and locked her weapons away. Then, wearing her nightgown and robe, she returned to the kitchen to make toast and pour a glass of milk while she told Butch about the situation with Catherine Yates, her dead daughter, Sandra, and her missing granddaughter, Lucy.

"Not a very happy story," Joanna concluded. "Here I should have been spending the weekend enjoying Jenny's birthday celebration with you and getting ready for our wedding. Instead, I'm busy worrying about who's killing whom and why."

"Which reminds me," Butch said, getting up to clear the table. "George called, too. Just a little while ago. He said it was something to do with Clayton Rhodes, but he also said that he and your mother were going to bed as soon as the news was over. He said he'd talk to you about it in the morning."

Joanna looked down at her watch. By then it was close to midnight. "It's almost morning right now," she observed. "If we're going to church tomorrow, we'd better get to bed."

"You go on, if you want to," Butch said. "I'll clean up the kitchen and then shove off for home."

"You mean you're not staying?"

"Waking up naked this morning with Jenny right there in the room made a believer of me," Butch said with a rueful smile. "No more sleep-overs for us until after the wedding. I don't want people to talk any more than they already do. But don't worry. I'll come out first thing in the morning and help with the animals."

"It's all right. Jenny and I can feed the animals."

"Well, I'll come fix you breakfast, then. We have to build up our strength so we'll be ready to clean that oven tomorrow afternoon."

Joanna laughed aloud at that. She came across the kitchen and hugged him close. "I love you, Butch Dixon," she said. "Thank you for caring about what Jenny thinks and about what people say."

Firmly Butch moved her away from him, leaving her standing in the middle of the room and safely out of arm's reach. "And I love you, but no more thanks like that," he said. "If you're not careful, I'll end up changing my mind and I'll stay over after all."

*   *   *

It was late in the afternoon before Lucy once more ventured out of her hiding place among the gigantic boulders scattered across the Texas Canyon landscape. Emotionally and physically exhausted, she had slept most of the day. Now chilly, lonely, and longing for the comfort of a soda or candy bar from a vending machine, she approached the fenced freeway rest area.

There were half a dozen eighteen-wheelers parked in the designated truck parking area, but there was only one car—an SUV—parked near the entrance to the rest rooms and the vending machines. There was a man standing leaning against it, talking on a cell phone. When Lucy was close enough to distinguish his features, she gave a gasp of dismay. It was the same man she had seen the night before— the man who had shot her mother.

Panicked and sobbing, Lucy fled back into the desert. *How did he find me?* she wondered. *How did he know I was here?*

 **NINE**

Sheltered by a wall of Texas Canyon house-sized boulders and huddled in her sleeping bag, Lucy tried to sleep. It was far colder than she had thought it would be, but she didn't dare start a fire. She was too close to the rest area. Someone might notice and come looking. The rocks in the ground beneath her—sharp-edged rocks that had seemed insignificant when she was choosing a place to put her bedroll—now cut into her back and legs.

Lucy was still shaken by what had happened earlier. She had gone down to the rest area to use the phone again, and her mother's killer was still there—waiting. Stunned, she had melted back into the desert before he or any of the half dozen truckers stopped there noticed her. The rest of the afternoon and evening and far into the night she had struggled to find answers. He must have known she was there, but how? What he wanted she didn't need to ask. He was looking for her—for Lucy—and for his computer disk. Once he found them, there was no doubt in Lucy's mind about what he would do—take the diskette and kill her, the same way he had killed Lucy's mother.

At last, as the sky gradually grew lighter in the east, Lucy slept. She was still sleeping hours later, when Big Red's warning screech issued an alarm. He had made that peculiar noise other times when they had been together on their solitary Cochise Stronghold adventures. And always that particular sound meant the same thing—a warning that someone was coming.

Panicked into full wakefulness, Lucy scrambled out of the bedroll. Standing shaking in the full morning sun, she looked skyward. Outlined against the blue sky, Big Red flew in frantic circles, pinpointing the position of something or someone who was coming toward Lucy's camping place from the south, from the direction of the rest area.

In a futile effort to keep warm overnight, Lucy had stayed dressed. Not only was she still wearing her jacket, she was also wearing her sneakers. Now she was glad she was. Grabbing only her backpack, she fled uphill and away from whoever it was who was coming—as if she didn't know.

In Cochise Stronghold, she had often tried to teach herself the things her ancestor, the Apache chief, Eskiminzin, must always have known. With careful practice she had taught herself to run long distances over rough terrain, leaving behind little or no trail. She did this now. Leaping from rock to rock, she sprinted for nearly a mile, leaving no discernible footprints to mark her passage. At last, gasping for breath, she squirreled herself into a cleft between two huge boulders, and there she stayed—listening, waiting, and wondering how long it would be before he somehow tracked her there as well.

Joanna Brady awakened Sunday morning as Jenny eased herself onto the side of the bed. "Where's Butch?" Jenny asked.

"He went home," Joanna mumbled sleepily. She would have liked nothing better than to roll back over and sleep a little longer, but Jenny was fully rested and ready for conversation.

"How come?"

"How come what?"

"Why'd he go home?"

"Because that's where he lives."

Opening her eyes, Joanna studied her daughter. Jenny was perched on the edge of the bed with her blond frizz of hair backlit by morning sun. In that light, she looked more like a haloed angel than a little girl. Joanna felt a sudden surge of thanksgiving that, despite Andy's death, Jenny seemed to be doing more than merely coping. She gave every appearance of being a well-adjusted, sweet, and relatively innocent child. When Lucinda Ridder's father was killed, Lucy had been almost the same age Jenny was when Andy died. Now, as a fifteen-year-old, Lucy Ridder was at best a runaway and at worst a homicide suspect.

Joanna reached over, grabbed Jenny by the shoulders, and wrestled her into a smothering bear hug.

"What was that all about?" Jenny demanded once she had wriggled loose.

"I love you is all," Joanna said, clambering out of bed. "Now that I'm awake, I suppose we'd better get out and feed those animals. They're probably hungry. Compared to the schedule Clayton Rhodes kept, you and I are a couple of slugabeds."

Butch showed up while Jenny and Joanna were out in the barn doing chores. By the time they finished and returned to the house, breakfast was ready. There were glasses of fresh-squeezed orange juice and bowls of steaming Malt-o-meal waiting on the table.

"We're a team," Butch said cheerfully when Joanna kissed him good morning. "A well-oiled machine."

The phone rang just as they were slipping into their

places in the breakfast nook. Jenny scampered off to collect the phone and brought it back to the kitchen.

"Who is it?" Joanna mouthed as Jenny handed her the phone.

Jenny merely shrugged and rolled her eyes. "How would I know?" she returned.

"Hello?" Joanna said.

"Joanna," Burton Kimball said. "Glad you're there. Sorry to bother you so early on a Sunday morning, but I tried to reach you several times yesterday. When you didn't return my calls, I was afraid you were out of town."

Burton Kimball was a Bisbee-area attorney. His practice included a good deal of criminal defense work, and Joanna wondered which of his clients was in such dire straits that Kimball would be working this early on a Sunday morning.

"Sorry about that," Joanna said. "I was out of town most of the day. Then, when we came back, I was called out on a case and didn't get home until it was too late to return anybody's calls. What's up?"

"It's about Clayton Rhodes," Burton Kimball said.

"Clayton Rhodes!" Joanna exclaimed. "How can you already have a client, since my investigators aren't close to having a suspect?"

"Mr. Rhodes *was* my client," Burton returned. "I did some estate planning for him. His daughter showed up on her broom yesterday afternoon. The funeral is tentatively scheduled for Monday. Even so, Reba Singleton insisted on having the will opened and read yesterday evening. I tried contacting you beforehand so you could be here when it was read, but—"

"Why would I need to be there?" Joanna asked. "As far as I know, Clayton's death resulted from natural causes. In any event—even in the case of an apparent homicide—

there's no need for a sheriff's department representative to attend the reading of a will."

"Not as a representative of the sheriff's department," Kimball responded. "You. Joanna Brady. The reason I wanted you in attendance is that you're a major beneficiary."

That stopped Joanna cold. "Me?" she asked dazedly. "I'm a beneficiary?"

"Yes. Clayton rewrote his will a year and a half ago. He left Rhodes Ranch to you—all three hundred and twenty acres of it. It's free and clear, house and all."

Joanna could barely believe her ears. "I don't get it. Clayton Rhodes left his place to me?" she stammered. "That's impossible! A ridiculous joke! You mean to say he left Reba out of his will entirely, that he disowned his own daughter in favor of me?"

"Not entirely. He and Molly had tons of savings bonds, as well as a whole bunch of certificates of deposit. There will be plenty of cash to pay final expenses, including all applicable income and estate taxes. Whatever money is left after taxes goes to Reba, but you're to have the property and whatever personal effects Reba doesn't want. You're to deal with those as you see fit. No strings attached."

Stunned, Joanna felt the blood drain from her face, causing both Butch and Jenny to cast worried looks in her direction. "What is it, Mom?" Jenny asked. "What's wrong?"

"Clayton left two letters—one for you and one for Reba," Burton Kimball continued. "I gave Reba hers last night. I was wondering if I shouldn't bring yours out to you this morning. I want you to be aware of everything that's going on because of Reba, you see. I'm concerned about her reaction. She and her father had been estranged for years—ever since her mother's death—but I'm afraid this still hit her pretty hard. I wouldn't be surprised if she didn't try to make trouble, if she hasn't already, that is."

"When did you read the will?" Joanna asked.

"Yesterday evening. She came to see me around noon, about as soon as she got to town, I guess. I don't think she even bothered to go to the funeral home before she showed up at my house—in a limo, no less—demanding to see the will right then. In all my years in practice, I've never seen anything like it. I tried to stall; told her there were other people involved who should be present as well, but when I couldn't reach you, I finally went ahead without you. She insisted. Have you seen her yet?"

"Briefly," Joanna said. "She was out here at the ranch yesterday afternoon. When we came home from Tucson. Her limo was stuck in my wash. The driver had to call Triple A to come pull it out."

"Did she say anything to you?" Burton Kimball asked.

"She seemed upset. She said something to the effect that I had killed her father by working him into the grave. She asked me about the status of the investigation. I told her that since Dr. Winfield had ruled Clayton dead of natural causes, there wasn't going to be any investigation. As soon as she heard that, she went off on a wild tirade about George Winfield having a conflict of interest in the case, but I didn't think anything of it. I chalked it up to her being overwrought. In situations like that, people end up saying all kinds of things they don't really mean."

"I believe she meant it, all right," Burton Kimball said softly. "She meant every word. After the will was read, she threw a fit. She ranted and raged and said that she'd had her suspicions, but now she was sure you had murdered her father and that George Winfield was helping you by covering it up."

"Mom," Jenny insisted. "What's going on?"

Joanna waved her to silence. "You don't think she's serious, do you?"

"Unfortunately, I do," Burton replied. "Now how can I get you that letter? You need to know what's in it. Should I bring it out to the house?"

"No," Joanna said quickly. "We'll be coming to town in a little while. We can stop by and pick it up on our way to church. Where will you be?"

"Linda and the kids are going off to church themselves," Burton said. "How about if I meet you uptown at my office. Say, forty-five minutes?"

Joanna looked down at her untouched bowlful of Malt-o-Meal that, without the benefit of milk and brown sugar, had now cooled and congealed into a hard gray lump. "Give us an hour," she said. "That's the soonest we can be there."

Two hours later, Joanna was sitting in a pew in Canyon United Methodist Church, while her pastor and best friend, the Reverend Marianne Maculyea, read the morning's scripture. Pregnant women are supposed to glow. That was especially true for Marianne, who was in the last stages of a long-sought but unexpected pregnancy. Her face was alight as she read the passage from Deuteronomy 30:19. "I have set before you life and death, blessing and curse; therefore choose life, that you and your descendants may live."

For years Joanna had sung in the church choir, but the countervailing pressures of work and single-motherhood had eventually made regular attendance at weekly practice sessions an impossibility. Sitting in the choir loft behind the minister, it had been necessary to remain both awake and properly attentive.

Now, though, seated discreetly in the fifth pew back,

Joanna paid scant attention to Marianne's sermon for the day, "Choose Life!" Instead, she was preoccupied with her own set of issues. Most of Joanna's wool-gathering focused on the letter in her purse, one Clayton Rhodes had laboriously written in ink in a spidery, old-fashioned scrawl. The letter had been dated barely two months earlier.

Dear Joanna,

By now you know of my intention to leave my place to you. I understand that if you marry Butch Dixon, it will be partially his, too.

I want you to know how much working for you these past few years has meant to me. When you're old, it's easy to get thrown on the scrap heap and forgotten. I've enjoyed getting to know Jenny and watching her grow. She's a sweet kid in a way my own daughter never was.

I've seen how you are with High Lonesome Ranch. I know how much it means to you, and how hard you've had to work to keep it. If I were to pass my place along to Reba, she would take the first offer to sell it and wouldn't care what became of it later. She may say this isn't fair and she may try to make you feel sorry for her, but don't fall for it. She treated her mother and me like scum. If she gets anything at all, it's more than she deserves.

I wish you and yours the best, Joanna. You and Andy and Jenny have always been good neighbors.

Sincerely,
Clayton Rhodes

Joanna's eyes had blurred with tears as she finished reading the text of the letter. After that, Burton Kimball had read aloud the applicable passages in Clayton Rhodes' will. Since being given the letter, Joanna had read it through only twice—once in Burton Kimball's office and presence, and again, aloud, when she returned to the Outback, where Butch and Jenny were waiting. Even so, sitting there in the church pew, Joanna could have recited the entire letter from memory. The words were etched on her heart.

"He can't mean this" was the first thing Joanna had said to Burton.

"He meant it all right," the attorney had returned calmly.

"But what about Reba? She's his daughter, after all."

"She's also a complete bitch, if you'll pardon the expression," Burton said. "The will was properly drawn and witnessed a year and a half ago. And, as I told you on the phone, it isn't as though she'll be left with nothing. After taxes, she'll still have a fair chunk of cash which, as far as I can tell, is all she's interested in anyway."

"A year and a half," Joanna echoed. "But the letter is dated . . ."

"There was another letter," Burton Kimball said kindly. "One that was written at the time we drew up the will. Clayton threw that one away and wrote this one after you and Butch Dixon announced your engagement. He told me he didn't want Butch to feel left out. This isn't in the letter, but Clayton told me he thought Butch was a fine young man. I guess the two of them had a long talk about the advisability of removing mesquite and trying to reintroduce native grasses."

Joanna nodded. "It is something we've talked about, but there didn't seem to be much point to doing it on a paltry little forty acres."

Burton Kimball smiled. "Now you'll have three hundred and sixty. That'll be a lot more work." The lawyer paused and smiled. "By the way," he added, "congratulations from Linda, and me as well. On your engagement, that is. When's the big day?"

"Next Saturday."

"Well, then. I'm sure Clayton would be happy to know that he's giving the two of you a terrific wedding present. The place will have to be appraised. The IRS will want us to establish current market value for estate-tax purposes. And, of course, that valuation will give you an official basis in the property should you later decide to sell it."

"What about the will?" Joanna asked. "Is it contestable?"

Burton's smile disappeared abruptly. "Every will is contestable if someone wants to go to the trouble, that is. However, Clayton stipulated that all costs related to contesting the will are to be deducted from the cash portion of the proceeds. In other words, if Reba tries to go against the will, she'll have to pay her attorney's expenses and mine as well. That's assuming, of course, that you want me to handle it. That would also apply to the expenses of any other attorney you might choose to represent you."

"Is that why Reba thinks I murdered her father?" Joanna asked. "State law dictates that people found guilty of killing someone aren't allowed to profit from their actions. If she can somehow cast enough suspicion on me, she'll be able to destroy the will without actually having to contest it."

Burton Kimball sighed and nodded. "Let me remind you that I'm also a damned fine defense attorney, but that is what I meant when I warned you that she might make trouble."

And now, as Joanna sat in church not listening to the sermon, that was what she was worried about, too. Clayton

Rhodes had probably been dead for several hours when she had found him in his exhaust-filled garage, but she had had no way of knowing that at the time. She hadn't been worried about preserving evidence when she smashed a hole in the door to get inside. She hadn't been wearing gloves or worrying about leaving a trail of fingerprints when she reached in through the driver's window to turn off the ignition key. She had been intent on saving the man's life.

Unfortunately, her fingerprints would be found there, and they wouldn't be wear-dated. If Reba set out to do so, she might be able to make the case that the prints had been placed on Clayton Rhodes' ignition key long before he died rather than after. The idea that Sheriff Joanna Brady herself could turn into a homicide suspect should have been laughable. It might have been, if it hadn't been so scary.

"Therefore choose life," Marianne was saying from the pulpit. "Choose it for yourself and for your children. Choose it with all your heart and all your mind and all your soul. Because it's how you choose life now that determines both the now and the hereafter. If you can't choose this simple living and breathing life, how will you choose eternal life? Because they go hand in hand, you see. It's like what that old fifties song says about love and marriage," she added, aiming a beaming smile in Joanna and Butch's direction. "You can't have one without the other. Therefore choose life. Let us bow our heads in prayer."

With his shaven head glowing deep-red, Butch reached over and folded Joanna's hand in his. "I told you we should have sat in the back row," he muttered under his breath.

After the closing hymn, Butch and Joanna went hand in hand as they worked their way down the center aisle to where the Reverend Marianne Maculyea and her husband, Jeff Daniels, stood greeting attendees. Wanting to have a private word with her best friend, Joanna stalled long enough to be last in line.

Once Marianne's early bouts of pregnancy-related nausea had finally subsided, she had gone on to have an uneventful and so-far uncomplicated pregnancy. Because Marianne would be officiating at the wedding, Butch and Joanna had set the ceremony for early April so as not to conflict with the baby's due date. The wedding was now less than a week away. According to Dr. Thomas Lee, Marianne's attending physician, the baby was expected in three.

Finished with shaking hands at the door, Marianne stood with one hand massaging her sore back and with the other resting on a belly so swollen that it left a telltale shelf protruding beneath her clerical vestments. With a squeal of joy, Jeff and Marianne's adopted three-year-old daughter, Ruth, escaped the nursery attendant and slipped under her mother's robe for a game of peekaboo with whoever happened to be nearby. As the last of the congregation headed for the fellowship hall and coffee hour, Jeff captured Ruth, scooped the squirming child into his arms, and carried her downstairs. Butch and Jenny followed, leaving Joanna and Marianne with a rare moment of relative peace and privacy.

Always attuned to what was going on with other people, Marianne gave Joanna a searching look. "Are you all right?" she asked. "You seemed pretty distracted during the service."

"What makes you say that?" Joanna countered.

Marianne smiled. "Because you missed not one but two of the in-crowd jokes I put in the sermon especially for you. What's going on?"

"Clayton Rhodes died and left me his place in his will," Joanna blurted.

Surprise washed over Marianne's face. "The whole thing?"

Joanna nodded.

"What about his daughter?" Marianne asked.

"I talked to Burton Kimball on the way to church this morning. According to him, she's not a happy camper. She may go so far as to try to accuse me of murdering her father."

Marianne's gray eyes turned dark and stormy. "You can't be serious."

"I am. Dead serious."

Marianne took a deep breath. "We need to get together and talk about this. We should also discuss any last-minute hitches or glitches in wedding plans. What are you and Butch and Jenny doing this afternoon?"

"Cleaning house," Joanna replied. "My new mother-in-law shows up tomorrow, remember? We're doing the oven, cabinets, closets—the whole bit."

"I have an idea," Marianne suggested. "I was supposed to have a steering-committee meeting this afternoon, but it's been canceled. Before you and Butch go tear into your house, how about if we all meet at Daisy's for lunch as soon as coffee hour is over? I'll con Jenny into looking after Ruth, and that way maybe the four of us will have a moment or two to think straight."

"Sounds like a plan to me," Joanna replied with a laugh. "I'm sure Butch will agree to anything that will delay working on the oven that much longer."

Joanna had barely set foot inside the fellowship hall when she was pounced upon by Marliss Shackleford, who had clearly been waiting just inside the door. It was an unfortunate piece of small-town life that both Sheriff Brady and her fourth-estate nemesis attended the same church— one which both of them refused to leave. Usually Joanna managed to avoid Marliss. This time she was trapped.

"It sounds as though you've had a busy few days of it," Marliss began sweetly enough. "It's too bad about what happened to Clayton. I know he's been such a help to you all this time. How are you and Jenny managing without him?"

"We're doing all right," Joanna said stiffly.

"And then, of course, you do have Butch. I understand he's something of a city slicker, but he seems bright enough."

"He is trainable," Joanna returned. "Just barely."

"I didn't mean to imply that he wasn't."

Of course, you didn't, Joanna thought. "Of course not," she said aloud.

"Have you spoken to Reba Singleton yet?" Marliss asked. "Clayton's daughter? She's in town, you know."

"We touched base," Joanna said. "That's about all."

"*The Bee* is trying to set up an interview for me with her. Molly and Clayton Rhodes were such old-timers around here that Clayton should get more than just the standard, run-of-the-mill obituary. It's a little out of my usual line of work, but I told my editor I'd be glad to write the piece for them. I'm sure Reba will be able to give me all sorts of insights into the kind of person her father was."

Great, Joanna thought. *That's just what I need. The poisoned daughter being interviewed by the original poisoned pen.*

"I'm sure it'll be very interesting," she said, sidling away. "Now, if you'll excuse me, Marliss, I need to catch up with Jenny before she fills up on cookies and punch and makes herself sick."

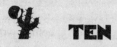

TEN

When it came time to park at Daisy's Café, Joanna was dismayed to see that the lot was full to overflowing. "Great," she grumbled. "If it's already this crowded, it'll take forever to get a table."

"Maybe not," Butch said cheerfully. "There's Jeff and Marianne's VW. If they're here ahead of us, maybe they've already snagged one. If nothing else, they'll have put our names on the list."

Jenny let herself out of the backseat and scampered into the restaurant. Meanwhile, Joanna studied some of the vehicles in the unpaved lot. A surprisingly large number of them looked familiar. In addition to Jeff Daniels' sea-foam green Bug, Joanna recognized Jim Bob and Eva Lou Brady's Honda and Angie Kellogg's aging Omega, along with Eleanor Lathrop's brand-new Buick. She also caught sight of the fire-engine-red Geo Metro driven by her secretary, Kristin Marsten.

Joanna looked back at Butch. "Wait a minute," she said. "Something's fishy here. Bisbee may be a small town, but it's a little too much of a coincidence for everyone I know to turn up at the same place at the same time. What's going on?"

"Why don't we go in and see," he said.

As soon as Butch held open the door, Joanna caught a glimpse of a bank of balloons lined up down the middle of the dining room. Once she saw the balloons, she knew she'd been had. A burst of applause, accompanied by shouts of "Surprise!" erupted from half the room, which had been screened off to create a semi-private banquet room.

Joanna turned on Butch. "It's a shower," she said accusingly. "Butch Dixon, you tricked me."

He tried his best to look contrite, but it didn't work very well. "I told you I hate cleaning ovens," he said. "I'll do almost anything to avoid it."

Accompanied by gales of laughter, Marianne Maculyea stepped forward, grabbed Joanna by the arm, and led her toward the far end of the room, where a mound of gifts had been stacked on one table. A grinning, self-satisfied Jenny stood next to the table.

"You were in on this, too, weren't you!" Joanna said accusingly.

Jenny nodded. "But I didn't tell."

"No, you certainly didn't."

"So we pulled it off?" Marianne asked.

"Completely."

"Good."

Just then, Joanna found herself enveloped in the warm embrace of her former mother-in-law, Eva Lou Brady. Eva Lou's exuberant greeting was followed by a reserved hug and a dignified peck on the cheek from Eleanor Lathrop Winfield, Joanna's own mother. Joanna pulled away from Eleanor in time to see Butch and Jim Bob Brady sidling toward the door.

"Wait a minute," she demanded. "Where do you two think you're going?"

"This is a shower," Butch said. "Girls' stuff," he added with a wink in Jenny's direction. "You can't expect us men to hang around here."

"But when will you be back? How will Jenny and I get home?"

He grinned. "I'm sure someone here will give you a ride. In the meantime, we're going up the street for a guy lunch. No girls allowed. Except for Ruth, of course, who already left with Jeff. But since she's just a baby, she doesn't count."

Butch followed Jim Bob out the door before Joanna could lob a rejoinder in his direction. By then an apron-clad Junior Dowdle had walked up behind her, grinning broadly and carrying a black baseball cap with the word BRIDE embroidered on the front.

"Put on!" he demanded urgently, handing Joanna the cap. "Put on now."

Knowing the cap would give her a terrible case of hat-hair, Joanna tried to weasel out of it. "Do I have to?" she asked.

"Put on!" Junior ordered again. Amid another burst of general laughter, Joanna did as she was told.

Within minutes, Joanna lost herself in the carefree mood of a wedding shower. Daisy Maxwell, owner of Daisy's Café, had provided platters of nachos, tacos, and mini burritos. For a change, instead of hustling around with a pencil in her beehive hairdo and taking orders, Daisy herself was seated among the guests while a wait staff that included her husband, Moe, took care of the shower guests as well as the other Sunday diners on the far side of the balloon barricade.

After lunch and pieces of a wonderful lemon chiffon cake, it was time for Joanna to tackle the mountain of gifts. She was assisted in the unwrapping process by Angie Kellogg, who had finagled a day off from her relief bartending job at the Blue Moon Saloon and Lounge up in Old Bisbee's Brewery Gulch. Angie, a former L.A. hooker, was someone whose rehabilitation Joanna and Marianne Maculyea had taken on as a joint project. Together they had helped her exit her previous line of work and had eased her way into a far more settled existence in Bisbee. Her new life came complete with a boyfriend named Dennis Hacker, an English biologist who specialized in reintroducing parrots into the wild forest lands of southern Arizona.

Angie's newfound happiness was a testimony to the fact that Joanna Brady was making a contribution with her own life—that her efforts were accomplishing some good. That afternoon it was especially gratifying for Joanna to see Angie laughing, talking, and seemingly completely at ease among a group of women in whose presence she would have been petrified and/or self-conscious only a few years earlier. It was also fun to see Angie, as designated maid of honor, set about the mundane task of stringing colorful package-wrapping ribbon through a paper plate in order to make the traditional shower ribbon bouquet.

Not far into the pile of gifts, Joanna was grateful the men had been banished to parts unknown. Angie Kellogg's carefully understated gift was a beautiful box of perfumed bath oils and powders. Other attendees' gifts, however, weren't nearly so restrained. There were several sets of sexy, slinky underwear, including a particularly racy black bikini-cut duo from Kristin Marsten, Joanna's secretary. There were two separate peignoir sets. One, from Joanna's mother, was a stylish but chastely cut long gown and robe in a demure cream. To Joanna's amazement, the one from Eva Lou Brady, her former mother-in-law, was a short, flimsy see-through froth of emerald lace and silk that left nothing to the imagination.

"Eva Lou!" Joanna exclaimed. "It's lovely, but where on earth did you get this?"

Eva Lou Brady blushed and beamed with pleasure. "Victoria's Secret," she said. "I ordered it from a catalog. You don't think I'd actually set foot in a place like that, do you? I'd be too embarrassed."

Glancing back at the growing pile of unwrapped lingerie on the table, Joanna looked around the room. "Are you guys trying to tell me something?" she asked.

Eva Lou nodded. "You're a little too practical for your own good at times," she said. "It's time you lightened up. Time you stopped taking everything so seriously."

"I'll try," Joanna said with a laugh. Then, ignoring the strictures about not breaking any strings at a wedding shower, she tore into the next package.

By two o'clock, the party was winding down. Most of the guests had left. Marianne was sitting on a chair with her feet up while Joanna and Kristin Marsten loaded the gifts into Eleanor Winfield's Buick. "I'll bet you were in on planning this, too, weren't you?"

Kristin, a good-looking blond, twenty-something, had been the previous sheriff's private secretary long before Joanna's election. Attached to the previous administration and resentful at having a female boss, Kristin had been difficult to handle at first. She and Joanna had lived through several stormy periods, not only right after the election but again when Dick Voland, Joanna's former chief deputy, had left the department. Things were better now. Joanna was somewhat concerned about the fact that Kristin was dating Terry Gregovich, her department's K-9 officer. However, since the secretary and deputy were being discreet about their relationship, and since they didn't hang around mooning at one another on the job, Joanna hadn't voiced too many complaints.

"I did help," Kristin admitted. "Reverend Maculyea wanted to have the party sometime during the week, but I told her she'd be better off having it on a weekend when I could make sure Chief Deputy Montoya was on call and looking after things."

"Is that why my beeper hasn't gone off even once today?" Joanna asked.

Kristin glanced shyly in her boss's direction. "Could be," she said. "I told Frank not to call you out unless it was a dire emergency."

"Thanks, Kristin, it must be working. I was beginning to worry that maybe my pager was out of order."

"I'll go get the last load of presents," Kristin told her. "You wait here."

Joanna was standing next to the open passenger door when she heard a car waiting to park in the next space. She moved out of the way. Only when the driver unfolded his long legs and stepped out of a late-model white Camry did she recognize Dick Voland. It was the first time she had encountered the man in person since their confrontation on the road to High Lonesome Ranch months earlier.

"Hello, Dick," she said, struggling to keep her tone of voice even. It was bad enough seeing him again after so many months. The fact that she had to peer up at him from under the brim of that ridiculous BRIDE-inscribed baseball cap made it that much worse. "How's it going?" she asked.

"Fine," Voland answered. When he hoisted his pants, Joanna noticed they were quite loose around the middle. His belt showed marks where it had once been fastened before a considerable loss of weight. Joanna could see that the man was in far better shape than he had been in those first unhappy months after his divorce when he had been drinking too much and not taking care of himself.

"You look good," she said. "You've lost weight."

Nodding, Dick Voland patted what had once been a bulging belly. "I've been working out again," he told her.

"I'll say," Joanna replied.

Just then Kristin emerged from the restaurant bearing the last load of gifts. On top of the stack was the box from Victoria's Secret. Kristin paused uncertainly when she caught sight of Dick Voland.

"Hello, Mr. Voland," she mumbled. "Good to see you."

As she bent over to put the armload of gifts in the car, the topmost lid caught on the side of the trunk door and spilled a flimsy froth of tissue-wrapped green nightgown out onto the ground. "Oh, no," she wailed. "I've probably ruined it."

Dick Voland reached down and picked it up, dusting it off as he did so. "No harm done," he said, holding it out to her. "A little bit of dust never hurt anything."

Embarrassed, Kristin ignored the proffered gown and fled back inside, leaving Joanna the task of dealing with the gown herself.

"Thanks," Joanna said as she stuffed it back into the box. Waiting long enough for her own blush to dissipate, she closed the trunk. When she straightened up, Dick Voland was still looming over her. He may have lost weight, but he was still six feet four. Joanna was wearing two-inch heels. The top of her baseball cap barely grazed the bottom of his chin.

"What can I do for you, Dick?" she asked, trying to put their conversation on some kind of businesslike basis.

For his part, Voland didn't appear to be any happier about the situation than Joanna was. Acting for all the world like a dumbstruck teenager, he stared down at his feet for some time before he spoke.

"Marliss told me about the shower. I didn't mean to upset anything, but I needed to talk to you."

"The shower's over. It's fine. What do you want to talk about?"

"It's awkward."

"What's awkward?"

Dick took a deep breath. "Look, Joanna. Reba Singleton has hired me to investigate her father's death. I told her I thought she was way off-base. I told her that you and I had worked together for a long time and that, in my opinion, she'd just be throwing her money away. So she said did I want her to throw her money in my direction, or did I want her to hand it over to someone else? I couldn't very well turn her down. I need the work."

He paused, then continued. "I wanted to warn you," he added. "Wanted to let you know what was going on so you wouldn't be blindsided by all this. I came by last night and left a message. I guess Butch didn't see fit to give it to you."

The last thing Joanna would have expected from Dick Voland was kindness. "Butch did give me the message," Joanna said, "but by the time I got home, it was already too late for me to return any calls. And, as you can see, so far today I've been caught up in a dozen other things."

Dick glanced toward the interior of the restaurant. Standing up, the bank of balloons was still clearly visible through the windows. "I'm surprised Marliss wasn't invited to the shower," he mused, as if puzzled by an unintentional oversight. "I'm sure she would have enjoyed it."

That one took Joanna's breath away. Surely Dick Voland understood that she and Marliss Shackleford weren't friends—would never be friends—any more than he would be buddies with Butch Dixon.

"It was a small shower," Joanna said defensively. "Family, mostly. But, Dick, thanks for the heads-up on this other thing, about Reba, I mean."

"You do know about Clayton's will then?" he asked.

"I do now. Burton Kimball called this morning and clued me in."

"She's something, Reba is," Dick said. "And she sure is on a tear about this. She's going to push it all the way to the end."

"Which is?"

"She wants me to gather enough evidence that she can present a case to the FBI."

"The Feds?" Joanna yelped in surprise. "You can't be serious."

"Serious as can be. She claims her husband is friends with some big-wig assistant director who specializes in investigating wrongdoing in local law-enforcement jurisdictions. She's also going to court first thing tomorrow morning to request an additional autopsy. Since Doc Winfield is your stepfather, she wants him to be required to turn over both his results and his tissue samples to another medical examiner for a second opinion."

Sighing and scuffing one foot on the ground, Voland looked even more ill at ease than he had before. "So I guess you could call this a courtesy call," he continued. "I'll be coming around to the department tomorrow morning, Joanna. I'll be asking for fingerprint information—on you."

The whole time Dick Voland was speaking, Joanna hadn't taken her eyes off his face. Rather than his usual bluster and bravado, she saw something else there, something she never would have expected to see—regret. She and Dick Voland had worked together for years. He had been her Chief Deputy for Operations, and he was someone Joanna had looked up to. At the beginning of her administration, while she had been fighting her way through an overwhelming mire of on-the-job training, she had counted on Dick

Voland's good sense and his years of law-enforcement experience for counsel and advice. Despite the unfortunate way things had ended between them, there remained a lingering respect—one that hadn't been entirely obliterated and probably never would be.

"My prints are on Clayton Rhodes' ignition key," she said. "I'm the one who found the pickup in his garage. The engine was still running. At that point I had no way of knowing whether Clayton was dead or alive. There wasn't time to go hunting for a pair of latex gloves. I had to shut the engine off."

Voland nodded. "I figured as much, but try explaining a concept like that to a crazy woman. It's hopeless. She didn't believe a word of it."

"No," Joanna agreed. "I don't suppose she did."

Just then Marianne Maculyea emerged from the restaurant. Catching sight of Dick Voland standing there talking to Joanna, she frowned with concern. "You've been out here a long time," she called across the top of Eleanor's Buick. "Anything wrong?"

Marianne Maculyea was one of the few people in whom Joanna had confided the real reasons behind Dick Voland's abrupt departure from the sheriff's department.

"No," Joanna said quickly. "Nothing's wrong, Mari. Dick here was just giving me a preview of what to expect tomorrow morning at work. And I appreciate it, too, Dick. I really do. Thanks."

"Okay, then," he said. "You're welcome. Guess I'd better be going. See you tomorrow." With that, he folded his lanky frame small enough to fit back inside the Camry and then drove off.

Joanna turned back to Marianne. "What is it, Joanna?" Marianne asked. "You can say there's nothing wrong, but I know better. I can see it in your face."

"Reba Singleton has hired Dick Voland to gather enough evidence against me to ask the FBI to investigate my involvement in her father's death."

"She's accusing you of murdering Clayton Rhodes?"

"That's right."

Marianne's eye blazed with anger. "That's the most ridiculous thing I've ever heard!"

"No, it's not. According to Burton Kimball, if Reba tries to go against her father's will, the expenses of that come straight out of her pocket. But if she can somehow prove that I'm responsible for his death, the state would be compelled to declare the will invalid. I don't know all the applicable statutes well enough. It may not even be necessary for her to make a murder charge stick. Criminal negligence might be enough to invalidate the will."

"But what's the point?" Marianne asked. "Reba Singleton seems to have plenty of money of her own. According to what I heard, she came to town yesterday in a chauffeur-driven limo after flying into Tucson International in a private jet. Why does she even care what happens to her folks' old place? It can't be worth that much money."

"I doubt it is," Joanna agreed. "I'm sure it's the principle of the thing. She regards Rhodes Ranch as hers. The fact that her father may have had other ideas about it is driving her crazy."

"What can I do to help?" Marianne asked.

Joanna smiled. "Listening helps more than you know," she said. "This isn't exactly the kind of problem I want to broadcast to the world. There aren't that many people I can talk to about it."

"Does Butch know?"

"He knows about the will. He doesn't know that Reba Singleton has hired Dick Voland. I don't think he'll be thrilled when he finds out."

"Are you going to tell him?"

"Absolutely. It'll give us something to talk about—while we're cleaning the oven and wiping down cabinets."

"What about a ride home?" Marianne asked.

Joanna shook her head. "Mother already offered," she said. "I'm sure it's just a ploy to fill my head with a whole other list of things that have to be done before the wedding. Still, I'd better ride with her and give her that much of a shot at me. I haven't exactly been sitting still this week."

"You never do," Marianne said.

"Look who's calling the kettle black," Joanna pointed out. "We're both card-carrying members of the Women Who Do Too Much Club. Speaking of which, what are you going to do after the baby gets here? Have you and Jeff found a live-in sitter yet?"

Marianne frowned. "We haven't, and I don't know what we're going to do. We can't really afford a nanny, but I know Jeff won't be able to keep track of Ruth and the baby at the shop. I'll have a few weeks of maternity leave right after the baby is born. What we've decided to do is not worry about the sitter situation until it's closer to time."

"In other words, cross the bridge when you come to it."

Marianne nodded. "Exactly," she said. "You should probably try doing the same thing with Reba Singleton and her going to the FBI. Don't worry about it until it happens."

Great advice, Joanna thought. *Easier given than taken— in both directions.*

The ride home with Eleanor Lathrop Winfield proved to be just what Joanna expected. Eleanor wanted to present her daughter with a complex litany of things that had to be done in the course of the next week, along with a detailed schedule by which each one of those assigned tasks had to be accomplished. Eleanor remained willfully oblivious to the fact that her daughter might have a few other concerns in her life in addition to her upcoming wedding.

"You're treating this whole thing far too casually," Eleanor complained. "An event like this doesn't come together without a little effort and cooperation, you know."

"I've told you before, Mother," Joanna said. "You need to talk to Butch about all these details. He's the one who's in charge of wedding plans and logistics on our end. I have my hands full just doing my job."

"What about your hair?"

"My hair?"

"Have you made your appointment at Helene's yet? Or has he made one for you? If the wedding starts at four, you should be in a chair in Helen Barco's shop no later than eleven. And since the wedding is going to be on a Saturday, somebody had better call for an appointment pretty soon because she could be all booked up."

"Mother," Joanna replied. "I'm sure I can fix my own hair that day without having to visit an adequate shop."

"I beg your pardon? A what?"

"I know Helen calls her place a beauty shop, but my results are usually adequate rather than beautiful. I prefer calling Helene's an adequate shop."

Eleanor Winfield gave a disapproving shake to her head. "There you go again," she sniffed. "You're just like your father—always making jokes. You're so like him at times, Joanna, I can hardly stand it. Part of the time Big Hank Lathrop was your basic a-number-one clown. The rest of the time he was out trying to save the universe, even if it meant leaving his own family out to dry.

"I almost feel sorry for Frederick at times," Eleanor added after a pause. Even now, less than a week before the wedding, Joanna's mother still refused to call Butch Dixon by anything other than his given name. "I doubt the poor man has any idea of what he's letting himself in for."

"I believe you're wrong there, Mother," Joanna said quietly, thinking back over the events of the last two nights. Both times she had left Butch minding the store, and both times he had come through like a champ. "Butch is nobody's dummy. I'm pretty sure he knows what's coming."

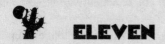

ELEVEN

Nine o'clock Monday morning found a bleary-eyed Sheriff Brady in her office and trying hard to concentrate on work. She had barely made her way through the first two letters by the time Chief Deputy Frank Montoya showed up for his morning briefing.

"How's the bride?" he asked cheerfully, popping his head in the door. "And how was the shower?"

"The shower was fine," Joanna replied, rubbing her eyes. "As for the bride, she's not doing all that well at the moment. Butch and I had a hell of a fight last night. Since I have yet to hear from him this morning, I have to assume we're still not exactly on speaking terms."

"Sorry to hear it," Frank said, setting a stack of incident reports down on the corner of Joanna's desk before easing himself into one of her two captain's chairs. "Pre-wedding jitters, I assume?"

"Some people would call it that, I suppose," Joanna replied.

The previous evening the oven had been sparkling clean and she and Butch had tackled cleaning grout on the kitchen counter when she had happened to mention Dick Voland's visit at the end of the shower.

Butch's reaction to the news had been instantaneous and in hindsight, quite predictable. "You can't be serious!" he

had exclaimed. "You mean you're actually going to cooperate with that jerk?"

"Of course I'm going to cooperate," Joanna replied.
"What do you expect me to do?"

"Ignore him."

"Butch, I can't do that," an exasperated Joanna had explained. "I've got nothing to hide. Besides, if I refuse to give
him what he needs, it'll make matters that much worse."

"I don't see how. I think he's got a hell of a lot of
nerve—"

"Dick Voland stopped by Daisy's to let me know what
was going down," Joanna said. "It was quite nice of him,
considering."

"And you're so naive, you fell for it."

"Fell for what?"

"The nice-guy routine," Butch growled. "Dick Voland
wasn't being nice. He doesn't know the meaning of the
word. He's a disgruntled ex-employee who came by to let
you know that he's about to stab you in the back. And while
he's at it, he wanted to ask you if you'd mind giving him a
hand."

"That's not how it was," Joanna said.

"Right."

"Butch, I happen to know Dick Voland better than you do."

"I'm sure *that*'s true."

That was where the conversation had ended, and the
evening, too. A few minutes later, Butch had stalked out of
the house and left for home. Energized by anger, Joanna had
kept on cleaning right up until midnight. She was angry with
Butch for flying off the handle and angry with herself for not
managing the issue in a more diplomatic fashion. The last
thing she had wanted to do the week before her wedding was
quarrel with Butch over Dick Voland. But the more she

scrubbed and cleaned and the more she thought about it, the more she began to wonder if perhaps Butch was right. Joanna had assumed a mutual respect existed between her and her former colleague. Was it possible that respect was totally one-sided?

Finally, worn out by work and worry both, she had gone to bed but not to sleep. In fact, she had tossed and turned until almost time for her alarm to sound.

Frank took a sip of his coffee. "Don't your new in-laws arrive today? I've heard rumors that they're always good for at least one fight."

"This has nothing to do with Butch's family," Joanna said. "The beef was over Dick Voland."

"Dick Voland? I would have thought Butch had moved beyond worrying about Dick Voland a long time ago. That's all water under the bridge."

"New water, new bridge," Joanna said. "Dick showed up at the shower yesterday afternoon."

"He was there?" Frank demanded. "How come? Who invited him?"

"He wasn't invited. He stopped by afterward to tell me that Clayton Rhodes' daughter, Reba Singleton, is on the warpath. She believes one way or another that I'm responsible for her father's death. She's hired Dick and wants him to gather enough evidence to bring the situation to the attention of the FBI."

At that juncture, Frank actually choked as a sip of steaming coffee caught in his throat. "Why, for God's sake, would she—"

"Because Clayton left me his place in his will."

"His place?" Frank blinked. "You mean Rhodes Ranch—the land, house, and everything?"

"All three hundred and twenty acres," Joanna replied.

"Reba is of the opinion that the prospect of receiving the ranch sooner rather than later was inducement enough for me to knock her father off. Never mind the fact that I had no idea about the contents of Clayton's will until yesterday morning, when Burton Kimball called to tell me what was happening."

"So Dick gets to sic the FBI on you," Frank grumbled. "And he had the gall to come by and gloat about it. That jackass—"

"He didn't come by to gloat," Joanna interrupted. "He came to warn me, Frank. To let me know what was happening. He's coming here to the department sometime this morning—probably any minute now—to pick up fingerprint information on me. I expect our people to give him their full cooperation, and courtesy, too," she added. "If he needs help collecting latent prints at the scene, he's welcome to request Casey Ledford's services. He shouldn't have a problem with that. As far as I know, at this point Doc Winfield and I are the only ones accused of any complicity. I don't believe anyone else in the department is under suspicion."

"Doc Winfield?" Frank repeated. "What did he do?"

"Clayton's autopsy, for one thing," Joanna answered. "But since George Winfield is also my stepfather, Reba Singleton is claiming conflict of interest. She's asking for a second-opinion autopsy. She's going before a judge to get a court order."

"Doc Winfield's gonna love that," Frank said.

Joanna continued. "I assume they'll ask the ME up in Pima County for assistance. The problem is, we've done so much work with them lately, that, for all I know, they might be considered contaminated as well."

Frank Montoya shook his head. "I can't believe it,

Joanna. You're really going to help Dick Voland open this can of worms?"

"The can's already open," Joanna said firmly. "And everybody in this office is going to cooperate with Dick's investigation. I've got nothing to hide or apologize for, and neither does George Winfield. The sooner we get this mess handled, the less outside interference we'll have to deal with. And now," she added, reaching for the stack of incident reports, "what all went on yesterday?"

"Do you want to read all those?" Frank asked.

"Not especially. Give me the *Reader's Digest* condensed version."

"In descending order, fifteen UDAs held for the INS, and four DWIs. Two each motor-vehicle accidents and domestic-violence incidents—no fatalities and no serious injuries in any of them. One of the inmates in the jail suffered a seizure of some kind and had to be transported down to the county hospital in Douglas. He's still there, under guard. In other words, all pretty much routine stuff."

"What about the Sandra Ridder investigation?"

"We had a team from the crime lab out at the scene—at the two scenes—pretty much all day yesterday. They picked up some trace evidence—threads, hair, that kind of thing—but there's no way to tell whether or not it has anything to do with what happened.

"Jaime and I picked up Catherine Yates and brought her in to George's office yesterday afternoon. She IDed the dead woman from the culvert as her daughter, Sandra Ridder. No surprises there, since we'd already pretty much figured that out on our own. According to the doc, he was scheduling the autopsy for sometime this morning. Still no sign of that missing Lexus."

"What about Lucinda Ridder?"

"She's still missing, too. Deputy Gregovich and Spike worked the problem all day yesterday. They had no trouble following her after she left the house. She stuck to the road for half a mile or so, then the trail disappeared. They lost her."

"So she either got in a vehicle or took off on her bike. Since the bike is missing, I'm betting on the latter. Can Spike follow a trail left by a bike?"

"Not as well as he can follow one left by a pair of human feet. On a hunch, I had him check out the crime-scene area over by Cochise Stronghold. They hit a jackpot there and picked up Lucy's scent again. She spent some time concealed in a dry creek bed, with her bike hidden nearby. She came out of hiding long enough to go over by the sign, then she disappeared into thin air again, same as she did before, when she left Catherine Yates' house."

"If she was at the crime scene when her mother was," Joanna mused, "she might have seen what happened."

"Or she might have been involved in what happened."

"You're still thinking Lucy might have had something to do with what happened to Sandra?"

Frank nodded. "It's possible," he said. "According to Catherine Yates, Lucy is desperately unhappy that her mother is getting out of jail. Embarrassed, probably, more than unhappy. It's like I said the other night. She sneaks up on her mother armed with a gun that she knows how to use. Maybe she goes to the sign for the same reason her mother did—looking for whatever was in that damned Tupperware bowl. Maybe she's still there when her mother arrives. That could just be a coincidence, or maybe Lucy knew that's where her mother would go the first moment she had a chance.

"One way or the other, regardless of what Catherine Yates told us about Lucy refusing to have anything to do with her mother, I think she was wrong. I'm pretty sure Lucy and Sandra did meet up that night."

"Why's that?"

"Remember the necklace Sandra Ridder was wearing when she was found?"

Joanna nodded. She hadn't seen the necklace, but she remembered hearing it described by Hal Witter. "The devil's-claw necklace?"

"Right. Well, guess what. According to Catherine Yates, that necklace actually belongs to her granddaughter. Lucinda Ridder was wearing it the last time Catherine saw her."

Joanna followed that line of reasoning for several long moments. "Maybe the whole thing was set up," she suggested at last. "Suppose Sandra Ridder contacted her daughter without Catherine Yates' knowledge and arranged for Lucy to meet her at the Cochise Stronghold in the middle of the night."

"Seems far-fetched," Frank said, "but I suppose it could have happened that way."

"And," Joanna continued, "if Spike and Terry can't pick up Lucy's trail after that, it probably means that Lucy left the scene on her bike or in a vehicle of some kind. The first question that comes to mind, then, is whether Lucy Ridder is a suspect or a fellow victim in this case. If she took a ride, was it voluntary or not? Did whoever drove off in the missing Lexus take Lucinda and Big Red and the missing bicycle along with him?"

"What would a UDA want with Lucinda Ridder and her red-tailed hawk?"

"Nothing good," Joanna answered with a slight shiver. "Not every illegal who comes across the line looking for work is a fine upstanding citizen."

"No," Frank agreed, "especially when you take into consideration the fact that Sandra Ridder was shot in cold blood."

"Getting back to the necklace," Joanna said. "Did you take a look at it?"

Frank nodded. "Doc Winfield showed it to Ernie and me before he returned Sandra's personal effects to her mother. That's when Catherine told us the necklace really belonged to Lucy— that Catherine's mother, Lucy's great-grandmother—had commissioned it made for Lucy's tenth birthday. It's a pretty little thing—two silver prongs that seem to be growing out of a tiny turquoise bead. Beautiful workmanship, and signed, too."

"Signed?"

"Catherine said it was made by a friend of her mother's— someone who lives over in Gallup, New Mexico. The signature was too small for me to read with the naked eye, but the doc had checked it out under the microscope. Vega is the name of the guy who made it. L. Vega."

"Valuable, do you think?" Joanna asked.

"Maybe," Frank responded. "Depends on the reputation of whoever made it."

"Try to find out," Joanna said. "I'd like to know more about the artist who made it and also about how much it cost. But more than that, I want to know why it's still here."

Frank wrote himself a reminder. "You mean why didn't whoever killed Sandra Ridder take the necklace at the same time they took the car?"

Joanna nodded. "Exactly. It stands to reason they would, if robbery was part of the equation."

"What if they only wanted the car?"

Joanna shook her head. "I've never yet met a car thief who wouldn't steal something else as well if the opportunity presented itself. By the way, what are Jaime and Ernie doing today?"

Detectives Jaime Carbajal and Ernie Carpenter, the Double Cs, as they were sometimes called, constituted the Cochise County Sheriff's Department entire Detective Division.

"Jaime was supposed to sit in on Sandra Ridder's autopsy this morning, but Doc Winfield had a conflict. So now they're both heading out to the valley. They'll most likely stop by and see Catherine Yates again, then they plan on going to Elfrida to interview Lucinda Ridder's friends and classmates. Jaime thinks that if Lucy had plans, she might have confided them to someone out there at the high school. After that, Jaime will go on up to Tucson. He has an early-afternoon appointment to see Melanie Goodson. He also plans on going out to Old Spanish Trail. He wants to nose around Mrs. Goodson's neighborhood to see if anyone there saw something out of line. Ernie will be coming back to Bisbee to sit in on the autopsy."

Joanna nodded. "Sounds as though that's all moving forward as well as can be expected." She pulled her desk calendar over in front of her. "On another front, what's coming up at the Board of Supervisors meeting this morning?"

"Routine stuff, as far as I can see," Frank told her. "Nothing major, as far as the department is concerned."

Months earlier, one of the sheriff department's previous investigations had uncovered a trail of graft and corruption, which had resulted in the abrupt resignation of a member of the board. Since then, Joanna had tried to maintain a low profile at Board of Supervisors meetings. Whenever possible, she sent Frank Montoya in her place.

"Nothing you can't handle?"

"Right." Frank pursed his lips. "What about the press, Joanna? I've already had a couple of calls from reporters this morning. I haven't returned any of the calls. I'm assuming they'll be asking questions about Clayton Rhodes, and about Sandra Ridder as well. How do you want me to handle this?"

"Refer all Clayton Rhodes inquiries to George Winfield's office. For the time being, his natural-causes ruling dictates our official handling of the case. Sandra Ridder's next of kin have been notified, so there's no need to hold back on her identification. For right now, we'll say that the victim's unnamed daughter, a juvenile, is missing and is considered a person of interest in the investigation of Sandra Ridder's death."

"What about Reba Singleton's accusations as well as Dick Voland's so-called investigation? How do you want those handled—containment?"

"Trying to squelch them isn't going to work, Frank," Joanna answered. "You and I both know that Dick and Marliss Shackleford are an item. She's not going to miss out on a chance to show me in a bad light, especially if she can do it with the help of insider information. She told me yesterday in church that she's going to be writing Clayton's obituary."

"Great," Frank said. "That should give her ample opportunity for a little gratuitous editorializing."

Just then Kristin Marsten's voice came over the intercom. "Sheriff Brady?"

"What is it?"

"I know you don't like to be interrupted during the briefing, but Casey Ledford is on line one. I told her you were busy, but she said this is important. She says she needs to talk to you right away."

"Thanks, Kristin. I'll take the call."

A year and a half earlier, a windfall of unexpected money had become available for Joanna's department to create its own Automated Fingerprint Identification System. Casting about for someone to get the system up and running, Joanna had stumbled on Casey, a young college dropout and a single mother supporting her four-month-old baby by waiting tables at the Copper Queen Hotel.

With a tiny baby to support, no college degree, and no law-enforcement training, Casey's application might well have gone nowhere. The good news was that her unfinished degree was in the Bachelor of Fine Arts program at the University of Arizona. She was a capable artist who was also savvy with computers. Joanna reasoned that she'd be able to use her artistic skills for the manual augmentation of prints necessary to make the AFIS scans work. What ultimately carried the day, however, was the fact that Casey Ledford was the only candidate who had applied for the job. In the intervening months, she had become a valued member of Joanna's team. If anyone remembered that the AFIS tech had no Police Science degree, it no longer mattered enough for people to mention it.

Joanna punched down the lit and flashing button that indicated line one. "Good morning, Casey. What's up?"

"Dick Voland is here and he—"

"He's asking for a copy of my fingerprints," Joanna supplied.

"That's right, and I told him—"

"I want you to give them to him," Joanna interrupted. "I also want you to give him whatever additional assistance he may deem necessary. If that includes going out to Clayton Rhodes' place and lifting prints, I want you to do that as well. Is that clear?"

"Yes, but—"

"No buts, Casey. This is important. Mr. Voland is to have your full cooperation. Is that clear?"

"Yes. I'll get right on it."

"Wait, Casey. Before you go, I have a question."

"What's that?"

"Have you had a chance to lift any prints off the water jugs Jaime Carbajal brought in from the Cochise Stronghold crime scene on Friday?"

"I tried," Casey replied. "But there weren't any."

"Not one? That's odd."

"Yes, I thought so, too. I've looked at several sets of those water jugs over the months I've been here," Casey said. "I've never seen one with no prints on it before. Since when did UDAs start either wearing gloves or wiping their jugs clean?"

"They don't as far as I know," Joanna said.

"Right," Casey said. "It's something that doesn't fit. One of the jugs still had some water in it. I've taken that down to the lab and asked Ernesto to check on it and see if he can tell where it came from."

"Probably from a well in Old Mexico or from somebody's stock tank somewhere between Pearce and the border."

"But how many towns in Mexico chlorinate and fluoridate their water?" Casey asked back.

"Not many," Joanna said. And then, seeing where Casey's line of thought was leading, she added, "Same goes for ranchers and stock tanks between here and the border. Is it possible to get a match on where the water came from?"

"Maybe," Casey said. "Ernesto's making some follow-up phone calls on that right now."

"Good work, Casey. Have him call me with his results. In the meantime, give Dick Voland whatever assistance he needs."

"Will do," Casey replied.

Sitting on the far side of Joanna's desk, Frank Montoya had followed enough of the conversation to know what was going on. "That Casey Ledford has a good head on her shoulders," he said. "It's a shame we have to keep her locked up in the print lab."

"Casey *likes* the print lab," Joanna reminded him. "She's good at what she does, and as long as she's not afraid to think outside the box from time to time, we have the benefit of her smarts in more than one direction."

"Sheriff Brady?" Once again Kristin's disembodied voice came over the intercom. "Is Chief Deputy Montoya still in there?"

"Yes."

"Would you tell him that Marliss Shackleford is out in the public lobby waiting to speak to him?"

Frank stood up. "Time to go earn my keep," he said. "Why do you suppose she wants to talk to me?"

"The last I heard, you were still our Media Relations officer," Joanna said.

"Media Relations!" Frank snorted, heading for the door. "For this I ought to qualify for hazardous-duty pay."

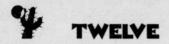

TWELVE

The bell on Joanna's private phone line jangled before the door finished closing behind Frank Montoya. Hoping the caller was Butch and wanting to compose herself and not sound too eager, she let the phone ring twice more before she answered. "Hello."

"So how is my partner in crime this morning?" George Winfield asked. "According to Reba Singleton, you and I are schemers of the first water—conflict of interest, collusion. The woman seems to have a whole laundry list of grievances. Is there anything you and I aren't guilty of?"

"How's it going, George?" Joanna said, swallowing her disappointment.

She felt more than a little guilty about talking to him. Despite his having left two separate messages on Saturday, all of Sunday had passed without Joanna actually speaking to the medical examiner. She had attempted to call him—once each at home and at the office—but when he hadn't answered after several rings, she hadn't left messages and she hadn't attempted to reach him again, either. She might have tried harder, if she had known exactly what to say.

Sheriff Joanna Brady cringed at the idea that the mere existence of a relationship between the two of them had caused the medical examiner's professional integrity to be called into question. It made her feel responsible and more than a

158

little embarrassed. She was also cautious. Eleanor Lathrop hadn't mentioned a word about the situation to Joanna during their ride out to the High Lonesome after the Sunday-afternoon wedding shower. Joanna had taken her mother's lack of comment to mean that Eleanor Lathrop Winfield was still in the dark about Reba Singleton's allegations. And, since George hadn't had nerve enough to broach such a touchy subject with his wife, Joanna thought it wise to follow suit. Still, given the seriousness of the situation, she hardly expected George to be joking around about it.

"Does Mother know what Reba Singleton is up to?" Joanna asked.

"Not exactly," George admitted. "At least not yet. I didn't want to discuss it with her and get her all wound up until you and I had a chance to talk. However, I just left Madame Singleton in the courthouse lobby in what can best be described as a state of high dudgeon. The way the grapevine works around here, it's probably only a matter of hours before Ellie hears about it and the you-know-what hits the fan. What's this about the FBI's being expected to ride to Reba's rescue at any moment?"

"As far as I know," Joanna told him, "all that's happened so far is that she's hired Dick Voland to investigate. His task assignment is to dig up enough evidence of wrongdoing to bring in the Feds."

"Dick Voland?" George Winfield asked. "Your ex-chief deputy?"

"That's the one."

"What is he now, a PI?"

"Right again. He was here at the department just a few minutes ago picking up fingerprints records on me. You see, since I'm the one who found the body, my prints are on Clayton's ignition key."

"Why, that ungrateful son of a bitch!"

"George," Joanna interjected. "Dick Voland is only doing the job he was hired to do. And give the man some credit. He did me the common courtesy of stopping by yesterday afternoon to clue me in about what was going on. Giving me that advance warning wasn't something he had to do. In fact, if Reba Singleton knew about it, I'm sure she'd be pissed as hell. Which reminds me, what was she doing in court?"

"Seeking a court order to require me to have another autopsy done by an outside medical examiner—with the county paying the tab, of course. She lost. Superior Court Judge Cameron Moore told her to take a hike. Then, once the hearing was over, she demanded that I release her father's body immediately, along with my results and tissue samples so she can hot-foot it up to Tucson for a second-opinion autopsy which she'll pay for."

"What did you tell her?"

" 'No dice, lady. You can't have it both ways.' If she wants a second opinion, fine. She's more than welcome to one. But I'm not sending my results out of town. And I'm not releasing tissue samples, either. That means Clayton Rhodes' body stays in my morgue until Ms. Singleton's second-opinion autopsy is complete. She wanted to know what she's supposed to do about a funeral. I told her that depends on how soon she can find some circuit-riding ME to come down here to Bisbee to do it. If Reba Singleton wants accountability, I'll show her accountability. In spades."

George Winfield wasn't joking now. He was hot. Joanna recognized that his earlier attempts at humor had been entirely for her benefit—to make her feel better. Clearly he was as disturbed by Reba's unfounded allegations as she was. And, far more than his earlier joking, knowing that *did* make Joanna feel better.

"I'm sorry I got you into all this, George," she murmured.

"You?" he demanded. "How did you get me into anything? Did you have any idea you were a beneficiary under Clayton Rhodes' will?"

"No."

"The man died of a cerebral hemorrhage, Joanna. You didn't cause that either. You could have turned that ignition key on and off a hundred times, and it wouldn't have made a speck of difference. There isn't an ME on the planet who isn't going to rule on Clayton's death the same way I did."

"It's still a hassle."

"So's having Dick Voland show up at your office asking for copies of your prints," George countered. "How are *you* doing?"

"I'm okay," she replied without enthusiasm. "We're trying to get a handle on that case that turned up over by Pearce."

"Sandra Ridder?"

"That's the one."

"I had planned to start the autopsy on her first thing this morning, but I ended up having to go to court instead. Thank God Judge Moore doesn't believe in wasting a man's time. But now both Detective Carbajal and Detective Carpenter have been called out of town. I won't be able to start the autopsy until one or the other of them gets back."

"That's fine," Joanna assured him. "As far as I can see, there's no big hurry. There'll be time enough for that later."

After she finished talking to George Winfield, Joanna hung up the phone. Then she sat staring at the face of it for several long seconds—wondering if it would ring again and willing Butch to be the first to call. When no call came through, she picked up the next piece of mail in her stack of correspondence—an invitation to attend the annual Arizona Sheriffs' Conference the last week in May.

She started to fill out the form. Would she attend? Yes. Would anyone be accompanying her? Yes. What kind of accommodations did she require—single or double? Smoking or nonsmoking? Two double beds, queen, or king? Frustrated, she tossed down her pen and reached for the phone, but when she picked it up to dial Butch's number, there was no dial tone.

"Hello?" she demanded into the silent receiver. "Hello? Hello?"

"Does this mean great minds think along the same lines?" Butch Dixon asked.

"My phone didn't even ring."

"That's right," he said. "I dialed and you answered before the ringer had a chance. Who were you calling?"

Joanna hesitated. "You," she admitted finally.

"So can we both say we're sorry at the same time and get this over with?" he asked. "And will you have a late breakfast or an early lunch with me? And could we do it right now, since my parents just called from El Paso? I'd like to have one last quiet meal for just the two of us before all hell breaks loose."

Relief washed over her. "Yes, yes, and yes," Joanna answered with a laugh. "I'd like that, too."

"Good. How soon can you get away?"

Joanna looked at the stack of correspondence on her desk. She needed to make as much headway on it as she could before the current day's batch arrived. "Let's make it eleven at Daisy's," she said. "That'll give me time to finish up what I'm doing. Which reminds me. The reason I was calling you was to ask if you'd like to attend the annual sheriffs' conference with me."

"You mean you weren't calling to apologize?"

"I was calling for both reasons," Joanna said.

Butch laughed. "In that case, when's the conference?"

"The week before Memorial Day. We finish up on Friday. It's up at Page. We could probably stay gone over that three-day weekend, too."

"Just you and me?" he asked.

"As long as we can find someone to take care of Jenny and the animals."

"Sounds good. Only what'll I do all day while you're in meetings?"

Joanna shrugged and glanced back at the form. When that told her nothing, she browsed through the brochure. "It says here that wives—"

"Wives?" Butch interrupted.

"It does say 'wives,' " Joanna told him. "Remember, at this point I'm still the only sheriff who's a woman. They're probably not used to the idea of sheriffs who show up with husbands in tow."

"I'm not used to it yet, either," Butch said. "Now, what does it say again?"

"That wives will be offered their choices of several tours, including a bus trip to Canyon de Chelly, visiting a trading post on the Navajo Nation, and possibly doing some antiquing."

Butch sighed. "Well," he said. "That's a relief, anyway."

"What's a relief?"

"I was afraid you were going to tell me we'd all be doing makeovers and having our colors done."

"I'm hanging up now," she told him with another laugh. "See you at lunch."

When she went back to working on the correspondence, it was with a good deal more energy. She started by filling out the registration form and authorizing the check that needed to go with it. Then she marched through the stack of mail. Would she come speak to the Willcox Kiwanis Club? Would she agree to be marshal of the Tombstone Heldorado Parade? Would she come to Douglas High School to be a part of their career-day program?

Responding to those requests and putting the various appointments into the calendar, Joanna was well aware that the job of sheriff consisted of far more public relations work than she had ever thought possible. No wonder her father, Sheriff D. H. Lathrop, had been at work so much of the time. It was also no wonder that his wife, Eleanor, had often been in an uproar about it.

How will Butch react to all those demands on my time? she wondered. He had been understanding enough in the past, but that was when they were just dating. Would his attitude change once he was at home keeping dinner warm for someone who never managed to make meals on time?

Finished with as much paperwork as she could handle right then, Joanna gathered up the stack of letters in need of envelopes and mailing. When she came out through her office door, her secretary was talking on the telephone. She hung up abruptly once she realized Joanna had stopped in front of her desk. Joanna noticed that Kristin seemed uncharacteristically flustered.

"Sorry," Kristin said hurriedly. "I didn't see you. Did you want something?"

"I'm going to lunch," Joanna said. "I'd appreciate it if you'd get these all copied, addressed, and mailed. I've already put the appointments in my calendar, but you may want to add them to yours as well so you'll know where I'm supposed to be and when."

"All right," Kristin said. "Any idea when you'll be back?"

"Probably no later than twelve-thirty."

Joanna started to walk away, then turned back. "How's Deputy Gregovich this morning?"

Kristin flushed. "He's fine," she stammered.

Joanna nodded. "Tell him hello for me next time he calls."

Out in the parking lot, Joanna stopped for a moment in the bright March sunshine. It wasn't especially warm, and once again a blustery, chill wind was blowing in out of the west. Up on the hillside behind the department, the only visible clumps of green were either bear grass or scrub oak. At nearly five thousand feet, the mesquite was still nothing but gaunt black trunks and branches. Spring would come to the high desert country eventually, but not quite yet. It was still too soon for the emerald-green mesquite leaves to burst forth in search of sunlight.

On her way to Daisy's Café, a place that seemed to be her home away from home these days, Joanna remembered something she had failed to ask Frank Montoya. She reached for her cell phone and caught him just as he was leaving for the Board of Supervisors meeting.

"Did you tell Terry Gregovich to keep an eye out for Big Red?" Joanna asked.

"Lucy's hawk? I think so," Frank answered. "But maybe not."

"Is Terry going back out there to look some more?"

"I don't think so. As I told you, he and Spike worked pretty much all day yesterday. They put in some pretty long hours. My understanding is that he's taking some comp time off today."

"And chewing up my secretary's workday by calling her on the phone," Joanna said.

"Want me to talk to him about that?"

"No," Joanna said. "If it gets to be too much, I'll handle it."

Butch was waiting for her on the sidewalk outside the restaurant. "Your mother called after I got off the phone with you," he said, as Junior Dowdle led them to a booth in the far back corner of the room.

"What did Eleanor want today?"

"To know whether or not I had scheduled hair and manicure appointments for you on Saturday morning."

"What did you tell her?"

"That I hadn't, but I would. And I did. You and Jenny both are due at Helene's Salon of Hair and Beauty on Saturday at eleven A.M. Helen Barco will handle the two hairdos. Helen's daughter-in-law will be on hand for your manicure." Butch frowned. "By the way, if Helen owns the shop, who's Helene?"

Joanna laughed. "When Slim Barco was making the sign for his wife's new beauty shop, he added the extra *e* because he thought it would make the place sound classier."

"Oh," Butch said. "I see."

"But you didn't need to make an appointment for me," Joanna continued. "I'm perfectly capable of doing my own hair."

"Tell that to your mother," Butch replied. "She insisted, and in case you haven't noticed, Eleanor Lathrop Winfield can be very persuasive."

"She's a bully," Joanna said. "Did she say anything else?"

"She wanted to know what's all this stuff about Clayton Rhodes' daughter?"

"What did you tell her?"

"Nothing. I'm not dumb enough to get sucked into that kind of deal. I told her that if she wanted information she'd have to go straight to the horse's mouth—to you." He grinned.

Joanna shook her head. "Great. That means I can expect

my phone to be ringing the moment I come back from lunch."

"Sorry," Butch said. "But I was afraid if I said anything more than that, I'd probably stick my foot in my mouth."

"You're right. I'm the one who should handle it. She is my mother, after all."

"She's also inviting us over for dinner tonight. You, Jenny, and me, and my folks as well. She wants us all to have a chance to get acquainted."

"What did you tell her on that score?"

"I asked her what time and told her we'd be there."

Joanna found herself bridling. She didn't like having someone else tell her where she'd be going and when, but then she thought better of it. After all, she had told Eleanor that Butch was in charge of wedding logistics. It was time to shut up, take her lumps, and let him do it.

"What time?" she asked.

"Six-thirty."

Daisy came and took their order. "What's going on at work today?" Butch asked after Daisy left for the kitchen.

As Joanna prepared to answer, she worried about restarting the previous night's quarrel. "Dick Voland came around for those fingerprints."

"Did you give them to him?"

"Casey Ledford did. I told her to."

"All right, then," Butch said. "I suppose you know what's best."

And that was the end of it. They went on to enjoy their lunch. They were done with their burgers and drinking coffee when Joanna's distinctive cell phone with its roosterlike ring crowed in her purse.

"Sheriff Brady," Tica Romero said when Joanna answered. "A call just came in from Tucson. The man first asked to speak to one of the detectives. When I told him neither of them was available, he asked to speak to the sheriff. Do you want me to patch him through?"

"Please," Joanna said. "What's his name?

"Quick," Tica said. "Mr. Jay Quick."

"And where's he from, again?"

"Tucson."

"Did he say what this was about?"

"No," Tica replied. "Just that it was important, and he wanted to speak directly to someone in authority."

"I guess that's me, then," Joanna said. "Patch him through."

Moments later a male voice came through the phone. "Hello? Sheriff Brady?" he said.

"Yes," Joanna said. "This is Sheriff Brady."

"Sorry," he said uncertainly. "I thought I was still talking to the nine-one-one operator. I didn't expect the sheriff to be a woman."

Joanna laughed. "You and a lot of other people, but I really am the sheriff. What's your name again?"

"Quick. Jay Quick. I live in Tucson."

"What can I do for you, Mr. Quick?"

"I just heard a report on the radio about a homicide down in your neck of the woods. The report said the dead woman's name was Sandra Ridder and that she had recently been released from prison. Is that true?"

"Yes," Joanna replied. "That's correct."

"And is that the same Sandra Ridder who went to prison several years ago for shooting her husband up here in Tucson?"

"That's also correct, Mr. Quick, but why are you asking? Do you know something about this case?"

He hesitated before he answered. "The report also said

that Sandra Ridder's daughter has disappeared and that she's a person of interest in her mother's death. Is that true as well?"

Joanna found herself sitting up straighter in the booth. Her grip on the telephone tightened, as though, by holding the device more firmly in her fist, she could somehow force Jay Quick to get to the point and tell her why he had called.

"Yes," she said smoothly, trying to keep from betraying her rising excitement. "Lucinda Ridder—Sandra Ridder's fifteen-year-old daughter—has been missing since the night her mother was killed. She is a person of interest in that case. She's not a viable suspect at this time, although in the course of our investigation, she may turn into one."

Now it was Joanna's turn to pause. She waited for Jay Quick to say something. When he did not, she continued. "Why are you asking these questions, Mr. Quick? Do you know something about the missing girl—something that would help us locate her?"

"Lucinda Ridder called my house at three o'clock last Saturday morning. She was looking for my mother. I wondered about it, but I didn't think anything more about it until a few minutes ago, when I heard about Sandra Ridder on the news."

"You say Lucy was calling your mother?"

"Yes. Evelyn Quick, my mother. Years ago she used to be Lucinda Ridder's ballet teacher at the Lohse Family YMCA here in downtown Tucson. Lucy sounded very upset on the phone, and what I had to say didn't help. My mother's dead, you see. She died two—almost three—years ago. When I told Lucy that, she just started sobbing. It broke my heart. I asked her what was wrong and was there anything I could do to help, but she said no, no one could help her now. Do you think it's possible that she killed her own mother, Sheriff Brady? She sounded desperate on the phone. The poor girl's been through so much trauma for someone her age. I wonder if she didn't just snap."

"Did you ask where she was? Get a phone number?"

"I asked, but she wouldn't tell me. I could hear what sounded like trucks in the background, though. My guess is she was using a pay phone at a truck stop."

"Whereabouts are you, Mr. Quick?"

"At my office. Quick Custom Metals out on Romero Road in Tucson."

"Give me your phone number. And your home phone number as well. I'll try contacting my detectives. If one of them can't meet with you this afternoon, I will."

As Joanna hung up the phone, Butch was looking at his watch. "And where exactly is this Mr. Quick?" he asked.

"In Tucson, on Romero Road."

"And you're thinking of going up there, seeing him, and still being back in time for dinner at your mother's?"

"I'm sure I can make it if I have to."

Butch sighed and shook his head. "Good luck," he said. "But I'm not holding my breath."

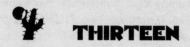

THIRTEEN

It was shortly after noon when Joanna left the restaurant. Her cell phone rang the moment she closed the car door. "I just got lucky," Frank Montoya said.

"Lucky," Joanna echoed. "Why, Frank, I didn't know you were even dating."

"Not that kind of lucky," he replied wryly. "I got to the Board of Supervisors meeting and found out it was canceled. They had their annual retreat over the weekend at a guest ranch up in the Chiricahuas. This morning the whole bunch of 'em is sicker 'n dogs."

"What was it?" Joanna asked. "Food poisoning?"

"I guess. That's what it sounds like. So since I happen to have all this unscheduled free time on my hands this afternoon, I was wondering if there was anything in particular you needed me to do."

"As a matter of fact, there is," Joanna said. "Hold on a minute. Let me give you a phone number." She reached into her pocket and pulled out the notebook in which she had jotted Jay Quick's number. Once she found it, she read it off to Frank.

"Who's this?" he asked.

"It's a telephone number Lucy Ridder called Saturday morning at three A.M. The man's name is Jay Quick. Years ago, Mr. Quick's mother, Evelyn, was Lucy Ridder's ballet teacher at the Lohse Family YMCA in Tucson. Not knowing that Evelyn Quick died some time back, Lucy called the son's house trying to reach her."

"That's a relief then," Frank breathed. "We may not know where Lucy Ridder is, but at least she's still alive."

"She was early Saturday morning," Joanna returned. "Naturally she didn't leave a number where she could be reached, but Mr. Quick told me he heard what sounded like eighteen-wheelers rumbling in the background. He thought maybe she was calling from a truck stop."

"Want me to find out where the call came from?" Frank asked.

Joanna laughed. "How did you guess? Out of my whole department, you're the best-suited to ferreting information out of faceless corporate entities and balky bureaucrats. Go get 'em, Frank."

"Was that a compliment or not?" he demanded.

"That's how it was intended."

"All right, then. Let me off the phone so I can see if I can live up to it."

Once Frank hung up, Joanna radioed into the department and asked to be patched through to either Ernie Carpenter or Jaime Carbajal. Since Jaime Carbajal was planning to go to Tucson that afternoon, she hoped he could also stop by and see Jay Quick.

"Where are you?" she asked, when the detective's voice came over the speaker.

"Between Elfrida and Douglas. We're on our way to a place east of Douglas, where a border-patrol officer reported spotting an abandoned white Lexus parked along the border fence."

"Melanie Goodson's missing Lexus?"

"According to license information, it's the very one. The

officer saw what he believes to be bloodstains in the back-seat. I've called up and canceled my appointment with Melanie Goodson. Ernie and I talked it over and decided that right this minute it's more important for us to check out the vehicle than it is to go running up to Tucson to interview secondary witnesses."

"That's probably a good call," Joanna agreed. "Are you going to try to change the appointment to later this after-noon?"

"No. Tomorrow should be plenty of time. Once we finish with the Lexus, Ernie and I will have to hotfoot it back to Bisbee. Doc Winfield is chomping at the bit to tackle the Sandra Ridder autopsy, and one or both of us should be on hand when he does it."

By that point in the conversation Joanna had driven as far as the traffic circle. At the intersection where she should have turned right to head back to the department, she made a last-minute decision. Since there was no chance Jaime Carbajal was going to go see Jay Quick that afternoon, Joanna decided to copy the Little Red Hen and do so herself. Instead of turning right, she went straight ahead.

"I'm on my way to Tucson right now," she said. "At three o'clock on Saturday morning, Lucy Ridder attempted to place a phone call to her old ballet instructor up in Tucson."

"She called somebody?" Jaime demanded. "Where is she, then? Is she all right?"

"I don't know the answers to any of those questions at the moment," Joanna told him. "I'm on my way to talk to the in-structor's son and see if I can learn anything more."

"With this kind of a new lead, do you want either Ernie or me to skip the Lexus and follow up on the Tucson deal in-stead?" Jaime asked.

"No, that's all right. I'm fine this way. Now tell me, did you and Ernie learn anything useful out in Elfrida today?"

"Not a whole lot other than the fact that Lucy Ridder wasn't the most popular girl in town," Jaime said. "I'd say she's probably right at the bottom of the heap in Elfrida High School's social pecking order. We didn't find a single person who would admit to being her friend."

"Sounds to me like we're dealing with the classic teenaged loner," Joanna observed, thinking of the disaffected youths who had, in recent years, wreaked schoolyard havoc with guns and/or explosives.

"And we're not the only ones worried about it, either," Jaime added. "We went out to the ranch and talked to Catherine Yates before we went to the school. She told us that, as far as she knew, Lucy's only friend was the damned hawk. Then, while we were at the school, the principal's secretary brought us a message that we should talk with a guy named Wayne Hooper."

"Who's he?"

"His wife, Agnes, drives Lucy's school bus. We spent quite a while with him. Somehow or other he found out we were in town and insisted on talking to us. He doesn't know Lucy Ridder personally, but claims his wife does. He says Lucy Ridder sounds like a weird kid. He's afraid she's going to show up at school with a gun and mow down everybody in sight. After we talked to Wayne, we tracked his wife down at the school district bus garage. Her take on the situation is a little different from her husband's. She says Lucy's never been any problem—that Wayne is pushing panic buttons for no reason. Agnes did say, though, that on Friday afternoon on the bus, Lucy Ridder looked unhappier than usual. Like she was upset. Like she didn't want to get off the bus to go home."

Joanna thought about that for a minute, trying to remember exactly what Catherine Yates had said about Sandra Ridder's release from prison and her expected homecoming.

"I'm pretty sure Catherine Yates told us that she had just heard on Friday afternoon that her daughter was being released from Perryville. But if Lucy was more upset than usual on Friday afternoon and if what was upsetting her was the unwelcome prospect of her mother's homecoming, then how did she know about it before she got off the school bus?"

"Good question," Jaime Carbajal said. "Maybe Catherine Yates called the school and told her so."

"That's one possibility," Joanna agreed. "But since Catherine knew all about Lucy's negative attitude toward her mother, I doubt it. No, I think Lucy herself had some kind of advance notice—probably from Sandra herself."

"You're saying maybe Lucy knew about her mother's upcoming release before Catherine Yates did?"

"Maybe," Joanna said. "Speaking of Catherine Yates, did she give you any more helpful information about either Sandra or Lucy?"

"Some, but not very much. According to Catherine, compared to her mother, Lucy's a peach. She said Sandy was a headstrong handful from the day she was born. By the time she hit junior high, she was in so much trouble that she spent several months in juvie. We don't know why she was sent up because the record was expunged once she turned eighteen.

"Then, in high school, Sandra more or less got her head screwed on straight. She started staying out of trouble and hitting the books. Since her father was an Anglo, she's not a full-blooded Apache, but she had enough Native American blood to win a BIA scholarship to the University of Arizona, where she majored in Business and Native American studies. She didn't graduate, though. Her senior year she got hooked up with a radical group called NAT-C."

"You mean like Hitler Youth?" Joanna asked.

"No, something called the Native American Tribal Council—NAT-C for short."

"That's an unfortunate acronym," Joanna murmured.

Jaime laughed. "Isn't it, though! NAT-C is made up of Indian radicals and wannabe Indian radicals from all over the country who take the position that the Indian wars never ended. Once Sandra got involved with the group, she quit school and hit the road with them doing demonstrations, picketing, that kind of thing."

"Is that where she met her husband?"

"No. They met later. By then, Sandra had given up demonstrating and had gone to work at Fort Huachuca. That's where she and Tom Ridder met—working on post. She was civil service, and he was career army—a staff sergeant."

"Was Tom Ridder a Native American?"

"Evidently not. When Tom got pushed out of the service, Sandra stayed on working at the fort. They rented a house in Tucson. She carpooled back and forth to Fort Huachuca, and Tom started a Tucson-based landscaping business."

"That's what he was doing at the time he was killed, running a landscaping business?" Joanna asked.

"That's right."

"But didn't you say just a few minutes ago that he was a staff sergeant in the army?"

"Right again," Jaime said.

"Going from staff sergeant to running a landscaping outfit is a pretty big step down," Joanna observed.

"That's what I thought, too. According to what Catherine Yates told us, one way or another, Tom Ridder got himself crosswise of his commanding officer. He left the army with a general discharge. I would expect that having one of those on your record puts a damper on potential career opportunities."

"Did Catherine give you any details on that, on what caused Tom Ridder to be booted out of the service?"

"No. We asked. If she knew, she wasn't talking."

"We should probably find out."

"Right. Ernie Carpenter has some fairly good connections out at Fort Huachuca. He'll take a crack at finding out those details; if not today, then first thing tomorrow for sure."

"Good work, Jaime," Joanna told him. "You two keep after it."

Once across the divide and out in the wide valley between the Mule Mountains and Tombstone, Joanna tried calling Kristin. It was only fair to let her secretary know that her lunch date in Bisbee had turned into an afternoon drive to Tucson. Unfortunately, Kristin was away from her desk. Several minutes later, Joanna's phone chirped its distinctive rooster-crow ring. The cell phone's caller ID readout told her Frank Montoya was on the line.

"Hello," she said. "What's up?"

"I traced that phone number for you," he said. "The U.S. West phone logs say it's a pay phone, all right, but not at a truck stop. The calls were made from that I-Ten rest area in Texas Canyon east of Benson."

"As the crow flies, that's only about fifteen miles or so from Catherine Yates' place," Joanna observed. "Less than that from Cochise Stronghold. But did I hear you to say calls? As in plural?"

"That's right," Frank said. "There are three different calls on that phone, all made within a few minutes of three A.M. Saturday morning. All of them went to different numbers in the Tucson area. The first one, at three straight up and down, is the one placed to your friend Mrs. Quick. That one lasted about six minutes. You'll never guess where the next one went."

"Where?"

"At three ten the log shows a call to one M. Goodson out on Old Spanish Trail."

"That has to be Melanie Goodson," Joanna repeated. "Sandra Ridder's old defense attorney, and the place where Sandra was supposed to be spending the night Saturday night. Is there a chance Lucy was calling there looking for her mother?"

"Could be. Or maybe she had reason to believe that she would soon be in need of a capable defense attorney, although Melanie Goodson hasn't worked as a public defender in years. Whatever the reason for the call, my guess is Lucy didn't connect with anyone in person. The call lasted for just over thirty seconds."

"Long enough to be picked up by an answering machine?" Joanna asked.

"Sounds like. The last call was placed at three-fifteen. That one went to a Catholic convent at Santa Theresa School in the twenty-four hundred block of South Sixth Avenue in South Tucson. Somebody took that one because the call lasted a full fifteen minutes."

"So there, at least, Lucy must have made contact with whoever it was she was looking for. What's that address again?"

Frank gave it to her, and Joanna jotted it on her dash-mounted message pad.

"It just so happens that I'm on my way to Tucson right now to see Jay Quick," Joanna told Frank. "If I finish up with him in time, I may stop by the convent and see if I can find out who it was Lucy was calling so early in the morning."

"Anything else you want me to do on this end?" Frank asked.

"Jaime and Ernie think they've located Melanie Goodson's missing Lexus. It was found abandoned out east of Douglas. They're on their way to the scene right now. Ernie was going to look into this tomorrow, but as long as you're in a bureaucracy-busting mood, how about if you call out to personnel at Fort Huachuca? See what you can find out about Tom Ridder and why he was run out of the army back in the early nineties. He was a staff sergeant when they booted him out, so my guess is the infraction was something more serious than an unauthorized walk in the park.

"When you finish up with that, call Terry Gregovich and tell him comp time's over for the day. I want our canine unit to get their butts up to that rest-area telephone in Texas Canyon and see if they can pick up Lucy Ridder's trail from there. Between Saturday night and now, lots of different people may have used that particular pay phone, but it won't be nearly as many as those hundred-plus Volksmarchers who went meandering through the crime scene out at Cochise Stronghold. We also need to schedule deputies to stop through the rest area overnight for the next several days to see if there are any regular three A.M. users of the rest area who might have seen Lucy Ridder and her sidekick red-tailed hawk."

"Anything else?" Frank asked.

"One. Have you seen Kristin?"

"She wasn't at her desk when I got back to the department."

"I wonder where she went. She didn't say she was going to lunch. Well, anyway, when you see her, let her know I'm on my way to Tucson. I probably won't be back until fairly late, but if you have any more good ideas, give me a call back."

As Joanna continued driving north toward Tucson, she puzzled over what it all meant. Why on Saturday night had Lucy Ridder succumbed to a sudden urge to reconnect with people from her distant past? For a fifteen-year-old, reaching back eight years was going back more than half her life. So the question was: Had she stayed in touch with these folks through all the intervening years, or was this series of phone calls a bolt out of the blue to all three recipients?

The fact that Evelyn Quick had died years earlier without Lucy's knowing about it made Joanna think the lightning-bolt option was actually the correct one. And if that was true, that meant the phone calls had to do with Sandra Ridder's sudden and—as far as her daughter Lucy was concerned—unwelcome release from prison.

Joanna also mulled what Jaime Carbajal had told her about Lucy Ridder being a loner. That wasn't much of a surprise. Anyone who would prefer the company of a red-tailed hawk to the company of people couldn't be called outgoing or even normal—whatever that might be. Joanna thought back to her own high school days in the years after her father died. She had grieved over D. H. Lathrop's death and blamed herself for it, too, since her father had been bringing Joanna and members of her Girl Scout troop home from a weekend camp-out when he was struck and killed by a drunk driver while changing a tire. Eleanor Lathrop may have been annoying at times and downright wrongheaded on occasion; still, Joanna had had the benefit of her mother's love and guidance during those years when she had felt her father's loss most keenly. Nonetheless, even with her mother's help, Joanna had felt like the odd man out at school. Kids her age might have had parents who were divorced, but when you were a sophomore or junior or senior in high school, hardly anybody else had a parent who was dead.

Bearing all that in mind, it was hardly surprising that Lucy Ridder was a loner. Her father was dead, and now so was her mother. And all those years she had lived with Catherine Yates—all during the time when the awful pain of losing her father would have been at its peak—Lucy had been in the care and keeping of someone who more or less thought Tom Ridder got what he deserved—of someone who thought Lucy's father's killer was being wrongly imprisoned. That had to have hurt. And even if it was true that Tom Ridder had physically abused his wife, it might not have made any difference to his daughter's broken heart. It seemed clear enough to Joanna that Lucy had loved Tom Ridder as much as or more so than she despised Sandra, her mother.

Joanna knew enough about domestic violence in families to realize that children—the innocent bystanders to those knock-down, drag-out battles—often end up choosing sides, and the sides they choose aren't necessarily the ones outsiders might expect. And, for a child coming from that kind of troubled background, it wasn't at all out of the question to think Lucy Ridder herself might have resorted to a violent solution to what she deemed an overwhelming problem.

But still, Joanna reasoned as she sped past the Triple-T Truck Stop on her way into Tucson, *that's no excuse.*

Just because the Bible talked about an eye for an eye and a tooth for a tooth didn't mean that the offending eye or tooth were there for anyone's taking. If Lucy Ridder had avenged her father's death by killing her mother, then fifteen years old or not, she would have to answer for that crime in a court of law.

Regardless of whether or not Lucy Ridder agreed with the judge's sentence, her mother had paid for her crime by spending eight years of her life in prison. Joanna could feel empathy for Lucy Ridder, but the bottom line was if Sandra Ridder's daughter turned out to be a killer, too, then the justice system would have to decide on an appropriate punishment—once Joanna's department delivered Lucy into their hands and assuming some wily defense attorney didn't figure out a way to get her off scot-free.

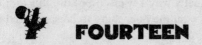

FOURTEEN

Quick Custom Metals on Romero Road was in a light-industrial complex near I-10 and Prince. Driving up to it, Joanna saw a glass-topped brick building that looked for all the world like an airport control tower, only there was no airport. Around the building was an expanse of green lawn.

When Joanna stepped out of the car, she was surprised by the difference in temperature between Bisbee and Tucson. Here, at a far lower elevation, the sun blazed down with an intensity that felt more like a Cochise County June day than a late-March afternoon. When she stepped into the company's front office, she was grateful to find it was fully air-conditioned.

A counter ran the length of the room. In front of it, an elderly silver-haired woman was engaged in a serious low-voiced conversation with a middle-aged man who stood behind the counter. It was clear from what was being said that the woman was in the process of having a sheet-metal custom-made coffin designed to hold the earthly remains of her beloved cat. The woman wanted to ascertain that the dimensions of the box would be large enough to accommodate her pet in a comfortable resting position without being crowded.

"Some cats like to curl up in a little ball, you know," she was saying. "But not my Sidney. He always preferred to stretch out flat on the cool tiles in the kitchen, more like a dog than a cat. So that's why I want to be sure this will be big enough. I don't want the poor thing to be scrunched up for all eternity."

It may have sounded like a bizarre request, but the man behind the counter seemed unfazed by it. "In that case, Mrs. Dearborn," he said, "you'd better bring us Sidney's exact measurements so there's no mistake. Where is Sidney now?"

"Still at the vet's," Mrs. Dearborn replied. "They're keeping him on ice there until I can come back with the coffin."

The man gave the woman an understanding smile. "Well, if you'll have the vet call me with the correct measurements, I'll have one of my men get right on it. And be sure that they measure him laid out just the way you want him. Once we have the dimensions, you'll have the box—the coffin— within twenty-four hours."

"Oh, thank you, Mr. Quick," Mrs. Dearborn murmured. "You are quick, too," she added. "Just living up to your name, I suppose, but you have no idea how much this means to me. I expect you'll be hearing from my vet, Dr. Winston, within the hour."

With that she gathered her purse from the counter, collected a crystal-knobbed cane, and hobbled her way toward the door. Joanna hurried ahead of her and held it open long enough for the woman to make her way out.

"Thank you, young lady," Mrs. Dearborn said. "That's a big help."

"Thanks from me, too," the man behind the counter said when Joanna turned back in his direction. "Sorry to keep you waiting. We're a little short-handed in the office today. Can I help you?"

"You are Mr. Quick, then?" Joanna ascertained.

"That's me," he said with a nod.

Joanna reached into her purse, extracted her badge and

ID, and held them up. "Sheriff Joanna Brady," she told him. "Is this a good time to talk?"

"Sure," he said. "Just a minute." He pulled open a door that led into a cavernous shop area. Sharp metallic-smelling smoke from a burning welding torch wafted into the office. "Hey, Leon," he called. "Kathy's still at lunch. Could you come watch the front counter for a few minutes?"

A few seconds later, a young man in a pair of faded blue coveralls riddled with burned spots came sauntering into the office. Once he arrived, Jay Quick ushered Joanna into his private office. His desk was a serviceable, battleship-gray metal one. The top of the desk, made of gray linoleum, matched not only the front and sides of the desk but the floor and walls as well. The whole room, from file cabinets to door, was covered with that same dull, unremitting gray. The effect might have been impossibly depressing if it hadn't been for the collection of copper-framed art prints that covered almost every available inch of wall surface. There were some Old Masters scattered here and there, but mostly the prints were colorful renditions of well-known Impressionists—Monet, Degas, and Renoir.

"Nice art," Joanna said, admiring the collection.

Jay Quick nodded. "I have my mother to thank for that," he said. "She may have come from a place most people think of as a backwater, but she maintained that living in Council Bluffs, Iowa, was no excuse for not knowing about the world outside the city limits—fine art and music included."

"She sounds like an unusual woman," Joanna said.

Jay nodded. "She was," he said. "I still miss her. But let's get down to business, Sheriff Brady. I'm sure you're not here to admire my framed art or discuss my mother. I'll be glad to give you whatever help I can, but I'm not all that sure what I can tell you."

"First, if you will, try to remember exactly what Lucy Ridder said to you on the phone."

"Not all that much. She did identify herself, of course. Said she was Lucy Ridder and that she was looking for Mrs. Quick. At first I didn't recognize the name and thought she wanted to speak to my wife. Finally, though, I figured out who she was and that she was trying to reach my mother. She said she wanted to talk to her—that she *needed* to talk to her. She made it sound important, like it was some kind of dire emergency."

"She didn't say what that emergency was?"

"No. Not even a hint."

"Do you have any idea why she would call your mother?" Joanna asked. "Were they close?"

"I don't know if 'close' is the right word," Jay said. "I know Lucy made a big impression on my mom—a favorable impression. And maybe that went both ways. I know Mother talked about Lucy for years afterward, always hoping that, wherever she was, she was all right."

"You told me on the phone that your mother was Lucy's teacher?"

"Not a real teacher, like at school. Mother was Lucy's ballet instructor at the Lohse YMCA. You see, all her life, Mom lived and breathed dancing. Even after she retired, she could never quite get it out of her system. When she came out here to visit us that one year, she heard that the Lohse YMCA downtown had lost its ballet instructor on a temporary basis. The woman had had a premature baby and was on extended maternity leave. The Y was strapped enough for funds that they couldn't handle having one person on maternity leave and, at the same time, pay to hire a replacement. Rather than see ballet lessons canceled for several months in a row, Mother volunteered to fill in. She worked at it that whole winter.

"I remember her telling me, a week or so after she started, about a little girl who came to her class, a little girl wearing thick glasses. When Mother asked her what she wanted, she said she wanted to be Maria Tallchief. Mother said, 'Oh, so you want to be an Indian?' The little girl said, 'I already *am* an Indian. I want to be a ballerina.'

"According to Mother, one of the nuns from Lucy's school had evidently given her a book to read about a young Native American woman who had gone on to become a world-class ballerina. Lucy couldn't have been very old at the time, only second grade or so, and the story made a big impression on her. So that's how Mother and Lucinda Ridder met. Once Lucy was in the program, she loved it. She came every day after school, either to take lessons or to practice. As I remember, she attended a Catholic school somewhere near downtown, and came to the Y on the bus."

"The school," Joanna interjected. "Was it Santa Theresa?"

Jay frowned. "Could be," he said. "I don't really remember. Anyway, she rode the bus from school to the Y every afternoon. Then, when the lessons were over, her dad would come downtown to pick her up."

"Her father," Joanna put in. "Not her mother."

Jay nodded. "Right. I believe her mother worked out of town—at Fort Huachuca, as I recall. Anyway, Lucy's mother came to pick her up just that once. As far as I know, it was the last time Lucy Ridder ever came to the Y."

"When was that?"

"The day of the murder," Jay answered. "That night was the night Lucy's father was shot and killed. Mother had told me about it even before we saw the news the next day and realized what must have happened."

"It was so unusual for Sandra Ridder to show up that your mother actually told you about it?" Joanna asked.

"It wasn't just that she showed up. It was how she looked when she got there. You see, Mother wasn't the violent type, and she lived a pretty sheltered life," Jay Quick explained. "Seeing something like that really shook her up."

"Something like what?" Joanna asked.

"The way Sandra Ridder looked that day. Her lip was cut and bleeding. There were cuts and bruises on her face. Her eyes were black and blue. One of them was almost swollen shut. She came barreling into the gym right after Mother's lesson had started, dripping blood on the floor and interrupting the whole class. Sandra ordered Lucy to go get her clothes on because they were leaving right then. Mother tried to tell Sandra that she shouldn't be doing that, that she shouldn't be driving. She tried to convince Sandra that she needed to be driven to a doctor or else to an emergency room, but Sandra wasn't having any of it. She just told Lucy again to come on. Now.

"Mother agonized about it for years afterward. She always wondered if she had shut down her class and insisted on taking Sandra to see a doctor, maybe none of it would have happened—maybe Tom Ridder wouldn't have died. Mother felt responsible, you see—felt as though there should have been something she could have done to prevent it. She blamed herself, and it haunted her. I don't think she ever quite got over it."

Joanna thought back to Clayton Rhodes' garage. Even now, if she closed her eyes, she could see him sitting there in the smoke, pale and limp, hunched over the steering wheel of his idling pickup. In that moment she knew exactly how Evelyn Quick must have felt. She understood the hopeless, hollow emptiness of thinking there must have been something she could have done. With an effort, she shook off her own nightmare to return to Evelyn Quick's.

"What happened then?" Joanna asked.

"The next day, once we heard what had happened—that Tom Ridder had been shot dead—Mother tried to get in touch with Lucy to see if there was something she could do or at least to offer her condolences. But as far as we could tell, there were no services of any kind held for Tom Ridder, at least not ones that were announced to the public. Mother tried calling the house several times, using the number the YMCA had in their records, but there wasn't any answer. It wasn't until months later, when the paper announced that Sandra Ridder was being sent to prison, that Mother learned Lucy had been sent to Pearce to live with relatives.

"The whole thing was terribly sad—all of it. As I said, Mother mourned about it for a long time. She said Lucy was an unusual girl, a kid with a lot of spunk. She said she was certain Lucy could have amounted to something someday. Maybe not in ballet, but in something." He paused before adding sadly, "I don't think this is what she had in mind."

"Let's go back to what you said before," Joanna interjected. "You mentioned that Tom Ridder was always the one who came to get Lucy at the end of her lessons."

Jay Quick nodded. "Always. That's what Mother said. Regular as clockwork. She said his pickup would be parked right outside the door in a loading zone whenever the lessons were over. I think that was the other thing that bothered my mother—that Tom Ridder had fooled her so completely. She said she never even suspected that someone who seemed so crazy about his little girl—so devoted—could, at the same time, have been so physically abusive with his wife. After the fact, I think Mother was concerned that if he had beaten his wife like that, he might have been doing the same thing to Lucy, although she said she never saw any sign of it. No bruises or cuts or anything like that."

"Obviously this whole experience made a big impression on your mother."

Jay Quick nodded. "She talked about it for years afterward. Every time she came to Tucson to visit—and she came every winter—she'd get to wondering whatever became of Lucinda Ridder. Once she even talked about taking a drive out to Pearce to try to find her, but we never quite got around to making that trip, and I don't think Mother ever did anything about it on her own."

"So, as far as you know, your mother and Lucy didn't maintain any contact after that?"

"Right. Not as far as I know."

"Lucy Ridder is fifteen now. Almost sixteen. Do you have any idea why, after all these years, she would try reaching your mother now?"

Jay shook his head. "None at all," he said. "I've been trying to figure that out ever since Saturday morning when she called. I've been wondering about it even more today, ever since I heard about this latest mess on the news."

"While I was on my way here, I had one of my officers trace the call that came to your house on Saturday morning," Joanna told him. "You were right about hearing trucks in the background, but Lucy's call wasn't placed from a truck stop. It came from a freeway rest area in Texas Canyon on the other side of Benson."

"What are you going to do now?" Jay asked.

"Look for her."

"Will you be able to find her?"

It was Joanna's turn to shake her head. "I don't know," she said. "We're trying, but the trail is several days old. I've just dispatched my canine unit to the rest area to see whether or not they can pick up her trail there."

There was a long, heavy pause. "What will happen

then?" Jay Quick asked. "Do you think she really did kill her mother?"

Joanna shrugged. "I don't know. I can't say for sure at this time, but it is a possibility. Lucy disappeared on the same night her mother was shot. According to Lucy's grand-mother, Lucy and her own mother have been estranged for years—for as long as Sandra Ridder was in prison. We be-lieve Sandra Ridder died of a gunshot wound, and we know from Lucy's grandmother that Lucy had a handgun with her when she ran away from home. As I told you on the phone, all those things don't necessarily make her a suspect, but they do make her a person of interest. We need to find her, talk to her, and ask her some questions."

Jay sighed. "I hope it's not true that she's a killer. But if it is—if it turns out Lucy Ridder really is responsible for her mother's death—then I'm glad my mother didn't live long enough to see it. Finding out that one of her favorite students ended up like that would have broken Mother's heart. I don't think she could have stood it."

Having gleaned as much information as possible, Joanna thanked Jay as he escorted her outside. "I appreciate all your help."

He nodded.

Joanna was about to climb into the Blazer when once again the control-tower-looking building caught her atten-tion. "What is that?" she asked. "It looks like it belongs on an airport."

"Right," Jay said. "It does. This complex used to be called Freeway Airport. When they rezoned the land and shut down the runways, the control tower became the only part of the airport they left standing. It's sort of a memorial, I guess."

The sound of a ringing telephone drew Jay Quick back

inside while Joanna climbed into her overheated Blazer. Once inside with the air-conditioning running, she used her cell phone to dial information. Seconds later a second call was answered across town at a convent on South Sixth Avenue.

"Santa Theresa's," a woman said. "Sister Emelda speaking."

"I'd like to speak to whoever's in charge," Joanna said uncertainly.

"That would be Sister Celeste, but she won't be home until after five."

"This is Sheriff Joanna Brady, from Bisbee. Is there somewhere else where I could reach her in the meantime?" Joanna asked. "It's urgent. I really do need to speak to her as soon as possible."

"She's over at the school," Sister Emelda said. "But she has a faculty meeting that's scheduled to start at three and won't be out until around four o'clock. Is that too late?"

Joanna glanced at her watch. It was only a little before three, but waiting until after four to speak to Sister Celeste would make it chancy for her to do an interview, drive out of town in rush-hour traffic, and still make it home to Bisbee in time for Eleanor Lathrop Winfield's command performance dinner.

"Could you give me her office number?" Joanna said. "Maybe I can catch her before she goes into the meeting."

"You can try," Sister Emelda said dubiously. "But one thing about Sister Celeste. She's very prompt, and she expects other people to be the same."

Seconds later, Joanna was speaking to a secretary at Santa Theresa School. "Sister Celeste, please," she said.

"Could I take a message, please? She's about to go into a meeting."

"This is Sheriff Joanna Brady from Cochise County," Joanna said. "And it's really quite important that I speak to her as soon as possible. I won't keep her long."

The secretary went off the line. Seconds later the phone was answered again. "Yes," a clipped voice said. "What can I do for you?"

"My name is—"

"You're Sheriff Brady," the woman interrupted. "I know all that. My secretary already told me. This is Sister Celeste. What is it you want?"

"We're investigating a homicide that occurred sometime overnight last Friday down near Elfrida," Joanna said. "We have reason to believe that a person of interest in that case—a girl by the name of Lucy Ridder—called your convent in the early hours of Saturday morning and spoke to someone there for some time—fifteen minutes or so. I was hoping I could speak to whoever that person was."

"I don't think so," Sister Celeste said abruptly. "In fact, I'm sure that would be quite impossible. Now, if you'll excuse me, I have to go."

With that, the line went dead. Joanna sat in the Blazer holding her cell phone, staring at it, and feeling as though a door had just been slammed shut in her face.

You may think it's impossible, Sister Celeste, Joanna thought. *But I will be back.*

Joanna was still sitting in the Quick Custom Metals parking lot and holding her phone when it came to life in her hand. When she answered, her caller turned out to be Detective Carpenter.

"Thought you'd like to know that we're having the Lexus towed to the impound lot," Ernie said. "Looks like our victim was there, all right. Or, if not Sandra Ridder, somebody else bled all over the leather upholstery. Casey Ledford came out to the site and did a preliminary look-see. She tried lifting prints from several places and couldn't find any."

"No prints again," Joanna breathed. "Just like all those plastic water jugs."

"Right," Ernie agreed. "I don't know about you, but I don't see one of your ordinary run-of-the-mill UDAs working that hard to keep his fingerprints out of sight and out of our computers. That suggests to me that whoever it is has been in some kind of hot water before, and he knows once we get a lock on his prints, we're going to get a hit on AFIS and know exactly who he is."

"Can you tell where whoever it was went after abandoning the Lexus?"

"I'd say the driver of the Lexus was picked up by someone driving a second vehicle. The driver went from one vehicle to the other without leaving any kind of prints we could cast. And the tire tracks of the second vehicle are in the roadway, so they've long since been obliterated by passing traffic. We'll probably pick up trace evidence from the car's interior that will help us get a conviction if we ever catch who did it, but for right now . . ."

"The Lexus is a dead end for identifying the suspect," Joanna supplied, "unless Casey can pull something out of the hat."

"How many low-life crooks do you know who are this cagey?" Ernie Carpenter asked. "Most of them never consider the possibility that they might get caught. In other words, Joanna, I'm getting a funny feeling about this case."

"What kind of feeling?" Joanna asked.

"Like we're supposed to think we're dealing with illegals when we're not."

"Who then, Lucy Ridder?"

"She's fifteen years old. I doubt very much that a kid her

age would know enough or be sophisticated enough about criminal procedures to wipe down prints. Besides, she doesn't have a driver's license."

"I don't think Lucy Ridder has a license to carry, either," Joanna said. "But that doesn't mean she doesn't know how to fire that twenty-two she stole from her grandmother."

"Point taken," Ernie said.

There was a momentary pause before Joanna spoke again. "What if all this has something to do with what went on eight years ago? Maybe it goes back to Tom Ridder's murder. Maybe that's why Lucy was trying to get in touch with all those folks from back then. Is Jaime there?"

"He's driving," Ernie replied. "I know better than let him talk on the cell phone when he's supposed to be concentrating on the road. What do you want to know?"

"He's talked to Melanie Goodson, hasn't he?"

Ernie was off the phone for a few seconds. "He says three times so far. Why?"

"Did she say anything about receiving a middle-of-the-night phone call around three o'clock on Saturday morning?"

Ernie passed along the question. "No," he said when he came back on the line "She never mentioned it. Do you want him to ask her about it?"

"Why don't I do it?" Joanna said. "After all, I'm right here in Tucson. Where's her office?"

"On Speedway. The street number is four fifty-eight."

"Tell him I'm on my way. And, Ernie?" Joanna added. "One more thing. When you get back to the department, I want you to ask Frank Montoya to get on the horn and try to get faxed copies of all the Tucson newspaper reports from back then that dealt with either Tom Ridder's death and/or with Sandra Ridder's prosecution. I'm convinced that what went on then has something to do with what's happening now, but I don't know what."

"This sounds suspiciously like we're operating on women's intuition again," Ernie said.

"Do you have a problem with that?" Joanna asked.

"Not at all," Ernie Carpenter told her cheerfully. "Whatever works works for me."

 **FIFTEEN**

When Joanna turned off I-10 onto Speedway Boulevard, the speed limit was signed at 35 miles per hour. Most traffic, including not one but two City of Tucson patrol cars, whizzed around Joanna at ten to fifteen miles above the posted limit. Meanwhile, knowing she'd be turning right somewhere beyond Fourth Avenue, Joanna stayed in the right hand lane stuck behind a Nebraska-licensed Buick whose snowbird driver was content to drive at five miles under.

I guess they got the name right when they called it Speedway, she thought.

Number 458 was one of those old stucco places that dated from the twenties or thirties. Most of the remaining houses on that stretch of Speedway seemed to come from that same pre-air-conditioning era and had been built along the same lines, with cavernously shaded front porches designed to keep out the worst of the afternoon sun. In the fifties and sixties, most of those old houses had fallen on hard times and decrepitude. Many had been carved up into boardinghouse-style living spaces for students attending the University of Arizona a few miles to the east.

It was possible there had been a similar house on the lot just to the west of number 458. If so, all sign of it had been erased, bulldozed into oblivion to make way for a smoothly paved parking lot that came complete with accents of blooming bright-pink verbena. Joanna parked her Blazer between a boxy bright-red Cadillac and a white Nissan Sentra.

Walking past them, Joanna forced herself to notice details about them—the gold emblem on the Caddy's trunk and the smashed left rear fender on the Sentra. That was one part of Joanna's law-enforcement training that was still giving her trouble. She constantly had to battle herself to notice and identify the vehicles she saw around her.

Walking from the lot to the office, Joanna found that in its new incarnation as a professional office, the former residence boasted a desert-friendly but beautifully Xeriscaped front yard that was alive with an abundance of drought-resistant blooms—verbena, purple sage, and desert poppies, accented here and there by clumps of prickly pear, agave, and barrel cactus. Not a single stray weed poked its nervy head out of the red-gravel-covered earth. Joanna knew from looking at it that, in the middle of the city, that kind of artfully created and impeccably maintained "natural" landscaping didn't come cheap.

Bathed in shadow from afternoon sun, the magnificent hand-carved mahogany front door with its brass-plated handle contained an oval of etched, leaded glass. The door may not have been part of the house's original equipment, but the look of it left little doubt that the house and door were full contemporaries, and if the door had been expensive back then, now it was even more so. Stenciled onto the glass in blocky gold letters were the words MELANIE J. GOODSON, ATTORNEY AT LAW.

Pressing down the old-fashioned thumb latch, Joanna let herself into dusky, air-conditioned comfort. The entryway floor was shiny, high-gloss hard wood. It was covered with a Navajo rug that spoke of both age and money. Joanna had seen rugs like that before, but the people she knew who owned those Native American treasures had long since declared them far too valuable to continue using them on floors.

"May I help you?" Behind the reception desk was a mid-twenties woman with a headful of loose auburn hair. She was decked out in suitably serious business attire—blazer, skirt, silk shirt, and heels. If it hadn't been for the seven or eight pierced earrings decorating both ears and a mouthful of very expensive orthodontia, Joanna might have taken her for Melanie Goodson herself.

"I'm Sheriff Joanna Brady from down in Cochise County," she announced, pulling out her ID. "I'd like very much to speak to Ms. Goodson."

"I don't remember Ms. Goodson having an appointment scheduled with anyone by that name for today." While the young woman ran a black-enameled fingernail down the page of a leather-bound appointment calendar to check, Joanna did her best to ignore the unfortunate and noticeable lisp caused by her braces.

No doubt the receptionist was intimately familiar with her boss's schedule. Hers was a form question worthy of nothing more than a form answer. "No," Joanna said, swallowing a bubble of annoyance. "One of my deputies had an appointment to see her earlier this afternoon, but he found it necessary to cancel. I'm sure Ms. Goodson will want to see me," she added. "It's about her missing vehicle."

"So someone has found it then?" a husky female voice asked from an open-doored office. "When will I be able to have it back? I hate driving rentals."

Joanna looked up in time to see a woman appear in a doorway just to the left of the reception desk. She was tall and good-looking but tending to be heavyset. Her highlighted hair was precision-cut in a timeless bob. She wore an ivory silk blouse with a pair of custom-made slacks, and her fingers carried a full contingent of heavily jeweled rings. *Here's a high-maintenance woman if I ever saw one,* Joanna thought. *Stylish and expensive both.*

"I'm Melanie Goodson," she said, holding out her hand. "Who are you again?"

"Joanna Brady. Sheriff Joanna Brady."

"Oh, yes. I've spoken to one of your deputies."

"Detective Carbajal?" Joanna suggested.

"Right. That's the one. I believe I was supposed to see him this afternoon, but he called in and canceled. Come on in."

Melanie Goodson led Joanna into a spacious, cove-ceilinged office that looked as though it had been carved from two separate rooms. The ornate white molding on the wainscoting, the lush floral draperies and muted grass-cloth wallpaper all announced their quality workmanship. In one corner of the room was a seating area that consisted of a polished coffee table, a wing chair, and an old-fashioned settee. Melanie Goodson settled into the chair and motioned Joanna onto the settee, which turned out to be far better-looking than it was comfortable.

"You never answered my question," Melanie said, pouring two glasses of ice water from a cut-crystal pitcher into matching glasses.

"What question?" Joanna asked after taking a grateful sip of the water.

"My car. When will I be able to have it back?"

"Probably not for some time. There are bloodstains inside it, Ms. Goodson. My investigators have reason to believe it was used to transport a homicide victim. I have a feeling my crime-scene investigators are going to need to keep it in our secure impound lot for some time. We'll no doubt need to hang on to it as evidence at least until this case comes to trial."

"You're saying whoever killed Sandra did it in my car?"

"I don't know for sure that's where the homicide actually took place, but the presence of bloodstains certainly indicates that a seriously wounded individual was in the car. Whether or not that person turns out to be Sandra Ridder remains to be seen."

Melanie shook her head. "They say no good deed goes unpunished, and it must be true. That's what I get for picking Sandra Ridder up at the prison gate and bringing her into my own home. Not only did she steal my car the moment my back was turned, she also managed to get herself killed in it. Well, no big deal. Maybe I can get my insurance company to total the damned thing so I can buy a replacement and get on with my life. Once you've driven a Lexus, a Caddy doesn't quite measure up, if you know what I mean."

"Of course," Joanna agreed, although, never having driven either a Lexus or a Cadillac, Joanna hadn't the vaguest idea of why Melanie might find her rented "Caddy" so objectionable. No doubt, Joanna would have found both of them equally acceptable and luxurious.

"Is that what you came to talk to me about?" Melanie asked. "The car?"

"Not entirely. Since I wasn't directly involved in investigating your vehicle, I don't know that much about it. Detective Carbajal was on the scene, and he expects to come talk to you about it tomorrow if you can work him into your schedule. No, the main reason I'm here is I wanted to ask you about something that came to my attention an hour or so ago."

"What's that?"

"A phone call you received around three o'clock Saturday morning. It was placed from a pay phone."

"What about it?" Melanie asked, her voice hardening. "How would you know whether or not I received a call in the middle of the night, to say nothing of the fact that it came from a pay phone?"

"From telephone-company phone logs. The one to you was part of a series of calls Lucy Ridder made that night, one right after another. Did she actually speak to you, or did the call go to a machine?"

Melanie Goodson frowned. "There was a call," she said. "I saw it on caller ID Saturday morning when I got up, about the same time I realized the Lexus was missing. And there was a message on it, sort of, although not a real message. All I heard was a voice—a girl's voice. She said my name, and then for several seconds she didn't say anything. There was just this breathing on the phone. I thought for a second or two that it was going to turn into one of those heavy-breathing crank calls. But then, whoever it was hung up without saying anything more."

"Did you happen to mention this to the Tucson cops when you reported your vehicle missing?"

"Report what?"

"The fact that you had received a strange middle-of-the-night phone call. Did it occur to you that the two events—your stolen car and the phone call—might be related?"

"I had no way of knowing they were," Melanie Goodson replied. "In fact, I never even considered it. I do a lot of defense work, Sheriff Brady. Phone calls coming in from pay phones at three o'clock in the morning aren't all that unusual for people like me, especially not on a weekend. No offense, Sheriff Brady, but DUIs are my bread and butter, which means three o'clock on a Saturday morning is a golden time for me.

"But if that's when Lucy Ridder called," Melanie added, "she was probably looking for her mother. I know Sandra had told someone—her mother, most likely—that she'd be staying with me on Friday night. Lucy probably expected that she'd be able to reach Sandra there. I imagine Lucy was excited at the prospect of seeing Sandra and didn't want to wait until the next day. I know if I hadn't seen my mother in eight years, I would have been."

"Lucy never went to visit her mother while she was in prison?" Joanna asked.

"No, not as far as I know."

"What about Catherine Yates, Sandra's mother?"

"Sandra told me that both her mother and her grandmother used to come, until her grandmother got too sick. But never Lucy."

"Did you ask her why?"

"I didn't have to. It's not too hard to figure out. Sandra was ashamed to have her daughter see her in a place like that. Lucy didn't want to come and Sandra didn't want her to, so they were in total agreement on that score. But when I picked Sandra up on Friday, she told me she was looking forward to seeing Lucy and explaining things to her."

"What things?"

"I don't know. I think there were things that occurred between Tom and Sandra Ridder—problems in the marriage—that Sandra refused to discuss with a seven-year-old child. But I think she thought that at fifteen, Lucy might be old enough to understand what all had gone on."

"What had?"

"Look, Sheriff Brady," Melanie Goodson said. "I'm sure you know all about the rules of client privilege. I can't tell you anything more than I just did."

"I do know about client privilege," Joanna conceded.

"And I've seen a number of working defense attorneys, but other than you, I don't know of one who would drive well over two hundred miles to bring back a client who had just been let out of prison or who then would let the same ex-con spend the night in his or her own home. That strikes me as a little unusual, Ms. Goodson. Care to explain that one to me?"

"Ever hear of guilt?" Melanie asked.

"You mean as in guilty or innocent?"

"No, as in guilty conscience. Sandra Yates Ridder and I go way back. We were friends at college—roommates for two years. It was one of those college things, and we both did it for a time—we went out protesting for NAT-C."

"The Native American Tribal Council," Joanna supplied.

Melanie nodded. "I'm part Cree; Sandra was part Apache. We figured it was a way of reclaiming our roots. Sandra even changed her name for a while. She called herself Lozen, after the Warm Springs Apache woman who fought with Victorio and Geronimo. The next thing I knew, she quit school. She told me she was going on the warpath—literally. She dropped out of sight for several years—long enough for me to graduate from the U., go to law school, and pass the bar exam. When I heard from her again, she had gotten herself in some kind of activist hot water and was ready to give up life on the road.

"I had a few contacts by then. Lozen went back to being plain old Sandra Yates and I helped her find a secretarial job out at Fort Huachuca. That's where she was working when she met Tom Ridder. I attended their wedding and that was the last I heard from her until the night Tom Ridder died. She called me up and told me she needed help. I was at her house the next morning when she reported Tom Ridder's death, and I was there with her when she surrendered to the police."

"And to suggest the plea agreement?" Joanna asked.

"Sandy came up with that brilliant idea all on her own. In fact, she insisted on it. And that's where my guilty conscience comes from. If I had been more experienced or tougher, I never would have let her do that. She was a victim, Sheriff Brady. Her husband had beaten her to a bloody pulp. I should have taken the case to court and used a domestic-abuse defense. If I had played the cards right, even if she'd been found guilty, she would have been locked up for three to five years at most. As it stands, I figure my inexperience cost Sandra Ridder a good five years of her life. My fault, Sheriff Brady. Don't you think I owed the poor woman a ride home? It's the least I could do."

"So why didn't you take her straight home?" Joanna asked. "On the one hand you said she was eager to get back to her daughter. Why, then, did she stay over, or *pretend* to stay over in Tucson for that extra night?"

"They let women out of the Manzanita unit in Perryville wearing whatever they happen to have on hand. Sandy showed up wearing a pair of used jeans, a pair of old tennis shoes, and somebody else's used sweatshirt. She told me she had some money. She wanted to go shopping on Saturday and get herself some decent clothes to wear home. She wanted to buy some makeup, have her hair cut and fixed. I think she wanted to go home looking like a human being instead of some kind of street person."

"And where was the money coming from to enable this combination makeover and shopping spree?" Joanna asked. "From you?"

"No, although I did offer. Sandy said that wasn't necessary, that she had enough money to get what she needed. I assumed her mother must have sent it to her, or she earned it and saved it. Prisoners do have jobs, you know."

Joanna considered Melanie's answer. In view of the fact that Catherine Yates claimed to have known nothing at all about her daughter's impending release until the very day it happened, it seemed unlikely that she had been the source of Sandra Ridder's cache of cash.

"Why do you think she stole your car?" Joanna asked.

"You're asking me? I have no idea. I suppose she wanted to go someplace and she didn't want me to know about it. When I went to bed around ten-thirty, she was tucked away snug as a bug in my guest room. When I woke up the next morning, she and the car were both gone. No note, no explanation, no nothing."

"Do you have a phone in your bedroom?" Joanna asked.

"Yes, why?"

"So do you turn off the ringer overnight?"

Melanie Goodson paused. "Well, no."

"If you went to bed at ten-thirty, you must have heard the phone ring at three A.M. So why didn't you answer? Why did you let the call go to the machine pickup, even though the caller might have been a well-heeled client in need of middle-of-the-night hand-holding over his latest DUI?"

"Come on, Sheriff Brady," Melanie said. "Why are you doing this? Are you trying to make out that I'm a suspect in stealing my own car?"

For no reason Joanna could put a finger on, she had the sudden sense that Melanie Goodson was lying. But why? What was she covering up? For the first time the thought crossed Joanna's mind that despite Melanie's claim of long-term friendship, the defense attorney might well have had some connection to Sandra Ridder's death. The problem was, Joanna understood that if she even hinted at Melanie's complicity, the entire tenor of the interview would change, with all the potential of what had been said and learned being ruled inadmissible and thrown out. Not wanting to jeopardize something critical to the investigation, Joanna backed off.

"I'm just trying to get a handle on what happened the night Sandra Ridder was killed," she said with what she hoped was a reassuring smile. "You say you went to bed at ten-thirty. I have a witness who places Sandra Ridder and your Lexus at the entrance to Cochise Stronghold, seventy miles or so away, at midnight. How did she get there so soon?"

"I always keep my car keys in a drawer in the kitchen," Melanie replied. "Sandra probably saw me put them away after we came home and knew where to go looking for them. So it's not like she had to hot-wire the damned thing in order to steal it. And now that the Eastern do-gooder fifty-five-mile-an-hour speed limit is history, anybody can make seventy miles in an hour and a half. In fact, most people can do it in a lot less than that."

Joanna glanced at her watch and was astonished to see how much time had passed. There were other nonthreatening questions she might have asked, but it was already after four. Her mother's command-performance dinner deadline was fast approaching.

"Speaking of speed limits," she said, rising to her feet, "I need to head out. I have a meeting in Bisbee at six-thirty, and I can't afford to be late. You've been very cooperative, Ms. Goodson. I appreciate it."

"Glad to help," Melanie Goodson said.

"And you have a lovely office, but then, I'm sure you hear that all the time."

"My partner and I like it."

"Partner?" Joanna asked. "I didn't know this was a joint practice. There's only one name stenciled on the front door."

"My partner's not an attorney," Melanie said with a ready smile. "Ed's a contractor who's into buying and rehabilitating old houses. He does the heavy stuff—the grunt labor. He gets all the permits, handles all the structural problems, and makes arrangements to bring the plumbing and electrical systems up to code. I oversee all the interior design work. It's a hobby of mine. In another life or if I hadn't been able to make it in law school, I might have become an interior designer instead. Once the places are rehabbed, we lease them out. This one happens to be the pick of the litter, which is why I'm here. As you can imagine, the lease rates are quite favorable."

"Nice workmanship," Joanna said admiringly as she made her way back to the outside office.

"Thanks," Melanie Goodson said. "I'm glad you like it."

Once back in her oven-hot Blazer, Joanna turned the air conditioner on high and rolled down the windows to let some of the heat blow out. While the hot air drained out and even though the clock was ticking, she wrote herself a note: "Have Jaime check with Melanie Goodson's neighbors to see if we can find out whether or not she really was home and asleep when Sandra Ridder took off in the Lexus."

Then, having done what she could do, Joanna headed out of town. Traffic wasn't all that bad getting to and on the freeway, and once she passed the exit to I-19, most of the local commuters disappeared as well. Out in the desert with mostly eighteen-wheelers for company, she dialed into the office. Despite the fact that she had called Kristin's number directly, the phone was answered by the switchboard operator.

"This is Sheriff Brady," Joanna said. "Where's Kristin?"

"She went home sick at noon," the operator said. "Is there anyone else you'd like to speak with?"

"How about Chief Deputy Montoya?"

"One moment."

"How's it going, Frank?" she asked when he came on the line.

"We're not having a real good day around here."

"Why not?"

"For one thing, our canine unit seems to have disappeared off the face of the earth. I finally broke down and called out Search and Rescue after all. I dispatched a crew out to Texas Canyon. I was afraid if we waited any longer—until however long it takes for Deputy Gregovich to resurface—there wouldn't be much chance of picking up Lucy Ridder's trail at the rest area."

"So with me out and with Kristin home sick . . ." Joanna began.

"Sick!" Frank snorted. "If she's sick, she's sure as hell not home. I went by her folks' place and checked. Her car wasn't there. And then, because I have a suspicious mind, I went by Terry's apartment, too. Guess what? His patrol vehicle is parked out front, and so's Kristin's Geo, but Terry's little four-by-four is nowhere to be seen. So wherever they are, they're together."

"What about Terry's pager?" Joanna asked.

"Turned off."

"Damn," Joanna muttered. "I had a feeling this morning that I needed to talk to her about this—to both of them, really—but I was in a hurry and I let it go."

"Do you want me to handle it?" Frank asked. "I'll be happy to haul them both on the carpet."

"No," Joanna said. "It's my job, and I'll do it—first thing in the morning. Give me their home numbers, Frank. I'll call them both right now and leave messages."

Frank located the two numbers in the departmental directory and read them off while Joanna jotted them down. "Anything else going on?"

"Ernie Carpenter came in a little while ago. He said they'd just finished up with the Sandra Ridder autopsy. No big surprises there. She died of a gunshot wound from a twenty-two. The doc recovered the slug. It evidently hit soft tissue only, so it's in fairly good shape. Jaime will bring it up to Tucson tomorrow and drop it off at the Department of Public Safety gun lab for analysis. And yes, I did warn the S and R guys to be careful and wear vests. I told them Lucy Ridder is to be considered armed and dangerous. I also told them that she's accompanied by a red-tailed hawk. I don't know whether or not Big Red should be considered danger-ous, but I suppose he could be."

"Anything else?"

"Are you planning to stop by the department on your way home?"

Joanna glanced on her watch. "Not really. I have a date at six-thirty. If I really push it, I'll just have time to go home and change—"

"That's why I asked. Butch stopped by a few minutes ago and dropped off some clothes for you to wear. I had him put them in your office."

"He did what?"

"He dropped off some clothing for you to wear to your mother's place tonight. He said your mother called and that she especially wanted you to wear some certain outfit. He was worried that you might be running late and not have enough time to go home and change, so he dropped the clothes off here thinking it would save you a few minutes. He also said that he and Jenny will feed the animals, pick up his folks from the RV park, and then meet you at your mother's place."

"I'll be a son of a bitch!" Joanna exclaimed. "I'm thirty years old. I've been elected sheriff, and I'm being married for the second time. How dare my mother still think she can tell me what to wear? That in itself would be bad enough, but here's Butch—my fiancé—helping her do it."

"I wouldn't be too hard on the man if I were you," Frank said.

"Why not?" Joanna demanded. "What did he say to you to get *you* on his side?"

"Butch didn't say a thing," Frank answered. "He didn't have to. If I were about to inherit your mother as my mother-in-law, I'm sure I'd jump when she said so, too."

"We'll just see about that," Joanna retorted. "No matter what Eleanor says, I'm sure what I wore to work today will be plenty good enough for my mother, and for meeting my new mother-in-law as well. And if it isn't," she added, "Eleanor Lathrop Winfield can go jump in the lake. Or else, she can send me home."

For a time after ringing off, Joanna was still so torqued with both Butch and her mother that she didn't trust herself to speak. Finally, after giving herself ten or fifteen miles of driving to settle down, she picked up the phone again and left almost identical messages on answering machines at Terry Gregovich's apartment and at the home of Kristin Marsten's parents. "Sheriff Brady. Be in my office tomorrow morning at eight o'clock sharp. Both of you. No excuses."

That should settle that hash, Joanna thought grimly. *And the only thing I have to worry about in between now and then is doing battle with my mother.*

 **SIXTEEN**

By the time Joanna finished driving the hundred miles between Tucson and Bisbee, she had cooled down considerably. The situation with Terry Gregovich and Kristin Marsten would be resolved the next morning one way or the other. And as for Eleanor . . . Joanna realized that she was just being Eleanor. How typical of her to want to pull off some elegant, sit-down meal to impress Joanna's incoming relatives. The problem was, just because Joanna *understood* what was going on with her mother didn't make it any easier to deal with. And it also didn't mean Joanna was going to knuckle under and obey.

She came over the divide and down into Bisbee's Tombstone Canyon just at sunset. There would have been plenty of time to run by the department, change into the specified outfit, and still be at Eleanor and George's house within five minutes of the appointed hour. Instead, Joanna drove straight to their place on Campbell Avenue.

Joanna was surprised to see Jim Bob and Eva Lou Brady's car parked out front right along with Butch's Subaru. Although Eleanor got along fine with Joanna's former in-laws, the down-home Bradys hardly qualified as the kind of elegant dinner guests Eleanor much preferred to have gracing her dining room.

As soon as Joanna opened her car door, her ears were assailed by the steady thrum of blaring mariachi music that seemed to emanate from George and Eleanor Winfield's backyard along with bursts of laughter and the party sound of several voices talking at once. The whole neighborhood was permeated with the tantalizing odor of meat cooking over open-air charcoal.

"A barbecue?" Joanna said aloud to herself. "My mother's having a barbecue?"

When it came to the Eleanor Lathrop Winfield Joanna knew, an outdoor barbecue was something totally out of character. In the months before D. H. Lathrop's death, he had devoted all his spare hours to planning and building a massive used-brick barbecue in the far corner of the backyard. During the construction process, Eleanor had disdained the whole idea. She claimed that if she had to have grilled meat, she much preferred going to a restaurant. Despite his wife's objections, Big Hank Lathrop had persisted. Once the grill was completed, D. H. had been inordinately proud of his do-it-yourself handiwork. Unfortunately, he had been able to use it only twice. Within two weeks of finishing the project, D. H. Lathrop was dead.

Once he was gone, his widow never once deigned to use the thing, and she hadn't allowed Joanna that privilege, either. For years the grill had sat untouched, protected from dust beneath a layer of multiple blue tarps. But now, with George Winfield in residence and from the looks of the smoke wafting skyward, the tarps were obviously long gone.

Just then the front door slammed open and Jenny came flying down the wooden steps. "Mom," she shouted. "You're home." She stopped two feet away, just inside the gate. "How come you didn't change clothes?" she added with a sudden scowl.

Jenny was wearing jeans, sneakers, and a Mickey Mouse sweatshirt. Her mother, on the other hand, was dressed for work in a dry-clean-only two-piece suit and a creamy blouse along with a pair of sensibly-low high heels.

"What's the matter with what I have on?" Joanna asked.

Jenny shrugged. "It's going to look pretty funny out in the backyard at Grandma's picnic table. Everybody else is wearing jeans and stuff."

"We're having a picnic?" Joanna asked. "It's only the end of March. Isn't this a little early for a picnic or a barbecue?"

Jenny shrugged. "It's what Mr. and Mrs. Dixon wanted." She paused. "They told me to call them Grandma and Grandpa Dixon, but I don't really want to. I mean, I just met them. It seems kinda weird."

"What are they like?" Joanna asked.

"Okay, I guess," Jenny replied, wrinkling her nose. "But they talk funny. Their words are so sharp they hurt my ears. And they think it's summer, because they're both wearing shorts. Shorts and white socks and black sandals. Ugh."

"They're from Chicago," Joanna said. "I think it's a lot colder there than it is here. Maybe this feels like summer to them."

"Maybe," Jenny said. "Anyway, when Butch introduced them to Grandma Lathrop this afternoon, she asked them if there was anything special they wanted for dinner. Mr. Dixon said what he wanted more than anything was Mexican food and he wanted to eat it outside. So Grandma Winfield went down to Naco and bought tamales and tortillas. And Grandpa Winfield is making *carne asada*."

"Who hired the mariachis?" Joanna asked.

"They're not real. That's just a tape on Butch's boom box. He said it would add atmosphere."

Butch met them just inside the door. "You didn't change,"

he said, frowning. "Didn't you get my message? Frank said he'd be sure to tell you."

Joanna sighed. "Frank did give me the message, but there wasn't enough time to go out to the department and still be here on time. I'm sure the clothes I'm wearing will work. I promise not to spill anything."

"It's not that," Butch said. "It's just that everyone else is dressed a lot more casually than you are."

"Don't worry," Joanna said. "I'll be fine. Now come on. Where are your parents? Let's go get the introductions out of the way so I can stop being nervous about meeting them."

Outside, Joanna found that the backyard was lit with a series of festive-looking lanterns complete with lighted candles. Predictably, three men—George Winfield, Jim Bob Brady, and a portly man in shorts, sandals, and socks, who made Jim Bob look slim by comparison—were clustered near the barbecue. Even across the yard, Joanna could see that Butch Dixon resembled his father, Donald. The older man was taller and much heavier than his son. In contrast to Butch's clean-shaven head, his father had thick, curly gray hair, but their facial features were almost identical.

Halfway down the yard, Eva Lou Brady sat at Eleanor's cloth-covered picnic table engaged in subdued conversation with a heavyset woman with thinning gray hair who looked to be in her mid-sixties.

"Come on," Butch said to Joanna, taking her hand and leading her down the backyard. "I'll introduce you to my father first."

They met Eleanor Winfield halfway to the barbecue. She looked her daughter up and down, pursed her lips, and said nothing, but Joanna got the message all the same.

"Dad," Butch was saying. "Here she is—the girl of my

dreams—Joanna Lathrop Brady. Joanna, this is my dad, Donald Dixon."

Donald Dixon turned away from the grill with its layer of thinly sliced beef, looked at Joanna's face, and beamed. "You can call me Don," he said, holding out a massive paw of a hand and pumping Joanna's eagerly. "Everybody does. And I'm delighted to meet you. Maggie and I have heard so much about you. Butch said you were just a little bit of a thing, and by God it's true!"

Despite the fact that it annoyed Joanna when strangers and new acquaintances made unsolicited comments to her size, she nonetheless managed to keep her smile plastered firmly in place. "Good things come in small packages," she responded, knowing that the comment sounded perky and stupid both, but Don Dixon seemed to like it.

"Right you are," he said heartily, slapping a beefy, snow-white, shorts-clad thigh. "I do believe my mother used to tell me the same thing. I just didn't pay any attention. Have you met Maggie yet?"

Hearing the Chicago twang in his voice—the hard-edged vowels—Joanna recognized what Jenny had meant. Don Dixon's accent hurt her ears, too.

"No," she said in answer to his question. "I just now got here."

"Well, by all means go over and be introduced. She's really looking forward to meeting you. She hasn't talked about anything else ever since we left Chicago."

Taking a deep breath and following Butch's lead, Joanna turned back to the picnic table. "Mom," Butch was saying when they arrived at the table. "This is Joanna Brady. Joanna, my mother, Margaret, but everyone calls her Maggie."

Margaret Dixon held out her hand. She smiled a thin

smile. "How do you do. Glad to meet you, Joanna. I've got my fingers crossed. Let's hope the third time's the charm."

Joanna saw the muscles tighten along Butch's jawline. "Mother!" he said.

"I'm sure Joanna knows what I mean," Maggie Dixon said quickly, waving away his comment as though it were a bothersome fly. "No doubt the two of you will be very happy. And since Butch is getting such a late start on settling down, it's probably a good thing you come complete with a ready-made family."

For months Butch had been hinting to Joanna that his mother was a difficult woman. He had warned that, in a competition of relative prickliness, Maggie Dixon would run Eleanor Lathrop Winfield a close race. Joanna had laughed off his comments, saying he was probably exaggerating or making things up. Now, all it took was that one exchange for Joanna to realize he was right. Maggie Dixon was going to be tough to like. Across the table and behind Maggie's back, even the perpetually easygoing Eva Lou Brady felt constrained to shake her head and raise a disapproving eyebrow.

Never one to retreat from a battle, Joanna motioned Butch to take a seat next to Eva Lou. Then, raising her skirt, she stepped over the picnic bench and sat down next to Maggie. Wanting to give Butch a chance to relax, Joanna dived into the task of making polite conversation.

"So how do you like Cochise County so far?" she asked as evenly as she could manage.

"It is warm," Maggie replied. "I'll say that much for it, and it's so dry here. My skin feels like it's going to turn brittle and break off. I'm used to a lot more humidity. My mother and her second husband retired out here," she continued. "They bought a place up in Sun City. That's how

Butch ended up coming out here years ago. But as far as I'm concerned, I could never see what it was about the desert that appealed to my mother so much, and it's such a long way from home. And now that Donald's retired from the post office, we prefer to spend our winters in Hot Springs, Arkansas. Ever been there?"

Suddenly the idea that Arizona was a long way away from both Chicago and Hot Springs, Arkansas, held some appeal for Joanna Brady. *Good,* she found herself thinking. *Let's keep it that way.*

"So how do you like being sheriff?" Maggie Dixon continued without bothering to wait for an answer. "That sounds like a difficult job for a woman. And isn't it dangerous?"

"At times, it's a difficult job for anyone—man or woman," Joanna replied. "And yes, it can be dangerous, but that can also be true of any job. You have to keep your wits about you."

"Well," Maggie said, shaking her head. "From what Butch writes about you and says on the phone, I can tell he's very proud of you. But you won't keep doing this, will you—I mean after you're married?"

"Why wouldn't I?"

"Well, you know how it is. It's the man's job to support his family. And then, if you got pregnant . . ."

Butch got up abruptly. "I think I'll go see if Eleanor needs any help," he said, leaving the battle of the picnic table under Joanna's sole direction.

Maggie turned and watched him go. "Now I suppose my son will be mad at me," she mused. "He's always accusing me of being nosy. But these are the kinds of things people need to talk about *before* they get married, not *after*. And I'm sure that's the mistake Butch made before—the other times he got married. He went into those relationships with no idea at all of what he really wanted. Of course, the first time, he and Debbie were both much too young. And with Faith, I don't think either one of them thought ahead very much, either. Faith's a very nice girl," Maggie added. "We still stay in touch from time to time. I'm sure you'd like her. She and her husband just had their second child—a little boy. I meant to mention that to Butch."

Months earlier, about the time Butch had asked Joanna to marry him, he had told her about his first two marriages and what had happened to them. She remembered all too well Butch relating the tale of his bitter divorce from a woman named Faith who had taken him to the cleaners both financially and emotionally as she abandoned ship in order to marry her husband's soon-to-be-former best friend.

Don't bother telling him, Joanna thought. *That's the last thing he needs to know!*

"Well?" Maggie asked. "Are you?"

Her tone implied that there was an unanswered question lingering in the air, one Joanna had somehow failed to hear.

"Am I what?" Joanna returned.

"Are you and Butch planning on having kids?" Maggie prodded. "The magazines are always filled with articles about women and their ticking biological clocks, but I think men's do, too. And at Butch's age—"

"Come and get it while it's hot," George Winfield announced as he walked by the table carrying a platter piled high with strips of broiled flank steak. "We're serving this buffet-style," he added. "Come into the kitchen and fill your plates. Those who want to can come back outside to eat."

"Let me give you a hand, Maggie," Don Dixon said, stopping by the table to help his wife rise from the picnic bench. While Don led Maggie into the house, Eva Lou stood up and wordlessly gave Joanna a sympathetic pat on the shoulder as she walked by. Meanwhile, a stunned Joanna stayed where she was. With a last flourish of trumpets, the mariachi music faded to nothing and the boom box clicked off, leaving the backyard in welcome silence.

"Are you all right?" Butch whispered near her ear a few moments later. "Would you like something to drink?"

Joanna shook her head. "I don't think George and Eleanor have anything strong enough," she returned.

Butch shook his head. "I can't believe she said that—the third one's the charm. She's something else, isn't she?" he added. "It's like that old saying about how absence makes the heart grow fonder. When I'm not around her, I always end up convincing myself that my mother can't possibly be as bad as I remember. Then, once we get within shouting distance of one another, it all comes back to me. Believe me, it's no accident my grandparents wound up retiring to Sun City. I'm pretty sure my stepgrandfather was looking for a way to get away from his stepdaughter. I don't think he or Grandma were the least bit unhappy that Mother hated Arizona. It seemed to suit both of them just fine."

"No wonder Eleanor doesn't bother you," Joanna said. "She may be a piker at times, but right now she seems mild by comparison."

"That's what I've been trying to tell you all along," Butch said with a rueful grin. "I told you that you just didn't know when you were well off."

Jenny came to the back door and stuck her head outside. "Aren't you two going to come inside and fill your plates?"

"In a minute," Butch called back, then he turned to Joanna. "Are you all right?"

"I'm fine, really," Joanna said. "Maggie takes some getting used to, is all. And how did we end up out here in the yard? Mother hates barbecuing and picnics and all the bugs that go with them. And she's not that fond of Mexican food, either. That's why I didn't worry about not changing clothes. I figured we were in for one of Mother's six-course sit-down extravaganzas."

"That was before she caught sight of my mother's hefty backside," Butch said. "I think the thought of Mother sitting on one of Eleanor's fine dining room chairs was enough to spark an instant change of menu and venue both. That's also about the time Eleanor decided to invite Jim Bob and Eva Lou along for the ride. I think she hoped they'd serve as leavening agents, but when I met Eva Lou on her way inside a few minutes ago, even she looked like she'd had enough."

"How do you tolerate her?" Joanna asked.

Butch shrugged. "I live in Arizona, and my parents live in Chicago," he said. Behind them, Joanna heard the back door slam. "Here they come," he added. "We'd better go fill our plates."

By the time Joanna and Butch reached the head of the serving line, everyone but George Winfield had abandoned the kitchen in favor of outside dining. George stood at the counter dealing out plates loaded with meat, tortillas, and steaming, freshly made tamales.

"How are the love birds doing?" he asked, as Joanna and Butch paused by the counter and began dishing up condiments.

"Fine," Butch and Joanna both said at once, then they burst out laughing.

"Sure you are," George agreed. "For somebody getting the third degree, you're both in great shape. Hey, would you two like to sit inside? My guess is the picnic table is already full to overflowing."

It was true. Six was the maximum number of diners that

could be accommodated at the wooden outdoor table. "But won't Eleanor be pissed?" Joanna asked.

"Let her," George said with a shrug. "After all, doing dinner this way was her bright idea. There's no reason we should all have to suffer."

In the end, the three of them settled at the kitchen table. The food was good. The tamales were thick and spicy. The tortillas were soft and see-through thin. And the strips of ancho-flavored steak had been grilled to spicy perfection. Until Joanna put the first bite of food in her mouth, she had no idea how hungry she was. For several minutes Butch, Joanna, and George ate in companionable silence.

"Your old friend Fran Daly was in town today," George said at last when he paused from eating long enough to unwrap the corn husks from his tamale.

Dr. Daly was the assistant medical examiner in neighboring Pima County. In the course of the past few years she and Joanna had been involved in several different joint investigations. After a somewhat rocky start, the two women had come to have a good working relationship.

"What for?" Joanna asked.

"She showed up to be Reba Singleton's hired gun," George Winfield replied.

"To do Clayton Rhodes' autopsy?" Joanna asked. George nodded. "How'd it go?"

"Pretty much the way I said it would," George replied. "Fran Daly says the same thing I did—Clayton Rhodes died as a result of a cerebral hemorrhage. That should get Reba off your back for good and all. And now that I've released the body and Little Norm Higgins from the funeral home has collected it, Reba should be off my back, too."

"When's the funeral?" Joanna asked.

"According to Little Norm, they've scheduled it for tomorrow at two. Reba says she wants to have it ASAP so she can get back home to California, which is good riddance as far as I'm concerned." He added, "And while we're on the subject of autopsies, I know what killed Sandra Ridder— loss of blood combined with peritonitis. If the Volks-marchers had found her in the morning and she'd been treated with massive doses of antibiotics, she might have made it. But as it was . . ." George shrugged.

Joanna glanced at Butch to see how he was handling this graphic dinnertime discussion. Chewing thoughtfully, he seemed unfazed.

"Will you be going to Clayton's funeral?" he asked Joanna, as if just then becoming aware of a pause in the previous conversation.

She nodded. "Yes, of course I am."

"And Jenny?"

"I don't know. I'll leave that up to her. When we first talked about it, I know she was planning on going. Why?"

"I want to take the folks out sight-seeing tomorrow," Butch said. "It's better than having my mother prowling around my house all day, looking through drawers and opening my cupboards. Besides, they've never been in southern Arizona. I wanted to show them the sights—the Wonderland of Rocks, Boot Hill, maybe even Kartchner Caverns."

"Sounds like a big day."

Butch nodded. "I'm hoping to wear them out. Maybe that way they'll be ready to go back out to the park at a decent hour in order to get some sleep. But if I have to be back in time to take care of Jenny after school . . ."

"Don't worry about Jenny, Butch," Joanna told him. "She'll probably go to the funeral with me. And, if need be, she can come out to the department after that and stay until it's time to go home."

"Good," Butch said. "That's one less thing for me to worry about."

Just then Eleanor stormed into the kitchen. "Just what do you three think you're doing hiding out in here?"

"Eating," George replied mildly.

"But the company is outside," Eleanor huffed. "We're all supposed to be out there together, so we can get better acquainted."

"I'm sure Butch knows his parents well enough," George returned. "But Joanna and I needed a little time to talk business. I didn't think you'd want your company meal disrupted by discussion about autopsies and such."

Eleanor's face fell. "You weren't really, were you, George?" She turned to Butch. "Is he telling me the truth? Were they really talking about autopsies at the dinner table?"

Butch sighed and shook his head. "I'm sorry to say they were, Eleanor. I swear to God!"

"Well!" she exclaimed. "I never!"

With that, Eleanor Winfield turned and flounced back outside, missing Butch's grin and George Winfield's answering wink. "I'll pay for that later," he said. "But it was worth it."

By then, though, Joanna's conscience was beginning to bother her. "Shouldn't someone go rescue Eva Lou and Jim Bob?"

"Naw," George said. "Don't worry. Those two have been around. They're perfectly capable of taking care of themselves."

 **SEVENTEEN**

By seven-thirty the next morning, Joanna was driving Jenny to school. "You're awfully quiet this morning," Joanna said. "What's going on?"

"Did you like them?"

"Who?"

"Did you like Butch's parents?" Jenny asked.

After years of telling her daughter that honesty was the best policy, Joanna decided a truthful answer was the best option. "Not very much," she admitted.

"Me, either," Jenny replied. "Mrs. Dixon seems really mean, and Mr. Dixon . . . well, he kept asking me all kinds of dumb questions. You know, the kind of questions grown-ups ask kids when they think they have to talk to them but they really don't have anything to say."

"I agree. They were both pretty annoying," Joanna said. "But remember, they say you can choose your friends, but you're stuck with your relatives."

"They're not *our* relatives," Jenny declared.

"They will be," Joanna told her daughter grimly. "Since they're Butch's relatives, they're going to end up being our relatives, too. We'll just have to do our best to figure out a way to get along with them."

"Okay," Jenny said, nodding. "But I'm not going to like them any better."

For the next few minutes, mother and daughter rode in silence. Finally, Joanna tackled another topic. "What about Clayton's funeral?" she asked. "Have you made up your mind yet about whether or not you're going to go?"

Jenny nodded. "I want to go," she said. Then, after a pause, she added, "No, that's not true. I don't *want* to go, but I'm going anyway. Clayton was my friend—our friend—and I want to be there."

"Good girl," Joanna said. "I'll call the school from my office and let them know that I'll be by to pick you up at one-thirty. Since the funeral's scheduled for two, that should be plenty of time."

Only after Jenny jumped out of the Blazer and slammed the door did Joanna let her mind focus on her scheduled coming-to-God meeting with Kristin Marsten and Terry Gregovich. She had watched the blossoming romance between her secretary and the K-9 officer with amused tolerance. As long as they had remained discreet about it and hadn't let their relationship get in the way of work, she had been willing to go along with it. Her department had no hard and fast rules about fraternizing between officers and staff as long as there was no inappropriate relationship between supervisors and reporting employees and as long as the relationship didn't interfere with the performance of respective duties.

Clearly, though, what had happened the day before was anything but discreet. Joanna knew all about young love. After all, she was in love herself. She didn't like being forced into taking a hard-nosed position, but as an elected administrator, it was her job to supervise her employees and see to it that they maintained a clear-cut line between love and duty. If Kristin and Terry weren't prepared to function with a suitable degree of separation between their professional and personal lives, then, as sheriff, Joanna had to be prepared to demand someone's resignation.

At the Cochise County Justice Complex, Joanna parked the Blazer in her reserved spot. As she stepped out of the SUV, she paused long enough to glance around the lot. It was only five of eight, but she noticed that both Kristin's red Geo and Terry's blue four-by-four were already in the parking lot. They were parked side by side in the farthest corner of the farthest row. So much for maintaining any kind of discretion.

Shaking her head, Joanna used the electronic keypad to let herself directly into her corner office through a private entrance—one that avoided her having to traverse the public lobby areas. Once in her office, she straightened her desk before squaring her shoulders and walking over to open the door that led to the outer reception area. A pale-faced, stricken Kristin sat at her desk. There were dark circles under her eyes, which were puffy and red. Across from her, Terry Gregovich sat on the waiting-room-style love seat, with Spike curled comfortably at his feet. The K-9 officer sat still and straight in his chair, his arms folded across his chest.

"You'd better come on in," Joanna announced to them. "Let's get this over with."

Kristin entered Joanna's private office first, followed by Terry and the dog. The two people sat on the captain's chairs across from Joanna's desk. As soon as Terry was seated, Spike circled three times and then settled in comfortably at his handler's feet. For a time, no one spoke.

"Well," Joanna said at last. "Would anyone care to explain exactly what went on around here yesterday afternoon and why you both seem to have gone AWOL at the same time?"

"I will," Terry said.

"No, let me," Kristin interrupted. "It was my fault. I'm the one who took off from work without really being sick. And I'm the one who told Terry that I had to see him no matter what—that we had to talk."

"Don't listen to her, Sheriff Brady," Terry said. "It isn't either her fault. I'm a big boy. I knew better than to turn off my pager, but I did it because I didn't want to be interrupted even though I had a feeling Spike and I might be needed again yesterday. If anyone deserves to be in trouble over this, I'm the one."

At the sound of his name, Spike raised his head, looked up, and thumped his bushy tail on the floor. When no orders were forthcoming, however, he sighed, put his head back down on his front paws, and closed his eyes once more.

Joanna sighed. "All right then," she said. "What was it that you needed to discuss that was so all-fired important that you were both willing to risk losing your jobs over it?"

"I was late," Kristin said in a small voice.

The way she said it, Joanna knew at once she wasn't talking about being late for work. "A whole week," Kristin continued after a pause. "And that's not me. I'm one of those women who's as regular as clockwork—every twenty-eight days."

Joanna felt her eyes widen. "You mean to tell me you're pregnant?" Kristin nodded miserably. "What happened? Weren't you using birth control?"

Kristin nodded again as two fat tears spilled out of her eyes and ran down her cheeks. "We were," she replied. "Condoms. But something must have happened to one of them. I couldn't talk to my mother—she'd have a fit—so I was planning to talk to you about it on Sunday, after the shower, to ask your advice. But then Dick Voland showed up and I lost my nerve. So I talked to a friend instead. She gave me the name of a doctor down in Agua Prieta who would take care of it for me, but . . ." At that point, Kristin buried her face in her hands and sobbed.

Joanna took a deep breath. It was déjà vu all over with a painful piece of her own life. She remembered all too well when she had been in Kristin's shoes in a similar situation; when she, after agonizingly considering whether or not to have an abortion, had finally been forced to tell Andy that she, too, was pregnant. She hadn't wanted to and had delayed for weeks, hoping she was wrong. Part of her reason for not wanting to tell was due to the fact that she and Andy had barely begun dating. She hadn't wanted him to feel trapped into marrying her, but as soon as he found out, he had insisted. He and Joanna had run off to Lordsburg, New Mexico, the very next weekend, to tie the knot.

And the knot had worked. Theirs hadn't been a trouble-free marriage, but it had been a good one. They had been in love and they had stayed that way. Together they had been happy. The only person who had seemed seriously offended by Jenny's early arrival had been Eleanor Lathrop, who had, as it turned out, her own long-hidden and hypocritical reasons for being opposed to shotgun weddings.

With a jolt, Joanna emerged from an instant replay of her own past with the sudden realization that reliving the misery of her own experience was doing nothing to alleviate Kristin Marsten's.

"She wasn't even going to tell me," Terry Gregovich was saying. "I could tell all last week that something was wrong, but I didn't know what it was. I thought we'd get a chance to talk about it over the weekend, but then I had to work all day Sunday. Yesterday morning, I called her here at work. I told her I knew something was up, and if she wouldn't meet me to tell me what it was, that I'd come here to her office and I wouldn't leave until I knew where I stood." He paused. "I was afraid there was somebody else and that she wanted to break up with me.

"So I told her I was picking up some burgers at the Arctic Circle and that she should meet me down at Vista Park. It was while we were there that she finally broke down and told me what was up. I asked her if she knew for sure. She said no, she only *thought* so. That's when I told her, we can't go around making decisions in the dark and that we had to have her tested so we'd know what was what. She didn't want to go to a doctor here in town or in Sierra Vista because she was afraid someone would talk. And she didn't want to get one of those pregnancy test kits from the drugstore for the same reason. So yesterday afternoon, I turned off my pager and we drove up to Tucson—to Planned Parenthood."

"And?" Joanna prodded.

Kristin looked up through teary eyes and nodded. "It's true," she said. "I'm pregnant."

"So what are you going to do?" Joanna asked.

"It's not how I wanted it to work out, Sheriff Brady," Terry answered. "It's not how either one of us wanted it. But I love Kristin, and she loves me, and both of us want this baby. So if you have to fire one of us, go ahead. You can have my resignation right now. If I go up to Tucson I can probably find another job that will pay as well or better than this one. If I'm going to be a husband and a father in the next little while, you'd better believe I'm going to take those responsibilities seriously."

Having said that, he reached out for Kristin's hand and held it tenderly, cradled between both of his.

"So what's the plan then?" Joanna asked. "Are you going to tell your parents?"

"I suppose," Kristin said. "I don't want to. Mother's going to kill me. And then we'll get married. I know my mother always wanted me to have a nice, big church wedding. So did I, but I guess we can't do that now."

"But we can, Kristin," Terry objected. "Don't you see? We can still have just the kind of wedding you want. There's no law that says you can't have a nice wedding and wear a long white dress if that's what you want to do. We don't have to go running off to some chapel in Vegas or to a Justice of the Peace somewhere. So what if it takes a month or two to put together a wedding? If there are people who stand around after the baby's born, counting months and pointing fingers, then it's their problem, not ours."

Joanna nodded. "Terry's right, Kristin. You can have as nice a wedding as you want."

"But how?" Kristin asked tremulously. "Terry and I both work. Weddings take a lot of planning, and I know my mother. She'll be so mad that she won't lift a finger." At that, Kristin once again burst into inconsolable sobs.

"If your mother won't help us, mine will," Terry said. "I know we can do it. It'll work out, hon. I know it will. Don't cry, please. We'll be fine."

Listening to him, he sounded so confident, so sure of himself, that Terry almost had Joanna convinced that it really would be fine.

"Is that what you want, Kristin?" Joanna asked kindly. "To marry Terry and keep the baby?"

"Yes," she whispered, "but how . . ."

"Do you attend church regularly?"

"I used to," Kristin said, sniffling. "My parents go to Cornerstone out in Sierra Vista. I tried it a few times, but I didn't like it."

Cornerstone in Sierra Vista was a nondenominational

megachurch made up of disaffected evangelicals from many denominations who had coalesced into a separate church of their own. Cornerstone's fiery pastor had been in the news for first blocking and then physically assaulting an elderly man who, along with his wife, had parked in the church parking lot while attending a weekday luncheon at a nearby senior center. The assault charges were eventually dropped but the incident had left both church and pastor with an unfortunate reputation in the community.

Even Marianne had been constrained to comment, telling Joanna at one of their weekday luncheons, "Cornerstone is longer on judgment and hellfire and brimstone than it is on forgiveness and the milk of human kindness." Joanna hoped, for Kristin's sake, that the same didn't hold true for the young woman's parents.

Joanna turned to her deputy. "What about you, Terry?" she asked.

He shrugged. "The last time I went to church I think I was about seven years old."

"So you're telling me that you'd both like to have a church wedding but neither one of you has a specific church in mind. Is that right?"

Terry Gregovich nodded. "That's about it," he said.

Joanna pulled a piece of paper loose from one of several half-used tablets of Post-its and jotted down a telephone number. "This is Reverend Marianne Maculyea's number up at Canyon United Methodist Church," she said. "Marianne's a good friend of mine, and she has a cool head on her shoulders. I'm sure she can help talk you through some of the decisions you both need to be making right now, the bottom line of which is—baby or no baby—do you really love one another enough to get married? Since Marianne doesn't know either one of you, she should be a truly impartial observer. Then, who knows, if you do decide on a church wedding, maybe Canyon would be a good place to do it."

Joanna passed the note across her desk. Kristin took it as if grabbing hold of a lifeline.

"Does that mean you're not going to fire us?" Terry asked.

Joanna shook her head. "It sounds to me as if the two of you were dealing with a life-or-death situation yesterday. Under the circumstances, I wouldn't call that a firing offense. A lot of people seem to think that police officers are cops first and people later. I happen to believe it's the other way around. On the other hand, you're not getting a walk. From now on, I expect your behavior to be above reproach. That goes for both of you. I know love is grand, but it isn't supposed to infringe on work. No hanging around the office mooning at one another when you're supposed to be out in the field, Deputy Gregovich. Do I make myself clear?"

"Absolutely. You can count on me, Sheriff Brady," the deputy replied.

"And if you want to take time off together," Joanna continued, "it has to be arranged in advance through proper channels. No more of this instant comp time or 'I feel a headache coming on, so I think I'll go home.' Understood, Kristin?"

The young woman nodded eagerly.

"Okay, then," Joanna said, "it's probably time we all went to work. Terry and Spike need to get over to Texas Canyon to help the Search and Rescue guys look for Lucinda Ridder. And I'm sure Kristin and I have a bale of incoming mail to handle. Right, Kristin?"

"Right."

Kristin and Terry stood up together. So did Spike. "There's one more thing I need to tell you," Joanna said. "If anyone were to track down the records, you'd be able to see that, taking Andy's and my wedding date into consideration, Jenny was born a lot sooner than she should have been. And since she weighed in at seven and a half pounds, we would have been hard-pressed to convince anyone that she was premature."

Kristin Marsten caught her breath. "Sheriff Brady, you mean the same thing happened to you?"

"It happens to a lot of people, Kristin, and I'm here to tell you it's not the end of the world. Talk to your parents about it. They just might surprise you."

Nodding and holding hands, Kristin and Terry left Joanna's office, closing the door behind them. Moments later there was a discreet knock.

"Come in," Joanna called.

Frank Montoya poked his head around the door. "Time for the morning briefing?" he asked, waving a fistful of manila folders.

"Past time," Joanna said. "Let's get cracking."

"I guess you didn't have a chance to have that little chat with Deputy Gregovich and Kristin," Frank suggested tentatively.

"But I did talk to them," Joanna replied. "The two of them left my office just a few seconds ago."

"Well," Frank said. "It doesn't appear that your talk did much good. You'd better give it another shot. When I came into the outer office just now, I caught them in the middle of a great big smooch. They broke it off, but they didn't even have brains enough to look guilty about it."

"Kristin Marsten and Deputy Gregovich aren't guilty, Frank. They're pregnant. They spent yesterday afternoon finding out for sure that it was more than just a late period and deciding whether or not to have an abortion. I think we

can say Kristin was legitimately sick even if she wasn't
home when you went by to check. They were in Tucson seeing a doctor from Planned Parenthood."

"Whoa! I'd guess that means you're not going to fire them."

"And I'd guess you're right. I told them no more monkey
business at work or during business hours, but we can probably overlook an engagement-launching smooch. Now let's
get down to business. What happened overnight?"

For the next forty-five minutes, Joanna and Frank went
over the chief deputy's usual collection of mundane stuff—
incident reports, jail menus, scheduling and vacation ap-
provals. None of it was critical, but it all had to be brought
to Joanna's attention.

"And here's the information you wanted me to find,"
Frank Montoya said when they had finally worked their way
down to the last folder in his stack.

"What's that?" Joanna asked.

"Faxes of the newspaper clippings on the Thomas Ridder
shooting. I also found out why he got thrown out of the
army. He decked a superior officer."

"So at least he didn't discriminate," Joanna said.

Frank frowned. "What do you mean by that?"

"Most of the men who beat up their wives don't have
balls enough to pick on someone their own size who might
hit back."

"Maybe you're the one who's discriminating, Joanna,"
Frank said. "Remember, the army discharged Thomas Ridder over whatever happened. Sandra Ridder's solution put
the guy away in a pine box—permanently. I'm not saying he
didn't deserve it, but I am saying there may have been other
possible solutions that Sandra Ridder never considered. And
the judge who sent her up must have thought so, too, or he
wouldn't have given her eight to ten."

"Point taken," Joanna said with a sigh. "Anything else?"

"Ernesto poked his head in my office a little while ago and told me to tell you the water is from Tucson. He said you'd know what he meant, but I don't."

"The water in the jugs with no fingerprints," Joanna supplied. "And if the water came from Tucson, the jugs probably did, too. Which means that whoever put them there wasn't a UDA from Mexico walking south into the US of A to find field-hand work."

"I see what you mean," Frank said. "Most of the UDAs are walking north, not south. So what else is going on that I don't know about?"

"Dr. Daly came down from Tucson yesterday and did Clayton Rhodes' second autopsy."

"And?"

"And nothing. She came up with the same results Doc Winfield did—cerebral hemorrhage."

"That's a relief then," Frank said. "At least we won't have to have the FBI snooping around here and sticking their noses into everybody's business. I wasn't looking forward to that."

"Neither was I," Joanna agreed.

"And we'll also have Reba Singleton off our backs."

"Right."

Frank was up and on his way to the door when Joanna thought to ask him about Ernie Carpenter and Jaime Carbajal.

"They took off for Tucson first thing this morning," Frank told her. "They had an appointment with Melanie Goodson. They were also going to take the slug that killed Sandra Ridder up to the Department of Public Safety satellite crime lab in Tucson. Why, do you have something for them?"

"I talked to Melanie Goodson myself yesterday afternoon," Joanna said. "And I had the distinct impression that she wasn't being forthright with me. She claims she was at home asleep when Sandra took off in her Lexus, but— despite having a telephone in her bedroom—she still claims she didn't hear Lucy's phone call when it came in around three A.M. She let the call be picked up by her machine."

"What do you want Ernie and Jaime to do about it?"

"I want them to bear that in mind when they talk to her. And when they finish up with everything else, I want them to go out to Melanie's neighborhood on Old Spanish Trail and check it out. There's always a chance that one of her neighbors saw or heard something unusual."

"There's a chance," Frank Montoya agreed. "But not a very big one. If I were you, I wouldn't hold my breath."

The moment Frank left Joanna's office, a much-relieved Kristin Marsten appeared with that day's worth of correspondence. For Joanna, dealing with the daily deluge of mail was an unending source of frustration. She worked for two golden and almost totally uninterrupted hours before her private-line phone rang.

"I hope you're happy," Eleanor Lathrop said. "I don't see how the Dixons could have felt very welcome when you and George and Frederick locked yourselves up in the kitchen that way. I suppose it could have been worse, though. If you had come outside and started discussing all those gruesome things . . ."

"Mother, look," Joanna said. "This is a complicated week for all concerned. It was wonderful of you and George to host last night's dinner, and I'm sure everyone enjoyed it. Those tamales were incredible."

"I'm glad *you* liked them," Eleanor sniffed. "The food was all right, but the atmosphere was so thick you could have cut it with a knife. Why, even Eva Lou was snappish with Maggie when she and Jim Bob were getting ready to leave."

She was snappish a lot earlier than that, Joanna thought. *I wonder what Maggie Dixon said that finally pushed even sweet-tempered Eva Lou over the edge?*

Joanna's unspoken question was never uttered aloud, but Eleanor Lathrop Winfield, chattering on, answered it anyway.

"All Maggie did was ask a few questions about Andy— nothing out of line as far as I could see, but all of a sudden Eva Lou stands up and says, 'I can't imagine why you'd be asking such a personal question.' It was an answer straight out of 'Dear Abby,' and I was absolutely floored. Can you imagine Eva Lou being so . . . well . . ." Eleanor Winfield paused as she groped for the proper word. "So outspoken," she finished at last.

When it comes to Maggie Dixon, Joanna told herself, *anything is possible.*

EIGHTEEN

The service for Clayton Rhodes was a simple affair held at Higgins Funeral Home and Mortuary up in Old Bisbee and conducted by Clayton's longtime pastor, the Reverend Lonnie Dodds of the Double Adobe Baptist Church. Reba Singleton sat stiffly in the front row and spoke to no one. Joanna and Jenny sat near the back. When the minister announced that Clayton had been preceded in death by his beloved wife, Molly Louise, and his infant son, Cyrus Andrew, Joanna reached over and squeezed Jenny's hand. Had it not been for Jenny, Joanna wouldn't have had any previous knowledge about the existence of Clayton's second child.

Because Molly Rhodes had been a behind-the-scenes linchpin in Bisbee's YWCA, the post-service social hour was held there. Always with a keen eye for spotting readily available refreshments, Jenny chose seats at a table within easy striking distance of silver trays laden with artfully arranged decorated cookies. A few minutes after Joanna and Jenny sat down, they were joined at the table by a tiny, bird-boned woman Joanna had never seen before.

"I'm Carol," she said, smiling cordially at Jenny. "Carol Hubbard from Tucson. Who are you?"

"I'm Jennifer Brady, and this is my mom, Joanna," Jenny answered brightly. "Mr. Rhodes was our neighbor. He used to feed our animals and stuff."

Carol looked at Joanna. "Oh, I know about you. You're the woman whose husband was killed, and now you've been elected sheriff. Isn't that right?"

Joanna nodded. "Yes. The name's Joanna Brady," she said, holding out her hand.

"Clayton spoke very highly of you—and of you, too, Jenny," Carol Hubbard continued. "And don't you have some kind of funny-looking dog? I seem to remember Clayton saying his name is Tiger."

"Tigger," Jenny corrected. "Not like the golfer. Like the character from *Winnie the Pooh*. And Tigger's really funny. He's half golden retriever and half pit bull, and he loves to jump."

"How did you know Clayton?" Joanna asked. "Are you a relative?"

"Oh, no. Nothing like that. Just friends. He and my first husband, Hank, met during the war," Carol Hubbard replied. "World War Two, that is. They were in the U.S. Air Force— the Air Corps back then. Hank was stationed in India with the Four Hundred Ninety-first Bomber Squadron and worked intelligence for them. According to him, his major task assignment was sobering up pilots so they were straight enough to fly the Hump. He was a voice major in college, though—a talented soloist—and later on in the war he was pulled into entertaining the troops. He and a group of other performers went to bases all over India and Burma putting on variety shows. That's where he met Clayton."

"Mr. Rhodes could sing?" Jenny asked.

Carol Hubbard laughed. "Actually, he couldn't sing a note, and he couldn't dance, either, but they had him in every show—moving his lips and acting like he was singing his heart out. You know how these days they have those traveling Broadway productions that go all over the country? I

believe they call them bus-and-truck shows. Well, this was
the same thing, only it was a plane-and-truck show. According to Hank, Clayton Rhodes was the best mechanic in
India. They flew from show to show in planes that were so
old and rickety that they were in danger of falling out of the
sky every time they took off, but by hook or crook Clayton
somehow managed to keep them running and in the air.
Hank and some of the others had wonderful voices. Hank
was the soloist for Saint Philips in the Hills up in Tucson for
many years after the war. But he always said that if it hadn't
been for Clayton, those shows in India never would have
gotten off the ground."

"So Clayton and your husband stayed in touch after the
war?"

Carol nodded. "You may remember seeing my husband.
He was a news anchor in Tucson for many years."

Suddenly the name finally clicked in Joanna's head, and
she remembered a handsome, smooth-voiced, silver-haired
man sitting at a television news desk. *That* Hank Hubbard.

"He was a big deal up in Tucson, but even so, there was
nothing Hank liked better than coming down here to Bisbee
for a few days and staying with Clayton and Molly. The two
of them—Clayton and Hank, that is—would go out hunting
in Clayton's old beat-up Ford. During the gas shortage back
in the mid-seventies he added an extra gas tank so they could
go as far as they wanted without having to worry about having to stop for gas.

"The two of them would come dragging home with whatever they'd caught—venison and javelina and dove, and
Molly—bless her heart—and I would figure out a way to
cook whatever it was on Molly's old woodstove." Carol
Hubbard paused. "Have you ever cooked javelina?" she
asked Joanna.

"Venison and dove, yes," Joanna said. "But I have to admit, no javelina."

Carol grinned. "The best thing to do with that is cook it the way the Indians do—in a pot of Anaheim chili paste and let it simmer for hours. Otherwise, it's tough as it can be. Still, the four of us had great times together. I know Rhodes Ranch was real life for Clayton and Molly, but for Hank and me, the time we spent there was like time apart—like camping out.

"Whenever we were with them it seemed as though we were a world away from the high-pressure life in Tucson. While we were there, we could afford to be ourselves— Hank and Carol. That's important sometimes, especially when you're in the public eye. It's easy to get too full of yourself, to take yourself too seriously. If Hank ever started getting all puffed up, Clayton was the one person who could throw Hank Hubbard off his high horse."

At that juncture Reba Singleton, accompanied by Marliss Shackleford, chose to make her grand entrance. She swept into the room and went straight to the head of the line, where she helped herself to a cup of coffee and declined an offer of cookies. Carol Hubbard regarded her behavior with a raised eyebrow. "Some things never change," she murmured.

"I beg your pardon?" Joanna asked.

Carol shook her head. "Molly and Clayton both would be embarrassed beyond belief to see their daughter behaving like that—pushing her way to the head of the line—but then it's not very surprising. Reba was always that way—pushy— from way back, from when she was tiny. She was the kind of child who wanted her way, and she wanted it now."

Joanna was tempted to ask, What went wrong? How could two people as squared away as Molly and Clayton Rhodes raise a daughter who was that screwed up? Instead, she allowed herself a discreet "You knew her back then—when she was little?"

"Yes, I'm afraid we did. One of the things Hank and I liked about coming down to see Molly and Clayton was that they didn't even have a TV set. It wasn't until Reba went away to college—to the university in Tucson—that she discovered that Hank, her father's dear old friend, was on television up there. Then she raised all kinds of hell with her parents because she wanted her dad to have Hank help her get on television, too."

"And did he?"

Carol nodded. "Of course he did. That's the kind of guy Hank was. Once Reba managed to pick up a degree in broadcast journalism, he put in a good word for her here and there. Hank knew people who knew people. That's how those things happen in broadcasting, through connections."

Jenny turned in her chair so she could watch Reba and Marliss making the rounds of the room. "You mean she's on TV, too?" Jenny asked, her eyes wide with wonder.

Carol smiled. "She was, but not anymore. It's sad but true that most male news anchors have a much longer shelf life than female anchors do. She's been off the air for years now. According to Clayton, she's been married and divorced several times since then, but she's always managed to marry up. I think her current husband is some kind of bigwig in computers out in Silicon Valley."

Carol shook her head and laughed. "My goodness. Whatever did you say to set my tongue to wagging so much? You must think I'm a terrible gossip."

Joanna looked around the room, scanning faces. "So is your husband here as well, Mrs. Hubbard?"

"My second husband," she corrected. "Hank died years

ago. A couple of years after that, Molly died as well, but Clayton and I remained friends. Force of habit, I guess."

"Why, Carol Hubbard," Reba Singleton said from just over Joanna's right shoulder. "I didn't know you were here. I almost missed you."

Carol held out her hand long enough for it to be pressed by Reba's ring-bedecked fingers. "Your father was such a good man," Carol Hubbard murmured. "And such a dear friend, too. I'm so sorry he's gone."

With a curt nod, Reba acknowledged Carol Hubbard's comment, then she rounded on Joanna. "Isn't it bad enough that you've taken away my father's ranch?" she demanded in a loud voice. "Do you have to steal his friends as well? Don't you have any shame? How dare you!"

As conversation in the rest of the room came to a complete standstill, Joanna felt her cheeks turn hot. "Reba," Joanna began. "Please."

"Please what?" Reba demanded. "Please shut up and don't let anyone know what you've been up to? Please go away so people won't know about your underhanded dealings and how you've cheated me out of my birthright?"

"Reba," Joanna said. "I've done nothing of the kind."

"The hell you haven't!" Reba Singleton snarled back while her whole body trembled in a fit of ill-suppressed fury. "I guess you don't want these nice people to know that their little Miss Goody Two-shoes of a sheriff is actually a double-dealing bitch! What I want to know is what makes you think you can get away with it? Who says I'm not going to stop you?"

Behind Reba, Marliss Shackleford's eyes widened. Like Joanna, she too must have feared that Reba's attack would escalate from verbal to physical. "Come on, Reba," Marliss said, grabbing the other woman by the arm. "Let's go."

They left then, leaving behind a silent room full of people and a stunned and flushed Joanna Brady. Reeling like the victim of a hit-and-run, Joanna could think of nothing at all to say. Gradually the level of conversation in the room resumed its former level, while Carol Hubbard shook her head.

"I take it from that she's learned about Clayton's will," Carol said in a low voice.

"You knew about that too?" Joanna asked in surprise. Clayton may have kept the news from Joanna, but obviously he hadn't kept it to himself.

"Oh, yes. Clayton told my husband and me all about it when he first had his will redrawn. He and Reba had that huge falling-out when Molly got so sick. Reba wanted her father to send Molly out to California to some specialist she knew about, and neither Clayton nor Molly wanted to do that. When they refused, everything went downhill in a hurry. It was right about then—right after Molly's funeral— that Reba went to court and tried to have her father declared incompetent. She wanted to be appointed his legal guardian so she could have power of attorney over him and manage his affairs. But Clayton fooled her. He hired his own attorney. The guardianship petition never went through."

"That was what the quarrel was all about?" Joanna asked.

"The quarrel was about control," Carol Hubbard replied. "Reba is the kind of person who has to be in the driver's seat at all times. Once Clayton beat her back, his first intention was to leave his ranch to the Nature Conservancy. But then Clayton changed his mind. He said he didn't think you'd ever want to actually move into his place because it's so old and run-down, but he knew you'd like having the land. I believe he told me you're planning to remarry soon?"

Blushing again, Joanna nodded. "This coming Saturday," she said.

"Well," Carol Hubbard said, rising. "I'm sure you and your new husband will be very happy together. Whoever he is, he's lucky to have found you. And your daughter, too. Now, I have to be going. It's a long drive back to Tucson, and we don't like being out after dark. My husband's night vision is none too good these days."

She held out her hand. Joanna shook it, and then Carol Hubbard was gone.

"She was nice," Jenny said a moment later. "Why couldn't Butch's mom be somebody like her?"

Joanna laughed and shook her head. "You know what they say: Some days you eat the bear; some days the bear eats you."

Jenny scowled. "What's that supposed to mean?"

"It means that Butch's mother is the way she is, and we're just going to have to learn to live with it and accept her the way she is."

"Even if we don't want to?"

"Even if."

By four o'clock, Joanna and Jenny were back at the Justice Complex. Jenny took her homework and disappeared into the empty conference room. In the meantime, Joanna headed into her office to go through her messages and return calls.

Talking about Butch had made her realize that she hadn't heard from him all day long, and she was missing him. However, having just made a big stink with Kristin and Terry about the hazards of mixing love and work, she was glad no calls from Butch had come in through the switchboard during the course of the day. "Do as I say, not as I do" wasn't the way Joanna Brady wanted to run her ship.

. Once the most pressing calls had been handled, Joanna went looking for Frank Montoya. "I take it your pager is still turned off?" he asked.

Guiltily, Joanna reached into her pocket, removed the pager, and switched it on. "Sorry about that," she said meekly. "I turned if off during the funeral and must have forgotten to turn it back on."

"No problem," Frank said, "but I didn't know you were back, and I thought you'd want to hear the news."

"What news? Did Search and Rescue locate Lucy?"

Frank shook his head. "No, but we think we've found her bike. At least we found somebody's bike. It was hidden in among some of those huge rocks in Texas Canyon about half a mile from the rest area. It looks like somebody took a sledgehammer to it and turned it into a piece of junk. There was also a canteen and a sleeping bag."

"Do you know for sure the gear is Lucy's?" Joanna asked.

"We haven't confirmed it yet, but we're pretty sure. Catherine Yates told us there was a leather thong tied to the handlebars to give Big Red something to hang on to. The bike S and R found had a leather thong on the handlebars."

"And Lucy?"

"No sign of her. She had been there, but she's evidently not there any longer, and there's no sign of that damned hawk of hers, either. But that's not why I called you. The real news is about Melanie Goodson."

"What about her?"

"She's dead," Frank said.

Joanna's jaw dropped. "She's what?"

"You heard me. Dead."

"When? What did she die of?"

"No way to tell. The Pima County ME's office says they

saw some signs of needle tracks, so maybe she overdosed. At any rate, she didn't turn up for work today. Nobody was really all that concerned because her first appointment wasn't until after one, when she was supposed to meet with Ernie and Jaime. According to her secretary, if she had worked late the day before, she sometimes didn't come in at all in the morning. By the time somebody started to worry and called Pima County to go out to her place on Old Spanish Trail to check on her, she'd been dead for some time."

Joanna shook her head. "This feels bad to me, Frank. This isn't some accidental overdose. She didn't look like even a recreational drug user to me. This has to be connected to Sandra Ridder and what happened to her. Did Ernie and Jaime go out to Melanie Goodson's house?"

"The last I heard, they were on their way, but it's Pima County's deal, Joanna. As you know, our relationship with the Pima County Sheriff's Department hasn't been exactly cordial of late, so don't hold your breath as far as interdepartmental cooperation goes. It isn't gonna happen."

"Can we get either Jaime or Ernie on the horn?" Joanna asked.

"I don't know. We can try. The last time I talked to Ernie, his cell phone was cutting in and out. The coverage may be pretty spotty out in that neck of the woods." Nonetheless, Frank picked up his phone and began dialing.

"How can the cell phone coverage be that bad?" Joanna asked. "Old Spanish Trail is in Tucson, for God's sake."

"Not *South* Old Spanish Trail," Frank told her. "From what Ernie told me, Melanie Goodson's house is out in the middle of nowhere, almost to Vail." He listened intently for several seconds, then shook his head. "Says he's left the service area."

"What's the phone company thinking?" Joanna asked.

"Angie Kellogg's boyfriend can make cell-phone calls from Skeleton Canyon—which *is* the godforsaken middle of nowhere—back home to England, but we can't call from here to Vail?"

"That's about the size of it," Frank told her. "The phone company doesn't have to think, and our two-way car radios don't stretch over the mountains that far, either. We'll just have to wait for one of them to report in."

"Waiting isn't something I'm very good at," Joanna said.

Frank Montoya grinned at her. "Really," he said. "I never would have guessed."

Joanna did a few more pacing-style turns around the office and checked on the progress of Jenny's homework. Finally, at five-thirty, she went back to Frank's office. "All right," she told him, "I'm leaving. Somebody has to go home and feed the animals. Leave word with Dispatch that as soon as either Ernie or Jaime comes within hailing distance, I want a call to me on *my* cell phone. Even if Jenny and I are out doing chores; I'll have the phone with me at all times."

After that Joanna cleared her desk of everything she'd left undone during the course of the day by stuffing a pile of untouched paperwork into a much-used briefcase. Taking work home was something she did by force of habit almost every night these days. Often she never even got around to opening the briefcase between leaving the office and returning the next morning. Still, it made her feel better somehow that her desk usually looked more or less cleared when she left work at the end of the day.

She and Jenny were home, had fed all the animals, and were on their way back into the house to fix dinner when the cell phone rang in Joanna's shirt pocket. Hoping the caller would be one of her two detectives, Joanna answered hurriedly.

"Congratulate me," Butch Dixon said. "It worked."

"What worked?"

"Butch Dixon Tour Guide," he said. "I've worn my parents out. I offered to take them out to dinner, but they said they'd had enough. All they wanted to do was go back out to the RV park and hit the hay. And all I want to do is come see you."

"Butch, really," Joanna began. "I've brought a briefcase-ful of work home. If I'm going to be gone for the better part of next week, there's a lot I need to get caught up on before we leave town."

"Please," he said. "Have pity on me. I've spent the whole day trying to dodge one of my mother's negative comments after another. 'Wherever did you get the odd idea that you could write a book?' is my personal favorite. As far as I'm concerned, that was the topper on the cake. What my ego needs now is a little dose of positive feedback from my two favorite people in the world. I promise, I won't try to talk. I'll sit in the corner quiet as a mouse and watch you work— make you work—if need be. And I won't even hint about spending the night."

By the time Butch finished his sad lament, Joanna was laughing at him. "All right," she relented. "But no more whining, either. I can't stand it when you whine."

"I don't like it either," Butch agreed. "I'm afraid my folks bring out the worst in me."

He was out at the High Lonesome within fifteen short minutes. By then Joanna had thawed out some ground beef and was frying corn tortillas for tacos. Jenny had chopped up tomatoes and onions and was busy grating cheese when Butch walked in the door.

"Boy," he said. "Are you two a sight for sore eyes! I've had about all of Maggie Dixon I can stand, and she's been in town for barely twenty-four hours."

Jenny wrinkled her nose. "You mean you don't like her either, even though she's your own mother?"

"That's about the size of it," Butch said.

Joanna's phone rang just then. When she dragged it out of her shirt pocket, Butch relieved her of the tongs. "I'll finish frying the tortillas," he said. "You talk on the phone."

"Where are you?" Joanna asked when she heard Jaime Carbajal's voice.

"Benson," he said. "We've given up for the day, and we're on our way home. Dispatch said you wanted us to call."

"I did—do," Joanna said. "How's it going?"

"Not too bad, considering. I guess Frank told you that we missed the boat when it came to talking to Melanie Goodson. And the nun you wanted us to talk to, the one who's the principal at Santa Theresa's . . ."

"Sister Celeste," Joanna supplied.

"Right. We didn't see her, either. She was out sick today, but we did have one bit of luck."

"What's that?"

"Not surprisingly, the Pima County homicide detectives weren't too thrilled when we showed up hot on their heels. Since they wouldn't let us anywhere near their crime scene, Ernie and I were stuck just sort of milling around down on Old Spanish Trail at Melanie Goodson's turnoff, which, by the way, seems to be paved from there all the way to her house. That had to have cost a fortune. Anyway, we were left cooling our heels there, and since people are just naturally curious when they see a couple of stopped police vehicles, we did manage to talk to some of Melanie's neighbors."

"Jaime, could you stop stringing me along and try getting to the good part?"

"We ended up talking to a lady named Karen Gustafson who lives just up the street, if you could call it that. It's a road, really. Anyway, she told us that she and her husband were coming home from Webb's Steak House on Friday night about ten when they saw Melanie Goodson's Lexus coming down the road. Karen said she was sitting in the car while her husband went over to the mailbox to pick up their mail. She said that when the car came by, she saw there were two people in it—Melanie Goodson and some other woman. The thing is, until we started asking her questions, she didn't even know Melanie's car had been stolen."

"Good grief!" Joanna exclaimed. "Pima County's supposedly investigating that case. What did they do, drop the ball?"

"I don't think they ever bothered to pick it up. Grand-theft auto evidently isn't a very high priority around here. In most cases they don't do much more than take the report over the phone. I believe Melanie Goodson got an in-person officer visit because of who she was and what she did for a living. Of course, now that she's dead, a possible homicide case is gathering a lot more attention than her stolen car did."

"Could it be that Melanie Goodson and Sandra Ridder both went to Cochise Stronghold that night?"

"That's how it sounds to Ernie and me," Jaime answered.

"But why would she go along?" Joanna asked.

"I don't know," said Jaime, "but my guess is, once we have an answer to the first question, we'll also know how come she's dead. She was Sandra Ridder's attorney, right?" Jaime asked.

"Right."

"And Ridder went to prison on a plea bargain. That means there was never any trial in regard to Tom Ridder's death, so maybe there wasn't much of an investigation, either," Jaime continued. "The detectives probably figured they had a slam-dunk domestic-violence case. Frank told us

Tom Ridder got thrown out of the army for assaulting one of the brass. And since Sandra was willing to stand up in front of a judge and accept full responsibility for plugging her husband, the detectives on the shooting case probably figured, why waste any more time digging any deeper? She goes to prison. The detectives clear one case and go on to the next."

Joanna considered the possibility. "So you're thinking the same way I am—that all this has to have something to do with Tom Ridder's death?"

"It's the only tie-in Ernie and I can think of."

"Me, too, Jaime," Joanna said. "And maybe we're on to something. Melanie Goodson told me that Sandra was planning to buy some new clothes, have her hair done, and pretty much get herself fixed up before she went on home to the Dragoons to see her mother and daughter. She also said she didn't have any money worries about her upcoming makeover and shopping spree. We need to find out whether or not Catherine Yates sent Sandra get-out-of-jail money or if she had savings from her prison wages. If neither of those options pans out, maybe she was expecting to collect some cash somewhere else. What if somebody else killed Tom Ridder and Sandra stepped up to the plate and took the rap for it? What if she knew who really did do it? Then, after all these years, she gets out of jail and decides to collect on that old debt. What would happen then?"

"Whoever she was trying to put the squeeze on might prefer some other medium of exchange—say a hot bullet in place of cold cash."

"Exactly," Joanna said. "And since Melanie Goodson was Sandra Ridder's attorney back then, she may have known about the connection as well. So where do we go from here?"

"I don't know about you," Jaime Carbajal said, "but I'm on my way home. Whatever we're going to do next will have to wait until tomorrow. If I don't get home in time to see at least the last couple innings of Pepe's game, Delcia is going to kill me."

"Your wife isn't going to kill you over missing a Little League game," Joanna said. "But if she does, we'll see to it that Delcia doesn't get any less of a sentence for knocking you off than Sandra Ridder did for shooting her husband."

"Thanks, boss," Jaime Carbajal said. "You're all heart."

 **NINETEEN**

Over dinner, Butch turned serious. "What's this I hear about Reba Singleton making a scene at Clayton's funeral?"

Joanna glowered at Jenny. "It wasn't a big deal," Joanna said. "She didn't mean anything by it."

"She did too," Jenny insisted. "She said you wouldn't get away with it. She sounded so mean when she said it, that it scared me. It really did."

"And now that I've heard about that," Butch said, "there's something worrying me as well. When I came home, there was a car pulling out of the drive onto High Lonesome Road, but Jenny tells me there was no one here but the two of you."

"What kind of car?" Joanna asked.

"I couldn't tell," Butch replied. "All I saw were headlights. Still, if someone came to the ranch without coming up to the house and talking to you . . ."

"It was probably somebody using the facilities," Joanna said. "People do it all the time, especially regulars who are stuck driving Highway Eighty on a weekly or monthly basis. It's a long pit-stop-free zone from Benson to, say, Rodeo, New Mexico. People will pull off the highway and then come up High Lonesome Road until they hit the dips. Figuring they're out of sight, they'll stop there to relieve themselves."

255

"Mom!" Jenny objected. "That's gross."

"It may be gross, but it happens," Joanna said. "I've seen them myself."

Butch shook his head. "In other words, I'm not supposed to worry about whether or not a crazed Reba Singleton was parked down by the mailbox because you think it was probably just some weak-bladdered guy who couldn't make it all the way from Bisbee to Douglas."

"Right," Joanna said, while Butch shook his head and rolled his eyes. Forty-five minutes later, dinner was over and cleared away. While Jenny and Butch settled down to play a game of dominoes in the breakfast nook, Joanna opened her briefcase and spread the contents out across the dining room table. Digging through the bale of paper, Joanna located Frank Montoya's file folder labeled "Ridder, Thomas Dawson."

The poor print quality on the faxed material made it difficult to read. There was no way for Joanna to tell which end of the process had the dying printer problem, but she suspected that if it was on the Cochise County Sheriff's Department's side of the equation, Frank Montoya probably had repaired it by now or was in the process of doing so.

Joanna read through the file's contents one page at a time. True to his nature, Frank had arranged the material in meticulous chronological order. The first item—a single piece of paper—contained a copy of Thomas Dawson Ridder's general discharge from the army. A separate document indicated he was being dismissed for cause, for behavior ill befitting an officer and a gentleman. Nowhere in the verbiage could Joanna find any indication that Ridder's ill behavior had to do with assaulting a superior officer. Joanna made a note to herself: "Ask Frank where he picked up info on the alleged assault."

Turning to a sheaf of copied newspaper clippings, Joanna discovered that the first newspaper account of the Thomas Ridder shooting incident was a small three-inch article in the *Tucson Daily Sun* that reported an unidentified male had been shot to death in his home on East Seventeenth Street in Tucson's downtown area. It added that detectives from the Tucson Police Department were investigating the shooting as either the interruption of a robbery in progress or possibly as a domestic-violence incident.

That kind of surface-only reporting was typical of newspaper accounts that are written immediately after fatality incidents and before officials have an opportunity to notify next of kin. The second article was a more in-depth piece in which the reporter revealed the full names of both victim and alleged assailant.

The article recounted that at the time of Sandra Christina Ridder's surrender and subsequent arrest, she had made a complete confession to investigators, saying that she had shot her husband in an effort to ward off another violent attack. Afterward, she had picked up her young daughter from a ballet class downtown and then had driven around for hours trying to come to terms with what she had done and also trying to decide what to do next. After disposing of the murder weapon at an undisclosed location, Sandra Ridder had finally contacted a friend, an attorney, who convinced her she should turn herself in to the authorities.

Toward the end of the article was a paragraph that answered one of the questions Joanna had planned to ask Frank:

Thomas Dawson Ridder, a self-employed landscape gardener, had recently been dismissed from the army, where he had served as Staff Sergeant with STRATCom at Fort Huachuca. He was brought up on charges for assaulting an

unnamed superior officer. Rather than face court-martial in
that incident, Ridder accepted a general discharge, left the
army, and moved with his wife and young child to Tucson.

While the child's mother is being held without bond in
the Pima County jail and with her father deceased, the Department of Child Protective Services has taken steps to remove the minor child from the family home. She has been
placed in the care of relatives.

Joanna stared at the end of the article for a long time after
she finished reading it. She went back into the text of the article and underlined the word "weapon." Then she made a
note in the margin. "Was this missing weapon ever found? Is
that maybe what was hidden in the Tupperware bowl?"
Then, as soon as Joanna wrote that comment, she had another thought.

*If Sandra Ridder drove all the way to Cochise Strong-
hold the night of the murder,* Joanna wondered, *if she knew
she was going to be arrested, why didn't she drop Lucy off
at Catherine Yates' nearby house right then, instead of
taking the child back to Tucson with her? Why had she put
her daughter in a position where she would have to be
shuffled around by a bunch of bureaucracy-wielding
strangers?*

If Joanna hadn't been a mother herself, she might not
have considered that question, but it was one she wished
she'd had a chance to ask Sandra Ridder in person. And she
hadn't been able to ask that question of Sandra's attorney,
Melanie Goodson, either. There was still one person she
might ask—Sandra's mother, Catherine Yates. After mulling
the idea for a few moments, Joanna dismissed that one as
well. It seemed unlikely to her that Sandra's mother would
have any more of an idea about the whys and wherefores of

her daughter's behavior than Eleanor Lathrop Winfield did about Joanna's.

The next article was a short one that recounted the plea-bargain hearing. In it Sandra admitted that some of the injuries she suffered that night had been self-inflicted. That, although she claimed her husband had beaten her on other unreported occasions, on the night in question he had not. She had shot him as he sat in his chair in front of the television news and then had staged the ransacking of the house and her own injuries in order to be able to establish a claim of self-defense.

In making his decision, the judge said that based on Sandra Ridder's account of self-inflicted injuries, he agreed with the prosecutor in disallowing any claim of self-defense. However, in view of Tom Ridder's known violent tendencies, the judge did find some mitigating circumstances. As a consequence, his judgment of voluntary manslaughter was one full step down from the prosecutor's previously arranged plea bargain of second-degree murder.

Studying that article, Joanna realized that one of the standard newspeak phrases was missing from the references to Melanie Goodson. Nowhere in that article or in any of the others was there any mention that Melanie Goodson was Sandra Ridder's "court-appointed" attorney. That meant that Melanie Goodson had taken on Sandra Ridder's case on a fee basis.

Joanna jotted down another note to herself. "Who paid Melanie Goodson's fee? Sandra's mother???"

The whole while Joanna had been working, Sadie and Tigger had been sprawled comfortably in the cave beneath the table. Now, acting in unison, the two dogs scrambled to their feet. Shoulder to shoulder, they dashed from the dining room into the living room, where they stood side by side, barking frantically at the front door.

As Joanna followed the dogs to the door, she remembered Butch's concern about the unidentified car that had been lurking at the entrance to High Lonesome Ranch. She looked out in time to see a pair of headlights pull up and stop at the gate. *Whoever it is doesn't know us very well,* Joanna thought. *If they did, they'd be coming to the back door instead of the front.*

"Who is it, Mom?" Jenny called from the kitchen.

Peering out between the window blinds, Joanna couldn't tell. The vehicle hadn't come far enough into the yard to trigger the motion-activated yard light located on the side of the garage. Feeling vulnerable and besieged, Joanna wished for the comforting presence of either one of her Glocks, but those were both under lock and key in her bedroom.

"Joey?" Butch asked. "Do you want me to go out and check?"

Before Joanna could answer, the car door swung open. In the dim illumination of the dome light, she caught a glimpse of Kristin Marsten's cloud of blond hair as she climbed out of her Geo.

Almost sick with relief, Joanna turned back to Butch and Jenny. "It's Kristin," she said. "From work. If you'll take these two barking dogs into the kitchen, I'll let her in."

As Jenny and Butch collected the dogs, Joanna opened the door in time to see Kristin stumbling forward. She fumbled with the gate latch. Once inside the gate, she staggered up the walkway and onto the porch looking for all the world as though she was drunk.

"Kristin!" Joanna exclaimed, stepping onto the porch. "What are you doing here? Is something wrong?"

Without a word, Kristin propelled herself across the porch. Sobbing, she fell against Joanna with such force that they both crashed into the wall.

"Kristin," Joanna insisted. "Tell me. What's happened?"

"My parents threw me out," Kristin wailed. "My father told me to get out, that he didn't want a daughter like me living in his house. He said that I had fifteen minutes to gather up what I needed and then he wanted me to clear out."

Joanna was horrified. "What did your mother say?" she asked.

"Nothing. She sat there the whole time and listened to Dad yell at me, and she never said a word. Not a single word. I didn't know where to go, Sheriff Brady. I couldn't go see Terry, not like this. He already feels bad enough. So I came here. What am I going to do? What's going to happen to me? Where am I going to stay?"

Joanna patted the younger woman's heaving shoulder. "Come on inside," she said. "It's cold out here. You're shivering. I'll fix you something warm to drink, and we'll try to decide what to do."

"Joanna," Butch said from just inside the door. "What's wrong? Is there anything I can do to help?"

Kristin had taken a step toward the door. Now, hearing another voice, she broke away from Joanna's hand and darted back across the porch. "I'm so embarrassed. I didn't know you had company. I don't want anyone else to know about this. I'll just leave," she insisted. "I'll go somewhere else."

Joanna reached out and captured one of Kristin's flailing hands. "No, you won't," Joanna said. "It's only Butch. You've met him, and I promise you he won't bite. Be sensible, Kristin. Come on in now, please."

"But I don't want him to *know*," Kristin pleaded. "I don't want *anyone* to know. But now everybody will. Who knows what they'll think. And say." Once again she burst into incoherent sobs.

"Please, Kristin. It doesn't matter what anyone says or thinks," Joanna said calmly. "This is your business and Terry's and nobody else's. That includes your parents. Come on. Let's get you inside and warmed up so we can talk things over and decide what to do. You said your father gave you fifteen minutes to pack. Do you have luggage along?"

Still sobbing, Kristin nodded. "It's in the car."

"Butch," Joanna called. "Kristin's going to spend the night. Would you mind bringing her luggage in from the car? Put it in Jenny's room."

"Oh, not Jenny's room. I couldn't do that," Kristin hiccuped as Butch walked past her on his way to the Geo. "Couldn't I sleep on a couch or something? I don't want to put anyone out . . ."

"Nonsense," Joanna said, bodily pulling her over the threshold and into the living room. "It's all right. Jenny won't mind." As Joanna guided Kristin toward the couch, she called to her daughter. "Jenny, where are you?"

"Right here."

"Go to your room and gather up whatever you'll need for tonight, and for tomorrow morning as well. Kristin's going to need to use your room tonight. You can sleep here on the couch. And as soon as Butch finishes bringing in the luggage, I'd like both of you to go to the kitchen and make some cocoa. I think Kristin needs some privacy."

Joanna was grateful when Jenny did as she was told without so much as rolling her eyes or asking a single question. Once Jenny and Butch had retreated to the kitchen and closed the door, Joanna turned back to Kristin, who had managed to stop weeping by then and was noisily blowing her nose.

"I never thought they'd throw me out," she choked miserably. "I always thought my parents loved me."

"They do love you," Joanna said. "They're just hurt is all."

"It's not like I'm a seventeen-year-old kid," Kristin continued. "I'm an adult. Even if I live at home. I have a job. Ever since I graduated from high school, my dad's made me pay room and board. You should have heard some of the awful things he said to me, some of the terrible names he called me." Kristin stopped and shook her head as another deluge of tears threatened to fall.

Joanna reached out and took Kristin's hand. "You're going to have to forgive your parents," she said softly. "Both your mother and your dad."

"Forgive them," Kristin echoed. "Why should I? My father's the one who called me a slut! He said I was no better than a common . . ." She faltered to a stop again, unable to continue.

"It doesn't matter what your father called you," Joanna said. "Forget about it. And it doesn't matter what he thinks of you, either. This has far more to do with you and Terry than it does with either one of your parents. Have either of you changed your mind about what we discussed this morning?"

Kristin shook her head, tossing her wild tangle of blond hair around her tear-ravaged face. "Just like you suggested, we made an appointment to talk to Reverend Maculyea," she said. "But the soonest she can see us together is tomorrow afternoon after work."

"But you and Terry still want to get married?"

"Yes. Terry offered to come home with me to talk to my folks so I wouldn't have to do it alone. He wanted to ask my father for my hand in marriage. Now I'm glad he didn't. My father probably would have taken after him with a baseball bat."

"Does Terry know where you are right now?" Joanna asked.

Kristin shook her head. "No," she whispered.

Taking the telephone from its cradle, Joanna passed the handset to Kristin. "Call him," she said. "Let Terry know where you are. That way he won't call your house and antagonize your parents any more than they already are. That way, too, in case he already has called your house, he won't have to worry about where you've gone. In the meantime, I'll give you some privacy. I'll go to the kitchen and see how that cocoa is coming."

Joanna started to walk away, but Kristin reached out and stopped her. "You're sure it's all right if I stay here tonight? You're sure you don't mind?"

"Yes, I'm sure," Joanna replied with a rueful smile. "After all, it's my fault. If you hadn't been following my advice about telling your parents what was going on, they still wouldn't know anything about it, so you'd still have a place to spend the night."

Leaving Kristin alone, Joanna headed for the kitchen. There she found Butch and Jenny standing at the stove peering into a pan of made but not yet steaming cocoa. "What's going on?" Butch asked.

"Kristin's having a little disagreement with her parents," Joanna explained. "She lives with them, and they asked her to leave the house tonight."

"That sounds like a big disagreement to me," Jenny said. "What's it all about?"

"It's private, Jenny," Joanna said after a moment's thought. "If Kristin wants to tell you, that's up to her, but you're not to ask—not under any circumstances. Is that clear?"

Jenny nodded and sighed. "Is it because I'm too young?" she asked.

"It's because it's nobody's business but Kristin's," Joanna replied. "Now, how about that cocoa? Is it almost ready?"

"Coming up," Butch said. "Jenny, get out the mugs, would you? I'll pour. We'll let your mother serve."

Minutes later, Joanna returned to the living room taking two cups of cocoa and leaving Butch, Jenny, and the two dogs still confined to quarters in the kitchen. Kristin was just hanging up the phone.

"You talked to Terry?" Joanna asked.

Kristin nodded. "You were right. He had already called the house, talked to my father—or had been yelled at by my father—and he was worried sick. He wanted to come right over, but I told him not to. That I was fine and that I was going to stay here overnight. I told him I'd meet him for breakfast in the morning—before work."

She took the cup of cocoa Joanna offered her, tasted it tentatively, and then set it down on the end table. "Is it true that the same thing happened to you and Deputy Brady? Or did you just say that to Terry and me this morning to make us feel better?"

"No," Joanna said. "It really did happen."

"And what did your parents do?"

"My father was already dead."

"And your mother?"

"She was upset," Joanna admitted. "She was actually very upset."

"And how long did it take her to get over it?"

"Never," Joanna said.

Kristin's eyes widened. "Never? You mean she's still mad about it?"

Joanna nodded.

"But you seem to get along all right," Kristin objected. "I

mean, your mother calls and talks to you. I saw her at the shower on Sunday. She seemed to be having a good time."

"We get along all right now," Joanna said. "About as well as we've ever gotten along, but that one issue is always between us. We hardly ever talk about it, but it's still there. That's probably how it will be with your father, too. Eventually he won't be so angry. In fact, once the baby's born and he's a grandfather, your dad will probably come around. But things have changed between you and him, Kristin. Your father is used to always having the last word. Now he's come up against a situation where you're making your own decisions without consulting him and without doing things the way he wants you to, either. He's just now learning the hard lesson that he's going to have to let you go, and he doesn't like it."

"You make it sound like an ordinary part of growing up."

"It is an ordinary part of growing up," Joanna said. "Being pregnant is a complicating factor, but it's not the only one. This may seem to be a big deal to your parents, but in the larger scheme of things, it's not important. You and Terry love each other. You're going to get married and raise this child together. That's what's important. That's *all* that's important."

Once again Kristin's blue eyes brimmed with tears. "When you first came to the department, Sheriff Brady, I didn't like you very much," she admitted after a moment. "I'm sorry I made things so tough for you."

Joanna smiled. "I didn't like you very much, either. I think we both felt threatened, and now we're over it."

"The same way my parents may get over this?"

"Exactly the same way," Joanna replied. "Just give them time."

By the time Kristin finished drinking her cocoa, Joanna

could see that the day's emotional upheaval had taken its
toll. "Go to bed, now," she said. "The bathroom's that way.
We have only one, so we'll all have to take turns. Once you
have a decent night's rest, you're going to see the world
through much different eyes. I have a feeling you haven't
been sleeping very well the last few nights. There's nothing
like tossing and turning to wear a person down."

"How did you know that?" Kristin asked.

"Believe me," Joanna replied, "it was more than a lucky
guess."

Once Kristin had retreated to Jenny's room and while
Jenny was in the bathroom getting ready for bed, Joanna
walked Butch out to his car.

"I couldn't help overhearing what she said to you on the
porch. How pregnant is she?"

"Just barely," Joanna said. "But remember, there's no
such thing as slightly pregnant. You either are or you aren't."

"If her parents threw her out, what kind of people are
they?"

"Fallible people," Joanna answered. "People who are
doing the best they can. They're like parents everywhere—
wanting what's best for their children and being upset when
results come short of the mark."

"Wait a minute," Butch said. "Are we talking about
Kristin Marsten's parents, or are we talking about some
other parents I could name?"

"All parents," Joanna said after a moment. "Your mother
and my mother included."

"No! You can't mean it."

Joanna reached up and kissed him. "But I do mean it,"
she said. "Maybe after all this time I'm finally growing up,
too. Now good night. Drive carefully."

Back in the house, Joanna hurried to clear the dining

room table of paperwork before Jenny emerged from the bathroom. By the time a pajama-clad Jenny headed toward the couch, Joanna had refilled the briefcase and snapped it shut.

"Mom," Jenny said, as Joanna stopped with her finger on the light switch.

"What?"

"Will you ever get so mad at me that you'll kick me out of the house?"

"I don't think so."

"Well, Kristin must have done something really awful for her parents to get that mad at her."

"It wasn't so very awful," Joanna replied. "And it's something a lot of people have done before her—your mother included."

"Really? Whatever it is, you did it, too?"

"Yes. Good night, now. I told you it was none of your business."

"Good night."

Thoughtfully, Joanna went into her own bedroom and undressed. When she first lay down on the bed, she thought she would have a hard time falling asleep. But she didn't. In fact, she fell asleep sooner that night than any night in recent memory.

Maybe it was because on that night she went to bed knowing that one way or the other, the long warfare with Eleanor Lathrop Winfield might finally be coming to an end. Well, maybe not a complete end, but at least Joanna could see the possibility of a truce.

# TWENTY

Joanna's eyes popped open with the sun, and her first thought on waking was, *Three days to go.* Most of the time she was able to compartmentalize her life enough that the wedding didn't overwhelm her, but that morning it all seemed to be too much. No matter how hard she tried, she'd never get everything caught up at work. And the same was true at home. She'd never have the house in the kind of shape she wanted it to be in before Jim Bob and Eva Lou came to stay for a week to look after Jenny and the ranch while Joanna and Butch went off on their honeymoon.

And where were they going on their honeymoon anyway? Butch knew because he had made all the plans, but other than telling her she needed to have her passport in order, he had told Joanna nothing. Their destination remained top secret.

"But what kind of clothes am I supposed to pack?" she had asked.

"Minimal," he had replied.

"What does that mean? Beachwear? What?"

He had shrugged. "Not beachwear," he had said at last, relenting. "But again, I'd bring along as little as possible."

By the time Joanna arrived in the kitchen, someone—Kristin, it turned out—was already in the shower. Joanna

269

went out to feed and water the animals. When she had finished her chores and came inside, Kristin was already dressed for work.

"I'm on my way to meet Terry for breakfast," she said. "I told him we'd better go early so neither one of us will be late for work."

"Good," Joanna said. "Are you feeling better this morning?"

"Much. I really did get a decent night's sleep for a change."

"And no morning sickness?" Joanna asked, thinking about the dreadful bouts of morning sickness that had almost hospitalized Marianne Maculyea during the early stages of her pregnancy.

"None."

"You're lucky then."

A momentary shadow crossed Kristin's face. "Right now, I don't really feel very lucky," she said.

"Well," Joanna said. "You'll just have to take my word for it."

The extra shower had taxed Joanna's aging hot-water heater. By the time Jenny emerged from the bathroom, Joanna had to settle for a very quick and barely lukewarm shower. On the way to work, Jenny seemed subdued.

"What's wrong?" Joanna asked.

"Is it going to be very different?" Jenny asked.

"You mean after Butch and I get married?"

Jenny nodded.

"It'll be different for all of us," Joanna replied. "We'll all have to learn to practice patience. Are you worried about it?"

"A little," Jenny admitted.

"How come?"

"Last night when I went to bed, I thought about Kristin's

parents—about them throwing her out. I know you said you wouldn't ever get so mad that you'd kick me out, but it could happen. What if you ended up loving Butch more than you love me? What if you had to choose?"

"Fortunately, I don't think that's something either one of us will have to worry about." By then they had pulled up at the gates of Lowell School. "Go now," Joanna urged. "Have a good day."

Jenny made no effort to move or even open the door. "Where do I go after school?" she asked.

Joanna frowned. "I'm not sure. I don't remember what Butch's plans are for today. I think you're supposed to go to his place, but if it turns out he's busy with his folks, we may have to make some other arrangement."

"See there?" Jenny asked, screwing up her face to keep from crying. "It's already happening."

"What's already happening?"

"You're not even married yet and you're already forgetting about me. You can't even remember who's supposed to take care of me after school!"

Joanna shook her head. This was the same eleven-, almost twelve-year-old daughter who was always insisting that she should be treated as though she were several years older than her chronological age. And yet, when the chips were down and when Joanna could have used a real almost-teenager, she found herself dealing with a child who had suddenly regressed to a petulant seven or eight.

"Go to Butch's," Joanna said. "If that's not going to work for some reason, I'll call the principal's office and have them send you a note."

Jenny shook her head, climbed out of the car, slammed the door behind her, and then trudged off through the school gate with her head down and shoulders slumped. She looked so sad, hurt, and alone that Joanna's heart ached for her. She wanted to leave the Blazer where it was, run after her daughter, and hold Jenny close in a reassuring hug, which Jenny probably wouldn't have wanted either—not there in front of the school where all her classmates could see. Besides, a glance at her watch said there was no time for that. There was no time either to steal a brief visit with Butch in his remodeled Victorian a bare three blocks from Jenny's school. Needing to hear his voice, Joanna called instead.

"So how's the bride on three days and counting?" Butch asked cheerfully.

"Medium," Joanna replied. "Jenny's gone all teary and insecure on me. And it didn't help matters that I couldn't remember whether or not you were going to take care of her after school."

"Let me look at the Gantt chart on my computer for a minute."

"Gantt chart?" Joanna demanded. "What's that?"

"You might call it a flowchart. It's a graphical project timeline. I downloaded it into my computer from the Internet. It's for keeping track of projects. It helps you make sure that all available resources are allocated properly. Since you put me in charge of logistics for this wedding, I live and die by my Gantt chart.

"Let's see. Your brother and sister-in-law fly in from D.C. this afternoon. Your mother will meet them at the airport, and then they're scheduled to have dinner with the Winfields. My folks want to take us out to eat tonight. It'll just be the five of us—you, Jenny, me, and the two of them. We'll probably go somewhere here in town. Mother had heard about the Copper Queen and wanted to eat there. I told her that would be fine.

"Tomorrow night will be the whole group of out-oftowners—sort of a pre-rehearsal-dinner dinner. I'm voting for pizza for that one—probably out at your place, since you have more room than I do. Friday's the real rehearsal dinner and—"

"Stop," Joanna interrupted. "It's too much. Let's just stick to one day at a time. All I want to know is yes or no— are you taking care of Jenny after school today?"

"Yes."

"Good. Let's leave it at that. You can tell me everything else I need to know from the whatever-the-hell-it-is chart when I need to know it."

"Gantt chart," he repeated. "With two *t*'s. But are you okay?" he asked after a pause. "You sound stressed."

I am stressed! she wanted to shout at him. *I'm stressed beyond bearing!*

"I'm all right," she answered carefully. "And I'm sure Jenny will be relieved to have a little bit of ordinariness back in her life for today at least."

"You're sure you're not mad at me or anything, are you?" Butch asked.

"I'm not mad, but I am on my way to work. I'm about to be late, and I'm worried about how I'll ever get caught up enough to be gone for a whole week. Do we have to stay away that long? Couldn't we come back a day or two early—maybe in time for Jenny's birthday?"

"No, we can't, Joanna. Definitely negative on that. I've talked it over with Jenny, and she's cool about us missing her actual birthday. Not only that, as your newly designated husband, I'm making it my first priority to see to it that you don't work yourself into an early grave. I'm going to start by insisting that you actually take your vacation time as vacation. Working vacations like sheriffs'-conference trips don't count."

"All right," she said. "If you're going to insist on taking care of me, the least I can do is stop griping about it."

"Good decision," he said.

Joanna made it to her desk right at eight, but when no one showed up for the morning briefing, she gathered up a collection of files and went searching for Frank Montoya and her two detectives. In the reception room outside Joanna's office, Kristin was at her desk and sorting mail when Joanna walked in. "Where is everybody?" she asked.

"The conference room," Kristin replied. "Chief Deputy Montoya said that since the Double Cs are coming, the conference room would be a better fit for the briefing than your office."

Joanna grabbed a cup of coffee on her way past the corner pot and then hurried into the conference room in time to hear Frank Montoya say, "We'll have to leave that up to Sheriff Brady."

"What are you leaving up to me?" she asked.

"Contacting Bill Forsythe, the new sheriff up in Pima County," Detective Carpenter replied. "If we're going to have any kind of information sharing on Melanie Goodson's death, OD or otherwise, we're going to have to let them know what we're up against on our end. What's more, the only way it's going to happen is from the top down, because it sure as hell isn't going to happen from the bottom up."

"I'll work on it as soon as we finish up here," Joanna said. "Now, what else have I missed?"

"Nothing much," Frank replied. "We were just sitting around jawing and waiting for you to show up."

Joanna took her place at the head of the table. The morning's stack of incident reports sat in front of her. She moved that aside in favor of Frank Montoya's Thomas Ridder file, which she had carried into the conference room along with her coffee cup.

"All right, gentlemen. Where do we stand on the Ridder murders, assuming of course that Melanie Goodson *is* connected? I'm guessing we still haven't found any trace of Lucy?"

Frank shook his head. "Other than her busted-up bicycle, no. S and R, along with Terry Gregovich and Spike, spent all day yesterday combing the rest area and the adjoining part of Texas Canyon. In the hills above the rest area they found a spot where it looked as though she might have camped out for a day or so. Then they followed a trail down as far as the highway, where it disappeared. S and R offered to go back out there today, but I told them not to bother. My guess is she's long gone."

"She got into a vehicle," Joanna suggested.

"Presumably, yes."

"What about the bird? Didn't Catherine Yates tell us that Big Red wouldn't be caught dead riding in a car?"

Frank nodded. "She did say that," he agreed. "But maybe Big Red is dead. After all, things do happen to hawks, especially around busy highways. And it's not what he's used to. Interstate Ten is a whole lot busier than the roads that lead to Cochise Stronghold."

Nodding, Joanna turned to her detectives. "What's happening up in Tucson?"

"I called Santa Theresa's first thing this morning to see when we could make an appointment to see Sister Celeste," Jaime Carbajal put in. "The lady who answered the phone told me she won't be in all day today, either. I should try calling back tomorrow."

"Sounds to me like you're getting the runaround," Joanna said.

"Sounds like it to me, too," Jaime replied. "I tried asking if maybe she was attending a meeting somewhere, thinking we might be able to catch up with her at lunchtime, wherever she is, but the secretary clammed up on me and said I'd have to talk to her once she returns."

"Great," Joanna sighed. "Now what about the Pima County detectives working the Melanie Goodson case?"

Ernie Carpenter shrugged. When he frowned, his eyebrows seemed to come together, forming a solid caterpillar of hair across his broad forehead. "What about them? Like I said before, they're not going to give us the time of day unless a specific order comes down to them from upstairs, preferably one signed in God's own handwriting."

Joanna scribbled Bill Forsythe's name on the top line of her day's to-do list. "I'll get right on it," she said. "Any information about when the Goodson autopsy will be completed?" she continued.

"Preliminary results today," Ernie said, consulting his own notes. "But it's going to boil down to toxicology reports, so you know that's going to take time—a week or so, most likely."

"Frank, what about you?" Joanna asked. "Do you have anything to add?"

"Fortunately, our working relationship with the City of Tucson PD is a little less troubled than our dealings are with Pima County," Frank answered. "Consequently, I did manage to lay hands on a copy of the original case file for the Thomas Ridder shooting."

"Complete with ballistics reports?" Joanna asked.

"Yes," Frank said. "I think so."

"Does it say what size bullet killed him?"

Montoya opened the thick file and thumbed through several pages before stopping to peruse one in particular. "Here it is," he said. "Says here he died of a twenty-two-caliber bullet wound. The slug hit him in the heart, killing him instantly."

"Was the weapon ever recovered?" Joanna asked.

Once again Frank consulted the file. "Not that it says here; why?"

"How soon can we get a ballistics report back from the DPS gun lab on the bullet that killed Sandra Ridder?"

"Today, probably, if I call up and ask them to rush it. But what's going on?"

"What if the murder weapon is what was hidden in Sandra Ridder's Tupperware bowl all this time?" Joanna asked. "All along I've been thinking that Sandra Ridder may have been killed with the gun Lucy lifted from her grandmother's place. But what if that isn't the case? What if she was killed with the same gun she used to shoot her husband years ago?"

"I'll call up to Tucson and check as soon as we finish up with this meeting."

"Would a twenty-two fit in that Tupperware container?" Jaime Carbajal asked.

"Sure," Frank said. "One of those little featherweights would fit in a minute."

Joanna turned to her detectives. "Ernie, what are you and Jaime doing today?"

"Paper, mostly. Then, if you can clear us to talk to those Pima County guys, I'd like to be able to shadow their investigation as closely as possible. Sandra Ridder's funeral is scheduled for this afternoon at two over in Pearce. I don't see any reason for both of us to go, so Jaime's going to handle that."

Joanna looked at the younger detective. "And here's something else you can take care of at the same time. I've gone through all the Tom Ridder material Frank gave me yesterday. Nowhere does it refer to Melanie Goodson as being Sandra Ridder's court-appointed attorney."

"Somebody paid the bill," Jaime said at once.

"Right," Joanna returned. "Since you'll be at the funeral, maybe you can ask Catherine Yates if she's the one who paid Melanie Goodson's fee. If it was somebody other than Sandra's mother, let's find out who that person was."

"Will do," Jaime said.

Joanna directed her next request to Detective Carpenter. "Ernie, you're the one with contacts out at Fort Huachuca. I want to know more about Thomas Ridder's dismissal from the army. He evidently punched out a superior officer, but that officer is never once mentioned by name. I want to know who he was and what the beef was all about."

"I'll see what I can do. Anything else?"

"Yes, there is one more thing. As you know, I'll be gone all next week. I'm going to expect you to give Chief Deputy Montoya here your utmost cooperation. With any kind of luck, things will stay pretty quiet, but we all remember what happened last summer as soon as Doc Winfield left town on *his* honeymoon."

"We'll keep things under control, Sheriff Brady," Ernie Carpenter assured her, standing up. "Don't worry about a thing."

The two detectives were almost to the door when Joanna called Jaime Carbajal back. "What happened at Pepe's game last night?" she asked.

A wide grin suffused her young detective's face. "I made it to the field in time for the last two innings, including Pepe's third home run of the season."

"And Delcia didn't kill you?"

"Not yet," Jaime answered, "but there's another game tonight."

"Get out of here," Joanna said.

Once the two detectives were gone, Joanna and her chief deputy turned their attention to the stack of incident reports. Forty-five minutes later, Joanna was back in her office and dialing Sheriff Bill Forsythe's number up in Pima County.

"What can I do for you, Sheriff Brady?" he asked.

"We have a murder down here in Cochise County with possible links to one of yours—the Melanie Goodson death out on South Old Spanish Trail."

"What kind of links?"

"One of Melanie Goodson's neighbors saw her driving her Lexus with another woman in the vehicle. Two hours later, our homicide victim was spotted with that same Lexus near a campground in the Dragoon Mountains down here in Cochise County. The next morning, Melanie Goodson called your office and reported the Lexus stolen, even though she herself was the last person seen driving it." Joanna paused for breath. "It seems to me that, based on all that, there should be enough connections to justify the sharing of information."

"That remains to be seen." Bill Forsythe replied. "I take it the officers in question are the same ones who were making nuisances of themselves out at our crime scene yesterday afternoon?"

"My detectives were doing their jobs," Joanna answered evenly. "They were asking questions. They had an early-afternoon appointment to speak with Melanie Goodson at her office. When she stood them up, it was for the very good reason that she was dead. Wouldn't you find that a coincidence worthy of asking questions, one of which has to be: 'Who didn't want Melanie talking to my investigators?' "

"Give me the name of the neighbor who talked to your guys," Forsythe said. "The one who claimed to have seen Melanie Goodson driving her car. Once my dicks talk to him or her, I'll see what I can do."

"What you're saying is, none of your 'dicks,' as you call them, have yet spoken to Melanie Goodson's neighbors."

"We're still very early in the investigation—"

"Can it, Sheriff Forsythe. You want your department to piggyback on my detectives' work and then you may or may not decide to share information with us. Is that what you're saying?"

"Not in so many words."

"The hell it isn't."

"Sheriff Brady, you don't have to get hysterical about it."

Hysterical? The word buzzed in Joanna's ear like an angry wasp.

Her voice dropped to the bare whisper that people who knew Joanna Brady well also knew as a warning to duck for cover. "Believe me, Sheriff Forsythe," she told him icily, "I'm a long way from hysterical. I am pointing out, however, that our two departments have a long-standing mutual-aid agreement—one that predates your election, and mine as well. I expect both of our departments to live up to the terms of that agreement."

"Right," Sheriff Bill Forsythe responded. "When pigs fly!" With that he slammed the receiver down in her ear.

A stunned Joanna Brady was still sitting with the phone in her hand when Kristin came into her office moments later carrying that day's stack of mail.

"Sorry," she said. "I didn't realize you were still on the phone."

"I'm not. That rotten SOB hung up on me. He had the gall to say I was hysterical. Do you believe it?"

"Well," said Kristin guardedly, "you do look a tiny bit upset—"

"Upset?" Joanna repeated, as flame rose in her cheeks. "I'll say I'm upset! First I'm going to solve these two

damned cases—his and mine both—with no help from him
or from those arrogant jerks he mistakenly calls detectives.
And then, after that—"

Joanna paused in mid-sentence while a faraway look
crossed her face and a slight smile curved her lips.

"What now?" Kristin asked. "What's so funny?"

"This," Joanna replied. "When Butch and I go to that Arizona Sheriffs' Conference meeting in Page the last week in
May, maybe I can lure Sheriff Bill Forsythe into a late-night
poker game and whip his ass."

"You can do that?" Kristin stared at Joanna in wide-eyed
amazement. "I didn't know you knew how to play poker."

"Neither does Sheriff Bill Forsythe," Joanna said grimly.
"But with any kind of luck, the man's sure as hell going to
find out."

An hour later, at lunch with Butch, Joanna told him about
the personality clash with her neighboring sheriff. "So basi-
cally, you're mad because you regard yourself as a woman
scorned," Butch philosophized. "Professionally scorned, but
scorned nonetheless."

"Forsythe wouldn't have talked to me that way if I were
a man," Joanna declared. "Men get mad; women get hysterical. Men are aggressive; women are pushy."

"Isn't there a chance you're being overly sensitive about
this?"

Joanna thought about it. "Maybe," she finally admitted
reluctantly, "but what do you suggest I do?"

Butch shrugged. "Seems to me like you already have a
handle on that." He grinned back at her. "Solve the two murders and then whip Forsythe's ass at poker. What could be
better than that?"

"Nothing," she replied. "Nothing at all."

TWENTY-ONE

Joanna was back from lunch and hard at work early that afternoon when Frank popped his head in her office. "What's happening?" she asked.

"Nothing much." Frank shut the door and came on into the office, settling into one of the chairs. "I faxed what information we had on the Tom Ridder murder weapon to the Department of Public Safety firearms expert at the lab up in Tucson. I just now got off the phone with the guy."

"What did he say?"

"That it's possible to get a match, but he won't be able to tell for sure unless he can put both bullets under the microscope."

"What are the chances of that happening?" Joanna asked.

Frank Montoya shrugged. "That depends on whether or not Tucson PD kept a bullet from that long ago. And, if the bullet does exist, stashed away in their evidence room, it further depends on whether or not anyone can lay hands on it for us in a timely fashion. I have someone up there looking for it, but she wasn't very encouraging. She said she'd get back to me, but she wanted to know if I understood that working on a closed ten-year-old case takes a backseat to working on something current. I tried convincing her that ours *is* a current case, but I don't know how successful I was. We'll have to wait and see."

He paused before continuing. "How'd you do with Bill Forsythe?" he added.

Joanna shook her head. "I don't want to talk about it," she said.

"That good," Frank mused.

"He wanted us to give him whatever we had, including the name and address of that neighbor of Melanie Goodson's, the one Jaime and Ernie talked to yesterday afternoon. Once we tell him everything we know, Forsythe will decide whether or not in his opinion we're worthy of having his department's cooperation."

"That's certainly big of him."

"Right," Joanna said. "That's what I thought. I guess we'll have to do this without him."

Just then Joanna's intercom buzzed. "Sheriff Brady," Kristin said. "There's someone out here to see you. Her name is Sister Celeste. I know she doesn't have an appointment, but she says she's driven down from Tucson to see you."

Joanna took her finger away from the intercom, muting her side of the conversation. "What do you think?" Joanna asked Frank.

"Is this the disappearing nun the Double Cs have been trying to make an appointment with for at least two days?" Frank asked.

Joanna nodded. "She's the one."

"How about if I scoot out the back door," Frank suggested, nodding toward Joanna's private entrance. "That way you can see her alone."

"That's not necessary, Frank," Joanna said. "Stay. We'll hear what she has to say together."

Seconds later, Kristin opened the door and ushered a tall, spare, horse-faced woman into the room. Wearing jeans, sweatshirt, and hiking boots, the woman looked as though she might have been an extremely physically fit phys-ed teacher in her late fifties or early sixties. She held out a strong, lean-fingered hand and shook Joanna's, pumping it forcefully.

"Sheriff Brady," she announced. "As your secretary told you, I'm Sister Celeste. I'm afraid I was a bit abrupt with you on the phone the other day, and I apologize. I was on my way into a faculty meeting that afternoon, and I didn't want to be late. But the truth is, in addition to being late, I also didn't want to speak to you right then."

"This is Frank Montoya, my chief deputy," Joanna said, motioning toward the chairs. "Won't you have a seat?"

Sister Celeste smiled. "I suppose when you heard a nun was outside, you expected someone in a habit. I do wear mine at work during the school week, but now that habits are optional, the rest of the nuns at Santa Theresa's and I have taken to having dress-down days occasionally. Sort of like casual-dress Fridays in the rest of the world. And the truth is, there are times when jeans and sweatshirts make a lot more sense."

"Yes, there are," Joanna agreed.

Sister Celeste appeared to be on edge about something, and Joanna was content to let her babble on about the weather and what a nice drive she had had without further interruption. Finally, pausing in the middle of her verbal torrent, the nun took a deep breath. "I suppose you'd like me to tell you why I'm here," she said.

Joanna nodded. "That would be helpful. I'm assuming it has something to do with Lucy Ridder's Saturday-morning phone call."

"Yes," Sister Celeste admitted. "Lucy did call me that morning."

"And you spoke to her for some time," Joanna prompted.

"That, too. About fifteen minutes or so, I'd say. She was very upset."

Perhaps she had just shot her mother, Joanna thought. "Where is Lucy now?" she asked.

"I know, but I can't say," Sister Celeste returned. "Or rather, I won't say. There's a difference."

Joanna's eyes narrowed. "Yes, there certainly is a difference. Sister Celeste, I must tell you that Lucy Ridder is wanted for questioning in regard to the death of her mother, Sandra Ridder. Are you aware that interfering with a homicide investigation and harboring a criminal are both serious felony offenses?"

Sister Celeste leaned back in her chair. "I am aware of that," she said. "It's a risk I'm willing to take."

"Why?"

Sister Celeste merely shrugged and said nothing.

"If you can't or won't say, why are you here?" Joanna demanded.

Sister Celeste leaned down and opened the large, satchel-like purse she had placed on the floor next to her chair. Rummaging through it, she pulled out a three-and-a-quarter-inch computer floppy disk. "I came to give you this," she said, handing the small blue diskette over to Joanna. "I'm hoping it will provide all of us with some much-needed answers."

"What's on it?" Joanna asked.

"I have no idea. According to Lucy, this is the reason her mother died. I tried looking at it myself on my computer at school, but it didn't work. I can see there are files. In fact, I tried using my disk utilities program on the thing. It told me that the disk is full, but I wasn't able to open any of the files, and I wasn't able to view them, either."

Joanna passed the disk along to Frank Montoya. "Mr. Montoya happens to be my department's resident nerd," she said with a smile. "Do you mind if he tries taking a look at it?"

"Not at all," Sister Celeste said. "I hope he has better luck with it than I did."

Taking the disk, Frank left Joanna's office for his own, leaving the two women alone together. They sat in silence for the better part of a minute, regarding one another, each sizing up the other.

"Are you aware that Lucy's mother's funeral will be held this afternoon?" Joanna asked at last.

Sister Celeste nodded. "I knew about it and told her, but I don't believe Lucy has any interest in attending. She and her mother weren't especially close."

An all-time understatement, Joanna thought before asking her next question. "What about Catherine Yates? If nothing else, shouldn't Lucy go to the funeral for her grandmother's sake?"

"I think Lucy should do what Lucy thinks she should do," the nun replied coolly.

Joanna was sorry to see that Sister Celeste's initial case of nerves had obviously been put to rest. Sitting across from Joanna as silent and impassive as a carved Buddha, the nun seemed totally unperturbed. Another curtain of silence settled across the room.

"Are you aware Lucy Ridder is armed and possibly dangerous?" Joanna persisted eventually.

"I know she has a gun," Sister Celeste answered. "For protection."

"Protection from whom?" Joanna asked. "From my officers?"

"From the people who killed her mother," Sister Celeste returned.

At that juncture, Frank Montoya reentered Joanna's office. "It's encrypted," he said at once, spinning the flat disk across the smooth surface of the desk. Joanna caught it in midair before it had a chance to fall to the floor.

"I can't do anything with it," Frank continued. "But I'll bet I know of someone who can."

"Who?"

"I was talking to Rich Davis, one of the local POs the other day—"

"PO?" Sister Celeste asked. "What's that?"

"Probation officers," Frank explained. "Rich told me about one of his new parolees who was recently released from a federal prison up in Oregon. His name is Fred Woodworth. He was sent up for two years, having helped himself to other people's money by using the Internet to hack his way into their accounts. He's evidently quite an expert in his chosen field. If I remember correctly, he also broke into several Federal websites—places like the FBI, for instance, and military installations where they don't take kindly to unauthorized visitors. He got some time taken off his sentence by serving as an informant on a few of his former cyber pals."

"Great," Joanna said. "Sounds like a great guy. What's he doing here? How did Cochise County get to be so lucky that he ended up in our backyard?"

"He's taking art classes down at Cochise College," Frank said. "The Feds relocated him here because Bisbee is a long way from all his former known associates."

"Isn't that a little naive?" Joanna asked. "If he's a computer hacker, all his friends are just a point and click away. Physical distances mean nothing."

"True, but one of the conditions of his probation is that he's not allowed to own or have unsupervised access to a computer. But I'm guessing that if we showed him the files on this disk, he could give us some idea of what they contain even if he couldn't come straight out and decode them. On the other hand, if we wanted to dink around with this thing, I could probably go up to Tucson and find someone at the university who'd be willing to take a look at it. Depends on how much time you want it to take."

Even without Frank saying it aloud, Joanna knew exactly what he was thinking. There was every chance that the encrypted files on Sister Celeste's disk might be the key to unlocking everything that had happened. Sure, they could go through channels and pull in other people to help them on this. No doubt, Bill Forsythe would be thrilled to put his own stamp on the effort. But time was of the essence, and Sister Celeste hadn't brought the encrypted disk to Sheriff Bill Forsythe. For whatever reason, she had delivered it into the hands of Cochise County's Joanna Brady.

"What are you proposing, Frank?" she asked.

"That we give Rich Davis a call and have him bring Woodworth in right away to take a look at this stuff. That's all."

"If the parolee works with us on this, won't he be breaking the terms of his probation and running the risk of getting in trouble again?"

"The Feds weren't above using his computer talents when it suited their purposes," Frank replied. "And I believe the operant word here is 'unsupervised.' We'll have him look at the disk right here in the department on one of our own computers. Before he even touches the keyboard, I'll take the computer off-line and out of our intranet. He won't be able to do anything we don't let him do."

"Call Rich," Joanna said. "See what you can do."

Nodding, Frank left the office. Once again, Joanna and Sister Celeste sat facing each other across the shiny expanse of Joanna's polished desk. "What changed your mind?" Joanna asked.

"Excuse me?"

"The last time I talked to you, you weren't willing to give me the time of day," Joanna said. "Today you walked into my office with a ready apology. And, if you hadn't been prepared to trust me, I'm sure you never would have handed over that disk. What happened between then and now?"

"I talked to a friend of mine," Sister Celeste answered. "He spoke very highly of you."

"And his name is?" Joanna prompted.

"Please," Sister Celeste said. "Don't ask me that right now. First let's see what's on the disk. I'd really like to wait that long, if you don't mind. If it turns out to be what I think it is, I'll tell you everything I know."

"Including where to find Lucy Ridder?"

She nodded. "Most likely," she said.

Although Sister Celeste seemed prepared to sit quietly with her hands folded and wait indefinitely, Joanna was feeling the siren call of all the paperwork she had not yet completed. It struck her as impolite to work on it with someone sitting there watching, but she was too short on work time to squander any of it.

"Would you like anything?" Joanna asked in an effort to be polite and at the same time pry the woman out of her office. "We have coffee, water, sodas?"

"No," Sister Celeste returned. "Nothing. I'm fine. In fact, I'm glad to have the opportunity to chat with you for a few minutes. I remember when you were elected, Sheriff Brady," she added after a time. "It was all over the news up in Tucson. All the nuns at the convent were quite proud of you."

"Really. How could they be proud of me? They don't even know me."

Sister Celeste smiled. "Maybe not, but what they were

seeing was someone knock down another male-only barrier.
Some of our more liberal sisters see every change as a step
in the right direction. They're convinced that as one job after
another is made available to women, that it's inevitable the
priesthood will eventually follow."

"What do you think?" Joanna asked.

"I've been a nun for more than thirty-five years," Sister Celeste responded ruefully. "I'm lucky to have worked my way
up to be principal at the school where I've taught for twenty of
those thirty-five years. It's progress, I suppose, but very slow
progress. I'm afraid, when it comes to something as deeply en-
trenched as the priesthood, I don't see that kind of fundamen-
tal change happening in my lifetime. You're much younger
than I, and it probably won't happen in your lifetime, either."

Joanna's phone rang. When she heard Frank Montoya's
voice, she turned on the speaker so Sister Celeste could listen in as well. "We're in luck," he said. "Rich said Fred
Woodworth should be out of class by now and back home in
Upper Bisbee. Rich is going to go see him. If he can find
him, he'll try to bring him here to the office."

"You told Rich what we needed?" Joanna asked.

"Yes."

"What did he say?"

"Just what I thought. As long as it's done under supervi-
sion, he doesn't think having Fred use one of our computers
will be a problem."

"And what about Woodworth himself? Does Rich think
he'll go along with the idea?"

Frank laughed. "He says Freddy Boy misses his computers so much that he'll be thrilled to do anything in order to
lay hands on a keyboard again. That's how the FBI talked
him into working for them earlier, when he was locked up at
Club Fed."

Sister Celeste stood up as soon as Frank got off the phone. "Look," she said, "I can see you have work to do, and this could take time. Why don't I go outside and wait until your deputy's pet hacker gets here."

"Thanks," Joanna said gratefully. "That would be a big help."

It was another forty-five minutes before Kristin called in over the intercom once more to announce the arrival of Rich Davis and Fred Woodworth.

"Put them in the conference room, Kristin," Joanna told her. "And then let both Frank Montoya and Sister Celeste know they're here."

Joanna had met Rich Davis on several occasions. He was a beefy fifty-year-old with thick glasses and a vestigial sense of fashion. On that particular day he was wearing a bright red plaid flannel shirt along with a food-stained and not-quite-matching blue silk tie. The probation officer's young charge was a baby-faced twenty-five-year-old with a peach-fuzz goatee. He looked more like a high school student than an ex-con. Fred Woodworth wore his hair in musty dreadlocks. His T-shirt was shot full of holes, and his stained, raggedy jams looked as though the addition of a single ounce of weight to the pockets would send the pants plummeting around his bare bony ankles, which stuck out of worn emerald-green high-topped sneakers.

Woodworth barely glanced at the people ranged around the conference room table as they were introduced to him. Instead, he stared greedily—almost hungrily—at the laptop computer Frank had set down on the table nearby.

"Has Mr. Davis explained the situation to you?" Joanna asked once he was settled on a chair.

Fred nodded, but said nothing.

"You do know that even though you're cooperating with

us in this instance, we have no power to change the terms of your parole?" Joanna continued.

Fred nodded again. "Rich told me that. But, hey. What the hell? I'm glad to help." He glanced in Sister Celeste's direction. "Sorry about that, Sister," he said. "Please excuse my French."

She smiled. "That's all right," she told him.

"So can we get started?"

Frank switched on the computer and passed it to Fred. Frank did it so carefully, so gingerly, that he might have been a nervous first-time mother passing the care and keeping of her precious newborn into the hands of a baby-sitter she didn't quite trust. As for Fred Woodworth, when he put his fingers on the keys and began making a series of rapid-fire typed commands, the rapt look on his face was almost sexual in nature.

After several minutes, Fred asked if he could download a program from the Internet. Frank plugged in a PCI modem and plugged the other end into a wall receptacle. Then, with Frank logging on and doing the keyboarding, they took ten minutes to download a file. Only then, when the computer was disconnected from the Internet, did Frank once again give Fred Woodworth access to the keyboard.

For Joanna, the entire process seemed mesmerizingly boring. At last Fred Woodworth stopped typing. Folding his arms behind his head and leaning back in his chair, he stared at the screen. "I guess it's a good thing you're all cops," he said at last.

"Why do you say that?" Joanna asked. "What's on it?"

Fred gave her a lopsided grin. "It's code, all right," he said. "I don't know where you guys got this, but if the Feds knew you had it, they'd probably shit a brick. Excuse me, Sister," he said again, eyeing Sister Celeste. "I keep forgetting."

"What is it?" Joanna asked.

"It's military code," he said. "It's the kind of thing they use for command and control procedures. And even though it's out of date, I'm sure it's still classified. They don't like to let any of this stuff out because inevitably, one set of encryption codes is built on top of another. If you have one of the base codes, you can usually extrapolate from there and figure out what's going on."

"So," Frank asked. "Can you tell us anything about this?"

Fred Woodworth smirked and shrugged. "Some. Compared to where we are now, this is pretty primitive stuff. I'd say these files date all the way back to the late eighties or early nineties. I can't say which branch of the service the files are from, but since Fort Huachuca is right next door here, my first guess would be army. If you want to know anything more about this, I'd suggest you call them."

Across the table from Fred Woodworth, Sister Celeste let out a long, audible sigh. "It's true, then," she murmured.

"What's true?" Joanna asked.

"What Lucy Ridder told me."

Joanna held up her hand. "Wait," she cautioned. "Don't say anything more right now. Mr. Woodworth? Mr. Davis? Thank you so much for all your help, but I believe that's all we need for right now. If there's anything more, we'll let you know."

Now it was Fred Woodworth's turn to sigh. Closing the lid on the laptop, he ran one finger regretfully and lovingly across it. "It was a pleasure," he said. "I'll be glad to help out anytime. Just give me a call."

He and Rich Davis stood up. Frank Montoya escorted the two men as far as the conference-room door. As soon as they stepped over the threshold and out into the reception room, Frank closed the door behind them and turned expectantly back to Joanna and Sister Celeste.

"What did Lucy tell you?" Joanna was asking.

"That her mother was a spy."

"A spy?"

"She said her father told her that Sandra Ridder was providing top-secret information to our enemies. I'd guess that would have been the Iraqis during the Gulf War."

For a second or two, both Joanna Brady and Frank Montoya were struck speechless. Before either one of them could comment, Sister Celeste stood up. "I'm sure you've heard enough," she said. "Now, if you'll be so good as to come with me, I'll take you to Lucy right away."

"Where is she?" Joanna choked, finding her voice at last.

"At Holy Trinity Monastery over in Saint David," Sister Celeste said. "The prior, Father Mulligan, is a good friend of mine, and I understand he's a friend of yours as well. He promised me he'd take care of Lucy and keep her safe and out of sight. Lucy Ridder is convinced that the man who murdered her mother came out to Cochise Stronghold that night looking for the computer disk. She's afraid that eventually he'll figure out who must have it. Once he does, he'll come looking for her as well."

"Wait a minute. Are you saying Lucy knew someone killed her mother?" Joanna asked. "How could she?"

"It's perfectly simple," Sister Celeste answered calmly. "Lucinda Ridder saw him do it."

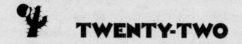

TWENTY-TWO

With Frank holding the door for her, Sister Celeste brushed past him and out of the office. For a time, Joanna made no move to follow. When she didn't, Frank pulled the door shut once more. "Do you want me to come along?" he asked. "To Saint David, I mean?"

Joanna shook her head. "I don't think so. I want you to get Detective Carpenter to tackle the Fort Huachuca situation ASAP. Tell him I want to know everything possible about Sandra Ridder's position when she used to work on post—who she worked for, what she did, how much money she earned, everything."

"Wait a minute," Frank cautioned. "If this really does turn out to be a legitimate spy case, won't we be stepping on jurisdictional toes?"

"Look at how old this case is, Frank," Joanna said. "It's been around at least as long as Sandra Ridder was in prison and probably a whole lot longer than that. What makes you think we're the first ones to discover it?"

"You're saying there may have been a cover-up?"

Joanna shrugged. "It could be. Look at what happened at Los Alamos. Let's solve Sandra Ridder's homicide *before* we send out for reinforcements and *before* we go jumping through any unnecessary bureaucratic hoops. If, in the process of doing that, we come across real evidence of espionage, then we'll pass it along to the Feds so they can follow it up. In the meantime, we're operating on hearsay eight-year-old evidence from a fifteen-year-old runaway and on the shaky technical assumptions of a convicted computer hacker. Talk about leaning on a pair of bent reeds. If we tried to call in the FBI based on what we have up to this point, they'd laugh themselves silly."

"Sister Celeste could have it all wrong," Frank suggested quietly.

"What do you mean?"

"Just because Sister Celeste thinks Lucy Ridder didn't kill Sandra Ridder, that doesn't necessarily make it true. Lucy may have lied to Sister Celeste, and she may lie to you as well, to say nothing of being potentially dangerous. Everybody seems to keep forgetting the kid has a gun."

"If Lucy Ridder killed her mother, who killed Melanie Goodson?" Joanna asked. "Are you suggesting that Lucy is responsible for that murder as well?"

"I don't know," Frank said. "I suppose it's possible."

"But not very likely," Joanna returned. "Somebody out there has gotten away with something for years. Once Sandra Ridder was let out of jail, maybe she threatened to blow the perp's cover. That's why Sandra Ridder is dead, and I'll bet that's why her attorney is dead as well. I'm with Sister Celeste on this one. I don't think Lucy had a thing to do with her mother's death other than possibly seeing it happen. And based on that—on the fact that she's both an eyewitness and thought to be packing around a computer disk full of classified material—I believe Lucy Ridder's life is in danger. Maybe her grandmother's is as well. Speaking of Catherine Yates, hadn't we better do something about her? Presumably, thanks to Sister Celeste's efforts, Lucy is safe at the moment. I want round-the-clock surveillance on Catherine

Yates' place. That way, if someone comes there looking for the disk, we might just nail them."

"Mounting a round-the-clock guard is going to cost money," Frank said. "Are you sure you want to do that?"

"Thanks for your budgetary concern, Frank. But if it's a choice between spending money or possibly saving a life, I'm in favor of the latter."

"All right," Frank agreed after a moment's hesitation. "I'll go round up Ernie, and we'll get started. But what about the disk?" He held it out to her. "It's evidence, isn't it?"

Joanna nodded. "The question is: evidence of what? Bag it, log it, and take it down to the evidence room. Somebody somewhere is going to want it eventually. When they do, I want to be able to lay hands on it at a moment's notice."

"Unlike Tucson PD and a certain missing bullet," Frank said.

"Right," Joanna returned. Frank Montoya opened the door once again. In the reception room, Joanna found Sister Celeste pacing impatiently back and forth in front of Kristin's desk. "Would you like to ride with me?" Joanna asked. "Or would you prefer to bring your own vehicle?"

"I'll ride with you if you don't mind," Sister Celeste returned. "We need to talk. On the way, I'll tell you what I know."

Joanna was surprised by the nun's response, but gratified as well. Sister Celeste may have had reservations about Joanna when she first appeared in the office, but those concerns had evidently been dealt with. Out in the parking lot, Joanna walked past her worn Blazer, choosing instead to drive Sister Celeste in the relative comfort of a departmental Crown Victoria.

"Were you the one who suggested Lucy sign up for ballet?" Joanna asked, once they were underway.

Sister Celeste regarded her with a raised eyebrow. "Yes," she said. "How did you know about that?"

"Jay Quick, the son of Lucy's ballet instructor, remembered something about one of the nuns at school giving a book to her—a book about a Native American ballerina."

"Maria Tallchief." Sister Celeste nodded. "I knew when I gave Lucy the book that it made a big impression on her. It seemed to help—to give her hope that somehow things could get better for her. She was so desperately unhappy, I had to do something."

"Why unhappy?" Joanna asked.

"Santa Theresa's is a barrio school," Sister Celeste answered. "We have lots of Hispanic students and quite a few Native Americans. Lucy was different."

"Different how?" Joanna asked. "She's Apache, isn't she? How much more Native American could she be?"

"She isn't full-blooded Apache," Sister Celeste replied. "And it shows. The other kids teased her and made her life miserable because she wasn't Indian enough to suit them. And then, once she arrived at her grandmother's place near Pearce, just the opposite must have been true. There she had too much Indian blood, and she was still an outsider."

"Which is why her best friend turns out to be a red-tailed hawk?" Joanna asked. Sister Celeste nodded. "Where is he, by the way?"

"Who, the hawk?" Sister Celeste asked. "Big Red is at the monastery, too. At the time Lucy called me, she said she and the bird would be hiding out in the hills near Texas Canyon. I suggested that she come to Tucson. I offered to come get her right then, early Saturday morning. I even told her she could stay at the convent, although we aren't really set up to accommodate boarders. Lucy refused. Said she couldn't come because of the bird. She said since she couldn't ride her bike on the freeway, she'd have to walk the whole way to Tucson because Big Red had never been in a car before and she didn't think he'd go in one.

"When she was talking about her pet bird, I was more or less envisioning something like a parakeet or parrot. I had no idea what kind of bird Big Red was or *how* big. Someone came to where she was right then, and she had to get off the phone. She said she'd call me back. I stayed by the phone all day long, but I didn't hear from her again until Sunday morning. When I talked to her that time, she was calling from a place called Walker Ranch. She told the people there that she had been hiking and gotten lost. She told me that someone bad had come looking for her Sunday morning, and she had run away, leaving everything behind—her bike, bedroll, water, and food. She said if it hadn't been for her hawk calling a warning, she would have been trapped. She said Big Red was the only reason she got away.

"That was the first I really understood Big Red is a hawk. The woman who lived at the ranch gave me directions, and I told her I'd be right there as soon as I could to pick them up. Overnight I had been racking my brain to think of a place where a girl and a bird would be welcome. Sometime around midnight I remembered my friend, Father Mulligan."

"At Holy Trinity in Saint David?" Joanna added.

Sister Celeste nodded. "Since Lucy was clearly so frightened, it seemed like an altogether more sensible place for her, and Holy Trinity is a retreat center that is set up to handle overnight visitors. Once I understood Big Red was a hawk, Holy Trinity seemed like a good place for him, too. Much better than the grounds at Santa Theresa's, which happen to be in the middle of Tucson. The only problem was getting them there."

"Wait a minute," Joanna said. "Don't tell me Lucy walked from Texas Canyon all the way to Saint David."

"Lucy's a very resourceful young woman, and I'm sure she could have walked that far," Sister Celeste returned. "But right then, she was at the end of her rope. I remembered how in some of the old romance novels I used to read, falconers would keep hoods over their birds' heads. So that's what I did—got Big Red a hood."

"Where?" Joanna asked, only half teasing. "What did you do, go to Pets-Are-Us?"

"I didn't have to. One of the sisters at the convent, Sister Anne Marie, is a real wizard with a Singer sewing machine. She whipped one right up. And when Lucy put it on Big Red, it fit perfectly—like it had been made for him, which, of course, it had. Once his eyes were covered, he got in the van just as nice as you please."

For several minutes the car moved through the bright desert afternoon sunlight with no further words being exchanged. When Sister Celeste spoke again, she took the conversation back several steps. "Back then, when I suggested Lucy take ballet, there was more to it than just the Indian situation."

"Oh?" Joanna replied. "What else?"

"When it was time for the first parent-teacher conferences that fall, Tom Ridder showed up by himself. I told him both parents needed to be involved in what was going on at school. I explained that things weren't going well for Lucy—that she wasn't fitting in and that she wasn't working up to her potential, either. I asked him if there were problems at home. He admitted that yes, there were. He said he and his wife were having marital difficulties. That things were so bad they might end up in divorce court. He said Lucy was the only reason he was hanging on and trying to hold things together."

"Lucy's grandmother claimed Tom Ridder had behaved violently with his wife," Joanna said. "And from what I saw of the record and legal proceedings, the judge who sent Sandra Ridder to prison seems to have said pretty much the same thing—that Tom Ridder was prone to violence. Prior to the murder, did you see any evidence that would support that?"

Sister Celeste shook her head. "No," she said. "I agree there was violence in the home, but I don't think Tom Ridder was the culprit. One day, Lucy came to school with a handprint-shaped bruise on her face. Remember, this happened back before there were state laws requiring school personnel to report instances of possible abuse to the authorities. I asked Lucy about it—asked if her father had hit her. I'll never forget what she told me. 'The only person in our house who hits people is my mom.' She said that her mother had a temper. That sometimes she would do mean things to Lucy and to her father as well, but Lucy insisted that no matter what people said, her dad never hurt anybody."

"And you believed her?" Joanna asked.

"I had no reason not to," Sister Celeste replied.

"Did you mention the possibility of Sandra Ridder's own violent tendencies to any of the detectives investigating Tom Ridder's death?"

Sister Celeste shook her head. "I kept waiting for someone to ask me about it, but no one ever did. I suppose I would have come forward eventually, but then, when Sandra Ridder pleaded guilty, it didn't seem as though what I had to say would make any difference one way or the other. After all, Lucy wasn't being left in the care of an abusive parent. Child Protective Services had shipped her off to live with her grandparents—a grandmother, I believe. The family sit-

uation was already in enough of a crisis. I didn't see any reason to heap fuel on the flames."

"Sheriff Brady?" The voice of Tica Romero came wafting into the car through the speaker in Joanna's police radio.

"I'm here, Tica. What is it?"

"We just had a call from Los Gatos PD out in California."

"Los Gatos," Joanna repeated. "What did they want?"

"They're looking for Reba Singleton. Her husband, Dennis, just finished filing a missing-persons report. The detective working the case wanted to know if anyone here had
seen her."

"Of course, I saw her," Joanna replied. "It was during the
reception at the YWCA after her father's funeral yesterday
afternoon. She bitched me out in public and then left in a
huff."

"No one's seen her since then?" Tica asked.

"Not that I know of. The last person I saw her with was
Marliss Shackleford," Joanna said. "Why? What's going on?"

"Mr. Singleton said he sent his corporate jet to Tucson International to pick her up, but she wasn't there to meet the
plane when it arrived. He contacted the limo company, but
they said her driver dropped her off at the airport late last
night. He claims he knew nothing about a private jet being
sent to get her. He says she asked to be dropped off at the
ticketing level. He assumed that meant she was catching a
plane. According to Mr. Singleton, she never showed up at
home. He hasn't seen or heard from her since. He seems
concerned that she may have been kidnapped and is being
held for ransom."

Joanna sighed. "Tell the detective we'll be happy to offer
whatever assistance he needs. Put him in touch with Frank
Montoya. He may be working with Detective Carpenter on
something else just now, but he needs to be aware of this.

And you might give Dick Voland a courtesy call as well. He was doing some work for Reba Singleton. He may know where she's gone off to. In any event, he should be notified about what's going on."

"Will do."

"Also," Tica continued. "Kristin wanted me to let you know that you're to contact Sheriff Forsythe up in Pima County. He left a number. Do you want me to give it to you?"

"Please."

While Joanna groped unsuccessfully for a pen or pencil, Sister Celeste found one. "I can take the number for you if you like."

"Thanks," Joanna said. Once Joanna signed off with Tica, Sister Celeste handed Joanna a scrap of paper with the phone number jotted on it. Rather than dial the number right then, Joanna stuffed the piece of paper into her pocket. Whatever it was Sheriff Bill Forsythe wanted, it would have to wait until after Joanna no longer had a listening and more than moderately interested passenger riding in her vehicle.

That year, neither winter nor spring rains had materialized in southern Arizona. According to local meteorologists, the previous six months had been the driest on record. As a result, not even the usually hearty mesquite and paloverde had yet leafed out. Coming through the barren, badly eroded gullies south of town, Saint David, with its patchwork of artesian-well-irrigated fields, seemed even more of a desert oasis than usual. Beyond the fields stood a line of ancient and majestic cottonwoods whose sturdy presence marked the path of the now dry San Pedro River bed as it wound through the valley that bore its name.

Holy Trinity Monastery was set in among a grove of

those old-growth cottonwoods just south of town and not far from the river itself. The monastery consisted of a tiny church, a ragtag collection of haphazardly parked mobile homes, as well as a library and a few other permanent buildings. It functioned throughout the year as a retreat center for Catholic clergy from the Tucson Diocese.

As soon as Joanna turned off Highway 80 into the parking lot, Father Thomas Mulligan emerged from his tiny adobe church and came striding across the gravel parking lot to meet the car. His white hair stood upright in the cool, blustery wind that caused his equally white robes to flap loosely around his long legs.

"Why, Sheriff Brady," he said, hand extended. "How good to see you again, although I wish it were under somewhat less stressful circumstances. We really must stop meeting this way. But that reminds me: How's my friend Junior doing these days?"

"As far as I can tell, he really seems to like living with his new guardians, Moe and Daisy Maxwell," Joanna told the priest. "He works at Daisy's restaurant most days—busing tables and washing dishes. He seems to like that, too. Every time I see him, it looks as though he's having the time of his life."

"I'll have to stop by and check on him one of these days," Father Mulligan said with a smile. "Now, I trust Sister Celeste has brought you up to speed with our latest little crisis? We do tend to gather unconventional strays around here."

Joanna looked around. "Where are they?" she asked.

"Big Red and Lucy? I'm afraid the hawk was keeping far too close an eye on the fish in our reflecting pond," Father Mulligan responded. "I suggested Lucy take him down by the riverbed in hopes he can rustle up something for dinner that isn't one of my prize-winning koi."

"Which way did they go?" Joanna asked.

Father Mulligan pointed. "Do you see that path between the church and the cemetery?" Joanna nodded. "Follow that," he said. "It'll take you right down to the river, but be careful. It's been so dry lately that the bank is crumbling in spots."

As Joanna set off in that direction, Sister Celeste made as if to follow. "I'll come, too," she said.

"No, Sister Celeste," Father Mulligan said firmly. "That's not necessary. Sheriff Brady will manage just fine on her own. I've seen this woman in action."

Sister Celeste made as if to protest, but Father Mulligan shook his head and took her by the arm. "Come on," he added. "Let's you and me go into the rectory and wait there. I'm sure Brother Gregory will be happy to pour us a nice cup of his special herbal tea."

Grateful to the priest for running interference, Joanna set off. Once she was out of sight behind the church and in the privacy of the well-kept cemetery, she stopped walking long enough to remove her cell phone from her purse. Fumbling Sister Celeste's slip of paper out of her pocket, she dialed Bill Forsythe's number.

"Sheriff Joanna Brady," she said to the woman who answered. "I'm returning Sheriff Forsythe's call."

The man who came on the line seconds later sounded far different from the person Joanna had spoken to earlier in the day. "Thanks for calling me back, Sheriff Brady," he said. "I just finished spending a good deal of time on the phone with Fran Daly. She's our assistant medical examiner."

"I know Dr. Daly," Joanna said coolly.

"Yes, I understand you do," Sheriff Forsythe said quickly. "She mentioned something to that effect. Anyway, she's completed the Melanie Goodson autopsy. She tells me the victim died of homicidal violence—smothered, to be exact. Whether it was done with or without the benefit of drugs remains to be seen. The toxicology report will take something over a week. At any rate, Dr. Daly suggested that we work in conjunction with your detectives on this one."

Thank you, Fran Daly, Joanna thought as she bit back the temptation to make some snide comment in return. "As you may have gathered," she said aloud, "I'm out of the office right now. So are my detectives. If you would call back down to my department and speak to my chief deputy, Frank Montoya, I'll direct him to give you whatever assistance you need.

"So," she added, testing the water, "do your detectives have any theories so far?"

Bill Forsythe paused momentarily. "Melanie Goodson has a real estate investment partner by the name of Edward Masters. My detectives have been trying to locate him for the better part of two days. No success so far, I'm afraid."

At that juncture, Joanna Brady might have volunteered the fact that she was about to interview Lucy Ridder, but she didn't. Sheriff Bill Forsythe had left her hanging earlier. *What goes around comes around,* she thought as she ended the call. Immediately afterward she dialed Frank's number. He didn't answer, but she left word on his voice mail about Sheriff Forsythe's sudden change of heart. Then, putting the phone away, Joanna started toward the river.

The groomed path that led from the church to the riverbank was an immaculately maintained mini nature trail complete with homemade hand-etched signs and arrows identifying the various plants along the way. Halfway to the river, Joanna caught sight of a huge shadow sweeping across the sky overhead. It was only after spotting the shadow that she caught sight of Big Red himself. Watching the magnificent hawk glide gracefully through the air, Joanna was stunned by the bird's tawny beauty and grace. She was still watching in transfixed wonder when the bird launched himself into a steep dive.

After plummeting for several seconds he disappeared from view, flying beak-down into a stand of tall, winter-dried grass. Joanna waited for the sound of a crash and the accompanying explosion of feathers. Neither came. Moments after disappearing, the hawk reappeared, holding in his powerful talons the squirming, writhing figure of some living creature—a field mouse, perhaps, or maybe a baby rabbit. Whatever prize Big Red had bagged, it was heavy enough to interfere with the big bird's complex aerodynamics. Coming up out of the tall grass, he had to struggle to become airborne once more. Flapping awkwardly, he disappeared into the lower branches of one of those age-old cottonwoods.

From his hidden perch he let out a blood-curdling screech—a cry of triumph, most likely—one that pronounced to all concerned a successful end to his hunt. That sound alone was enough to raise the hackles on the back of Joanna's neck, but then his cry was followed almost immediately by an answering screech that sounded so much like the first as to be almost indistinguishable. This one came from far closer to Joanna, and from the ground rather than from the sky or a sheltering tree branch. Searching for the source, Joanna spotted a young woman sitting on a tumbled boulder in the middle of the sandy, bone-dry riverbed.

In the spot where Joanna stood, the bank was some eight feet high. Climbing gingerly, Joanna scrambled down, cringing as the powder-dry dirt gave way beneath her every step. Once on flat ground, Joanna trudged over to where the girl was sitting and sank down nearby on a neighboring boulder. Lucy Ridder, sitting cross-legged with her chin raised, didn't even glance in Joanna's direction. Instead, she continued to stare through her thick glasses up into the tree branches where Big Red had disappeared.

"How'd you learn to do that?" Joanna asked.

"Do what?" Lucy asked.

"The bird call," Joanna answered. "You and he sounded just alike."

"Big Red taught me," Lucy said. She grimaced and then turned her face toward Joanna. "I guess you're the sheriff."

Joanna nodded. "Sheriff Brady," she said. "Joanna Brady."

Lucy sighed. "Father Mulligan told me about you. He likes you and says I should talk to you, tell you what happened."

"It would be nice if you did," Joanna agreed.

Two enormous tears leaked out from under the thick lenses of Lucy Ridder's glasses. They slipped down her cheeks and then dripped, unchecked, onto a worn blue flannel shirt that was several sizes too large for her.

"My mother's dead," Lucy said. "For years I hoped she would die in prison so I'd never have to see her again. But now that she really is dead, I wish it hadn't happened. I wish I'd had a chance to talk to her, to ask her the reason. Why did she have to do it?"

"Why did she do what?" Joanna asked.

"Why did she have to kill my father?"

"I don't know the answer to that," Joanna said. "But it's why I'm here. To find out."

Lucy blinked. "About my father?"

"About both of them," Joanna said. "During the last few days, I've become convinced that what happened to your father years ago is related to what happened to your mother last week. And I think you know that as well."

Lucy Ridder nodded once. "Yes," she said with a ragged sigh, and then she began to cry.

TWENTY-THREE

Several minutes later, when Lucy Ridder finally stopped sobbing and turned to face Joanna, the full force of the afternoon sun struck a shiny knot of silver dangling on a chain at the base of the girl's throat.

"That's a beautiful necklace you're wearing," Joanna said. "What is it?"

Unconsciously, one of Lucy's hands strayed gracefully to her throat and clasped shut around the necklace. "Grandma Bagwell, my grandmother's mother, gave it to me before she died," Lucy said. "It's a devil's claw."

"May I see it?" Joanna asked.

Shrugging, Lucy's hands went to the clasp. Within seconds Joanna was cradling the gleaming silver-and-turquoise amulet in her own hand. The two tiny pronged horns of the devil's claw seemed to grow out of an equally tiny turquoise bead. She hadn't seen the necklace George Winfield had given to Catherine Yates along with Sandra Ridder's other personal effects, but she was sure this one was similar, if not an exact copy. The two necklaces were so alike that even Catherine Yates had been fooled into believing the one Sandra had been wearing actually belonged to her daughter.

"It's lovely," Joanna said. "What does it mean?"

"Indians use devil's claw to weave in the patterns when they make baskets."

"I know," Joanna said. "I've seen them before."

"Grandma Bagwell, my great-grandmother, used to say that people can make baskets without using devil's claw, but that's what they need to make the basket interesting, to make it tell a story. When she gave me the necklace, she told me it was because she thought I was interesting, too."

"Did you know your mother had a necklace just like this—one that's almost identical?" Joanna asked after a pause. "She was wearing it when she died. When your grandmother saw it, she thought it was yours."

Once again Lucy's eyes clouded over with tears. "No," she whispered. "I didn't know that. Grandma Bagwell must have given her one at the same time. But why? I thought when Grandma Bagwell gave this one to me it meant I was special, but I guess I was wrong."

"I'm not so sure about that," Joanna offered. "Maybe she thought you were both special. That in your own way you both had interesting stories to tell."

"No," Lucy Ridder said, shaking her head.

Still holding the silver necklace in her hand, Joanna studied Lucy Ridder as the blustery late-March wind sifted through her light brown hair. Of the Native Americans Joanna had met, most had black, straight hair very unlike Lucy Ridder's, which was both light brown and wavy. Behind the girl's glasses her eyes were a striking gold-flecked hazel rather than deep brown. If this anguished young woman really was the great-great granddaughter of a famed Apache chief, it certainly didn't show in her features. But there could be little doubt that many of Lucy Ridder's ancestral instincts were still alive and well. After all, she had somehow summoned both the patience and skill to befriend, tame, and train a wild red-tailed hawk.

"My job is studying patterns," Joanna said quietly, as she

handed the necklace back to Lucy, who gazed at it as though it were no longer the treasure she had always assumed it to be. "Not the devil's-claw patterns woven into baskets," Joanna continued. "As sheriff, it's my job to study the patterns left behind when people die—when they're murdered."

"Like my father and my mother," Lucy murmured.

Joanna nodded. "Let me ask you something, Lucy. When a basketmaker weaves patterns with devil's claw, do they always mean the same thing?"

"Not always."

"But they may be connected, right? One may be different from the next one—from the one before it—but they're still related."

"Yes."

"I think something similar has happened here," Joanna said. "I think what's happened in the past few days with your mother may be related to what happened to your father years ago. And now someone else is dead as well."

"My grandmother?" Lucy asked.

"No. The latest victim is Melanie Goodson."

"My mother's attorney?" Joanna nodded.

Lucy shuddered. "She's dead because I called her," Lucy wailed, shaking her head and rocking back and forth. "I didn't mean to cause trouble for her, too. I didn't mean for her to be killed. I just knew I needed help, and I didn't know who to ask."

"Please, Lucy," Joanna said, trying to console the girl. "Don't blame yourself. Melanie Goodson was your mother's attorney when your father was killed. That makes her part of the pattern, too. Before I can make sense of what's happening now, I need to learn everything I can about what happened back then. As far as I can see, you're the only one left who can tell me what I need to know. If you will, that is," she added.

For several long seconds Lucy Ridder made no reply. She sat gazing intently into the concealing branches where Big Red had disappeared. Finally she turned away from the tree and focused her penetrating hazel-eyed gaze back on Joanna.

"Why should I?" she asked hopelessly. "What good will it do? My father's dead. Nothing I can tell you will bring him back."

"Or your mother, either," Joanna added. "Lucy, listen to me. My father died when I was just a year younger than you are now. My daughter, Jenny, was seven when her father was killed—the same age you were when you lost your father. Not knowing the answers about why those things happened to my father and to my husband could have haunted Jenny and me for the rest of our lives. Finding out and knowing the truth about what happened to my dad and my husband didn't bring either one of them back, but it did make it possible to go on.

"You're right. What we learn now won't bring either one of your parents back. They're gone. But they say the truth will set you free, and I believe that's the case. Finding out what really happened to Sandra and Tom Ridder is the only way you—Lucy—will be able to put these awful things behind you. It's the only thing that will allow you to move forward. Otherwise, you'll be stuck, and you're too young and have far too much potential to let that happen."

"What potential?" Lucy asked despairingly. "I'm nobody. I'm nothing."

"Evelyn Quick didn't think so," Joanna said. "That's not what she told her son. And Sister Celeste doesn't think so, either. That's why they're both worried about you. That's why Jay Quick called and told us about your phone call. It's why Sister Celeste came looking for you and brought you here to a place where she believes you'll be safe." She paused then, giving her words time to soak in. "Tell me what happened that night, Lucy. Please."

"First the one car drove up. My mother got out, went over to the sign, and started moving the rocks. The person who was driving didn't help her. Whoever it was stayed in the car and I never saw who it was. Then another car drove up. It belonged to a man from the campground—a nice man who stopped and asked my mother if she needed any help. She said no, she was fine. As soon as he left, she went back to moving rocks. That's when the other man showed up."

"Did you know who he was?" Joanna asked. "Had you ever seen him before?"

Lucy shook her head. "And I didn't hear him drive up, either. He must have parked far enough down the road that I never heard or saw his car. Mother didn't hear him either, until it was too late."

Lucy's lip trembled. "I could have warned her," Lucy said. "I could have told her, but I didn't. I kept quiet the whole time he was yelling at her and hurting her. He said she had something that belonged to him, something he wanted. But I knew that wasn't true. He was looking for the disk, and I had that right there in my backpack. If I had come out from where I was hiding and given it to him, maybe he wouldn't have shot her. Maybe she wouldn't be dead."

"You don't know that," Joanna said. "Maybe you'd both be dead. You mustn't blame yourself."

"But I do. Anyway, the next thing I knew, there was the gun. They struggled over it; wrestled over it. Then the gun went off while they were rolling on the ground. Pretty soon the man stood up, but my mother didn't move after that. The man picked her up—she was limp, like a rag doll. He dragged her over to the car and shoved her into the back-seat."

"Did you see where the gun came from?" Joanna asked. "Was the man who attacked your mother carrying it?"

"No," Lucy said. "I'm sure it was my mother's gun—the same one she used to kill my father. She hid it there beneath the sign the night she shot him. I saw her do it. It was tiny, and she hid it in a plastic bowl along with that stupid computer disk. When I took the disk, I left the gun where it was. It killed my father, and I didn't want to touch it.

"Anyway, after the man threw Mother into the car, he got in, too—in the front seat on the rider's side. I heard a woman's voice then—the driver, I guess—say, 'Now you've done it, you stupid bastard!' And he said, 'Just shut up and drive. Get us the hell out of here.' And they left."

"Lucy," Joanna said. "This all happened in the middle of the night. It was freezing cold that night. I was out in it, too. What were you doing out there?"

"Hiding. Big Red and I wrapped up in a bedroll. He helped me keep warm."

"But why did you go there in the first place?"

"I had to know. Mother said she was coming home. At least, that's what she told Grandma Yates and that's what she told me, but I knew all along it was a lie. I don't think she cared if she ever saw either one of us again. The only reason she came back at all was to get the diskette, just like I knew she would."

"And how long were you there waiting?" Joanna asked.

"I had to wait until Grandma fell asleep before I could sneak out of the house. And it took time to walk and ride there in the dark, but I got there in plenty of time. I was already hidden in the bedroll when they drove up."

"The man with your mother," Joanna said.

"He wasn't *with* my mother. He came later. She was already there, moving the rocks."

"Tell me about this man," Joanna urged. "Had you ever seen him before that night?"

"No," Lucy said. "Not that I remember. But I've seen him since then."

"You have?" Joanna demanded. "When?"

"The next day. He came to the rest area late Saturday afternoon. Big Red and I had been hiding in among the boulders just above the road. I was coming down to use the pay phone and get a candy bar. That's when I saw him. He was parked by the phone and stayed there for a long time. As soon as I saw him, I knew he was looking for me—and for the diskette. And I knew he'd kill me if he found me, so I stayed out of sight."

"Did you notice what kind of car he was driving?"

Lucy shook her head. "I don't know much about cars. It was gray—silver, I mean. And foreign, but that's all I saw."

"Did you tell Sister Celeste about him?"

"I was afraid to. I was afraid if she knew someone like that was looking for me, she might not help me anymore."

Joanna paused to get her bearings. "Tell me about this computer diskette. You said it was hidden in the plastic bowl along with your mother's weapon."

"Right," Lucy said. "She hid them both that night—the night she shot my father."

"I know how hard it is to talk about, Lucy," Joanna prodded gently. "But I need you to tell me about that night—as much as you can remember."

Lucy took a deep breath. "Mother came to the YMCA looking for me. We were in the middle of class, but that didn't matter. She just barged right in. She told me to get

dressed, that we had to leave. Her face was all bloody. Her
lip was cut. She looked awful. Mrs. Quick tried to tell her
that she shouldn't be driving, that she needed to see a doctor. But she kept yelling at me to come on. And so I did."

"What happened then?"

"She turned around in the car and said to me, 'All right,
where is it? It isn't at the house, and it isn't in his truck.
Give me your backpack.' So I gave her my backpack, and
she dug through it until she found the diskette right where
Dad put it."

"Your father gave you the diskette?"

Lucy nodded. "At lunch. He came to school that day and
told Sister Celeste he had to talk to me. He took me across
the street to the bakery. I can't remember the name exactly.
Something about a cave, I think. He bought us both dough-
nuts, but he was too upset to eat his. When he tried to tell me
what was going on, he started crying. He told me my mother
had done something bad at work, and that he had just found
out about it. He said he was afraid she was going to get into
serious trouble, that she might even have to go to jail if anyone ever found out."

"Did he say what kind of trouble?"

"He said Mom had a boyfriend at work and that the two of
them were doing stuff together—secret stuff. Like spies or
something. And then he told me he was going to talk to
Mother about it and get her to quit. That's when he gave me
the diskette to keep for him. He said if Mother knew about it
that she'd really be mad at him. He said once he talked to her,
he'd take it back and get rid of it so nobody else would find it.

"As soon as she took it away from me that night while we
were parked outside the Y, I should have known right then
Dad was dead, that she'd already killed him. And that's why
she did it, too. She killed him because she thought he was

going to tell on her, but he never would have. Mother was beautiful, and my dad loved her no matter what she did. I think he loved her even more than he loved me. It's the same thing with Grandma Yates—she loved Mom better, too. The only people who ever really loved me were Sister Celeste; my ballet teacher, Mrs. Quick; and Grandma Bagwell, my great-grandmother, although now that I know she gave Mother a devil's claw . . ." Without warning, Lucy's voice faded away into nothing.

Joanna tried to draw her away from that particular hurt. "Let's go back to the diskette," she urged. "You said your father gave it to you for safekeeping while he confronted your mother about whatever it was she was doing. Then your mother came to get you and took it away. What happened next?"

"We drove out to Cochise Stronghold. It was night when we got there, and cold, too. My mother cried the whole way there, and she kept saying stuff I couldn't understand. It sounded like she was mad at everybody. She told me to lie down and go to sleep. I kept peeking out, though. The whole time we were driving there, I thought we were going to Grandma Yates' place. Instead, we went straight to the entrance of Cochise Stronghold.

"When Mother opened the door to get out of the car, she told me to go to sleep. But I didn't. I saw everything she did. First she pulled loose a bunch of rocks. She had a little plastic bowl along with her, the kind she used to take along to work when she packed a lunch. First she put something shiny into the bowl. That must have been the gun—a tiny gun. Then she added the diskette and closed the bowl's lid. She put the bowl in among the rocks, then she covered it. When she came back to the car, I pretended to be asleep. Since we were so close to Grandma's house, I thought we'd go there and say hello and maybe have something to eat, but we didn't.

"Mother drove us straight back to Tucson. On the way, I fell asleep for real. I don't remember going home, and when we got there, she must have carried me into the house. When I woke up the next morning, the house was full of police, and Dad was sitting in the chair in the living room. He was dead."

Lucy sighed and shuddered, as though the effort of relating the story had been too much for her.

"What happened next?"

"Some man—a detective, maybe—came to the house and asked me a whole bunch of questions. He kept asking me if my father ever hit my mother. And I said, 'I never *saw* him hit her.' Then he asked if Dad ever hit me, and I told him no. I kept waiting for him to ask me if my mother hit people or if she was a spy and did bad stuff, but nobody ever did. Then it was like they forgot all about me and nobody bothered to ask me any more questions. I figured out later that was because Mother confessed. She told them she did it. After that, a woman came to talk to me and told me they were going to send me to live with my grandmother and my great-grandmother.

"After I got there, I tried to tell a few people about what Dad said my mother had been doing, but no one would listen. Not even Grandma Bagwell. She and Grandma Yates both said my father was dead because he was a bad man and because he had beaten up my mother. I told them they were wrong about that—that it was my mother who was bad. I tried telling them the same thing Dad had told me about Mother getting into trouble at work. I thought if there was a trial, lawyers would ask me questions and I would have to tell them the truth, the whole truth, and nothing but the truth.

"But there wasn't any trial. My mother said she shot Dad because she was tired of him beating her up. Afterward she said she was scared. She picked me up from ballet and then drove all over half the night trying to decide what to do. She said she didn't know what happened to the gun—that she had thrown it away somewhere. But that wasn't true, either, because I found the gun in the bowl along with the diskette."

"And when was that?"

"I don't know," Lucy answered with a shrug. "A long time later. I was only a little kid then. I turned eight the next summer. Grandma Yates didn't like me wandering around in the hills by myself, but Grandma Bagwell did. She said it was neat. The fact that I liked to be out scouting by myself proved I was a 'real' Apache, just like her grandfather Eskiminzin.

"Anyway, one day I went to the rock pile all by myself. I dug up the bowl, found the diskette, and took it home. I wanted it because Dad had given it to me to take care of. I wanted to know what was on it. I kept it hidden in another plastic bowl—one of Grandma Yates' this time. I hid the bowl out in the shed because I didn't want Grandma Yates to find it when she was cleaning my room. I knew it was from a computer, and I kept waiting for a chance to look at it. Finally, when I got to high school, there was a computer in the library. I tried looking at it there, but it must have been the wrong program or something. Or maybe the disk got wrecked when it was in plastic all those years. There wasn't anything there."

"That's not true," Joanna said quietly. "There is something there."

Lucy swung around to face Joanna. "Really?" she demanded. "What?"

"I don't know. It's encrypted."

"What does that mean?"

"It means most people can't read it because it's written in a top-secret code—a government code. As far as we can tell, it seems to contain command and control codes for the military."

Lucy's mouth dropped open and her eyes widened. "Does that mean my father was right the whole time? My mother really was a spy?"

Joanna nodded. "Possibly," she replied, "although at this point we can't say for sure."

"See there?" Lucy was almost shouting now. "I told you so. I was glad when they sent Mother to prison, and I'm glad, too, that she's dead now. Unlike my dad, she deserved what she got. I loved my father, Sheriff Brady. I hated it when people thought he had been mean to her, when they thought he was the kind of man who would beat us—beat both of us—when he didn't—not once, not ever."

"Let's go back to the other night for a moment," Joanna said.

"Why?" Lucy asked.

"I need you to finish telling me what happened. It's the only way we're going to find out who killed your mother."

"I don't care who killed my mother. I already told you," Lucy said fiercely. "I'm glad she's dead. What does it matter who killed her?"

"Lucy," Joanna said, "you told me that the whole time your father's death was being investigated, no one ever asked you about your mother's alleged spying or about her having a boyfriend. Right?"

Lucy nodded. "So?"

"That means no one ever knew about it—no one in authority, that is. Whoever investigated that case always assumed that the motive behind your father's murder was related to what was going on between your parents. Domestic violence is a handy catch-all, especially when your father was already on record for being violent."

"You mean that thing that happened back while he was in the army?" Lucy asked.

Joanna nodded.

"That was my mother's fault, too," Lucy declared. "She and my dad were in a bar together. Like I said, that was before my father quit drinking. He told me he got mad because Mother was flirting with some other guy. Dad hit him and knocked him out. He didn't find out until later that the guy was a superior officer. They made Dad leave the army over that, but he said he didn't mind. He said by then the army was driving him crazy anyway."

"Is that when he stopped drinking?"

"Yes," Lucy said. "I liked him a lot better after he did. From then on Dad was different somehow. Nicer. Happier—until that morning at the bakery, the morning when he came to tell me about Mother. He cried the whole time he was telling me. Not really crying like a baby does, but there were tears in his eyes. He had to keep brushing them away. I pretended like I didn't see them, but I did."

"Your mother admitted that some of her injuries that day were self-inflicted," Joanna said quietly. "What if she isn't the one who shot him? What if someone else did? And what if someone else beat her up?"

Lucy seemed stunned by the very suggestion. "Is that possible?" she asked. "If Mother didn't do it, why did she say she did? Why would she go to prison for something she didn't do?"

"I don't know," Joanna replied. "Maybe she was scared. Maybe going to prison wasn't as scary as what might have happened to her if she hadn't. And it looks like it worked. As long as everyone had your mother pegged for being a killer, no one but you and your father ever suspected her of being a spy. Which is why we have to find out who killed your mother. Remember those devil's-claw patterns woven into baskets? What if the person who killed your mother is the same person who killed your father and he's gotten away with it all these years?"

"What more can I tell you?"

"After they drove away that night, what did you do?"

"I was scared," Lucy said. "I knew I had what he wanted. I was afraid he might shoot me, too, or maybe even Grandma Yates, so I didn't want to go home. That's when I decided to run away for good. When I left Cochise Stronghold, I was going to ride my bike to Tucson. I forgot about the freeway and that I couldn't ride my bike on it. On the way, I kept trying to figure out who I could ask for help. I finally made up a list—my ballet teacher, Mrs. Quick; my mother's lawyer, Ms. Goodson; and Sister Celeste, my teacher from Santa Theresa's. By the time Big Red and I made it as far as the rest area in Texas Canyon, I was too tired to ride any farther. And it seemed safe. There was a vending machine there with candy bars and drinks and a phone. That's where I made phone calls to the people on my list."

"You had money?"

"Enough. Mrs. Quick's son told me she was dead, so that didn't work. I called Ms. Goodson, but when her answering machine came on I didn't know what to say so I left my name but I didn't leave a message. There was no way for her to call me back. Finally, I reached Sister Celeste. We talked, but someone came up to use the phone. I told her I'd call her back later, but I never had a chance to call again until Sunday morning.

"I was asleep in my bedroll when Big Red woke me up

and told me someone was coming. I don't know for sure it was him, but I ran away and left everything behind. I didn't dare go back for it."

"I don't know if it was your mother's killer," Joanna said, "but whoever it was who found your camp, he broke up your bike and tore up everything else you left there."

Lucy's eyes were wide. "That means Big Red saved my life," she said.

"I believe so," Joanna returned. "So what happened then?"

"I hid for a while. Then, later, I started walking. I walked until I came to a ranch. I told the lady I had gotten lost while I was out hiking with my family. She let me use the phone. I called Sister Celeste, and she came to get me. She brought a hood for Big Red, otherwise he never would have gotten in her car. And we've been here ever since while she and Father Mulligan tried to decide what to do."

"What about your gun?" Joanna asked, remembering for the first time the .22 Catherine Yates claimed Lucy had taken along with the bedroll and extra clothing.

Lucy shrugged. "Sister Celeste told me to give it to Father Mulligan, and I did," she said. "But it was no big deal. It wasn't loaded, and I forgot to bring along any ammunition."

A relieved Joanna was gearing up for her next question when her cell phone rang. She was tempted to ignore it. "Aren't you going to answer that?" Lucy asked, shaming Joanna into it.

"Hello."

"Joanna!" Butch Dixon breathed. "Thank God I caught you. Where are you?"

Quickly, Joanna looked at her watch. It was only five. Certainly she wasn't already late for dinner. Besides, the breathless urgency in Butch's voice boded something far more serious than that.

"I'm in Saint David," she answered. "I really shouldn't be interrupted right now. I'm in the middle of an interview."

"You've got to come home right now!"

The ferocity in Butch's order took Joanna's breath away. "What is it?" she demanded. "What's happened?"

"I'm leaving the vet's right now. Dr. Ross says whatever the poison is, both dogs got into it. She's administering an emetic, and she's hoping we got them here in time."

"Poison?" Joanna repeated. "Did you say poison?"

"Yes. Both dogs, Tigger and Sadie. Jenny is in the treatment room with them. She's been a brick, but I've called Eva Lou. She and Jim Bob are coming here to take Jenny home with them, then I'll go back out to the house. Deputy Howell is there keeping an eye on things."

"Butch, what the hell has happened?"

"Just come home, Joanna," he begged. "Please. You're not going to believe me if I try to tell you. You'll have to see it with your own eyes."

TWENTY-FOUR

Joanna left Holy Trinity in such a hurry that she didn't take time to track down Sister Celeste and say she was going. After scrabbling her way back up the crumbling, sandy bank, she did turn back to wave at Lucy Ridder, but Lucy didn't respond. Instead, she walked over to the cottonwood and proceeded to coax Big Red down out of the tree and onto her shoulder.

Even in her own turmoil, Joanna was moved by the wonderful simplicity in that act and by the visible bond of trust that existed between the lonely girl and the bird she had rescued and raised. It was nothing short of miraculous that Lucy—a child whose life had been torn apart by forces beyond her control—could find comfort in caring for something else. Joanna had no doubt that Lucy's concern for Big Red accounted for the young woman's very survival. Had she not saved a little hatchling from starvation, the grown bird wouldn't have been there to warn a sleeping Lucy that someone dangerous was headed for her camp in Texas Canyon.

Speeding toward home with her lights flashing and siren blaring, Joanna couldn't get that thought out of her mind. There were only three people who could possibly have known that Lucy Ridder was calling from the rest area pay phone—Jay Quick, Sister Celeste, and Melanie Goodson.

Jay Quick had called his concerns to Joanna as soon as he put Lucy's name together with the fact that Sandra Ridder had been murdered. Sister Celeste had done everything humanly possible to protect Lucy from whoever was following her. That left only Melanie Goodson—someone who had lied about receiving a middle-of-the-night phone call but someone who was also dead.

That meant that at the moment, Bill Forsythe was the only one working on the single real lead in the case. *Tomorrow,* Joanna promised herself. *Tomorrow I'll get Ernie and Jaime playing catch-up ball.*

Once past Tombstone, between there and the Mule Mountains, Joanna kept her blue lights flashing behind the Crown Victoria's grille. The speedometer hovered right around 95 miles per hour. She made no effort to listen to the chatter on the police radio. In fact, she actively blocked it out. Butch had said she needed to see it—whatever it was—for herself. No matter what, it couldn't possibly be that bad, could it?

She tried to imagine what the crisis might be. Butch was all right, and he had said Jenny was fine. And since Jim Bob and Eva Lou were coming for Jenny, they must be okay as well. But the dogs—Sadie and Tigger. Who would have ventured onto High Lonesome Ranch and poisoned Jenny's dogs?

After puzzling over the problem for several minutes, Joanna wondered if it wasn't possible that the dogs had simply gotten into something they shouldn't have. Tigger especially was always sticking his nose into places where it didn't belong. That was especially true when it came to porcupines. To her knowledge, Joanna kept no harmful chemicals lying around the place, but maybe there were some she didn't know about—maybe something Clayton Rhodes had used in the course of his chores during his last few days on the ranch and had neglected to put away. Even so, thanks to Butch's prompt action, the dogs were being cared for by Bisbee's newly arrived vet. Joanna prayed that Dr. Millicent Ross would be able to work her curative magic.

Maybe the house was hit by a fire, she thought. *If it is, we'll rebuild. It won't be that bad.* Then, a little later she added, *Please, God. Whatever it is, don't let it be that bad.*

Coming through the highway cuts between Bisbee and the Double Adobe turnoff, Joanna scanned the upper reaches of the Sulphur Springs Valley. In the spot where she knew her house to be, she saw the telltale pulsing glow of lights from any number of emergency vehicles. There were lots of lights, but there was no dark smudge of smoke rising skyward, no layer of smoke drifting north across the valley. So no, it wasn't a fire then, or, if a fire had occurred, someone had put it out much earlier.

Joanna slowed down and turned off, first onto Double Adobe Road and then onto High Lonesome. The whole situation seemed weird to her. On the one hand she was a police officer responding to the report of an incident. It could have been an ordinary car wreck or homicide, except this one was different. When she arrived, the smashed car or worse would belong to her. How was that possible? How could it be?

Turning onto the one-lane track that led to her house, she saw that the pulsing halo of lights was much larger, much brighter. Usually she recognized the separate tire tracks that traveled her mile-long dirt access road. This time there were too many strange tracks for her to be able to identify any of them. When Joanna reached the wash, she had to slow to a crawl. The Crown Victoria, built far lower to the ground than Joanna's Blazer, had a difficult time negotiating the rugged terrain where first Reba Singleton's limo and subsequently the tow truck as well as numerous other vehicles had torn the established roadbed to pieces.

Once through the wash, Joanna sped up again, only to be forced to a stop once more when she broke through the grove of mesquite and found her way blocked by a clot of emergency vehicles. That was when the reality of the situation finally hit home. Whatever had happened, it was serious enough to have brought all these people out in the early-evening twilight. And it had happened here, on High Lonesome Ranch, in Joanna Brady's own safe haven.

She looked at the house. From the outside it *seemed* all right. There were lights on throughout, and they cast a comforting, familiar glow. *See there?* Joanna told herself as she took a deep breath. *It's going to be fine.*

She stepped out of the Crown Victoria and took stock of some of the nearby vehicles scattered haphazardly around on the roadway. There were Frank Montoya's Civvie, Ernie Carpenter's Ford van, Butch's Outback, and even Dick Voland's new Camry. She noticed the vehicles and the small clutches of people standing here and there. The groups of onlookers all seemed to be watching her questioningly, waiting for direction, perhaps—waiting for her to tell them what they should do. She heard the sound of a few voices, of people speaking to one another in the low, earnest, and self-consciously controlled voices usually reserved for guests at funerals, for broadcasters at golf tournaments, and for stunned bystanders at fatality auto accidents.

Butch Dixon detached himself from a trio of men and walked toward her. His face materialized through Joanna's growing fear like a ship emerging from a cloud of fog. She tried to read the messages written on his features—concern, anger, and more besides.

"Are you okay?" he asked, reaching for her and pulling her close.

"I'm fine, Butch," she said with a catch in her throat. "At least I *think* I'm fine. What's happened here? What's going on?"

He took her hand. "Come inside," he said grimly. "You'll see."

As soon as Butch opened the back door, Joanna caught the whiff of a jarring mix of odors. The sharp smell of mustard, hot sauce, peanut butter, vinegar, and ammonia all came flowing at her in an eye-watering mix.

"Watch your step," Butch murmured, steadying her by holding on to her elbow. "There's lots of broken glass and lots of water, so it's all terribly slippery."

Once at the doorway to the kitchen, Joanna realized he was right. Nothing Butch could have said on the phone could possibly have prepared her for the wanton destruction that had been visited on her house. She felt her pulse quicken, felt the disbelieving panic rising in her throat. For a few seconds, she could barely breathe. The oxygen came into her mouth and throat but didn't seem to pass from there to her lungs.

Months earlier, watching a television newscast, Joanna had seen the image of a dazed woman pawing through the splintered remains of her tornado-shattered home. Now, as her own pulse accelerated and as she fought back a rising sense of panic, she remembered the disbelief written on that woman's face and knew exactly what she had been going through in those awful moments—knew exactly what she had been thinking and doing. That unknown woman—that stranger—had been searching through the shattered wreckage of her home for some sign or shred or crumb of her former life. Now Joanna Brady was doing the same thing.

Standing in the doorway of her own destroyed kitchen, it seemed impossible to Joanna that any such particle existed. The devastation, beyond anything she could have imagined, was almost complete. Cupboard doors had been wrenched off their hinges and the contents of the faceless, broken shelves swept out onto the floor. Broken jars and bottles of food mingled with the remains of shattered glassware, of broken plates and dishes and serving bowls. Plastic bottles that hadn't shattered on impact—the brand-new bottle of Log Cabin pancake syrup, a half-used gallon of Wesson Oil, a partially full container of Palmolive dishwashing detergent—had all been opened and poured over the mess, with the empty bottles allowed to fall in place.

All the kitchen drawers had been pulled out, emptied, and then used as sledgehammers on the counter and the breakfast nook, smashing to pieces Andy's carefully routered Formica and demolishing the drawers themselves in the process. And all around—on the walls, the ceiling, the light fixtures—were zany fingerpaint patterns of squirted colored matter—mustard, ketchup, barbecue sauce, hot sauce—crusted with crumbs of thrown cereal and flour and sugar.

The refrigerator lay on its side, with the hacked-off end of an electrical cord dangling from the back of it like an amputated appendage. On the counter was a line of broken appliances also devoid of cords. The kitchen sink had evidently been plugged up and filled to brimming, which accounted for the soup of inch-deep soapy, greasy water that covered the floor.

Stunned beyond speech, Joanna simply looked at Butch. He shook his head. "You'd better come see the rest," he said. "Then we'll talk."

If anything, the dining room was worse. The buffet had been turned over on its side, spilling out and smashing all of

Joanna's good china and crystal. Someone had taken her good flatware—the monogrammed silver Eva Lou had given her—and had used that to gouge long scars in the smooth surface of the oak dining room table and in the upholstery of every chair.

The top of the buffet was where Joanna had kept her treasure trove of framed family pictures—casual and professional photos of Joanna and Andy; and of Joanna, Andy, and Jenny together. There were pictures of Jenny with Santa Claus and a set of ever-changing school pictures. All of those were gone. Not only had the glass been broken and the frames been bent beyond recognition, the pictures themselves had been torn out and pulled to pieces.

Unable to move, Joanna braced herself by holding on to the scarred surface of the dining room table. From that vantage point she looked as far as the living room. There, every piece of upholstered furniture had been sliced with short, jagged cuts. Handfuls of stuffing had been pulled out through the holes in great white globs of cotton. The drapes on the windows had all been cut off halfway up the walls. The blinds behind the drapes had been wrenched from their moorings.

Shaking her head, still speechless, Joanna started toward the bathroom. "You can't go in there at all," Butch said.

"Why not?"

"All the fixtures were broken off," he said. "I've turned off the water, but the drywall is soaked. It's so full of water, the walls and the ceiling may come down at any minute."

Shaking her head in astonishment, Joanna headed for her own bedroom. There it was the same story all over again. Drawers had been torn out, upended, and then smashed to smithereens. The bedding and the bed itself had been sliced to pieces, as had most, if not all, of her clothing. Joanna had left the gifts from her Sunday-afternoon bridal shower neatly stacked in one corner of the room. The boxes had all been torn open and the contents ripped to shreds. What remained had been piled into a heap in the middle of the room, where the better part of a gallon of bleach had been poured over it.

In fact, nothing seemed to have escaped the destructive frenzy, not even the creamy silk dress—still in its distinctive Nordstrom bag—that Joanna had planned to wear for her wedding ceremony on Saturday afternoon. Seeing the ruined dress, a single involuntary sob escaped her lips.

"It'll be okay," Butch whispered. "Don't worry."

Joanna took a deep breath. Standing in the middle of her wrecked bedroom, she finally regained the power of speech. "This had to take hours," she managed.

Butch nodded grimly. "Whoever it was must have turned up this morning right after you and Jenny left and made a day of it. That's why Dr. Ross is so worried about Sadie and Tigger. It may be touch and go for them because the poison was in their systems for such a long time."

Stunned, Joanna looked at him. "You mean they could die?"

Butch nodded, his eyes dry but red. "They could," he said.

Unable to say anything more, Joanna turned away from Butch so he wouldn't see the tears blurring her own eyes. When she did so, she caught sight of the shattered top of her rolltop desk—the place where she kept her various weapons under lock and key.

"My Colt Two Thousand is missing," she said as a sudden chill passed over her body. She had stopped using the Colt due to dependability problems, but she also knew that when it did fire, it was a powerful and deadly weapon.

"I know," Butch said. "I noticed that, too."

"What about Jenny's room?"

"It's fine," Butch said.

It sounded to Joanna as though he was telling her that to soothe her rather than because it was the truth. "Fine?" she demanded. "What do you mean, fine?" Even she could hear the threat of hysteria rising in her voice. "You mean, like this is fine?" she asked, swinging one arm to encompass the wreckage of her bedroom.

"I mean it's fine," Butch said. "Whoever did this left Jenny's room entirely alone. It's untouched. Nothing is broken; nothing wrecked. Now come on. We have to go back outside."

"I don't want to go outside," Joanna protested.

"We have to," Butch insisted. "Frank Montoya didn't think you should come in here at all, not until after the crime-scene techs have had a chance to process the scene. But I told him that wouldn't work—that you'd have to see it firsthand. The only way I got him to agree to that was to promise we wouldn't touch anything and that we'd come back out as soon as you had seen it for yourself. Come on."

Joanna tried to dodge away, but he caught her hand and pulled her toward the doorway. "Really, Joanna. You've seen enough. Standing here in the mess isn't going to make it any better."

"But who would do such a thing?" Joanna murmured. "Who could possibly hate me this much?"

"Good question," Butch said, leading her back the way they had come. "It's what we were talking about outside just before you drove up. Dick Voland was telling us he had a call from Reba Singleton late last night." Butch paused. "She's missing, by the way. Did you know that?"

"Of course I knew that," Joanna replied. "I'm the one who told Dick about it in the first place."

"What you maybe don't know is that Reba's husband had her served with divorce papers at her B and B here in Bisbee yesterday afternoon after the funeral and just before she was getting ready to leave town."

"He what?"

"You heard me," Butch replied. "He had the divorce papers served on the poor woman just hours after her father's funeral. The no-good son of a bitch must have been planning it for days. No wonder she didn't go flying straight home when she was supposed to. I'd be a missing person, too, if somebody had pulled that kind of asshole stunt on me."

A power surge of mind-clearing anger erupted in Joanna's head. "So that's what happened!" Joanna exclaimed. "Dennis Singleton did Reba dirt, and so she turned it all on me."

"That's the general consensus," Butch agreed.

"How could he do such a thing?"

Butch shrugged. "Some men are all heart," he said.

Looking around the mayhem that had once been Joanna's home, she saw the damage in a new light—as the manifestation of a broken woman's rage and hurt and utter despair. In her outrage, Reba Singleton had focused her anger on property—on things. Dennis Singleton, on the other hand, had aimed his heart-seeking missile directly at his wife's very soul. As Joanna grasped both those concepts, her perspective shifted. A toggle switch in her head went from OFF to ON.

"Where's Dick Voland now?" she demanded.

"Outside," Butch replied. "At least that's where he was when I left everybody else to go meet you."

They were crossing the dining room and heading back

toward the shattered kitchen when something bright and sparkly reflected back the light from the broken chandelier and caught Joanna's eyes. Up against the mopboard and almost out of sight behind the swinging door was a tiny piece of glassware—Joanna's maternal grandmother's cut-glass toothpick holder. Seeing it, Joanna realized that the light pink Depression-era piece had been knocked out of the buffet along with everything else. Something must have cushioned its fall because it had landed without breaking. Spilling a thin trail of toothpicks, it had rolled across the floor and come to rest in a place where it was almost out of sight and hidden away from the frenzy of ongoing devastation.

Escaping from Butch's grasp momentarily, Joanna bent over and scooped up the fragile piece. Holding it up to the light, Joanna examined it for cracks and chips, but it was perfect. All this while she had managed to hold her tears in check. Now they burst through and threatened to overwhelm her. Seeing the glowing toothpick holder was like catching sight of the first rainbow after a terrible thunderstorm. And, like a rainbow, the delicately colored glass held a promise that perhaps the worst was over and that somehow, someday, the sun would shine again.

With a sigh, Joanna plunged the piece deep in her pocket.

"Wait a minute," Butch objected. "I told you I promised Frank that we wouldn't touch anything as long as we were in here."

"Too bad," Joanna said. "This toothpick holder belongs to me, and I'm keeping it. If it turns out this is the only thing in the whole house with usable fingerprints on it, that's too bad as well. In that case, we're going to have a hard time catching the perp who did this."

Butch looked at her. "It sounds like Sheriff Brady is back," he said. "I think you're going to be okay."

She nodded. "I will be okay," she agreed. "Seeing all this was a shock to the system, but this is all stuff—inanimate objects. I'm far more upset about what happened to the dogs. What about Kiddo and the cattle?"

"They seem to be fine."

"Good."

"There is one thing that really pisses me off," Butch added.

"What's that?"

The shadow of a grin played around the corners of his mouth. "Here we spent all that time and effort on Sunday cleaning your damned oven," Butch told her. "In all this mess, nobody's ever going to notice—not your mother, and not mine, either."

Hearing his good-natured grousing, Joanna felt some of the strain drain out of her own body. After all, this was Butch Dixon's way of dealing with a crisis—to make light of it if at all possible. Under most circumstances, it would have been Joanna's preferred way of coping as well, but she allowed herself only the smallest of giggles. She didn't dare laugh out loud. It would be only the merest of baby steps to go from dissolving into real laughter and then tumbling downward into a fit of hysterics and unstoppable tears. Right that minute, none of those were acceptable options.

As Joanna and Butch emerged from the house, Frank Montoya and Ernie Carpenter met them on the back porch. Concern was written large on both men's anxious faces. "Are you all right?" Frank asked.

"I'm okay," Joanna assured him with far more certainty than she felt. "Where's Dick?"

"Dick Voland?" Frank returned. "He left a few minutes ago. He said he was going to track Reba Singleton down and try to talk to her."

"You let him walk away just like that?" Joanna demanded. "Did anyone happen to tell him that my Colt Two Thousand is missing from the locked desk in my bedroom? What if an unsuspecting Dick Voland walks right up to Reba Singleton and she blows him to kingdom come?"

"We tried to stop him," Frank said. "But he wouldn't listen."

"Was he wearing a vest?"

Ernie Carpenter shook his head. "I don't think so. If I remember right, he never much approved of wearing the damned things."

Joanna glared at the detective. "Sounds like somebody else I know," she said. "But let's all remember, Dick Voland is a civilian now. If he's injured or killed as a result of his involvement in what ought to be a police action, you can bet there's going to be hell to pay. Our department will be caught in a hail of lawsuits that will take the wind out of our budget for years to come. Let's go."

"Go where?" Ernie asked.

"To where this all started," Joanna replied in exasperation. "And where I'm guessing Reba Singleton means for it to end—to Rhodes Ranch."

Ernie and Frank immediately turned on their heels and headed for their respective vehicles. "Hey, you two. Don't leave without me," Joanna yelled after them. "I'll catch up in a minute."

"So will I," Butch added at once. "I'm coming, too."

"No, you're not," Joanna returned. "You don't have a weapon, you don't have a vest, and you don't have a badge. That means you're staying here."

"Like hell—!"

Just then a pair of headlights came careening into the yard. Dodging around the clutch of parked vehicles, it skidded to a stop next to the gate and scattered a team of crime-scene techs who were gathered there assembling their materials.

"Joanna Brady, what on earth is going on?" Eleanor Lathrop demanded. She slammed the car door shut behind her and came tottering up the uneven walkway in a pair of high heels. "We were all just getting ready to leave for our dinner reservation when Eva Lou called and told us something dreadful had happened out here—something about the dogs being poisoned and I don't know what all else."

"Sorry, Mom," Joanna said hurriedly. "I have to go. Ernie Carpenter and Frank Montoya are waiting for me." Neatly sidestepping her mother's trajectory, Joanna dashed for the gate, leaving Butch Dixon trapped behind her.

"But what's going on?" Eleanor Lathrop Winfield insisted.

"Don't worry," Joanna called back over her shoulder. "I'm sure Butch will explain everything."

# TWENTY-FIVE

Not wanting to drive either of the Crown Victorias over such rough terrain, Frank commandeered Deputy Howell's Bronco for the short trip to Rhodes Ranch. They were crossing the wash when Joanna's cell phone rang.

"She's here," Dick Voland said, as soon as Joanna answered. "She's here at her father's place."

"I figured as much," Joanna said. "We're on our way. What's happening?"

"She's swinging."

"She's what?"

"Swinging. There's an old rope swing in one of the cottonwoods between the house and the barn. She's swinging on that."

"Be careful, Dick," Joanna warned. "She's armed. My Colt Two Thousand is missing from the house. I'm guessing she has it somewhere on her person. Have you spoken to her?"

"She doesn't even know I'm here," Dick replied. "I turned off my lights driving up the road and hiked in the last few hundred yards. I suggest you do the same."

"Where are you?"

"Out of sight on the far side of the house."

"Aren't you afraid she'll hear you talking on the phone?"

"Not right now," Dick replied. "She's singing at the top of her lungs. If she stops, all bets are off."

"What's happening?" Frank asked. "What's going on?"

Keeping the earpiece glued to her ear, Joanna explained to Frank what she had learned. "Ask him if he's got a plan," Frank said when she finished.

"Don't bother," Dick said. "I heard that. My only plan right this minute is to wait for reinforcements."

"What's she singing?" Joanna asked.

"What do you mean?"

"What song?"

"What the hell does that have to do with the price of tea in China?"

"It might give us some idea of what Reba Singleton's mental state is right now," Joanna said. "Listen for a minute and see if you can tell."

"Sounds like 'When You Wish Upon a Star,' something like that," Dick Voland said. "Isn't that from one of those Walt Disney movies, *Sleeping Beauty,* maybe?"

"*Pinocchio,*" Joanna told him. "It's Jiminy Cricket's song."

"So?"

"I don't know. What's she doing now?"

"Still swinging, pumping like mad."

Joanna picked up the radio and called Dispatch. "Tica, tell Ernie to pull over. We'll all get out and walk from here. And one more thing. Where's Detective Carbajal?"

"Over by Pearce with Catherine Yates. You told him he should go there after attending Sandra Ridder's funeral. At last report, he was still there."

"Good," Joanna said. "Glad to hear it."

Seconds later, Ernie's Econoline van pulled over to the side of the road. Frank followed suit. While leaving High Lonesome Ranch, Joanna had stopped by her Crown Victoria long enough to pull on a pair of sneakers. Now, as she and Ernie and Frank started up the rocky track to Clayton Rhodes' place in Mexican Canyon, Joanna was grateful she had done so. She was also thankful that there was enough moonlight so that, once their eyes adjusted to the lack of headlights, the three officers were able to see well enough to walk safely.

Moving along, Joanna couldn't help but be amazed. In the few minutes since leaving her damaged house and during the ride in Deputy Howell's Bronco, she had moved beyond the scope of her own personal crisis and slipped back into her role as sheriff. It seemed she couldn't be both victim and police officer at the same time, and that was just as well.

"Dick is asking how you want to handle this," Frank asked. While Joanna had been on the radio with Dispatch, Frank Montoya had maintained the cell-phone link with Dick Voland.

"Can he see if she's holding the weapon?" Joanna asked.

"Negative on that," Frank answered a little later. "He can't see it, but she's wearing a heavy jacket of some kind. It could be concealed in a pocket."

"I want to try to talk her down," Joanna said.

"Talk!" Frank exploded. "She's got your Colt, Joanna, and you want to talk?" Through the phone, she could hear Dick Voland's angry objections as well.

"First we're going to get the lay of the land," Joanna continued. "I don't remember where that swing is in relation to the house. Is it closer to the front or the back?"

"Dick says back."

"Okay, so I'll go to the back of the house and try to talk to her from there. One of you can come with me to back me up. The others should stay up near the front."

"Shouldn't someone go around and try to come up behind her?" Frank asked.

"You mean, so if shooting breaks out, we can wing one of our own in the process?" Joanna asked. "I don't think so."

"You're right," Frank agreed. "Not a good idea." Then, after a pause, he said, "By the way, Dick said to tell you now she's switched to that song from *The Wizard of Oz*—'Somewhere Over the Rainbow,' Dick thinks it's called."

"Fortunately, neither one of you will ever end up on 'Name That Tune.' " Joanna told them. "I'm sure Reba Singleton remembers them from when she was a little kid. From a time when the world wasn't such a scary, uncertain place. My guess is she's wishing she could go back there."

"Don't we all," Ernie Carpenter breathed. The road was rising sharply, and the detective was having to huff and puff in order to keep up. "I still don't think talking is going to do any good. I vote we lob a canister of tear gas under the tree and catch her when she gets off the swing."

"And what happens if she falls out of the swing and breaks her neck in the process?" Joanna asked. "We're doing this my way and talking first."

"Okay," Frank Montoya said. "You're the boss."

By the time they reached the gate to the yard, they could hear the singing. Dick Voland came to the gate to meet them. "Climb over the fence," he advised in a whisper. "I tried opening the gate. It squeaks like a son of a bitch."

Joanna hiked up her skirt and scrambled over the fence. Dick Voland was there to break her fall as she landed. "Are you wearing a vest?"

He shook his head.

"Armed?"

"Yes."

"All right," Joanna said. "Frank, you're with me. Dick, you and Ernie stay on the front porch and out of sight unless this thing goes in the toilet. Understood?"

"You can't—" Dick Voland began.

"I can and I will," Joanna declared. "Front porch or nothing. Front porch or go down the road. Which?"

"Front porch," Voland agreed glumly.

As Joanna and Frank made their way around the side yard, walking past thorny rosebushes and clumps of sharp-edged pampas grass, Reba Singleton tuned up with another song—a Teresa Brewer–like rendition of "I Saw Mommy Kissing Santa Claus." The singing was plaintive. Sad. With a sudden jolt of insight, Joanna realized why Jenny's room hadn't been touched. Jenny was a child, and in her torment, so was Reba Joy Singleton.

"Reba?" Joanna called softly, once she and Frank were in position.

The singing stopped. The swinging did not. There was a steady creak from a rope rubbing on a tree bough. That didn't change.

"Who is it?"

"You know who it is," Joanna said softly.

"How do you like being left with nothing?" Reba demanded. "How does it feel?"

"I'm sorry about your husband," Joanna said. "What he did must have hurt you very badly."

"How do you know about that?" Reba asked sharply. "Who told you?"

"Dick Voland," Joanna said. "You're the one who told him."

"Oh, that's right," she said. "I guess I did. And it did hurt. Dennis has a girlfriend, you know. Some guppy bimbo half his age that he picked out of the shallow end of the gene pool. He says he has to marry her because she's pregnant. Do you believe it? He's probably been planning this for months. I wouldn't be surprised if he hasn't moved most of his money offshore. That's why I wanted this place. I'm not completely stupid. I saw it coming even if I didn't want to admit it in public. I wanted this place so I'd have somewhere to run to if it came to that."

"Did your father know what was going on between you and your husband?"

"Are you kidding? We hadn't spoken in years. But now that I've been here, I remember how much I hate it. Everything but this swing. When I was little, I used to pretend that whenever I was in this swing I could see over the mountains. The whole time I was swinging, I told myself that someday I'd get out of here. And you know what? I did. I got away whole, and I'll be damned if I'll come crawling back. You can have this awful, godforsaken house. I don't want it."

She paused. "I'm sorry about what I did to your house. It was like I was crazy. Maybe I *am* crazy. But I'll get Dennis to pay for it. After all, it is his fault."

"Do you have an attorney?" Joanna asked.

"No. If you're going to arrest me, I suppose I'll need one."

"I mean a divorce attorney," Joanna said.

The steady squeak of the rope began to slow. "I do have one of those," Reba Singleton said thoughtfully. "Joyce Roberts is her name. I've used her several times through the years. She's really quite good."

"Have you been in touch with her about your current situation, about what's going on with Dennis?"

"No."

"I have a cell phone here," Joanna said quietly. "You're welcome to use it, if you'd like to call her and get her on the job." For several seconds there was no sound, only the ever-slowing scrape of the rope. "And, if what you suspect is true—if your husband is busy moving assets offshore—you probably don't have a moment to lose."

There was another long pause. "You'd let me do that?" Reba Singleton asked. "You'd let me use your telephone?"

"Sure. But first, let me ask you something. When you were in my house, did you take a gun?"

"Yes."

"Where is it?"

No answer.

"Where?"

"It's in my pocket."

"Put it down, Reba," Joanna ordered calmly. "Put it down on the ground so no one gets hurt."

"I'm not going to hurt anyone else with it. I was going to use it on myself."

"You don't want to do that," Joanna said. "You want to stick around and give Dennis Singleton what he deserves, and I'm sure Joyce Roberts will be more than happy to help you do it."

There was another long, long silence after that, followed eventually by a soft thud in the grass. "There," Reba said. "I dropped the gun. Now can I use the phone?"

TWENTY-SIX

Walking back to the cars, Joanna was almost giddy with relief. She had taken what could have been a terrible situation and had turned it around. Her strategic calls—her critical decisions—had transformed something that might have turned SWAT-team ugly into pass-the-cell-phone and not pass-the-ammunition.

"What do you mean, we're not going to arrest her?" Frank Montoya demanded.

"Just what I said. We're not. Her attorney is making arrangements for Reba to check into a hospital in Tucson for ten days of psychiatric evaluation. This way she pays for it. If we arrest her, we pay. Which of those two choices sounds like a better idea to you? Not only that, Reba says she's willing to sign a statement acknowledging her culpability. She's also going to have her attorney draw up a letter outlining her willingness to pay for all damages. If the letter isn't forthcoming by the time she's dismissed from the hospital, fine; we can arrest her then. But in my opinion, the Cochise County Jail can't afford to house someone who's used to flying in and out of town on board a private jet."

Frank shook his head. "Think how it's going to look. People will say you didn't have her arrested because of what was going on between the two of you concerning her father's will."

"And people will say the same thing if I do have her arrested, only then we'll have to deal with everything else," Joanna countered. "I want Reba Singleton free to leave the hospital, go straight home, and start working on her divorce proceedings, in which, by the way, I wish her the best of luck."

Just then Tica Romero's voice came over the radio again. "What is it this time?" Joanna asked.

"I have a call from Detective Carbajal. He's still with Mrs. Yates. She's wondering where her granddaughter is and wants to know when she can see her."

So much had happened between the last time Joanna had spoken to Jaime Carbajal and right then that she had to think hard about what he knew and didn't know. Joanna turned to Frank. "Has anyone told him about the diskette?"

"I did," Frank said. "At the same time I let him know Lucy Ridder had been found. I just didn't tell him *where* she had been found."

Joanna nodded. "Patch me through to him, if you can, Tica," Joanna said. "I think we'll do better talking directly than with you passing messages back and forth."

"Wait," Frank said during the pause while they waited for Tica to make the connection. "There's something else neither one of you know—something I forgot to tell you in all this other excitement. Two things, actually."

"What?"

"For one thing, the evidence clerk in Tucson pulled off a small miracle. She found the bullet from Tom Ridder's case and shipped it over to the state crime-lab gun unit. And guess what? It matches the bullet that killed Sandra Ridder."

"I already knew that," Joanna said. "Lucy told me."

Frank made a face. "Nothing like spoiling a guy's fun," he grumbled.

"What else?" Joanna asked.

"Ernie Carpenter spent all afternoon working with his connections at Fort Huachuca."

"And?"

"There's no official record that Sandra Ridder ever worked on post. We have anecdotal evidence that she worked there. That's what people have *told* us. If so, however, every single official reference to her has been deleted from the computer records. Right this minute there isn't even so much as a parking pass with her name on it."

"That's crazy," Joanna said. "It doesn't make any sense."

"Maybe not," Frank replied. "But consider this. The hacker who lifted those encrypted codes was no lightweight. How hard would it be for someone like him to delete a person's job and personnel records?"

"Not very," Joanna said after a moment's thought. "In fact, probably not hard at all."

"That's what I thought," Frank said.

"Sheriff Brady?" Jaime queried.

"Yes."

"I just heard about what happened at your house," Jaime Carbajal said. "Is everyone okay?"

Joanna found the switch from case to case—from official to personal—jarring and disconcerting at the same time. "We're all fine," Joanna answered after a moment. "Except for the dogs. They're still at the vet's. The last I heard, Dr. Ross couldn't tell if they're going to make it or not."

"How bad is the damage to your place? And is Reba Singleton really the one who's responsible?"

"The damage is pretty bad," Joanna conceded, flashing back to her last look at her devastated kitchen. "And yes, Reba did do it, but she's been handled. As of now, I'm convinced she's no longer a threat to herself or others. Even so, her attorney in California requested that she be checked into a hospital for evaluation. And no, we're not placing her under arrest at this time. What's going on with you?"

"I've spent the whole afternoon here with Catherine Yates—ever since the funeral. So far, there's been no sign of trouble. She was overjoyed to hear Lucy has been found, and she's frantic to see her granddaughter. She's willing to come see her tonight if that's possible."

Gauging her own diminished personal resources, Joanna shook her head. She had been through far too much that day to think through all the ramifications of sending someone back to Holy Trinity to pave the way for a late-night visit from Catherine Yates. And Lucy Ridder had been through too much as well. Right that second, Joanna hoped Lucy was bedded down and sleeping in the peaceful warmth and safety of one of Holy Trinity's retreat accommodations.

"No," Joanna said. "Tell her the reunion will have to wait until tomorrow. I interviewed Lucy myself, but only partially. We were interrupted halfway through. I want you and Ernie to have a chance to talk to Lucy in person before anyone else does, although, since she's a juvenile, we may have to allow the grandmother to be present while we talk to her. What Lucy has to tell us is going to be important, Jaime. She witnessed her mother's murder, and she may be able to ID the killer."

"Whoa! You mean she saw it go down?"

"That's what she said. So in addition to an interview, we'll need a composite drawing as well. As an eyewitness we have an obligation to keep Lucy safe, which is what she is right now. Tell Catherine Yates if she wants to discuss this with me, she should come to my office first thing tomorrow morning."

"We've been talking all day. She's been telling me . . ."

As Jaime began speaking, the Bronco Joanna was riding in emerged from the mesquite grove on High Lonesome Ranch and came to a stop behind the group of vehicles parked bumper to bumper outside Joanna's fenced yard. If anything, more people were in attendance now than had been earlier, when Frank Montoya and Joanna had set off for Rhodes Ranch.

"Where did all these yahoos come from?" Frank muttered.

"Look, Jaime," Joanna interrupted. "I can't talk anymore right now. I can't even think, and you've been on duty far too long as well. Have Tica send someone out to relieve you. I'll see you at the briefing in the morning. All right?"

"Fine."

"Good call," Frank said, as Joanna returned the radio microphone to its holder. "I was afraid you were going to send someone back over to Saint David. We can all do only so much, and that goes for you personally as well. Are you sure you should be at the briefing in the morning? Shouldn't you take the day off and tend to this mess?"

Joanna was touched by his concern. She shook her head. "Mess or no mess, I'll be at the office in the morning," she told him. "I'm still getting married on Saturday afternoon, and I'm still taking Friday and all next week off for my honeymoon. You can bet your butt I'll be at the briefing tomorrow morning."

"Suit yourself," Frank said.

From inside Joanna's house came periodic flashes of light, indicating one of the crime-scene techs was taking photographs. The burst of adrenaline that had fueled her body and kept Joanna going through the Reba Singleton crisis seemed to dissipate, leaving her drained and exhausted.

"Frank, please go tell whoever's taking those pictures to stop," Joanna said wearily. "If we do end up prosecuting this case, the evidence the crime techs have now—fingerprints, photos, and whatever else—will have to do. I want everyone to clear out of here. Now."

Ahead of the Bronco, illuminated in the headlights, Marliss Shackleford came hotfooting it toward them. Suddenly Joanna was struck by her own vulnerability. It was one thing to be tackled by the press in her role as sheriff. That was an assumed risk—part of the game. It was something else entirely to be targeted because you were the innocent and unwilling victim of someone else's act of violence.

"That goes double for her," Joanna added, nodding in the approaching reporter's direction as Frank exited the vehicle. "I want Marliss Shackleford out of here before now, if that's possible."

Frank laughed. "I'll see what I can do. Does that mean you're not granting interviews?" he added, slipping smoothly from chief deputy into his other departmental function—that of Media Relations officer.

"Right," Joanna said. "My only comment is no comment, and I'm not setting foot outside this vehicle or rolling down the window until you get rid of her."

Joanna watched while Frank and Marliss engaged in a long, heated debate. With the windows closed, it was impossible to hear exactly what was being said, but from Marliss' wild gesticulations it was pretty clear what was going on. Finally, with a departing wordless glare in Joanna's direction, Marliss stalked away.

Seconds after Frank walked off as well, Butch showed up and opened the car door. Joanna tumbled out of the Bronco and into his arms. She had been tough and strong long enough. Now all she wanted was to be held and comforted and told everything would be all right. Butch Dixon was happy to oblige.

"Come on," he said. "I'm taking you home."

"To your house?"

"Where else? I certainly can't leave you here."

"Shouldn't I go inside and get a nightgown for tonight and something to change into tomorrow morning?"

"Sweetie pie," he said. "The whole time you've been gone, I've been inside your house and looking over the damage. What you're wearing is what you've got."

"There's nothing left?"

"Nothing salvageable. But there is some good news."

"What's that?"

"I talked to Dr. Ross a few minutes ago. She says she thinks both dogs are going to pull through. Come on."

Joanna looked up at Butch through suddenly tear-dimmed eyes. That was just about the time a photographer from *The Bisbee Bee* caught the two of them in mid-embrace. Joanna started to object, but Butch took her hand.

"Forget it," he said. "They got what they came for. Let them have it."

"Wait," she said. "What about Kristin? I'm sure she was planning on spending the night tonight as well."

Butch nodded. "Fortunately for Kristin, all her stuff was in Jenny's room, which means it's fine. She'll be spending the night at Terry's. I don't think she minded very much," he added with a smile.

An hour later, with a peanut-butter-and-jelly sandwich and single stiff Scotch under her belt, Joanna lay next to Butch in the queen-sized bed of his Saginaw-neighborhood home. "Remember, we weren't going to have any more sleep-overs before the wedding," she said wistfully.

"This isn't a sleep-over," Butch returned. "You're a refugee."

"With all this going on, maybe we should postpone the wedding," Joanna hinted.

"No."

"The honeymoon, then. What if we took it later?"

"No. If anything, we need the honeymoon more than ever."

"But, Butch. How are we going to get the mess cleaned up? It's so much—"

"Don't you mean how am *I* going to clean up the mess? Well, *you* don't have to. As the guy on that "*Red Green* Show" says, we're all in this together. I've talked to a whole lot of people tonight. When Frank Montoya came back and shut down the crime-scene investigation, people were ready to go to work cleaning up right then.

"I sent everyone home tonight, but they'll be back first thing in the morning. Jeff and Marianne will be there. Angie Kellogg and her boyfriend, that parrot guy. Jim Bob and Eva Lou. My folks. Your brother and his wife, to say nothing of your mother and who knows who else. And the fact that all those people will be doing salvage and cleanup means you don't have to. You go to the department and do what you have to do in order for us to be out of town next week. Besides, it's not going to be that bad. Except for the bathroom and kitchen the repairs are mostly cosmetic. Once we clean things up and dry the place out, it will be livable again. But maybe we don't want to do that."

"Don't want to do what?"

"Live there. I've been reading articles in newspapers and magazines about a contractor from Tucson, a guy named Quentin Branch, who specializes in building rammed-earth houses. The house is actually constructed so the walls are made of layers of compacted dirt. A lot of time, whatever soil needs to be moved from the site in order to make way for construction can be worked into the construction of the house itself rather than having to be hauled off in dump trucks. Due to the miracle of natural insulation, rammed-earth houses are warm in the winter and cool in the summer. If we did that and built from scratch, we'd be starting married life fresh in a place that didn't belong to somebody else first, either to you and Andy, or to me. It could be our place, Joanna, yours and mine."

"It sounds like you've been giving this idea a lot of thought," she said quietly.

"I have," Butch admitted. "Long before what happened today. I've been worried about how all our furniture was going to fit into one place. How we'd all survive with that one bathroom and still be friends, to say nothing of lovers."

"You were worried about that?" Joanna asked. Butch nodded. "So was I. I couldn't figure out how it would work, but now it's not nearly such a problem since all my furniture is wrecked."

"Not all of it," Butch said. "Jim Bob and I were talking about how to repair the damage to the dining room table and the buffet. But going back to what we were talking about— what would you think of the idea of building a new place?"

"I guess we could think about it," Joanna conceded. "After all, thinking doesn't cost anything."

At nine o'clock the next morning, feeling grubby in her clothing from the previous day, Sheriff Joanna Brady hurried into the conference room just in time for the morning briefing. Frank Montoya and the two detectives were already present and drinking coffee.

"Hi, guys," Joanna said, trying to keep things on a businesslike basis. She knew from meeting with Kristin Marsten a few minutes earlier that on the morning after the disaster at High Lonesome Ranch expressions of sympathy tended to erode her emotional control.

"Sorry I'm late," she announced breezily. "I just got off the phone with Lucy Ridder. I've made arrangements for her to come here to be interviewed by Frank and Ernie and to do the composite drawing. I was in such a hurry yesterday that I forgot to bring Sister Celeste back here to the department to pick up her car. Right this minute, it's still out in the parking lot, so she'll be coming along with Lucy. That way, she can give Lucy some moral support and pick up her car at the same time. And since Sister Celeste already met you, Frank, I told her you're the one who will come to Saint David to pick them up."

"Good enough," Frank said. "How soon?"

"As soon as you can get to Saint David after we finish up here. So where do we stand?"

"I already told Jaime about the computer thing," Ernie Carpenter offered. "About Sandra Ridder's work record being erased out at Fort Huachuca. He has some thoughts on the subject."

All eyes in the room focused on Jaime Carbajal. "Which are?" Joanna urged.

"I started to tell you about this last night. When I was talking to Catherine Yates yesterday afternoon, she finally admitted that she hadn't been entirely truthful when she spoke to us earlier. She told us she knew weeks earlier that Sandra was due to be released from prison. It seems somebody from the Justice Department came to Sandra several months ago. Whoever it was told her that somebody had finally gotten around to investigating allegations of security leaks that had occurred at Fort Huachuca back in the early nineties.

"He told her that investigators had somehow tied her into

a plot that involved the lifting of top-secret command and control codes from STRATCOM for delivery to the Iraqis. The agent from the Justice Department offered her a sweet deal—an early out, full immunity from prosecution, and witness-protection status if she would tell them everything she knew. Sandra Ridder was nobody's dummy. According to Catherine, she agreed to the deal and then upped the ante by offering to deliver an actual diskette containing encrypted codes in exchange for an extra cash bonus."

"Any idea which agent made the deal?"

Jaime Carbajal shook his head. "None. My guess is that something like this is going to be damned difficult to trace from this end or from the bottom up."

Joanna nodded. "Full-immunity packages don't get passed out by lower-echelon players. I'll give Adam York a call over at DEA. He may have some idea as to where we should start looking. But here's my real concern: Why didn't Catherine Yates bother to tell us any of this earlier?"

"She was afraid to," Jaime answered. "Sandra had sworn her to secrecy. She told her mother that the other people involved—the people she used to work with—would kill her in a minute if they knew she was spilling the beans. She said that's what they did to Tom Ridder. He found one of the disks before she had a chance to deliver it. Ridder hid the diskette and threatened to blow the whistle on the entire Fort Huachuca operation. Whoever was running the show tried to get the diskette back, but Ridder wouldn't tell where he'd hidden it. So they killed him, and convinced Sandra to take the fall for it. They told her that if she didn't plead guilty to Tom's death and keep the conspirators' involvement out of it, they'd kill Lucy the same way they killed Tom Ridder."

"And she believed them?" Joanna said.

"Evidently. If I'd been in her shoes, I think I would have, too."

"You're saying Sandra Ridder spent all those years in prison in order to *protect* her daughter—to save Lucy's life?"

"That's what Catherine Yates told me."

"Assuming she's telling the truth now, that is," Joanna said. "At this point, I'm not sure I'd believe a word she says. What do you think, Ernie? Does any of this relate to what you told us about Sandra Ridder's civil-service existence being erased from Fort Huachuca records?"

"Possibly," Ernie Carpenter replied. "It could be part of a witness-protection protocol. I'm not entirely sure how that stuff works."

"Another question for our source at Justice whenever we manage to find one," Joanna said. "One other thing keeps bothering me. I know what our pet hacker said about even old encryption codes being valuable. Still, how valuable can they be? Three people are dead right now, and it could easily have been four.

"Melanie Goodson has to have been involved from the get-go. When Lucy placed those three rest-area calls that night, she thought she was calling people who would help her. And two out of the three—Sister Celeste and Jay Quick—did try to help. I'm guessing Melanie Goodson traced the call—possibly through caller ID—and then sent somebody out to the rest area looking for Lucy."

Jaws dropped all around the conference table. "Are you saying somebody came to Texas Canyon looking for Lucy?" Frank Montoya demanded.

"That's exactly what I said. And you'll never guess who it was, folks—the same guy who shot Sandra Ridder the night before. He came there and spent the afternoon hanging around the phone booth. And Sunday morning he came looking for her again. If it hadn't been for Lucy's pet hawk calling out a timely warning, we'd have another victim on our hands. I figure there's only one way an eight-year-old computer disk can still be worth the price of four separate lives. Whatever was happening back then must still be going on."

"Wait a minute," Ernie said. "That would mean whoever pulled Sandra Ridder's records might have had nothing at all to do with the Justice Department and everything to do with keeping suspicion from falling on him."

"Exactly," Joanna said. "And someone with that kind of time-in-place shouldn't be all that difficult to find. My brother, Bob Brundage, has spent the last six years of his life working in the Pentagon. He's out at the house today cleaning up the mess, but he might be able to point us in some likely directions. One of you might give him a call, or I'll talk to him when I go out there at lunchtime and see if he has any ideas."

"What about Sheriff Forsythe?" Frank Montoya asked. "Has he heard any of this?"

"How could he when we're all hearing it for the first time? We'll take this morning to track down the leads we have now. Once we do that, interview Lucy Ridder, and have the composite drawing in hand, I'll call Sheriff Forsythe personally. In the meantime, I don't see any need to rush. After all, he wasn't in any hurry to help us. Anything else?"

"Yes," Ernie Carpenter said. "I want to know about your dogs. How are they?"

Joanna took a deep breath. "I talked to Dr. Ross first thing this morning. When Reba Singleton checked into the Copper Queen Hospital for observation before transport to Tucson, she had a whole collection of pharmaceuticals and designer drugs in her purse—antidepressants, sleeping pills, muscle relaxants, whatever. She told us she slipped the dogs a double dose of her Valium. It knocked them out for the better part of twenty-four hours, but it's not fatal, and there shouldn't be any long-term damage. Now that they've slept it off, they're on their feet and ready to come home."

"That's a relief," Ernie said. "And how are you?"

Joanna looked from one face to the other. "Grateful," she said at last. "It could have been so much worse."

The meeting broke up several minutes later. Back in her office, Joanna found she already had a stack of messages. She was reaching for the phone to return the first one when it rang before she could pick it up.

"Joanna, how are you?" Eleanor Lathrop Winfield asked without preamble. "Are you all right?"

"I'm fine, Mother," Joanna replied. "I guess I'm a little tired, but otherwise fine. How are you?"

"Busy," Eleanor replied briskly. "Maggie Dixon, Eva Lou, Marcie, and I just came back from the house." Marcie Brundage was Joanna's sister-in-law, the wife of a brother who had been put up for adoption by Joanna's not-yet-married parents. Only recently, after the death of his adoptive parents, had Bob Brundage sought out his birth family.

"The men are busy as can be," Eleanor rattled on. "They've brought in a Dumpster to clean the mess into. Milo has an insurance adjuster on the scene monitoring everything that's broken and keeping track of whatever's being hauled out. That way, in case Reba Singleton *doesn't* pay up, you'll at least be able to file an insurance claim."

Milo Davis of the Davis Insurance Agency had once been Joanna's boss. Even now, several years later, he remained her insurance agent.

"Watching all that stuff being thrown out was just too

hard on Eva Lou," Eleanor continued. "She couldn't bear to watch, since so much of your furniture used to be hers. I'm sure Butch noticed how upset she was. I believe that's why he suggested we girls run some errands for him. He gave us a list. We're off to Tucson to see what we can do about it."

The idea of Joanna's sister-in-law, her former mother-in-law, her mother-in-law-to-be, and her mother all driving around in the same car together struck terror in Joanna's very soul. There was no telling what might happen. "What kind of list?" she asked warily.

"Never you mind," Eleanor replied firmly. "But I do have one piece of wonderful news."

"What's that?"

"I talked to a girl from Nordstrom's. I called their company headquarters up in Seattle, and guess what? Once I told them what had happened, they managed to locate another dress just like your wedding dress—same size, same color, everything. They found it in their store in San Francisco. They're Fed-Exing it out today—this afternoon. It should arrive here in Bisbee tomorrow. Early afternoon, one-thirty at the latest. What do you think of that?"

The fact that her wedding dress no longer existed had been such a huge stumbling block in Joanna's mind that she hadn't even allowed herself to think about it, much less go searching for a solution. Now she didn't have to. Eleanor had solved the problem for her.

"I can barely believe it, Mom," Joanna said with a lump in her throat. "In fact, it's pretty damned wonderful—and so are you."

"Thank you, Joanna. Now don't you worry. I'm sure we'll soon have everything under control."

After Joanna put down the phone, she buried her face in her hands and allowed herself the luxury of a good cry. It was only when she finished crying and was blowing her nose that she realized one other important thing about that conversation with her mother. For the very first time, in all the months Eleanor Lathrop Winfield had known the man, she had called her future son-in-law Butch instead of Frederick.

It indicated a sea change in her mother's attitude, and that was pretty damned wonderful, too.

TWENTY-SEVEN

That morning the phone calls and messages that came to Joanna's office gave telling testimony as to what was right with small-town America. One of the first messages came from Daisy Maxwell, who left word that her husband Moe would be taking enough food to feed a work crew of fifteen out to High Lonesome Ranch at lunchtime. If the crew was larger than that and more food was needed, just give her a call.

The messages included expressions of sympathy, concern, and outrage. There were offers of replacement furniture and appliances, offers to do free repairs and painting, to say nothing of offers of places to stay while the repairs were being made. The outpouring of sympathy was similar to the ones that had occurred when Andy died. The difference was, at the time of her husband's death, Joanna had been in too much emotional pain to appreciate or even notice the many kindnesses of friends and neighbors. This time she noticed, and she was overwhelmed with gratitude.

Between calls and while she waited for Frank Montoya to return to the Justice Complex with Lucy Ridder, Joanna tried to work. She attempted to call Adam York but was unable to reach him. She dealt with some of her routine paperwork, but that day Joanna Brady's heart wasn't in the task of conquering her current batch of mail. Around eleven she checked in with Detective Carpenter.

"What's happening, Ernie? Any luck tracking the witness-protection offer?"

"Not so far, but we're working on the problem. It would help if everyone I asked didn't think I was pulling some kind of April Fool's stunt."

"Keep after it," Joanna told him.

About eleven-thirty, Frank Montoya called her on her private line.

"We stopped for lunch on the way, but we're driving into the parking lot right now," he said. "How about if we use your private entrance so we don't have to drag Lucy and Big Red in through the front lobby?"

"Are you telling me you brought the bird along?" Joanna asked.

"He's wearing his hood," Frank said. "Lucy refused to come without him."

"Okay, then," Joanna said. "And you're right. You'll be better off bringing them in the back way. You know my door code, don't you?"

"Yes."

A minute or so later, Frank ushered Lucy Ridder, Sister Celeste, and Big Red into Joanna's office through her private entrance. The red-tailed hawk, with his head swathed in a black hood, perched quietly on Lucy's shoulder.

"Mr. Montoya told us what happened to your house," Lucy Ridder said, stopping beside Joanna's desk. "I'm sorry it happened."

"Thanks," Joanna replied. "So am I, and I appreciate your concern. But let's get back to you. Did Mr. Montoya tell you what we're going to need from you today, that you'll be interviewed by our two homicide detectives—Detectives Carpenter and Carbajal?"

"Yes."

"And that later on, after the interview is over, we'll have an artist help you create a composite sketch of the man who killed your mother?"

"Yes, he told me that, too." Lucy turned and surveyed the room. "Will my grandmother be with me when I talk to the detectives?"

Joanna glanced at Frank. After what Jaime Carbajal had said the night before about Catherine Yates' eagerness to see her granddaughter, Joanna had expected the woman would have met her at the door first thing that morning. In the flurry of taking phone calls and returning messages, the fact that Catherine had yet to show up had somehow escaped Joanna's notice. As a juvenile, if Lucy Ridder demanded that her grandmother be present, the interview would have to be delayed until Catherine Yates' arrival.

"I thought she'd be here by now, but she isn't," Joanna said carefully. "If you're worried about her coming, I'll be glad to bring her to the interview room as soon as she arrives."

Lucy nodded, then she brightened. "Since Grandma's not here, can Sister Celeste come in with me? I'd feel better if she did."

Joanna knew her detectives wouldn't appreciate an extra person being added into the mix. "Sure," she said, after a moment's consideration. "That'll be fine."

As soon as Frank took his charges and left for the conference room, Joanna picked up the phone, dialed Dispatch, and spoke to Larry Kendrick.

"Who's on duty at Catherine Yates' house over by Pearce?" she asked.

Several seconds passed while Joanna listened to the clatter of computer keys. "Deputy Ken Galloway," Larry returned.

"Has he checked in lately?"

"Not for an hour or two. Why?"

"He's supposed to be keeping an eye on Catherine Yates, and I expected her to show up here by now. See if you can raise him by radio and find out what's going on."

Once Joanna was off the phone, she glanced at her watch. It was noontime. By rights it was past time for her to head out to High Lonesome Ranch to see how things were going and to cheer on the work crew's efforts. It wasn't fair to let the responsibility for her problem fall entirely on other people's shoulders. Still, she knew she could trust Butch to oversee things. She had faith that he would be able to sort out which of her shattered possessions should be kept and which should be thrown away. And, just like Eva Lou, it was easier on Joanna not to be there in person. She didn't want to witness the sad process of watching her past being thrown, item by item, into a Dumpster.

The phone rang. "Yes."

"This is odd," Larry Kendrick said. "I've tried raising Deputy Galloway several times, but he doesn't answer."

"I don't like the sound of that," Joanna said.

"Me neither," Kendrick returned. "Deputy Pakin is over near the airport in Douglas right now. I've dispatched him to go to Pearce and check things out."

Before Joanna had a chance to think about what that all might mean, her intercom buzzed. "A Mr. Jerry Reed to see you," Kristin Marsten announced.

Who the hell is Jerry Reed? Joanna wanted to ask. *Why don't you ever get enough information?*

Shaking her head, she bit back her sudden attack of irritation. "Send him in," Joanna said.

The man Kristin showed into Joanna's office was tall, broad-shouldered, and handsome. In Bisbee, where most men didn't bother with suits and ties, Jerry Reed was wearing a perfectly pressed double-breasted suit along with an immaculate white shirt and an understated red-and-blue tie.

"Pleased to meet you, Sheriff Brady," he said, extending his hand. "My name is Jerry Reed. I'm a special investigator for the Attorney General's office."

"Which one?" Joanna asked.

He laughed. "*The* Attorney General," he said, reaching into a pocket and extracting his ID. "The U.S. Attorney General."

Joanna took the proffered leather wallet and examined the picture identification before handing it back to him. "To what do I owe the pleasure?" she asked.

Jerry Reed eased himself into one of Joanna's captain's chairs. "I'll cut right to the chase, Sheriff Brady. I believe you have something that belongs to us—to our department, that is—and I've been sent to retrieve it."

Jerry Reed's tone of voice—his very attitude—put Joanna Brady on edge. She didn't like the way he had walked into her private office and, without an appointment, had helped himself to a chair. Through the years Joanna had worked several joint operations with any number of exemplary federal and state officers. On occasion, though, she had come to loggerheads with a few individuals. Each time, the conflict had grown out of some visiting fireman's patronizing and overbearing attitude toward Joanna and her department and out of Joanna's greatly reduced ability to tolerate same.

"And what would that be?" she asked, leaning back in her own chair and wishing she were wearing something more businesslike and tidy than yesterday's somewhat grubby clothing.

"Please don't be coy, Sheriff Brady," Jerry Reed said. "It doesn't suit you. I'm talking about the diskette Sandra Ridder promised to give us. I understand from Catherine Yates that it has somehow come to be in your department's possession. My department wants it back."

"I've been given to believe the diskette contains top-secret military command and control information," Joanna said. "What makes you think I'll give it to you?"

Reed seemed stunned to hear that Joanna knew that much about the diskette's top-secret contents. "How do you know what's on the disk?" he growled.

"It doesn't matter how I know," Joanna returned smoothly. "The point is, I do. Currently, that disk is evidence in one of our ongoing homicide investigations, and I'm certainly not handing it over."

Reed reached into another inside pocket and pulled out a document. "Before you paint yourself into a corner, Sheriff Brady, you may want to take a look at this. It's a properly drafted subpoena, signed by a Federal judge, requiring you to produce the diskette and hand it over to me at once."

He passed the subpoena across the table. Joanna examined it and handed it back. As far as she could tell, it seemed to be in order. "Are you the one that offered Sandra Ridder a ticket into the witness-protection program?" she asked.

"I'm not at liberty to say."

"And wasn't there supposed to be a cash bonus if Sandra Ridder turned the diskette over to you?"

"Really, Sheriff Brady. Our negotiations with Ms. Ridder were and are entirely confidential. They have nothing at all to do with the situation here."

"That's not true, Mr. Reed," Joanna said. "Sandra Ridder is dead, but her daughter—her only heir, Lucy Ridder—is very much alive. If a cash bonus was due Sandra Ridder for turning this mysterious diskette over to you, then the money should be due her daughter as well."

"Sheriff Brady," he said, looking somewhat agitated that Joanna was unwilling to capitulate. "Sandra's daughter isn't handing it over to me. You are. And I didn't come here to play "Let's Make a Deal." This is a serious matter, and I'm not leaving your office without taking that disk with me."

Instinct told Joanna something was amiss, but she couldn't tell what. "Very well," she said. "Wait here, and I'll go get it. Since it's down in the evidence room, that may take some time. Please make yourself comfortable."

Outside her private office, Joanna pulled her cell phone out of her pocket and dialed 4-1-1.

"U.S. West," a disembodied voice said. "How can I help you?"

"I want to be connected to the office of the Attorney General of the United States in Washington, D.C. My name is Sheriff Joanna Brady. Please tell whoever answers that this is extremely urgent—a matter of life and death."

While Joanna waited impatiently for the connection to be made, she poked her head into Frank Montoya's office and waved frantically for him to follow her. Then she hurried down the long hallway and out toward the public lobby, with her chief deputy padding along behind. She stopped at a locked supply-room door and opened it with her key.

"What's up?" Frank demanded, following her into the supply room. "What's going on?"

"There's a man in my office who says his name is Jerry Reed. He claims he's a special investigator for the U.S. Attorney General. He comes to us armed with a subpoena and demanding that we hand over Sandra Ridder's diskette."

With that, Joanna passed Frank the phone. "I've placed a call to the Attorney General's office in D.C. You talk to whoever answers, and don't put down the phone until you find out whether or not Special Agent Jerry Reed is legitimate."

"What are you going to do in the meantime?"

"Give him the disk." Joanna reached up to a top shelf and pulled down a single computer disk—a blue one—from a box of blanks.

Frank's eyes widened. "You're going to give him a phony?"

Joanna nodded. "Why not? What's he going to do, pop it into my computer to check it out before he ever leaves my office? If it turns out Reed is for real, we'll tell him I made a mistake, and that our evidence clerk gave me the wrong disk. If he isn't—"

"Hello," Frank was saying into the phone. "No, this isn't Sheriff Brady. I'm her chief deputy, Frank Montoya. We have a serious incident unfolding here that may involve one of your investigators. I probably need to speak to someone in Operations."

Leaving Frank to sort through the layers of Federal officialdom, Joanna started back toward her office. Outside the door, Kristin flagged Joanna down and handed over the receiver from Kristin's desk phone. "I know you're in a hurry but I think you're going to want to take this."

"Hello."

"Sheriff Brady," Larry Kendrick said. "Deputy Pakin just arrived at the Yates' place out in the Dragoons. He says Deputy Galloway's patrol car is there, but he's not. Neither is Catherine Yates, although her vehicle is there as well. He says her house looks as though it's been ransacked, and there are signs of a struggle."

Like a zoom photo lens shifting into focus, Joanna suddenly felt as though she knew what was going on. "Listen, Larry," she said urgently. "Call down to Motor Pool. Tell Danny Garner someone's going to be leaving the department in the next few minutes. I have no idea what kind of a vehicle he's driving, but before he goes, I want at least one and preferably two sets of spike strips laid down across the entrance to the Justice Complex. If I'm wrong about this and we've got the wrong guy, we'll owe the Feds a new set of tires. If I'm right, we may save several lives."

"How do we know the guy you want is the only one who'll run over the strips?"

"We don't," Joanna replied. "Depending on how long he takes to leave, we may be buying a whole bunch of people new sets of tires. Just do it."

Glancing down at the diskette in her hand, Joanna realized something was missing. Returning to her office with a naked computer disk and trying to pass that off as the real one wasn't going to cut it. She hurried across to the conference-room door, poked her head into the room, and motioned Ernie Carpenter away from the interview.

"What the hell do you want?" the detective demanded irritably once he was outside and had shut the door. "Sheriff Brady, you know better than to interrupt—"

"Shut up and give me an evidence bag," Joanna said. "And a label, too. Date it yesterday, and sign Frank's name to it."

"Me sign Frank's name? Are you crazy?"

"Hurry, Ernie. There's not much time. A man's going to be leaving my office any minute. I want you and Jaime Carbajal out in the parking lot in a car and ready to follow him. Whatever you do, don't drive out the front entrance. Danny Garner is laying down two sets of tire spikes. When the guy gets out of his vehicle, nab him."

"On what charges?"

"How about impersonating an officer, for openers?"

"Wait a minute. Are you saying Jaime and I are supposed to quit right in the middle of the interview and go chase after this other guy?" Ernie asked. "Who the hell is he?"

"It's possible he may be a Federal agent," Joanna said. "But I don't think so. Now please, Ernie, just do as I say."

Exasperated and shaking his head in disapproval, Ernie Carpenter handed over the doctored evidence bag and then headed back into the conference room for Jaime. Joanna dropped the disk into the bag and then hurried back to her office. Inside, after closing the door behind her, she found Jerry Reed standing next to the window studying the birds milling around the outdoor feeder that had been a gift from Angie Kellogg.

"It took you long enough," Reed said testily.

"Sorry about that. We're breaking in a new evidence clerk," Joanna said with what she hoped was a convincing sigh. She handed him the evidence bag with the disk clearly visible. "Our old guy retired," she continued. "He could find stuff with his eyes shut. This new one is taking her own sweet time to get acclimated."

Reed seemed greatly relieved once the bag was in his hand. "I'd better be going then," he said, sidling toward the door.

Wanting a few more minutes for her assets to get in position, Joanna stalled for time. "As I told you earlier, the disk you're holding is part of one of our homicide investigations. I'm sure you know that procedures are everything these days. I'd appreciate it if you'd sign and date this receipt which shows you're taking charge of the disk. I also need to know where and how to contact you if and when our case comes to trial."

"I already told you, Sheriff Brady," Reed objected. "The contents of this disk are top secret. I couldn't possibly testify about them in open court."

"Please don't misunderstand," Joanna said with a smile. "We'd merely want you to testify as to the existence of the disk. We certainly wouldn't require you to divulge the actual contents."

Reed sighed. "Very well," he said.

Making a huge show of it, he took the receipt Joanna offered him. Then he pulled out a fountain pen and scribbled his name, the date, and a telephone number across the receipt. "Thank you so much," Joanna said. "Believe me, my department and I are always happy to be of service."

She walked Jerry Reed to the door and then escorted him all the way to the public lobby. Halfway down the hall, Lucy Ridder was emerging from the women's rest room. Reed rushed past her without a sideways glance, but Joanna caught the look of utter terror that passed across the girl's face. She gasped and started to say something, but Joanna silenced her with a shake of her head and a finger to her own lips.

"We'll see you then, Mr. Reed," she said, once he was safely out of the hall and beyond the locking security door. "Drive carefully."

Closing the door behind him and making sure it was properly latched, Joanna turned back to Lucy. "That was him, wasn't it?"

Lucy Ridder nodded. "That's the man who killed my mother," she said.

Just then Frank Montoya came racing down the hall.

"Where is he?" he demanded. "You didn't let him get away, did you? I don't know who this guy is, but he's phony as a three-dollar bill."

"He won't get away," Joanna returned. "Right about now, he should be driving over the tire spikes I had Danny Garner put down just inside the gates to the Justice Complex. Ernie Carpenter and Jaime Carbajal should be Johnny-on-the-spot to pick him up."

Frank stopped and looked at her. "How'd you do that?" he asked.

Joanna tapped the side of her head. "Kidneys," she said.

"I beg your pardon?"

"Never mind," Joanna said with a laugh. "It's the punch line to an old shaggy-dog story Marianne Maculyea taught me when we were in sixth grade."

"But it doesn't make any sense."

"Right," Joanna agreed. "It didn't make sense then, and it doesn't now. You'll just have to take my word for it."

About that time, Joanna's cell phone rang in Frank's hand. With a disgusted shake of his head, he handed it over to her.

"Mom?" Jenny sobbed into the phone. "Is that you?"

"Jenny. What's the matter? Where are you?"

"In the principal's office. We got out of school early today because it's a teacher-in-service day. I went to Butch's house, but the door is locked and nobody's home. Grandma and Grandpa aren't home either. Everybody's too busy today, and they just forgot all about me. Nobody even loves me."

"That's not true, Jenny. We do love you, and you're right. We are busy. Just stay there in the office. I'll be down to get you as soon as I can."

"Good," Jenny sniffled. "When can we go get the dogs?"

Listening to her weeping child made Joanna's heart hurt. She could remember times when Eleanor had been busy as well. "If it's not one thing," she used to say, "it's three others."

"I don't know what time exactly," Joanna said. "But it'll be before dinner. You can count on that."

TWENTY-EIGHT

Joanna and Jenny picked up the dogs and took them home to High Lonesome Ranch. Out in the front yard stood an overflowing Dumpster, but Joanna chose not to go near enough to see the unsalvageable debris. There was no point in it. Instead, tentatively, she made her way into the house.

"What do you think?" Butch asked.

The mess was gone. The broken glassware and food had been cleaned up and carted away. Someone had replaced the sliced cord on the back of the refrigerator. It was plugged in and humming away in an otherwise almost empty kitchen. The walls and ceiling had been scrubbed down, although shadows of mustard and stains of hot sauce remained visible. Those wouldn't disappear until after a coat or two of paint. The cupboard doors and drawer fronts were mostly missing, and the broken shelves were still broken. The rest of the house was in much the same condition. With the better part of the furniture hauled away, the place had a strange, unoccupied echo to it as Joanna and Butch walked from room to room. Only Jenny's room remained the same as it had been before.

"Amazing," Joanna murmured. "How did you do all this?"

"I had good help," Butch replied. "I still can't believe how hard people slaved away. I was afraid Jim Bob was going to work himself into a coronary. No matter what I said, he wouldn't stop or even slow down. Jeff Daniels and your brother were the same way, and my father was no slouch, either. Marianne was here with Ruth for a while, but with all the broken glass lying around, we decided it was best for her to go back home. Besides, the woman's eight and a half months pregnant and in no condition to be hauling broken furniture outside to a Dumpster. The stuff that isn't broken we packed in boxes, but I'm afraid there isn't much of that."

Joanna nodded. "Thank goodness all the photo albums Mom gave us—the ones she kept nagging us about and the ones Jenny and I have been working on a little at a time—were in the top of the closet in Jenny's room, which means they weren't touched. If we'd lost them, they would have been irreplaceable. Everything else is replaceable."

"Still," Butch said gently, putting his arm around her shoulders. "It's a hell of a loss."

"It would have been a lot worse if I'd had to face the job of cleaning up on my own," Joanna told him. "Thank you, Butch. You don't know how much this means to me."

He pulled her close and kissed the top of her head. "Yes, I do," he said.

For obvious reasons the pre-rehearsal-dinner dinner, which had originally been slated for High Lonesome Ranch, had been moved to a different venue. The party ended up being held at George and Eleanor Winfield's house on Campbell Avenue, but the menu remained the same—an all-you-can-eat pizza feast from Bisbee's Pizza Palace. The dinner guests, most of them exhausted from a day of heavy physical labor, arrived tired, hungry, and thirsty but ready to switch gears from clean-up crew to wedding-festivity attendees.

The four women who had been dispatched to Tucson earlier in the day didn't pull into the carport until after the pizza had been delivered. They, too, seemed tired but happy. "We shopped till we dropped," Eva Lou announced, massaging her feet.

"We could have done more," Eleanor put in, "but Butch said not to. Take a look at what we brought, Joanna. Tell us what you think."

One at a time Joanna rummaged through the bags. There were several new sets of underwear—none of it quite as racy as the ones Joanna had been given during Sunday afternoon's shower, but it was still all very nice. There were two dresses that, with the addition of a blazer, would be fine for work. There were two lovely blouses, two pairs of slacks, and three pairs of shoes—including a replacement of the wedding shoes to match the dress that was scheduled to arrive the following afternoon. There was enough new clothing in the shopping bags to see Joanna through several days, but not much beyond that. On thinking about it, Joanna decided that was fine. Nice as these selections were, she much preferred doing her own shopping.

"Don't you want to try these things on?" Eleanor suggested.

Joanna looked around at a roomful of expectant people and begged off. "Please, Mom," she said. "They're wonderful, and all the sizes look perfect, but I'm worn out. Couldn't we pass on the fashion show for tonight?"

"I'm sure that will be just fine, won't it, Ellie," George Winfield said before his wife could answer. "Besides, the food is here and getting cold. Time to eat."

"I suppose," Eleanor agreed, although Joanna could see she wasn't thrilled about it.

Marianne Maculyea and Jeff Daniels arrived shortly

thereafter. Marianne's eyes were red, as was her nose. "You look awful," Joanna said, after Jeff took Ruth out to the kitchen to fill a plate. "What's the matter? You look like you've spent the afternoon crying."

"I have."

"What's wrong?"

"After Ruth and I got home from the ranch, I put her down for a nap. I was just starting to pick up the house when the doorbell rang. There was a strange woman standing on the front porch, someone I had never seen before. She gave me this."

Marianne reached into her pocket and pulled out a letter.

"What is it?" Joanna asked.

"Read it."

Joanna looked down at the envelope. The return address said "E. Maculyea, P.O. Box 8751, Safford, Arizona." "Your mother?" Joanna asked.

Marianne nodded wordlessly. From the time Marianne Maculyea had left the Catholic Church in order to become a Methodist minister, she had been at war with her parents, Timothy and Evangeline. There had been a partial thaw in hostilities at the time Jeff and Marianne had lost Ruth's twin, Esther. Marianne's father had come to both the hospital and funeral. Her mother had not. For years, being at war with their respective mothers had been one of the glues that had held Joanna and Marianne's friendship together.

"Read it," Marianne said.

Joanna unfolded the letter and read:

Dear Marianne,

This letter will introduce you to Julie Erickson. She is a nanny who lives in Tucson. Your father and I know two different families for whom she has worked in the past ten years. Please interview her and get to know her. If you decide she would fit in with yours and Jeff's needs, please let us know. After the baby is born, your father and I will pay Julie's wages for a six-month period. That should give you enough time to get back on your feet.

Love,
Mom

Joanna looked up from the letter. "Did you like her?" she asked.

"The nanny?" Marianne returned. "She was wonderful. Perfect. In fact, she was still there when Ruth woke up. The two of them hit it off right away, and you know how stand-offish Ruth can be with strangers sometimes. It's a miracle, Joanna. An answer to a prayer."

"Yes," Joanna agreed, giving her friend a hug. "It's an answer to more than one."

TWENTY-NINE

At nine o'clock Friday morning, Frank was in Joanna's office for the morning briefing. "As soon as we're done with this, I'm leaving," she told him. "I worked all day yesterday. I'm not working today."

"Right," he said. "You stumble into a hornet's nest that's going to create jurisdictional wrangling from here to next Tuesday, and you bail out on me."

"I can't help that." Joanna grinned. She was feeling good that morning. On top of the world. "If you ever decide to get married," she added, "remind me that I owe you that extra half day off. Now, what's the deal? How are Ken Galloway and Catherine Yates doing, for starters?"

"Catherine Yates is still under observation at Copper Queen Hospital. Deputy Galloway is out and fine. We're lucky they were found when they were. If you hadn't put down the spike strips and if your phony Agent Reed had managed to make it off departmental grounds, they might well have suffocated before someone found them and hauled them out of his trunk. I think he planned to use them as bargaining chips if need be, but you outfoxed him there, Joanna. Jaime and Ernie nailed Ed Masters before he had a chance to get away."

"Who the hell is Ed Masters anyway?" Joanna asked.

"Melanie Goodson's silent real estate partner for one, but

before he retired from the army, Major General Edward P. Masters was director of military intelligence at Fort Huachuca."

"Bingo," Joanna said softly.

"You'd better believe it. The FBI is working behind the scenes to re-create Sandra Ridder's work record. I'm pretty sure they're going to find that she worked for Masters or for someone connected to Masters. He may even be the guy Tom Ridder punched out in the bar, but nobody knows that for sure because we're being systematically pushed out of the loop. The Feds don't want us rocking any boats until they can find out if there are still any active participants out on post. But there have been hints that Sandra Ridder had done something off the wall in her NAT-C days, something that left her open to blackmail when she tried to leave her past behind. There's also some indication that she thought it would be easier on Lucy if she went to prison for manslaughter rather than being sent up on charges of being a spy."

"So she did cop a plea in order to protect her daughter?"

"That's how it looks. In addition to that, Special Investigator Warren Borden, the guy who really made the witness-protection deal with Sandra Ridder, is due in town from D.C. this afternoon. I've been directed by his boss—Madame Attorney General herself—to turn the encrypted diskette over to him. He tells me that yes, the monies due to Sandra Ridder for delivery of said diskette will be paid directly into her estate."

"Maybe Lucy Ridder will be able to get a second chance at taking ballet lessons after all," Joanna mused. "Where is she, by the way?"

"As far as I know, she's still over at the hospital. Later on this afternoon, she and Big Red will be heading back to

Saint David and Holy Trinity. They'll stay there at least until after Catherine Yates is released from the hospital."

"How did this all happen?" Joanna asked. "If Borden was all set to put Sandra Ridder in the witness-protection program, how did things go so wrong?"

"Special Investigator Borden thinks Sandra must have mentioned her deal to Melanie Goodson, thinking, of course, that Melanie was her dear friend. Except it turns out that Melanie was far better friends with Ed Masters than she ever was with Sandra Ridder. As soon as Masters got wind of what was happening, he was prepared to go to any length and do whatever was necessary to put the genie back in the bottle."

For the next little while, Joanna and Frank sorted through the standard daily concerns. She had been afraid of losing control by being gone for such a long period of time, but after being forced to let go of most of her earthly possessions, leaving her job behind for a week no longer seemed like such a big deal. Frank would be fine without her. So would her department.

When the briefing was over and Frank left the office, Joanna sat looking in wonder at her surroundings. It seemed almost incomprehensible that tomorrow would be her wedding day, but it was true. Once the replacement wedding dress showed up, maybe it would all seem real.

Her intercom buzzed. "Sheriff Brady?" Kristin said. "There's a long-distance call for you from someone named Joyce Roberts. She says she's an attorney. Do you want to talk to her, or should I have her talk to Chief Deputy Montoya?"

"No," Joanna said. "This is Reba Singleton's divorce attorney. I'll take the call. Sheriff Brady here," she added a moment later when the Joyce Roberts' call was put through. "What can I do for you?"

"I've just spoken to Dennis Singleton's attorney. I've put him on notice that if Dennis wants to avert a costly lawsuit, he'd do well to speak to your attorney and arrange to settle all damages caused by his egregious treatment of his poor unfortunate wife. Do you have an attorney in mind, Sheriff Brady?"

"Yes," Joanna replied. "Just a minute and I'll look up Burton Kimball's number. I'm sure he'll be glad to handle this matter for me."

"Does he drive a hard bargain?" Joyce Roberts asked.

"Probably."

"Good. The tougher he is, the better."

"How's Reba?" Joanna asked.

"Contrite about what she did to you, but mad as hell at Dennis," Joyce returned. "And that's good. I believe she's going to be a whole lot tougher on Dennis than he thought she was going to be, and getting all the prescription drugs she was taking out of her system is going to help. I can hardly wait to tear that bastard apart in court. Do you want me to call this Burton Kimball, or are you going to do it?"

"I will, to begin with," Joanna said. "But give me your number. I'll have him give you a call."

Half an hour later, as Joanna was getting ready to leave the office, she popped her head out the door. "Okay," she said to Kristin. "I'm out of here. Is everything under control?"

"We found the perfect dress," Kristin said, bubbling with happiness. "I just talked to my grandmother, and she's going to go buy it today. She told me that just because my dad is her son doesn't mean he isn't a creep."

"Have you and Terry set a date?"

"We wanted to check with you first. What about the week after you get back?"

Joanna smiled at her. "I'm sure that'll be fine," she said.

"But talk to Chief Deputy Montoya right away and get it worked into the rotation schedule."

"We will," Kristin said. "Thank you."

"You're welcome," Joanna said.

Eleanor had called to say Joanna's dress had been delivered to the Winfields' house on Campbell Avenue. On the way to pick it up, Joanna drove past the Copper Queen Hospital and spotted Father Mulligan walking in the rose garden out front. Parking in the lot, she walked up to him.

"What are you doing here?" she asked.

"Lucy wanted to come see her grandmother. While we wait for visiting hours, Lucy and Big Red are fooling around out back. Want me to go get them?"

"I will," Joanna said.

Behind the hospital, in a clearing below the retaining wall that held the hospital's helicopter pad, Joanna found Lucy Ridder standing and staring up at the sky. High overhead, Big Red floated above her in long, effortless circles.

"Aren't you worried that a helicopter might need to land?" Joanna asked.

"No," Lucy replied without looking away from the hawk. "He'll come if I call him. We'll get out of the way."

Lucy stopped watching the bird and turned to face Joanna. On her neck were not one but two tiny devil's-claw amulets, both of them dangling on one silver chain. Lucy must have followed Joanna's gaze.

"Grandma Yates gave me the other one," Lucy said. "She told me she thought my mother would have wanted me to have it. She says I should have them made into earrings. What do you think?"

"I think your grandmother's right," Joanna told her.

"About the earrings?" Lucy asked.

"About your mother wanting you to have this."

"And was she really a bad person?"

Joanna considered her answer. "No," she said, softly. "I don't think she was bad. I think she made mistakes, but I also think she loved you very much."

Just then a terrible screech rent the air. Looking up, Joanna saw Big Red plummeting out of the sky, diving beak first straight for her head. Thinking she was under attack, Joanna covered her face with both arms and dodged to one side. When she opened her eyes, the bird had settled, nonchalantly, on Lucy Ridder's narrow shoulder. As Joanna watched, he nuzzled up to her and buried his head in her hair. All the experts would have told her such a relationship was impossible, and yet Joanna was seeing it with her own eyes. And something made her think that the old Apache chief, Eskiminzin, wouldn't have been the least bit surprised.

"And I think your great-grandmother was right as well," Joanna added after a moment as she dropped her arms and attempted to regain a little of her dignity. "It's all part of the pattern."

"What do you mean?" Lucy asked.

"I mean," Joanna told her, "that your mother was an interesting person, and so are you."

🌵 EPILOGUE

The wedding was beautiful, although Joanna didn't realize it at the time. Only later, later, when she saw the pictures, would she finally notice how much fun everyone seemed to be having. Her dress was beautiful, and the flowers were gorgeous. The bride was radiant, so was the groom, so was the flower girl, and so was the mother of the bride. If anybody cried, Joanna didn't see it.

She and Butch left the reception at Palominas while the party was still in full swing and drove as far as Tucson to spend the night. Early Sunday morning found them standing in a check-in line at Tucson International Airport. "So," the clerk said with a smile as she examined the passports Butch had presented for identification purposes along with their tickets. "Is Paris your final destination today?"

Butch nodded. "Have you ever been to Paris before?" the clerk continued.

"I have, but my wife hasn't," he replied.

Meanwhile Joanna had been struck speechless. Up to that very moment, Butch Dixon had refused to divulge where they were going.

"Paris?" she blurted. "That's where we're going—Paris, France?"

Butch shrugged. "It's April, isn't it? Paris is supposed to be lovely this time of year. At least, that's what I've been told. And it should be a pretty nice place for you to buy those new clothes. You sure as hell need them."

ACKNOWLEDGMENTS

I wish to thank all the many people who were involved with the Bisbee Kiwanis Club's successful Helipad Project and with the creation of this book. As my mother would say, "Whoever you are, you know who you are."

—JAJ

Here's a glimpse of J.A. Jance's next thrilling Novel of Suspense

PARADISE LOST

Available September 2001 in hardcover from William Morrow

It was late on a hot and sunny Friday afternoon as the four-vehicle caravan turned off Highway 186 and took the dirt road that led to Apache Pass. In the lead was a small blue Isuzu Tracker followed by two dusty minivans. A lumbering thirty-five-foot Winnebago Adventurer brought up the rear.

Sitting at the right rear window in the second of the two minivans, twelve-year-old Jennifer Ann Brady was sulking. As far as she was concerned, if you had to bring a motor home complete with a traveling bathroom along on a camping trip, you weren't really camping. When she and her father, Andrew Roy Brady, had gone camping those few times before he died, they had taken bedrolls and backpacks and hiked into the wilderness. On those occasions, she and her Dad had pitched their tent and put down their bedrolls more than a mile from where they had left his truck. Andy Brady had taught his daughter the finer points of digging a trench for bathroom purposes. Jenny's new scout leader, Mrs. Lambert, didn't seem like the type who would be caught dead digging a trench much less using one.

The Tracker was occupied by the two women Mrs. Lambert had introduced as council-paid interns, both of them former Girl Scouts and now History Majors at the University of Arizona. Because the assistant leader, Mrs. Loper was unavailable, they were to help Mrs. Lambert with chaperone duties. In addition, they would be delivering informal lectures on the lifestyle of the Chiricahua Apache as well as on the history and aftermath of Apache Wars in Arizona.

History wasn't something Jenny Brady particularly liked, and she wondered how much the interns actually knew. What she had noticed about them was that they both wore short shorts, and they looked more like high school than college girls. But then, she reasoned, since they were former Girl Scouts, maybe they weren't all bad.

Behind the little blue Tracker rolled two jam-packed minivans driven by harried mothers and loaded to the gills with girls and their gear-bedrolls, backpacks, and the scattered crumbs and associated debris left over from their now consumed sack lunches. Once the mothers finished discharging their rowdy passengers, both they and their empty minivans would return to Bisbee. They were due back Monday at noon to retrieve a grubby set of campers after their weekend in the wilderness.

Behind the minivans, Mrs. Lambert and one of her twelve charges lumbered along in the clumsy looking Winnebago. The motor home belonged to a man named Emmet Foxworth, one of Faye Lambert's husband's most prominent parishioners. Upon hearing that the U.S. Forest Service had closed all Arizona campgrounds due to extreme fire danger, most youth group leaders had canceled their scheduled camp outs. Faye Lambert wasn't to be deterred. She simply made alternate arrangements. First she had borrowed the motor home and then, since public lands were closed to camping, she petitioned a local rancher to allow her girls to use his private range land.

Even Faye Lambert had to admit that borrowing the motor home had been nothing short of inspired. She might have taken on the challenge of being a Girl Scout leader, but she had never slept on the ground in her life. Having the motor home there meant she could keep her indoor sleeping record unblemished. Also, since the ranch obviously lacked camping facilities, the motor home would provide both restroom and cooking facilities in addition to the luxury of running water.

Cassie Parks, seated in the middle row of the second minivan, turned around and looked questioningly at Jenny through thick, red-framed glasses. "Who's your partner?" Cassie asked.

Cassie was a quiet girl with long dark hair in two thick braids. Her home, out near Double Adobe, was even farther from town than the Bradys' place on High Lonesome Ranch. Cassie's parents, relative newcomers who hailed from Kansas, had bought what had once been a nationally owned campground that had been allowed to drift into a state of ruin. After a year's worth of back-breaking labor, Cassie's parents had completely re-furbished the place, turning it into an independent, moderately priced RV park.

When school had started the previous fall, Cassie had been the new girl in Jenny's sixth grade class at Lowell School. Now, with school just out, the two girls had a history that included nine months of riding the school bus together. Much of that time they had been on the bus by themselves as they traveled to and from their outlying Sulphur Springs Valley homes. They also belonged to the same scout troop. In the course of that year, the pair of girls had become good friends.

If Jenny had been able to choose her own pup-tent partner for the Memorial Day weekend camp out, Cassie would have been it. But Mrs. Lambert, who didn't like cliques or pairing off, had decided to mix things up. She had shown up in the church parking lot with a sock filled with six pairs of buttons in six different colors. While the twelve girls had been loading their gear into the minivans, Mrs. Lambert had instructed each one to pull out a single button. To prevent trading around, as soon as a button was drawn, Mrs. Lambert wrote the color down on a clipboard next to each girl's name. Jenny had already drawn her yellow button when she saw Cassie draw a blue one.

The last girl to arrive in the parking lot and the last to draw her button was Dora Matthews. Glimpsing the yellow button in Dora's fingers, Jenny's heart sank. Of all the girls in the troop, Dora Matthews was the one Jenny liked least.

For one thing, Dora's hair was dirty, and she smelled bad. She was also loud, rude, and obnoxious. She couldn't have been very smart because she was thirteen years old and was still in a sixth grade classroom where everybody else was twelve. Mrs. Lambert usually brought Dora to troop meetings and was always nice to her even though Dora wasn't nice back. Two months before school was out, Dora and her mother had returned to Bisbee and moved into the house that had once belonged to Dora's deceased maternal grandmother, Dolly Pommer. All their lives, the elder Pommers had been movers and shakers in the Presbyterian Church. Out of respect for them, Faye Lambert had done what she could for their newly arrived daughter and granddaughter.

That also explained why Dora Matthews was now the newest member in Jenny's Girl Scout troop.

Not that Dora was even remotely interested in Girl Scouts—she was far too mature for that. She was into cigarettes. And boys. She bragged that before she and her mother had moved back to Bisbee, she'd had a boyfriend who had "done it" with her and who had wanted to marry her. Dora claimed that was why her mother had left Tucson—to get her daughter away from the boyfriend, but Jenny didn't think that was the truth. What boy in his right mind would ever want to marry someone like Dora?

"Guess," Jenny muttered dolefully in answer to Cassie's question.

Behind her thick glasses, Cassie Parks' brown eyes widened in horror. "Not Dora," she said, wrinkling her nose.

"You've got it," Jenny replied and then lapsed into miserable silence. She hadn't wanted to come on the camping trip to begin with. It was bad enough that Grandma Brady had insisted she bring her stupid sit-upon, but having to spend the weekend with Dora Matthews was far worse than anything Jenny could have imagined. After two whole nights in a pup tent with stinky Dora Matthews, Jenny would be lucky if she didn't stink, too.

Slowly the four vehicles wound up the dusty road that was little more than a rutted track. On either side of the road, the parched desert was spiked with spindly, foot-high blades of stiff, yellowed grass. Heat shimmered ahead and behind them, covering the road with visible rivers of mirage-fed water. At last the Tracker pulled off the narrow roadway and into a shallow, scrub-oak dotted basin. Kelly Martindale and Amber Summers leaped out of the Tracker and motioned the other vehicles to pull in behind them. By the time the motor home had maneuvered into place, all the girls had piled out of the minivans and were busy unloading. Dora, who had been accorded the honor of riding along with Mrs. Lambert in the motor home was the last to arrive. She hung back, letting the other girls do the work unpacking.

"All right, ladies," Mrs. Lambert announced, as soon as the minivans drove away. "You all know who your partner is. Take tents from the luggage compartment under the motor home. Then choose your spots. We want all the tents up and organized well before dark. Let's get going."

Each pair of girls was required to erect their own tent. Of all the girls in the troop, Jenny had the most experience in that regard. While Mrs. Lambert and the two interns supervised the other girls, Jenny set about instructing Dora Matthews on how to help set up theirs.

When it came time to choose a place for the tent, Dora selected a spot that was some distance from the others. Rather than argue about it, Jenny simply shrugged in agreement. "Fine," she muttered. Without much help from Dora, Jenny managed to lay the tent out properly, but when she asked Dora to hold the center support pole in place, Dora proved totally inept.

"Don't you know how to do anything right?" Jenny demanded impatiently. "Here, hold it like *this!*"

Instead of holding the pole, Dora grabbed it away from Jenny and threw it as far as she could heave it. The pole landed in the dirt and stuck at an angle like a spear.

"If you're so smart, Jennifer Brady, you can do it yourself." With that, Dora stalked away.

"Wait a minute," Mrs. Lambert said, picking up the pole and walking toward the still unraised tent. "What seems to be the problem, girls?"

"Miss Know It All here thinks I'm stupid," Dora complained. "And she keeps telling me what to do. That's all right. If she's so smart, she can have the stupid tent all to herself. I'll sleep outside."

"Calm down, Dora," Mrs. Lambert said reasonably. "These aren't called two-man tents just because they hold two people. It also takes two people working together to put them up. Now come over here and help."

Dora crossed her arms and shook her head. "No," she said.

"Look here, Dora," Mrs. Lambert cajoled. "The only reason Jenny knows so much more about this than you do is that she and her dad used to go camping together sometimes. Isn't that right, Jenny?"

Jenny thought about her father often, but hearing other people talk about him always brought the hurt of his death back with an intensity that made her throat ache. Jenny bit her lower lip. She nodded but said nothing.

"So come over here and help, Dora," Mrs. Lambert continued. "That way, the next time, you'll know what to do."

"I don't want to know how to pitch a tent," Dora stormed. "Why should I? Who needs to learn to pitch tents anyway? These days people live in houses not tents."

Rather than waste any more time in useless discussion, Mrs. Lambert turned to Jenny. "Never mind. Here, Jenny. Let me help. We'll have this up in no time. Besides, we're due at the evening campfire in twenty minutes."

"Campfire!" Jenny exclaimed. "It's too hot for a campfire. And it isn't even dark."

"In this case, campfire is only a figure of speech. With the desert so dry, it's far too dangerous to have one even if there aren't any official restrictions here. We won't be having a fire at all. I brought along a battery-powered lantern to use instead. When it comes time for storytelling, we can sit around that."

"Storytelling is for little kids," Dora grumbled. "Who needs it?"

Mrs. Lambert didn't respond, but Jenny heard her sigh. For the first time it occurred to her that maybe her troop leader didn't like Dora Matthews any more than the girls did.

It was almost dark before all the tents were up and bedrolls and packs properly distributed. As the girls re-assembled around their makeshift "campfire," Jenny welcomed the deepening twilight. Not only was it noticeably cooler, but also, in the dim evening light, no one noticed the mess she had made of her sit-upon.

Once all the girls were gathered, Mrs. Lambert produced bags of freshly popped microwave popcorn and a selection of ice-cold sodas, plucked from the motor home's generator-powered refrigerator. Taking a refreshing swig of her chilled soft drink and munching on hot popcorn, Jenny decided that maybe bringing a motor home along on a camping trip wasn't such a bad idea after all.

"First some announcements," Mrs. Lambert told them. "As you can probably guess, Mr. Foxworth's motor home has a limited water storage capacity for both fresh water and waste water as well. For that reason, we'll be using the rest-room as a number two facility only. For number one, you can go in the bushes. Is that understood?"

Around the circle of lantern light, the girls nodded in unison.

Jenny raised her hand. "What about showers?" she asked.

"No showers," Mrs. Lambert said with a smile. "When the Apaches lived here years ago, they didn't get to take showers every day. In fact, they hardly took showers at all, and you won't either. Unless it rains, and that doesn't appear to be very likely. The reason, of course, is that since we don't have enough water along for showers for everybody, no one will shower. That way, when we go home, we'll all be equally grubby.

"As for meal preparation and cleanup, we're going to split into six teams, of two girls each. Because of limited work space in the motor home, two girls are all that will fit in the kitchen area at any given time. Tomorrow and Sunday, each tent will do preparation for one meal and cleanup for another. On Monday, for our last breakfast together, Kelly, Amber, and I will do the cooking and cleanup honors. Does that sound fair?"

"What if we don't know how to cook?" Dora objected. She had positioned herself outside the circle. Off by herself, she sat with her back against the trunk of a scrub oak tree.

"That's one of the reasons you're here," Mrs. Lambert told her. "To learn how to do things you may not already know how to do. Now," she continued. "It's time for us to hear from one of our interns. We're really lucky to have Kelly and Amber along. Not only are they both former Girl Scouts themselves, they also are well versed in the history of this particular area.

"When I first came to town two years ago, one of the things I offered to do was serve on the textbook advisory committee for the school board in Bisbee. In my opinion, the classroom materials give short shrift to the indigenous peoples in this country, including the ones who lived here before the Anglos came, the Chiricahua Apache. It occurred to me that there had to be a better way to make those people come alive for us, and that's why I've invited Kelly and Amber to join us on this trip. Kelly, I believe we should start with you."

Kelly Martindale stood up. She had changed out of her shorts into a pair of tight-fitting jeans and a plaid long-sleeved shirt. Her dark hair was pulled back into a long pony-tail.

"First off," she said, "I want you to close your eyes and think about where you live. I want you to think about your house, your room, your yard, the neighbors who live on your street. Would you do that for me?"

Jenny Brady closed her eyes and imagined the fenced yard of High Lonesome Ranch. In her mind's eye, she saw a framed house surrounded by a patch of yellowing grass and tall shady cottonwoods and shorter fruit-bearing trees. This was the place Jenny had called home for as long as she could remember. Penned inside the yard were Jenny's two dogs, Sadie, a long-legged, bluetick hound, and Tigger, a comical looking mutt who was half-golden retriever and half-pit bull. Tied to the outside of the fence next to the gate, saddled with Jenny's new saddle and bridle and ready to go for a ride was Kiddo, Jenny's sorrel gelding quarter horse.

Kelly Martindale's voice imposed itself on Jenny's mental images of home. "Now, just suppose," she said, "that one morning someone showed up at your house and said that what you had always thought of as yours wasn't yours at all. Supposing they said you couldn't live there anymore because someone else wanted to live there instead. Supposing they said you'd have to pack up and go live somewhere else. What would you think then?"

In times past, Jenny would have been the first to raise her hand, the first to answer. But she had found that being the sheriff's daughter came with a downside. Other kids had begun to tease her, telling her she thought she was smart and a show-off all because her mother was sheriff. Now, in hopes of fitting in and going unnoticed, she tended to wait to be called on rather than volunteering. Cassie Parks suffered no such qualms.

"It sounds like what the Germans did to the Jews," she said with a shudder.

Kelly nodded. "It does, doesn't it? But it's also what the United States government did to Indian tribes all over this country. And the reason I know about it, is that very thing happened to my great, great, grandmother when she was just a little girl—about your age. Her people—the Apaches—had lived here for generations—right here in the Chiricahuas, the Dos Cabezas Mountains, and in the surrounding valleys. When the Whites came and the Apaches tried to defend their lands, there was a war. The Apaches lost that war and they were shipped off to a place called Fort Sill, Oklahoma. My great, great grandmother was sent there, too. Although she and her family were prisoners, she somehow fell in love with one of the soldiers guarding the camp. They got married, and she went to live with him back east in Arkansas. But that's why I'm here in Arizona. It's also why I'm a history major. I'm trying to find out more about my people— about who they were, where they came from, and what happened to them."

"For example, this place." Kelly raised her hand and swept it around the tree-dotted basin where they were camped. "During the Apache Wars, this place was the site of a good deal of fighting mostly because up there—in the canyon—there's a spring. Wagon trains came through here for that very reason—because of the availability of water. In the 1850's Nachi, Cochise's father, attacked one of those trains. Thirty people were killed and/or mutilated. Two of the women were sold down in Mexico. But you have to remember, as far as the Apaches were concerned, they were defending their homeland from unwelcome invaders.

"In later years, the dirt road we followed coming up here from the highway was the route for the Butterfield Stage

Line. There were several fierce battles waged around the Apache Pass Stage Stop. During one of those battles, Mangas Coloradas, another Apache chief whose name in English means Red Sleeves, was shot and seriously wounded. In the next few days, as we explore this area, I want you to remember that, to some of us, Apache Pass is just as much a sacred battlefield as places like Gettysburg in Pennsylvania or the Normandy beaches in France are to other people."

"Will we find arrowheads?" Dawn Gaxiola asked.

"Possibly," Kelly replied. "But arrowheads won't necessarily be from the time of the Apache Wars. By then, bows and arrows were pretty much passé. The U.S. soldiers had access to guns and gunpowder, and so did the Indians."

"What about scalping?" Dora Matthews asked. For the first time she seemed somewhat interested in what was being said. "Did the Indians do a lot of that?"

"There was cruelty and mutilation on both sides," Kelly answered. "A few minutes ago, I mentioned Mangas Coloradas. When Red Sleeves was finally captured, the soldiers who were supposedly guarding him tortured him and then shot him in cold blood. Mangas was big—six foot six. After he was dead, the soldiers scalped him, cut off his head, and then boiled it so they could send his skull to a phrenologist back east who claimed his head was bigger than Daniel Webster's.

"Yuck!" Dawn said with a shudder. "And what about that other thing you said earlier—a friendologist or something. What's that?"

"Phrenologist, not friend," Kelly corrected. "Phrenology was a supposed science that's now considered bogus. During the 1880s, phrenologists believed they could tell how people would behave by studying the size and shape of their heads.

"But getting back to the Apaches, you have to remember that history books are usually written by the winners. That's why Indians always end up being the bad guys while the U.S. soldiers who turned the various tribes out of their native lands are regarded as heroes or martyrs."

"You mean like General Custer?" Cassie asked.

Kelly smiled. "Exactly," she said. "Now, tomorrow Amber and I will be leading a hike up to the ruins of Fort Bowie. But wherever you go tomorrow or later on, when you visit places like the Wonderland of Rocks or Cochise Stronghold, I want you to bear in mind that Anglos weren't the first people here. I'd like you to look at the land around here and try to see it through some of those other people's points of view."

Abruptly, Kelly Martindale sat down. After that, Mrs. Lambert saw to it that the evening turned into the usual kind of campfire high jinks. There were games and songs and even an impromptu skit. Finally, a little after ten, she told the girls it was time for lights out and sent them off to their tents.

"It's so early to go to bed," Dora muttered, as she and Jenny approached their tent. "I never go to bed at ten o'clock. I'm going for a walk."

"You can't do that," Jenny said. "You'll get in trouble."

"Who's going to tell?" Dora demanded. "You? Besides, I need a cigarette. If I smoke it here, Mrs. Lambert or those two snooty college girls who think they're so rad might smell the smoke and make me put it out because I might start a fire or something. You wanna come along?"

Jenny was torn. On the one hand, she didn't want to get in trouble. On the other hand, she wasn't ready to go to sleep yet, either. Not only that, their tent seemed to be far enough away from the others, that it was possible no one would notice if they crept out for a little while.

"I'll go," she said, after a moment's hesitation. "But first we'd better climb into our bedrolls and pretend like we're going to sleep."

"Why?"

"Because I'll bet Mrs. Lambert will come around to check on us, that's why."

"Okay," Dora grumbled. "We'll do it your way."

It turned out Jenny was right. Ten minutes after they lay down on their bedrolls, they heard the stealthy rustle of shoe leather approaching through dry grass. Moments later, the light from a flashlight flickered on the outside of the tent.

"Everybody tucked in?" Faye Lambert asked.

"Tucked in," Jenny returned. With the tent flap closed, the stench of Dora's body odor was almost more than Jenny could bear. She could hardly wait for their leader to go away so they could slip back out into the open air.

"Well, good night then," Mrs. Lambert said. "I've made out the duty roster. The two of you will be cleaning up after breakfast. Is that all right?"

"It's fine," Dora told her. "I'm better at cleaning up than I am at cooking."

The lantern light disappeared. Jenny listened to the sound of Mrs. Lambert's retreating footsteps and then to the slight squeak as the door to the motor home opened and closed. Kelly Martindale and Amber Summers were sleeping in their own two-man tent. Mrs. Lambert would spend the night in the motor home.

"Shall we go then?" Dora demanded.

"Wait a few minutes longer," Jenny cautioned.

Ten minutes later, the two girls cautiously raised the flap on their tent and let themselves out. Walking as silently as possible, they slipped off through the scrub oak. While waiting in the tent, their eyes had adjusted to the lack of light.

Once outside, they found the moonlight overhead surprisingly bright. Walking in the moon's silvery glow, they easily worked their way over the near edge of the basin. Within minutes they were totally out of sight of the other campers. At that point, Dora sank down on a rock and pulled two cigarettes out of the pocket of her denim jacket.

"Want one?" she asked.

Jenny shook her head. "I don't think so," she said.

"Come on," Dora urged. "What are you, chicken? Afraid your mom will find out and put you in jail?"

For the second time that evening, Jenny was aware of the burden of being the sheriff's daughter. She wanted nothing more than to be accepted as a regular kid. This dare, made by someone she couldn't stand, was more than Jennifer Ann Brady could resist. "Okay," she said impulsively. "Give me one. Where do you get them?" she asked, as Dora pulled out a lighter. She lit her own cigarette first, then she lit Jenny's.

"I steal them from my mother's purse," Dora admitted, inhaling deeply. "She smokes so much that she never misses them long as I only take a few at a time."

Jenny took a few tentative puffs, holding the smoke in her mouth and then blowing it out again. Even that was enough to make her eyes water.

"That's not how you do it," Dora explained. "You're supposed to inhale—breathe the smoke into your lungs—like this."

She sucked a drag of smoke into her lungs, held it there, and then blew it out in a graceful plume. Jenny's game effort at imitation worked, but only up to a point. Moments later she found herself bent over, choking and gagging.

"You're not going to barf, are you?" Dora Matthews demanded.

"I think so," Jenny managed.

"Well give me your cigarette, then. Don't let it go to waste."

Jenny handed over the burning cigarette. Embarrassed, she stumbled away from where Dora sat, heaving as she went. Twenty yards farther on, she bent over a bush and let go. In the process she lost all her popcorn and Orange Crush from the campfire along with the lunch Eva Lou Brady had packed for her ever so carefully. Finally, when there was nothing left, Jenny lurched over to a nearby tree and stood there, leaning against the trunk, gasping and shivering and wishing she had some water so she could get the awful taste out of her mouth.

"Are you all right?" Dora asked from behind her. She was still smoking one of the two cigarettes. The smell of the smoke was almost enough to make Jenny heave again, but she managed to stave off the urge.

"I'm all right," she said shakily.

"You'll be okay," Dora told her. "The same thing happened to me the first time I tried it. You want an Altoid? I always keep some around so Grandma can't smell the smoke on my breath."

With shaking hands, Jenny gratefully accepted the proffered breath mint. "Thanks," she said and meant it.

The two girls stood there together for some time, while Jenny sucked on the breath mint and Dora finished smoking the rest of the remaining cigarette. When it was gone, Dora carefully ground out the butt with the sole of her shoe. "I wouldn't want to start a fire," she said with a laugh. "Somebody might notice. Then we would be in trouble."

They were quiet for a time. The only sound was the distant yip of a coyote answered by another from even farther away. Then, for the first time that evening, a slight breeze stirred around them, blowing up into their faces from the valley floor below. As the small gust blew away the last of the dissipating cigarette smoke, Jenny noticed that another odor had taken its place.

"There's something dead out there," she announced.

"Dead," Dora repeated. "How do you know?"

Jennifer Ann Brady had lived on a ranch all her life. She recognized the distinctively ugly odor of carrion.

"Because I can smell it, that's how," Jenny returned.

The slight softening in Dora's voice when she had offered the Altoid disappeared at once. "You're just saying that to scare me, Jennifer Brady!" Dora declared. "You think that because they were saying all that stuff about Apaches killing people and all, that you can spook me or something."

"No, I'm not," Jenny insisted. "Don't you smell it?"

"Smell what?" Dora shot back. "I don't smell anything."

Jennifer Brady had seen enough animal carcasses along the road and out on the ranch that she wasn't the least bit scared of them, but she could tell from Dora's voice that the other girl was. It was a way of evening the score for the cigarettes—a way of reclaiming a little of her own lost dignity.

"Come on," Jenny said. "I'll show you."

Without waiting to see whether or not Dora would follow, Jenny set off. The breeze was still blowing uphill, and Jenny walked directly into it. After watching for a moment or two, Dora Matthews reluctantly followed. With each step, the odor grew stronger and stronger.

"Ugh," Dora protested at last. "Now I smell it, too. It's awful."

Their path had taken them up and over the ridge that formed one side of the basin where the troop had set up camp. Now, the girls walked downhill until they were almost back at the road that had brought them up into the basin. And there, visible in the moonlight and at the bottom of the embankment that fell down from the graded road lay the body of a naked woman.

"Oh, my God," Dora groaned. "Is she dead?"

Jenny's neck prickled as hair on the back of it stood on end. "Of course she's dead," she said, wheeling around. "Now come on. We have to go tell Mrs. Lambert."

"We can't do that," Dora wailed. "What if Mrs. Lambert finds out about the cigarettes? We'll both be in trouble then."

Jenny was worried about the same thing, but the threat of getting in trouble wasn't enough to stop her. Neither was Dora Matthews.

"Too bad," Jenny called over her shoulder. "I'm going to tell anyway. Somebody's going to have to call my mom."

The Joanna Brady Mysteries by
New York Times Bestselling Author

An assassin's bullet shattered Joanna Brady's world, leaving her policeman husband to die in the Arizona desert. But the young widow fought back the only way she knew how: by bringing the killers to justice . . . and winning herself a job as Cochise County Sheriff.